"An exciting and well-written horror story. . . . A brilliant and furious tale . . . as skillful as the whisper of the surgeon's blade."

—Whitley Strieber, author of Catmagic

The water lying on the sagging brick walk was clear and unrippled, and along one edge was a shadow that was neither the tree in the yard nor the eaves nor himself crossing over.

The shadow didn't move.

It suggested something much larger, much darker, than he had first imagined, but when he examined the sidewalk, the yard, the stoop behind him, he saw nothing.

The shadow was still there, and when he kicked at the water to rough it, it remained unmoved.

He stamped a foot into the puddle and watched the shadow slip over his toes.

The shoe yanked back and he looked up quickly, then sighed his relief aloud. A cloud. It was a black patch of cloud. Nothing more.

He had his hand on the doorknob when he heard the noise behind him.

Soft. Hollow. Slightly uneven, stones dropping lightly onto a damp hollow log.

It was coming up the w

Pet

OTHER BOOKS BY CHARLES GRANT

THE OXRUN STATION NOVELS

the Pet

Charles L. Grant

A TOM DOHERTY ASSOCIATES BOOK

This is a work of fiction. All the characters and events portrayed in this book are either products of the author's imagination or are used fictitiously.

THE PET

A Tor Book
Tom Doherty Associates, LLC
175 Fifth Avenue
New York, NY 10010

www.tor.com

Tor® is a registered trademark of Tom Doherty Associates, LLC.

ISBN: 0-812-51848-9
Library of Congress Catalog Card Number: 85-52254

First edition: June 1986
First mass market edition: May 1987

Printed in the United States of America

0 9 8 7 6 5 4 3

For Kathryn.
Because.

ONE

A cool night in late September, a Wednesday, and clear—
the moon pocked with grey shadows, and a scattering of stars
too bright to be masked by the lights scattered below; the
chilled breath of a faint wind that gusted now and then,
carrying echoes of nightsounds born in the trees, pushing
dead leaves in the gutters, rolling acorns in the eaves, snapping hands and faces with a grim promise of winter.

A cool night in late September, a Wednesday, and dark.

*. . . and so the boy, who really wasn't a bad kid but
nobody really knew that because of all the things he had
done, he looked up in the tree . . .*

And from the Hudson River to a point midway across New
Jersey, the land climbed in easy steps toward the Appala-
chian chain. The forests were gone and so were most of the
pastures, replaced by communities that grew in quick time
into small towns and small cities, pieces of a jigsaw fit too
close together.

One piece was Ashford, a piece not the largest, settled on

1

the first of those low curving plateaus, its drop facing south, low hills at its back. From the air it was indistinguishable from any of its neighbors—just a concentration of lights, glints on the edge of a long ebony razor.

. . . and he saw the crow sitting on the highest branch in the biggest tree in the world. A big crow. The biggest crow he had ever seen in his life. And the boy knew, he really and truly knew, that the crow was going to be the only friend he had left in the world. So he talked to the crow and he said . . .

The park was in the exact center of town, five blocks deep and three long blocks wide, surrounded by a four-foot stone wall with a concrete cap worn down in places by the people who sat there to watch the traffic go by. At the north end was a small playing field with a portable bandstand erected now behind home plate, illuminated by a half-dozen spotlights aimed at it from the sides; and the folding chairs, the lawn chairs, the tartan blankets and light autumn jackets covered the infield, protecting the large audience from the dust of the basepaths and the spiked dying grass slowly fading to brown.

A student-painted banner fluttered and billowed over the bandstand's domed peak, unreadable now that twilight had gone, but everyone knew it proclaimed with some flair the approach of Ashford Day in just over a month. The concert was a free preview of the events scheduled for the week-long celebration—a century-and-a-half and still going strong.

The high school band members sat on their chairs, wore their red uniforms with the black and gold piping, and played as if they were auditioning to lead the Rose Bowl parade. They slipped through ''Bolero'' as if they knew what it meant, marched through Sousa as if they'd met him in person, and they put fireworks and rockets, Catherine wheels and Roman candles exploding and spinning into the audience's imagination, into the dark autumn sky, when they bellowed and strutted through the "1812 Overture."

At the rim of the field, back in the bushes where the lights didn't reach, there were a few giggles, a few slaps, more than a few cans of beer popping open.

. . . do you think it'll be all right?

The parents, all the relatives, the school board, and the mayor applauded as if they'd never heard anything quite so grand in their lives.

The bandmaster beamed, and the band took a bow. There were no encores planned, but the applause continued just the same.

. . . and the crow said, it'll be just fine as long as you know who your friends really are.

In the middle of the park was an oval pond twenty feet wide, with a concrete apron that slanted down toward the water. It wasn't very deep; a two-year-old child could wade safely across it, but it reflected enough of the sun, enough of the sky, more than enough of the surrounding foliage to make it seem as if the depths of an ocean were captured below the surface. Around it were redwood benches bolted to the apron's outer rim. Above them were globes of pale white atop six bronze pillars gone green with age and weather. Their light was soft, falling in soft cowls over the quiet cold water, over the benches, over the eleven silent children who were sitting on them now. They didn't listen to the music, though it was audible through the trees; they ignored applause that sounded like gunshots in the distance; instead, they listened to the young man in pressed black denim who crouched at the apron's lip, back to the pond, hands clasped between his knees.

His voice was low, rasping, his eyes narrowed as he sought to draw the children deeper into the story.

"And so the boy said, how do I know who my real friends are? Everyone hates me, they think I'm some kind of terrible monster. And the crow, he laughed like a crazy man and said, you'll know them when you see them. The boy was a little afraid. Am I a monster, he asked after a while, and the crow didn't answer. Are you one of my friends, the little boy asked. Of course I am, said the crow. In fact, I'm your best friend in the whole wide world."

The children stirred as the applause faded, and they could hear the first of the grown-ups drifting down the central path. The young man frowned briefly. He thought he had planned the story better, to end just as the band did, but he had gotten too carried away, elaborating and posturing to get the kids laughing so they wouldn't be bored. Now he had lost them. He could see it in their eyes, in the shifting on the benches, in the way their heads turned slightly, too polite to ignore him outright though their gazes were drawn to the black-topped walk that came out of the dark on its way to the south exit.

"Crows don't talk," one ski-capped boy suddenly declared with a know-it-all smile as he slipped off his seat.

"Sure they do," a girl in a puffy jacket argued.

"Oh, yeah? You ever hear one, smarty?"

"Bet you never even saw one, Cheryl," another boy said. "I'll bet you don't even know what they look like."

The girl turned, hands outstretched. "Donald, I do so know what one looks like."

The others were lost now, noisily lining up as if choosing sides for a game. The crow's supporters were outnumbered, but they made up for it with indignant gestures and shrill protests, while the mocking opposition—mostly boys, mostly the older ones—sneered knowingly and laughed and punched each other's arms.

"Everyone knows what a crow looks like," Don said, in such a harshly quiet way that they all turned to look. "And everyone knows what the biggest crow in the world looks like, right?"

A few heads instantly nodded. The rest were unconvinced.

Don smiled as evilly as he could, and stood, and pointed to the nearest tree, directly behind them. Most of them looked with him; the others, sensing a trick and not wanting to give him the satisfaction, resisted.

Until the little girl put a hand to her mouth, and gasped.

"That's right." He kept pointing. "See? Right there, just out of the light? Look real hard now. Real hard and you won't miss it. You can see his feathers kind of all black and shiny. And his beak, right there by that leaf, it's sort of gold and pointed like a dagger, right?"

The little girl nodded slowly. No one else moved.

"And his eyes! Look at them, they're red. If you look real hard—but don't say anything or you'll scare him away—you can see one just over there. See it? That little bit of red up in the air? It looks like blood, doesn't it. Like a raindrop of blood hanging up there in the air."

They stared.

They backed away.

It was quiet in the park now, except for the leaves.

"Aw, you're fulla crap," the ski-capped boy said, and walked off in a hurry, just in time to greet his parents strolling down from the concert. He laughed and hugged them tightly, and Don without moving seemed to stand to one side while the children broke apart and the oval filled with voices, with feet, with faces he knew that thanked him for watching the little ones who would have been bored stiff listening to the music, and it was certainly cheaper than hiring a sitter.

He slipped his hands into his jeans pockets and rolled his shoulder under the black denim jacket and grey sweatshirt.

His light brown hair fell in strands over his forehead, curled back of his ears, curled up at the nape. He was slender, not tall, his face almost but not quite touched by a line here and there that made him appear somewhat older than he was.

Within moments the parents and their children were gone.

"Hey, Boyd, playing Story Hour again?"

He looked across the pond and grinned self-consciously. Three boys walked around the pond toward him, grinned back, and roughed him a bit when they joined him, then pushed him in their midst and herded him laughing toward the bike stand just inside the south gate.

"You should've been there, Donny," Fleet Robinson told him, leaning close with a freckled hand on Don's arm. "Chris Snowden was there." He rolled his eyes heavenward as the other boys whistled. "God, how she can see that keyboard with those gazongas is a miracle."

"Hey, you'd better not say stuff like that in front of Donny the Duck," said Brian Pratt solemnly. Then he winked broadly, and not kindly. "You know he doesn't believe in that kind of talk. It's sexist, don't you guys know that? It's demeaning to the broads who jerk him off on the porch."

"Drop dead, Brian," Don said quietly.

Pratt ignored him. With a sharp slap to Robinson's side he jumped ahead of the others and walked arrogantly backward, his cut-off T-shirt and soccer shorts both an electric red and defiant of the night's early autumn chill. "But if you want to talk about gazongas, you crude bastards, if you're really gonna get down in the gutter, then let me tell you about Trace tonight. Christ! I mean, you want to talk excellent development? Jesus, I could smother, you know what I mean? And she was waiting for it, just waiting for it, y'know? I mean, you could see it in her eyes! Christ, she was fucking asking for it right there on the stage! Oh, my god, I wish to hell her old man wasn't there, he should've been on duty or something. Soon as she put down that stupid flute I'd've planked her so damned fast . . . oh god, I think I'm dying!''

Robinson's hand tightened when he felt the muscle beneath it tense. "Don't listen to him, Don. In the first place, Tracey hasn't talked to him since the first day of kindergarten except to tell him to get the hell out of her way, and in the second place, he don't know nothing he don't see in a magazine.''

"Magazine, shit," scoffed Jeff Lichter. "The man can't even read, for god's sake.''

"Read?" Pratt said, wide-eyed. "What the hell's that?''

"Reading," explained Tar Boston, "is what you do when you open a book." He paused and put his hands on his hips. "You remember books, Brian. They're those things you got growing mold on in your locker.''

Pratt sneered and lifted his middle finger. Robinson and Boston, both heavyset and both wearing football jackets over light sweaters, took off after him, hollering, windmilling their arms as though they were plummeting down a hill.

Ahead was the south gate, and beyond it the lights of Parkside Boulevard.

Jeff stayed behind. He was the shortest of the group, and the only one wearing glasses, his brown hair reaching almost to his shoulders. "Nice guys.''

Don shrugged. "Okay, I guess.''

They walked from dark to light to dark again as the lampposts marked the edge of the pathway. Jeff's tapped heels smacked on the pavement; Don's sneakers sounded solid, as if they were made of hard rubber.

"How'd you get stuck with that?" Lichter asked with a jerk of his thumb over his shoulder.

"What, the story stuff?''

"Yeah.''

"I didn't get stuck with it. Mrs. Klass asked me if I'd watch Cheryl for a while. Said she'd give me a couple of bucks to keep her out of her hair. Next thing I knew I had a gang.''

"Yeah, story of your life, I think.''

Don looked but saw nothing on his friend's face to indicate sarcasm, or pity.

"She pay you?''

"I'll get it tomorrow, at school.''

"Like I said—story of your life.''

At the bike stand they paused, staring through the high stone pillars to the empty street beyond. Pratt and the others were gone, and there was little traffic left to break the park's silence.

"That creep got away with another one, you know,'' Jeff said then, looking nervously back over his shoulder at the trees. "The Howler, I mean.''

"I heard.'' He didn't want to talk about it. He didn't want to talk about some nut over in New York who went around tearing up kids with his bare hands and howling like a wolf when he was done. Five or six by now, he thought; once a month since last spring, and now it was five or six dead. And the worst part was, nobody even knew what he looked like. He could be an old man, or a woman who hates kids, or . . . or even a kid.

"Well, if he comes here,'' Lichter said, glaring menacingly at the shadows, his hair wind-fanned over his eyes, "I'll kick his balls right up to his teeth. Or get Tracey's old man to arrest him for unlawful mutilation.''

Don laughed. "What? You mean there's such a thing as lawful mutilation?''

"Sure. Ain't you never seen the dumb clothes Chris wears? Like she was a nun sometimes? That's mutilation, brother, and she ought to be arrested for it.''

They laughed quietly, shaking their heads, sharing the common belief that Chris Snowden's figure was more explosive than dynamite, more powerful than a speeding bullet, more likely to cause heart attacks in every senior class male than failing to make graduation.

Lichter took off his glasses and polished them on his jacket. "I'll tell you, she's enough to make me wish I was a virgin again."

This time Don's laugh was strained, but he nodded just the same. He wasn't a prude; he didn't mind talk about sex and women, but he wished the other guys would quit their damned bragging, or their lying. If they kept it up, one of these days he was going to slip and get found out.

"So, you start studying for the bio test next week?" Lichter asked, his sly tone indicating he already knew the answer.

"Yeah, a little," he admitted with an embarrassed grin. "Should be a snap."

"Right. A snap. And if it isn't, you and I will be standing outside when graduation comes around." He sighed loudly and looked up at the stars. "Oh, god, only eight more months and the torture is over."

The wind kicked up dust and made them turn their heads away.

"School," Jeff said then, with a slap to his arm.

"Yeah. School."

Lichter nodded, left waving at a slow trot, veering sharply right and vanishing. Don knelt to work the combination of the lock he had placed on the tire chain, then straddled the seat and gripped the arched handlebars. They were upright, cranked out of their racing position less than ten minutes after he had brought it home from the store. He didn't like hunching over, feeling somehow out of control and forever toppling unless he could straighten his back. He pushed off, then stopped as soon as he was on the sidewalk. To the right, far down the street, were the hazed neon lights of Ashford's long shopping district; directly opposite was the narrow island of trees and grass that separated the wide boulevard into its east and west lanes; to the left the street poked into a large residential area whose houses began as clean brick and tidy clapboard and eventually deteriorated into rundown brownstone and aluminum siding that had long since faded past its guarantee.

He glanced behind him and smiled suddenly.

On the path, just this side of the last lamppost, was a feather. A crow's feather twice as long as a grown man's hand. It shimmered almost blue, was caught by the wind, and tumbled toward him.

He waited until it fluttered to a stop against the bike's rear tire, then shook his head slowly. Boy, he thought, where were you when that kid opened his big mouth?

But as Jeff would say—the story of his life. Honest to god giant crows were not in his stars.

Tanker Falwick swore impotently under his breath. Thorns in the red-leafed bush had snagged his coat sleeve and held it fast, and he couldn't move quickly without making a hell of a racket. He slapped at them angrily while he rose and peered over the wall. And groaned with a punch to his leg when he saw his last chance for decent prey getting away. The boy was turning, bumping his ten-speed down off the curb and across the street. Away from the park, in spite of the moon.

It was too late. Goddamn, it was too late.

"Shit!" he said aloud, and yanked his arm until the thorns came loose. "Fucking shit!"

A glance up at the moon riding over the trees, and he swore again, silently, hoping that the squirrel he'd killed earlier wouldn't be the only meal he'd have tonight. There hadn't been much meat and its heart had been too small, and twisting off its head didn't give him near the same satisfaction as tearing out a kid's throat.

Several automobiles sped past, a half-empty bus, a pickup with three punks huddled and singing in the bed, a dozen more cars. None of them stopped, and when he headed back into the trees, he couldn't hear a thing except his paper-stuffed shoes scuffling wearily through the leaves. He hushed himself a couple of times before finally giving up. He wasn't listening, and there was, most likely, no one else around to hear.

The whole place had just been filled with damned kids, just filled to the rafters with them, and every opportunity he'd had to introduce himself to one had been thwarted in one way or another.

A large dirt-smeared hand wiped harshly over his mouth, not feeling the stiff greying bristles on his chin, on his sallow cheeks, on the slope of his wattled neck. He sniffed, and coughed, and spat into the dark. Then he drew his worn tweed jacket over his broad chest, hunched powerful shoulders against the wind, and moved toward the center path. He waited in the shadows for a full five minutes, then stepped out and took a deep breath.

He didn't like it back in there. He didn't like it at all despite his affinity with the best parts of the dark. There were too many noises he didn't understand, and too many shadows that trailed after him as he trailed the children who were scurrying after their parents.

A lousy night, all in all—except for the music.

He stopped at the oval pond, checked the path, and knelt on the apron, then leaned over and scooped some of the cold water into his mouth.

The music was nice. Not bad for a bunch of fucking dumbass high school kids, and he had even recognized some of the tunes. He had been hiding behind a patch of dense laurel just to the left of the bandstand, nodding, humming silently, and applauding without sound at the end of each number. He had also been hoping that one of the punks would have to take a leak during the program and wouldn't be prissy about heading into the bushes. Tonight he wasn't fussy about the sex; one of the boys would have done just as nicely as one of them young whores.

When that didn't work and he couldn't move anyone over to him through the sheer force of his will, he had moved down toward the south entrance since that's where the fewest of the audience had headed when it was over. He was hoping for a stray, but the little ones were too good, too well-behaved, like those who were at the pond while that other kid, the older one, the punk bastard in black denim, told them a preposterous story about a stupid giant crow.

And the big ones, the punks, the snot-nosed creeps who made up most of his fun, they stuck together like glue right to the street. Especially the whores.

He rocked back on his heels and dried his face with a sleeve.

That had been a close one, that one had, the moment with the black denims. Suddenly the punk had pointed right to the tree where he had been concealed, and he thought for sure he'd been caught, the cops would be on his ass, and he'd be fried without a trial. Then the kid had jabbered on about this dumb creature of his, and there was an argument, and Tanker was able to slip away without detection.

That, he thought smugly, was the easy part—because he was a werewolf.

The realization of his condition had been a long time coming, starting shortly after he had been handed his separation pay and papers. They said he had lost his touch with the new recruits; they said he wasn't living up to the image of the "new army"; they said he drank too much; they said it was against the new rules to hit the little snots when they didn't obey his commands. They said. They, who weren't hardly born when he had first signed his name in that pissant office in Hartford. And they said he ought to be able to find a pretty good job somewhere, that his pension and the job would take care of him for the rest of his life. After thirty years, though, the rest of his life wasn't all that far away.

He left Fort Gordon, Georgia, as he had arrived—on foot, his belongings slung over his shoulder. Refusing several offers of a ride, he walked into Augusta, put his things into a locker at the bus station, then went out and beat the shit out of the first kid under twenty he could find.

There had been a full moon that night, and though a number of people saw and chased him, he had escaped. He noticed the connection right away because he had been running ahead and behind his shadows the whole time, and he decided then and there that the moon would be his charm. It would help him in civilian life make a fortune and spit on those young bastards who thought they knew what the military was all about.

It didn't, though. It had plans for him he hadn't known at the time.

As winter passed, and the jobs passed, and he was constantly in trouble for mouthing off to spineless, candyass bosses usually two decades his junior, he realized that.

As the money ran low, and his friends stopped their loans, and the police looked at him more closely the more his clothes began to fade, he realized that.

The moon had other plans.

Another winter, and a third luckily mild. But the fourth was spent freezing to death in an overcrowded shelter for homeless men in New York City. Humiliation compounded when he was interviewed by a bleeding-heart liberal television reporter and he had tried to explain about his service to the country, and all the reporter wanted to know was if he could get a decent night's sleep in the same room with fifty other old men.

Old men.

Old man.

Christ, he had turned into an old man and he hadn't even known it.

That's when the moon came to him again. Last winter. To save him and show him what werewolves could do.

He had been stumbling along Eighth Avenue, popping into one porn place after another in hopes of getting a free peek at some tits since he hadn't the stuff to find some piece of his own, when a guy in tight jeans and leather jacket did something to his ass as he passed by. Tanker had frozen, turned slowly, and saw the look in the kid's eyes. Blank, like they were dead.

He had almost thrown up, but looked up and saw the moon, looked back to the young hustler and let himself smile. He still had good teeth, still tried to exercise when he had the food in him, and it wasn't hard, in that two-by-four hotel room that smelled like piss and pot, to tear the sonofabitch apart.

The moon winked.

And Tanker howled before he rolled the punk and left.

It wasn't the sex, it was the age.

"Babyfucks," he muttered. That's what they all were— babyfucks taking on the world like they knew what they were doing, leaving good men like him behind to fill up the gutters and the bars and the steps of churches that locked their doors at night.

Babyfucks who didn't know the power of Tanker Falwick, the power of the man who had personally seen the rise and the fall of the armored First Cav, who had crushed Nazis and Fascists and gooks beneath his treads, and who couldn't understand why a tank had to have all them damned computer things inside when all a man had to do was aim the fucking thing and run the enemy down. It was as simple as that, and he didn't need a babyfuck TV screen in his lap to tell him how to do it.

They said he was untrainable in the ways of the new army;

they said he was unstable because he fought them every step and trench of the way; they said he had to keep going to the babyfuck shrink or they'd muster him out and leave him on his own.

They said.

But they didn't say anything about the moon, and how it felt on his face, and how the blood felt when he found the kids and tore out their throats and tore out their guts and sipped a little red and gnawed a little meat and howled his signature before moving on.

They didn't say anything about that.

He rose, skirted the pond, and headed for the ball field and the large thicket where he had watched the concert. He would sleep there tonight and hope for a bit of luck tomorrow, for something more than a squirrel to keep the moon his friend. He needed some badly. He needed something to fill his stomach and something to leave behind and something to remind all those babyfucks that Tanker Falwick was still around. He couldn't do it anymore in New York, in the state or the city, because they had found the alley lean-to where he lived when the black hooker with the blonde hair saw him one morning dressed in fresh dripping red. But he didn't mind because there was a whole country out here just waiting to learn.

First stop, then, this burg, whatever name it had.

He didn't care. All he knew was that it had a lot of kids who thought they were going to live forever.

Despite the fact that it was a school night and his parents didn't like him staying out so late when he had to get up so early, Don decided not to go home right away. Instead, he pedaled across the boulevard, over the center island, and headed east until he reached his street. He turned into it and kept going, not looking left except to note that the station wagon wasn't in the driveway, so his folks still weren't home. And that was all right with him because it was getting harder to stand their sneaking around him as if he didn't know what was going on.

He had no idea where he was headed, only that he didn't want to get warm just yet. He liked the autumn nights, the way the air felt like thin ice on a pond, crisp and clean and ready to shatter as soon as you touched it; he liked the trees so black they were almost invisible, and the way the leaves were raked into huge gold and red piles in the gutters, and the way they made the air smell tart and smoky; he liked the sounds of things on an autumn night, sharp and ringing and carrying a hundred miles. It was somehow comforting, this stretch of weeks before November, and he wanted to enjoy it as long as he could. Before he had to go back; before he had to go home.

He scowled at himself then and slapped the handlebar, slamming his hair away from his high forehead with a punishing hand. That wasn't really fair. He really didn't have such a bad life, not really, not when you thought about it. The house was large enough so that everyone had his privacy, and old enough so that it didn't look like all the others on the block; his room was pretty big, and he never wanted for a decent meal or decent clothes, and he was fairly confident he would be going to college next fall if he kept his grades where they were, nothing spectacular but not shameful either.

But he didn't want to go home.

Not just yet.

There were two high schools in town—Ashford North and Ashford South. He attended South, where his father was the principal, and he had to work like a dog to get his competent grades because he was the honcho's kid and favoritism was forbidden. Norman Boyd had been in charge there for five years before his son became a freshman, and Don was as positive as he could be without proof that his father had met with all his prospective teachers privately before school began, perhaps one at a time in his office, and told them that while he didn't expect them to curry favor by giving the boy good grades just because he was who he was, neither did he expect them to punish Don if decisions were made that they didn't agree with.

Don was to be treated just like any other student, no better and no worse.

He was sure that's what had happened. And sure now they were ignoring their boss since it looked more and more as if the faculty was going to walk out at the end of next month over a salary and hours dispute that had erupted last May.

His father didn't believe him.

And neither did his mother, who taught art in Ashford North.

Besides, she was too busy anyway. She had all her lessons and projects to prepare for and grade, she had her private painting to do whenever she could take the time and get back into Sam's old bedroom, and she had the Ashford Day Committee that was beginning to keep her out of the house and his life most nights of the week.

And somewhere in between, when she thought about it at all, there was little Donny to look after.

Damn, he thought as he turned the corner sharply, nearly scraping the tires against the curb; little Donny. It wasn't his fault that Sam had died, was it? Sam, whose real name was Lawrence but called Sam because his mother said he looked like a Sam; Sam, who had been five years younger than Don, and had died screaming of a ruptured appendix while the family was on vacation, camping out in Yellowstone. Four years ago. In the middle of nowhere.

Sam, who was a shrimp and liked listening to his stories.

It wasn't his fault, and nobody really blamed him for not telling them about Sam's pains because he wanted to go so badly, but he was the only child left and godalmighty they

were making absolutely sure he wouldn't leave them before
they were good and ready to let him go.

He swung around another corner, slowed, and looked down
the street as if he'd never seen it before. It was an odd
sensation, one that made him close his eyes, and open them
again slowly to bring it back into proper focus.

Slower then, the bike on the verge of wobbling.

It was much like his own street—homes dating back to the
Depression and beyond to the turn of the century, all wood
and brick and weather-smooth stone, with small front yards
and old oaks at the curbside, the sidewalks uneven and the
street itself in deep shadow, where the leaves still on their
branches muffled the streetlights' glare.

And several cars parked at the curbs.

Nothing at all out of the ordinary, and ordinarily he would
have ridden right on. But tonight there was something different, something he couldn't see, something he thought he
could feel. It seemed familiar enough—Tar Boston lived
halfway down, in a green Cape Cod with white shutters and
no porch—and yet it wasn't the same.

Slower still, as if someone were behind him, pulling a cord
and drawing it beneath the tires.

He closed one eye, opened it, and gripped the handlebars a
bit tighter.

The cars.

It was the cars.

No matter what color they were, they were dark—gleaming
dark, waiting dark. The facets of their headlamps glowing
faintly like spidereyes caught by the moon, and the windshields pocked with the onset of frost. Their sides reflected
black; their tops reflected the shadows of dying trees. They
were giant cats from the jungle somehow transformed, and
all the more menacing for it.

Finally he stopped in the middle of the street and watched
them, licked quickly at his lips and imagined them waiting

here just for him, waiting for him to tell them what to do. A stable of cars. No. An army of cars. Patiently waiting for the order to kill.

His mouth worked at the start of a smile while he nodded to them all and told them his name.

From somewhere down the block, just past the middle, an engine rumbled softly.

Metal creaked.

A chassis rocked slowly back and forth in place.

He bit at his lower lip; he was scaring himself.

A headlamp winked.

Tires crackled as if they were frozen to the blacktop.

Jesus, he thought, and wiped a palm over his mouth.

The engine died.

Metal stopped shifting.

There was only the faint hiss of late downtown traffic.

He pushed off again and barely made the far corner without swerving off the road, then headed rapidly back up the boulevard toward home. A bus grumbled past him, exhaust clouding his face. He coughed and slowed again, watched as the amber lights strung along its roofline vanished when the street shrank into the dark that hung below the lighted sky above the next town.

Jesus, he thought again, and made himself shudder. He knew it was only heat escaping from the engines, released from the metal frames, that someone had only been warming up a motor in a garage. That's all it was. Yet he made himself think of something else, like what it was like to live in a place where the cities and towns weren't slambang against each other, like they were here, all the way to New York.

Spooky, he decided.

All that open space, or all those trees—spooky as hell, and anyway, Ashford wasn't all that bad of a place.

He turned into his block again, saw the station wagon in

the driveway, and pulled up behind it. After wiping his hands on his jeans, he walked the bike through the open garage door. There was no room inside for the car—too many garden tools and cartons and a thousand odds and ends that somehow always managed to be carted out here when there was no place immediate anyone could think of to put them. Like an attic with its house buried a mile below the ground.

He hesitated, and wiped his hands again as a sliver of tension worked its way across his back. Then he opened the door and stepped into the kitchen.

"I thought," his mother said, "you'd been kidnapped, for heaven's sake."

TWO

_T_he light was bright; he squinted to adjust.

She was standing at the sink with one hip cocked, rinsing out a cup while the percolator bubbled noisily on the counter beside her. Her hair was dark and long, reaching almost to the middle of her back, and when she pulled it together with a vivid satin ribbon the way it was now, she looked almost young enough to be one of her own students. Especially when she smiled and her large eyes grew wide. Which she did when he walked up and kissed her cheek, shucked his jacket, and draped it over the back of a chair.

He was going to tell her about the cars, changed his mind when she looked away, back to her cleaning.

"I was riding."

"Good for you," she declared, glowering at a stain that would not leave the cup. "Fresh air is very good for you. It flushes out the dead cells in the blood, but I guess you already know that from biology or something."

"Right."

A glance into the half-filled refrigerator and he pulled out a can of soda.

"But that gassy junk, dear, is bad for you," she said, setting the cup down and rinsing out another. There was a stack of dirty dishes in the sink, soaking in hot soapy water. Maybe tomorrow she would get around to washing them all. "It's not good to drink that stuff before you go to bed. It lies there in your stomach not doing anything but making you burp and giving you nightmares."

"Am I going to bed?"

She tsked at him and pursed her lips. "Donald, it is now"—she checked the sunflower-shaped clock over the stove—"forty-seven minutes past ten o'clock. Exactly. You have school tomorrow. I have school tomorrow. And I'm tired."

The percolator buzzed at her and she pulled out the plug.

"You didn't have to wait up for me if you're that tired, you know, Mom."

She dried the cups and poured the coffee, everything perfectly timed. "I didn't. Your father's been on the phone since we walked in the door. By the way," she added as he headed for the living room, "I saw that Chris playing the piano tonight. She's really quite pretty, you know it? Are you going to take her to the do?"

"I don't know," he said, still walking away. "Maybe."

"What?"

"Maybe!" he called back, and under his breath: "On a cold day in hell, lady."

Chris Snowden was the new girl on the block, and in this case it was literal. She and her family had moved in three doors down in the middle of last August. Her hair was such a pale blonde it was nearly white, her skin looked so soft you could lose your fingers in it if you tried to touch it, and, Brian Pratt's crudeness aside, she had a figure he had seen only in the movies. She was, at first glance, a laughable stereotype—cheerleader, brainless, and the football team captain's personal choice for a consort. Which she had been for a while, while everyone nodded, then professed shock and puzzlement when she started dating the president of the student council. She didn't need the grades, so he wasn't doing her homework, and she didn't need the ride to school, because it was only five blocks away and she walked every morning—except when it rained and she drove her own car, a dark red convertible whose top was always up. Then just last week it was known she was on her own again, and those who decided such things decided she was only sleeping around.

Don puffed his cheeks, blew out, and sighed.

Chris's father was a doctor in some prestigious hospital in New York, and if Don's mother had her way, he would be taking her to every event of the town's century-plus birthday— the Ashford Day picnic, party, dance, concert, football game, whatever. A full week of celebration. But even if he wanted to, he knew he didn't have a chance.

Just as he reached the front hall and was about to turn right into the living room, he heard his father's voice and changed his mind.

"I don't give a sweet Jesus what you think, Harry. I am not going to take a position one way or another."

Great, Don thought gloomily; just great.

The position was which side of the dispute to be on; Harry was Mr. Harold Falcone, his biology instructor and president of the teachers' union.

"Look," his father said as Don poked his head around the doorway, "I've pushed damned hard for you and your people since the day I walked into that place, and you know it. I got money for the labs, the teams, for the goddamned mainte- nance, for god's sake, so don't you dare tell me I don't sympathize."

Norman Boyd was sitting in his favorite chair, a monstrous green thing with scarred wood trim and a sagging cushion. His back was to Don, and it was rigid.

"What? What? Harry, goddamnit to hell, if my mother

hadn't taught me better, I'd hang up on you right now for that kind of nonsense. What do you mean, I don't give a shit? I do give a shit! But can't you see past your wallet just this once and understand that I'm caught between a rock and a hard place here? My god, man, you're screaming crap in one ear and the board is screaming crap in the other, and I'm damned for doing this and damned for doing that, and double damned if I don't do a thing—which is exactly what I feel like doing sometimes, believe me.''

He tapped a long finger on the handset, looked up at the high plaster ceiling, and used his free hand to rake through his greying brown hair. A deep breath swelled his chest beneath a white crewneck sweater; the tapping moved to the top of his thigh.

"I will be at the negotiations, yes. I've already told you that." He shifted. "I will not—" He glanced over his shoulder. "Yes, of course my contract is up for renewal at the end of this year. I know that, you know that, the board knows it—for Jesus's sake, the whole damned world knows about it by now!" He saw his son and grimaced a smile. "What? Yes! Yes, damnit, I admit it, are you happy? I do not want to jeopardize my job and my future just because you assholes couldn't come to terms over the summer. No," he said with acid sweetness, "I do not expect your support either if I decide to run for office."

He grinned then and returned the handset to its cradle on the floor beside him. "The creep hung up on me. He ain't got no manners, and that's shocking in a teacher. Hi, Don, saw you talking to the kids tonight. You change your mind about joining us and being a teacher, carrying on the new family tradition?"

"Dad," he said, suddenly cold. "Dad, there's a big test next week. Mr. Falcone is my teacher."

"I know that."

"But you were yelling at him!"

"Hey, he won't do anything, don't worry about it."

Don squeezed the soda can. "You always say that."

"And it always turns out, right?"

"No," he said softly. "No, not always." And before his father could respond, he said, "See you tomorrow. It's late. Mom wants me in bed."

He took the stairs slowly in case his father wanted to join him, but there was nothing but the sound of his mother bringing in the coffee, and the start of low voices. He heard his name once before he reached the top landing, but there was no temptation to eavesdrop. He knew what they were probably saying.

Dad was wondering if there was anything wrong, and Mom would tell him it was all part of growing up and Donny was really in a difficult position and perhaps Norm shouldn't lose his temper like that at the boy's teachers. Dad would bluster a bit, deny any problems, finally see the point, and reassure his wife that none of the faculty would dare do anything out of line, not if they wanted his support in the strike.

It was getting to be an old story.

Great, he thought as he pushed into his room. I'm not a son anymore, I'm a weapon. An ace up the old sleeve. If I fail, it isn't me, it's the teachers getting even; if I get an A, it isn't me, it's the teacher kissing ass. Great. Just . . . great.

He slammed the door, turned on the light, and greeted his pets by kicking the bed.

"I don't understand it," said Joyce Boyd from her place on the sofa when she heard the door slam. "He's a perfectly normal boy, we know that, but he hardly ever goes anywhere anymore. If we hadn't insisted tonight, he would have stayed home, playing with those damned things he has upstairs."

"Sure he goes out," Norm said, lighting a cigarette, crossing his legs. "But with all your zillion civic projects and that

Art League thing—not to mention the Ashford Day business—
you're just not home long enough to see it.''

Her eyes narrowed. ''That's a crack.''

''Yeah, so?''

''I thought we agreed not to do that anymore.''

He studied the cigarette's tip, the round of his knees, and
brushed at an ash that settled on his chest. The coffee was on
the table beside him, growing cold. ''I guess we did at that.''

''I guess we did at that,'' she mimicked sourly, and pulled
her legs under her. A hand passed wearily over her eyes.
''Damn you, Norman,'' she said wearily, ''I do the best I
can.''

''Sure you do,'' he answered without conviction. ''Whenever you're around.''

''Well, look at him, will you?'' Her lips, thin at best,
vanished when her mouth tightened. ''When was the last
time you spent an evening with him, huh? I don't think that
poor boy has seen you for more than a couple of hours in the
last two weeks.''

''I have a school year to run,'' he reminded her tonelessly,
''and a possible strike on my hands. Besides, he sees me at
the school every day.''

''Not hardly the same thing, Norm, and you know it.
You're not his father there, not the way it should be.''

He pushed himself deeper into the chair and stretched out
his legs. ''Knock it off, Joyce, okay? I'm tired, and the boy
can take care of himself.''

''Well, so am I tired,'' she snapped, ''but I have to defend
myself and you don't, is that it?''

''What's to defend?''

Her eyes closed briefly. ''Nothing,'' she said in mild
disgust, and reached over a pile of manila folders for a
magazine, flipped the pages without looking, and tossed it
aside. She picked up a folder—schedules for Ashford Day.
She was one of the women in charge of coordinating the

entertainment from the two high schools. She dropped that as well and plucked at her blouse. "I worry about all that running he does too."

He was surprised, and he showed it.

"What I mean is," she said hastily, "it's not really like jogging, is it? He's not interested in keeping fit or joining the track team or cross-country. He just . . . runs."

"Well, what's wrong with that? It's good for him."

"But he's always alone," she said, looking at him as if he ought to understand. "And he doesn't have a regular schedule either, nothing like that at all. He just runs when he gets in one of his moods. And he doesn't even do it here, around the block or something—he does it at the school track."

"Joyce, you're not making sense. Why run on cracked pavement and take a chance on a broken leg or twisted ankle when you can run on a real track?"

"It just . . . I don't know. It just doesn't feel right."

"Maybe it helps him think. Some guys lift weights, some guys use a punching bag, and Donald runs. So what?"

"If he has problems," she said primly, "he shouldn't . . . he shouldn't try to run away from them. He should come to us."

"Why?" he said coldly. "The way you've been lately, why should he bother?"

"Me?"

Her stare was uncomfortable.

"All right. We." And he let his eyes close.

A few moments later: "Norman, do you think he's forgotten that animal hospital stuff?"

"I guess. He hasn't said anything since last month. At least not to me."

"Me either."

He opened his eyes again and looked at the empty fireplace, ran a finger absently down the crooked length of his nose. "I guess, when you think about it, we didn't handle it very well. We could have shown a little more enthusiasm."

"Agreed." She rubbed at her knees.

Norm allowed himself a sly look. "Maybe," he said with a glance to his wife, "we ought to do like that couple we read about in the *Times*, the one that claimed they solved their kid's mind-shit by taking him to a massage parlor." He chuckled quietly. "That's it. Maybe we ought to get him laid." He laughed aloud, shaking his head and trying to imagine his son—not a movie star, but not an ogre either—humping a woman. He couldn't do it. Donald, as far as he was concerned, was almost totally sexless.

"Jesus," she muttered.

"Christ, I was only kidding."

"Jesus." She reached again for the magazine, gave it up halfway through the motion, and stood. "I'm going to bed. I have to teach tomorrow."

He waited until she was in the foyer before he rose and followed.

"You don't have to come."

"I know," he said, "but I have to be principal tomorrow."

At the landing she turned and looked down at him. "We're going to get a divorce, aren't we?"

He gripped the banister hard and shook his head. "God, Joyce, do you have to end every disagreement with talk of divorce? Other people argue like cats and dogs and they don't go running for a lawyer."

He followed her down the hall, past Don's room, and into their own. She switched on the dresser lamp and opened their bathroom door. Her blouse was already unbuttoned by the time he had sagged onto the bed and had his shoes off. Standing in the doorway, the pale light pink behind her from the tile on the walls and floor, she dropped the blouse and kicked it away. She wasn't wearing a bra, and though he could not see her face, he knew it wasn't an invitation.

"I know why," she said, working at the snap on her slacks.

"Why what?"

"Why you don't love me anymore."

"Oh, for god's sake." His shirt was off, and he dug for his pajamas folded under the pillow.

"No, really, I know. You think Harry and I are having an affair. That's why you're so hard on him. That's why you make an ass of yourself when you talk to him like you did tonight."

"You're full of it," he said unconvincingly. He put on his top, stood, and unfastened his belt, zipper, and let his trousers fall. "I figure you have better taste than that."

She turned away to the basin, running hot water and steaming the light-ringed mirror. "You don't have to pretend, Norman. I know. I know."

Except for her panties she was naked. Her breasts were still small and firm, her stomach reasonably flat for a woman who'd had two children and didn't exercise, and her legs were so long they seemed to go on forever. He watched as she leaned forward to squeeze toothpaste onto her toothbrush; he watched while she examined herself in the mirror, turning slightly left and right. He watched, and he was saddened, because she didn't do a thing for him.

It's a bitch, he thought; god, life is a bitch.

He wriggled under the covers, rubbed his eyes to relieve them of an abrupt burning itch, and looked at her again. "Are you?" he asked at last. "With Harry, I mean."

"You bastard," she said, and slammed the door.

The overcoat wasn't going to be enough, but Tanker had nothing else to use as a blanket. The leaves covered most of him, and the brush kept away most of the wind, but it still wasn't enough.

What he needed to relax was one of them whores. Like the

one up in Yonkers. Tits breaking out of her sweater, teenage
ass as tight as her jeans. When he yanked her into the alley
and clubbed her with a fist so she wouldn't scream, he had
known once again he wouldn't be dying without getting a
piece. Her eyes had crossed when he dropped her on the
ground, and she'd spat blood at him when he slapped her
again; but she was warm, no doubt about it. She was warm
right up until the moment he had opened her throat with his
knife, and had finished the job with his nails grown especially long.

She had been warm, and now he was cold, and he decided
that the next one would have to be one of them whores.

He shivered, huddled deeper under the coat and the leaves,
and closed his eyes, sighed, and waited for sleep.

Waiting an hour later, eyes wide and watching.

It was the park.

The moon was up there, still guarding him, still whispering him his orders, but there was something else, something
in the park that was waiting just for him. He tried scoffing at
it, but the feeling wouldn't go away; he tried banishing it
with a determined shake of his head, but it wouldn't go
away.

It was out there, somewhere, and if it hadn't been for the
moon, he knew he'd be dead.

Tomorrow, he promised himself, crossing his heart and
pointing at his eye; tomorrow he would have a whore, and
then get the hell out.

And if the moon didn't show, he'd kill somewhere else.

The door was open just enough to let a bar of light from
the hallway drop across the brown shag rug, climb the side of
the bed, and pin him to the mattress. Don lay on top of the
covers, head on the pillow, hands clasped on his stomach,
and checked to be sure his friends were still with him.

Above the headboard was a poster of a panther lying in a

jungle clearing and licking its paw while it stared at the camera; on the wall opposite, flanking the door, were posters of elephants charging with trunks up through the brush, their ears fanned wide and their tusks sharply pointed and an unnatural white. Elsewhere around the large room were pictures and prints of leopards and cheetahs running, eagles stooping, pumas stalking, a cobra from the back to show the eyes on its hood. On the chest of drawers was a fake stuffed bobcat with fangs bared; on the low dresser was a miniature stuffed lion; in the blank spaces on the three unfinished bookcases were plaster and plastic figurines he had made and painted himself, claws and teeth and talons and eyes. And above the desk set perpendicular to the room's only window was a tall poster framed behind reflectionless glass—a dirt road bordered by a dark screen of immense poplars that lay shadows on the ground, shadows in the air, deepened the twilight sky, and made the stars seem brighter; and down the road, just coming over the horizon, was a galloping black horse, its hooves striking sparks from hidden stones, breath steaming from its nostrils, eyes narrowed, and ears laid back. It had neither rider nor reins, and it was evident that should it ever reach the foreground, it would be the largest horse the viewer had ever seen.

His friends.

His pets.

After examining them a second time, he rolled over and buried his face in the crook of his arm.

His parents refused to allow real animals in the house, at least since Sam had died and they had given the kid's parakeet to an aunt in Pennsylvania. Because of the memories; and it didn't seem to make a difference that Don had loved the dumb bird too.

When he pressed for a replacement—any kind, he wasn't fussy—his mother claimed a severe allergy to cats, and his father told him reasonably there wasn't anyone around the place long enough anymore to take adequate care of a dog. Fish were boring, birds and turtles carried all manner of exotic and incurable diseases, and hamsters and gerbils were too dumb to do anything but sleep and eat.

He had long ago decided he didn't mind; if his parents weren't exactly thrilled about what he wanted to do with his life, why should he fuss over the absence of some pets?

Because, he told himself; just because.

And suddenly it was summer again, the sun was up, and he was down in the living room, bursting with excitement. Both his folks were there, summoned from their chores in the yard and waiting anxiously. He could tell by the look on his mother's face that she expected him to say he was quitting school to get married, by the look on his father's that he'd gotten some girl pregnant.

"I know what I'm going to study at college," he had said in a voice that squeaked with apprehension, and he bolstered his nerves by taking his father's chair without thinking.

"Good," Norman had said with a smile. "I hope you'll get so rich I can quit and you can support me in a manner to which I would love to become accustomed."

He had laughed because he couldn't think of anything else to do, and his mother had hit Norm's arm lightly.

"What is it, dear," she'd asked.

"I'm going to be a doctor."

"Well, son of a bitch," his father had said, his smile stretching to a proud grin.

"Oh, my god, Donald," Joyce had whispered, her eyes suddenly glistening.

"Sure," he said, relieved the worst part was over and there was no scene to endure. "I like animals, they like me, and I like learning about them and taking care of them. So I might as well get paid for doing what I like, right? So I'm gonna be a veterinarian."

The silence had almost bludgeoned him to the carpet, and

it wasn't until several seconds had passed that he realized they had misunderstood him, that they had thought at that moment he had meant he was going to be an M.D.

Joyce's smile had gone strained, but she still professed joy that he was finally decided; his father had taken him outside after a while and told him, for at least the hundred-millionth time, that he was the first member of the Boyd family to get a college education, and Donald would be the second. He said he hoped with all his heart the boy knew what he was doing.

"Being a teacher, and now a principal," Norman had said, "is something I'm not ashamed to be proud of, son. Being a vet, though, that's not . . . well, it's not really anything at all, when you think about it. I mean, helping cats instead of babies isn't exactly my idea of medicine."

"But I like animals," he had argued stubbornly. "And I don't like the way people treat them."

"Oh. Dr. Dolittle, I presume?" his father had said lightly.

"Yeah. Maybe."

"Don." And a hand rested on his shoulder. "Look, I just want to be sure you're positive. It's a hell of a step, making up your mind about something like this."

"I wouldn't have said it if I wasn't."

"Well, at least think about it, all right? As a favor to me and your mother. It's only August. You have a full year to graduation, and even then you really don't have to make up your mind. Some kids take a lot of time. You just take all the time you need."

He had wanted to shout that he had done all the thinking he had to on the subject; instead, he had only nodded and walked away, and had walked and run for the rest of the day. When he finally returned home, nothing was said about the announcement, and nothing had been said since.

He grinned now in his bed; he wasn't quite as thick as his father thought him—he knew they were hoping he would come to his senses and decide to treat rich old ladies instead of little old poodles.

What they didn't know was that he didn't want to work with poodles or Persians or dachshunds or Siamese; what he wanted was to work with the live equivalents of the pets in his room.

They'd scream bloody murder if they knew about that.

But he didn't mind, because nothing they could do would make him change his decision; now if he could only stop minding the sound of them arguing.

The voices in their room, as if at his command, stopped, and he undressed quickly and got into bed. Stared at the ceiling. Wondered if he was soon going to become part of a statistic. Jeff Lichter's folks had divorced when he was ten, and he lived with his father two blocks over. He was an all-right guy, nothing wrong there, but Brian Pratt lived with his mother, and whether it was because of the divorce or not, Brian was practically living on his own.

Nuts, he thought, and rolled onto his stomach, held up his head, and looked with a vague smile at the panther, then over to the horse, then the otters on the nearest bookcase. There were no names for any of them, but he shuddered to think of what Brian or Tar would say if they ever found out he sometimes talked to them all. Just a few words, not whole conversations. A touch on one for luck before a test, a wish on another that he would meet The Girl and wouldn't have to suffer the guys' teasing anymore, a wish on still another that he would wake up in the morning and discover that he had turned into a superman.

He grinned.

Don the Superman! Leaping tall buildings at a single bound! Carrying Tar Boston over the park and dropping him head-first right into the pond. Saving Chris Snowden from a rampaging Brian and letting her be as grateful as she wanted.

Using his X-ray vision to see through Tracey Quintero's baggy sweaters just to check if anything was really there.

Don the Superman.

"Don the jerk," he said.

It was funny, when he thought about it, how the little kids were the only ones he could really talk to. For some reason most of them thought his stories were pretty okay, except for that one little monster tonight. A laugh was muffled by the pillow. A good thing the brat's parents had come along just then, or he would have had them all really seeing that giant crow in the tree.

And damn, wouldn't that be something!

Don the Superman, and his giant pal, Crow!

Just before he fell asleep, he wished he could wake up and discover that he was the handsomest kid in the entire city, maybe the whole state, maybe even the whole world.

Just about anything except waking up to see plain old Don Boyd still there in the bathroom mirror.

THREE

The next seven days slipped into October on the back of a lost football game in which Brian dropped three sure touchdowns and Tar and Fleet each fumbled once, an article in the weekly newspaper implying that the Ashford South principal was delaying successful contract negotiations by his refusal for political reasons to support the people he led, and a series of grim reports on New York television's early evening news programs concerning the Howler—since his last victim had died almost two weeks before, the police theorized he had either committed suicide or had left the state, a notion adopted by Don and Jeff with an accompanying shiver of macabre delight.

On Tuesday morning Chris Snowden walked to school only a block ahead of him, and he could not decide whether to try to catch up and hope for a conversation, maybe she'd throw herself into his arms, or hang back and just watch. In the cafeteria he and Jeff scowled at the offering of scorched macaroni and cheese, and decided that Chris was probably into older men these days—college guys, if not their fathers.

Then Don watched Tracey Quintero pick up her tray and

carry it to the gap in the wall where a worker was waiting to scrub it down for the next user.

"Hey, Jeff, do you think it's possible for someone to be in love with two women at the same time?"

"Sure. I think."

"It has to be possible. I mean, different women have different things to offer a guy, right? And a guy can't find everything he wants in one woman, right? So he has to find them in different women, right?"

Jeff looked at him sideways. "What?"

"It makes sense, don't you think?"

"It makes sense if you're crazy, sure."

"Well, I'm not crazy, and it makes sense, and I think I'm in love."

"Lust," Jeff corrected. "It's lust."

"What a pal."

"Well, hell, Don, that's nuts, y'know?"

"I thought you agreed."

"I did too until I heard what you said."

He poked at the macaroni, stabbed at the cheese crust, and sighed as he opened a carton of milk. As he drank, Chris walked in, alone, saw him, and smiled and walked out again.

"God," he whispered.

"Maybe she likes you."

He didn't dare believe it; he didn't even know her.

"Or," said Jeff as he rose to leave, "she knows your old man and wants to polish a few apples, if you know what I mean."

Don sagged glumly, and Jeff realized his mistake, could do nothing about it, and hurried out. Don watched him go, then rose and followed slowly. Lichter had reminded him about a girl he had gone with as a sophomore. He thought he had found a one-way express ticket to heaven the way she treated him, trotted after him, made him laugh, and taught him the preliminaries of making love. Then, one day at his locker, he had overheard her talking with Brian, giggling and swearing on her mother's grave that the only reason she saw him was because of his father.

"I am not working one minute more than I have to to get out of here," she'd said. "And what tightass teacher's gonna flunk me when I'm messing around with the principal's kid?"

Several, apparently, after he broke it off that next Friday night. He had confronted her, she had denied it, and he had lost his temper, forgetting one of his parents' cardinal rules: never yell or threaten because it cheapens you and puts you on the defensive, because a threat made has to be carried out or it's worthless; if you're going to threaten, make sure you can do it.

She had laughed at him.

And though she was gone before the end of the year, he felt no satisfaction. All her leaving had proved was that she had been right, and smiles in his direction were seldom the same anymore.

On Wednesday he saw Chris again, and she ignored him.

It should have made him feel better; instead, he felt lousy, especially after his guidance counselor told him how expensive it was going to be to study veterinary medicine. His father was going to have a fit, and his mother might even relent and permit him to get a job to help defray the expenses.

He almost forgot Thursday's biology test.

"The meeting's over by now," Joyce said.

Harry Falcone punched at the pillows behind his back and watched with a lopsided grin as she dressed. "Tell him it ran late."

"They always run late. He doesn't believe it, you know."

Falcone shrugged; he didn't care.

When she was finished, she turned to look at him, the sheet just barely over his groin, his dark curly hair in matted tangles over his face. Patrician, she thought; put a toga on him and he'd look like a Roman senator about to slice up an emperor.

His smile exposed capped white teeth. "Thinking about seconds?"

She was. She hated herself for it, but she was. She wanted those hands on her rough not gentle, she wanted the weight of him crushing her into the mattress, she wanted the forgetfulness his sex brought—and she wanted to cut his throat for what he was making her do to her family.

"No."

"Too bad," he said. "Once the strike starts, it'll be hard seeing you."

Gathering her hair so she could tie on the ribbon, Joyce walked out of the room and picked up her coat. A hesitation— did she leave anything behind Norman would notice?—before she opened the apartment door.

"Hey," he called from the bedroom.

She waited.

"Nice lay, kiddo."

Bastard, she thought, slamming the door behind her, wincing as she headed for the fire exit and took the stairs shakily.

It was stupid, and it was the stuff of dreamlike romance— that a man would come along and sweep her off her feet, carry her into the sunset and unheard of ecstasy. She had told herself a thousand times that it was partly Norman's fault, that his preoccupation with running the school and unofficially running for mayor had somehow left her behind. She was no longer his partner, but a woman expected to remain ten paces back in his shadow.

The catch was, she'd never been able to keep a secret from her husband. Her eyes, too large for deception, betrayed her every night, and she was positive he was taunting her, tormenting her so she would admit it to his face.

And as she drove home, making sure she approached the house from the direction of the building where the meeting was supposed to have been held, she put a hand to her breast and felt the residue of Harry's touch.

It would be a hell of a lot easier, she thought, if she could just decide if staying with Norman was mere habit, or real love. And if it was the latter, what would Harry do if she broke the affair off?

The temperature slipped just before dawn, and the ground was covered with crackling frost, the first of the season. It ghosted the windshields and sugared the lawns, and as he walked to school he watched his breath puff to clouds. It was a good feeling, and he took long strides to force himself awake. He hadn't been sleeping long the night before, when something inside reminded him about the exam. He had awakened instantly and sat at his desk until just before sunrise, alternately reading his notes and talking with the galloping horse who had no pity for his error.

When his mother came home from the committee meeting, he had gone rigid, expecting a scolding for being up so late, and was surprised when she passed the door without stopping, sounding for all the world as if she were crying.

At the end of the block he turned left, having studiously avoiding staring at Chris's house. He crossed the street and moved more briskly, keeping his eyes wide, hoping a good strong wind would slap some sense into his foggy brain.

On his left were small houses crowded together on small lots, smothered by trees and azaleas and evergreen shrubs. Two blocks later they were stopped by a high chain link fence almost buried under swarms of ivy that rolled over its top. A large manicured lawn began on the other side, sweeping back and down the slope toward practice fields and the stadium, sweeping ahead of him toward the bulk of the school itself—a building of red brick and greying white marble, two stories in front and three in back, where the land fell away; tall windows, wide tiled corridors, an auditorium that seated over eight hundred, built in the 1930s and never replaced.

Ashford North, on the far side of town, had been constructed in 1959, was brick and white marble, one story with tinted windows, and it looked like a factory.

From the sidewalk Don climbed three steps to a wide concrete plaza that led to a dozen more low steps and the glass front doors. Paths were worn brown over the grass to the side entrances, and there were faces in the classroom windows watching the students hurrying, dawdling, daring the first bell to ring before they stepped inside.

He didn't wait, though a few called his name; he pushed straight in and swerved left to the banks of multicolored lockers at the end of the hall. A fumbling with the combination lock, and he grabbed the books he needed for his first three classes. A few rushing by greeted him with yells, but he only waved without turning; he was tired, and he didn't want to talk to anyone until, if he were lucky, he finally woke up.

He didn't.

He almost fell asleep in trig, actually dozed for a couple of minutes in English, and in German sat with his fingers pulling on either side of his eyes to keep them from closing. None of the teachers noticed. None of his classmates did either.

Just before ten-thirty he passed the glass-walled front office and saw his father standing at the chest-high reception counter with Mr. Falcone. They were speaking softly, heatedly from the way his father slapped a newspaper against his thigh and the way he swiped the side of his hawk's nose as if he were boxer; and as he moved on with a worried frown, the biology teacher stormed out of the glass-walled room and nearly collided with him. There was no apology; the man marched on, and Don's throat went dry. The voice of the corridor buzzed until he had a headache, and he stumbled back to his locker, took out his biology notebook and text, and floated into study hall, where he tried to concentrate on the lessons.

His mother didn't care about his father anymore.

He flipped open the book and toyed with the transparencies that displayed in garish color the inner workings of a frog.

His father didn't care about his mother. Once, last night while the room was dark and they had started arguing again after Joyce had returned, he thought he heard Mr. Falcone's name.

The quick breakfast he had made for himself suddenly curdled and threatened to climb into his throat, making him swallow four times before he knew he wouldn't throw up. Without realizing it, then, he moaned his relief, and only a muffled giggling behind him gave warning that Mr. Hedley was coming down the aisle.

"Mr. Boyd?"

He looked up into a pair of horn-rimmed glasses. "Yes?"

"Are you having a little do-it-yourself choir practice back here, Mr. Boyd?"

The giggling again, and outright laughter from Tar and Fleet on the other side of the large room.

His face grew warm. "No, sir."

"Then may I suggest you remain a bit more silent so that the rest of us can get on with our work?"

"Yes sir, I'm sorry."

"Thank you, Mr. Boyd." Hedley turned, Don's stomach churned again, and he inadvertently managed to make his acidic belch sound like another groan. Hedley reversed himself slowly. A small man, nearly as wide as he was tall, with a dark plastered fringe of red hair and a thick twitching mustache. "Mr. Boyd, perhaps you didn't hear me."

He felt perspiration gathering coldly under his arms. They were all watching him now, waiting for him to brave it out the way Tar would, or Brian. But he could only blink and gesture helplessly at his abdomen, pantomiming an upset stomach because the acid was climbing again and he felt his cheeks begin to burn.

Hedley clasped his tiny hands behind his back and rocked on his heels. "Mr. Boyd, this, as you may have learned from your study of American history, is a democratic society. There is no privilege here. None. You will therefore remain silent, or you will remain for detention."

He nodded glumly.

The giggling stopped immediately as the man headed back for his desk.

Privilege, he thought bitterly; the sonofabitch. Why couldn't he have gone to Ashford North the way his mother wanted him to? Nobody cared if your mother taught art.

Even if your mother didn't care for your father.

He clamped a hand over his mouth and tried to resume studying, but the words blurred and the pictures swam like muddied fingerprints, and when he was out in the hall again, the mobs pushed and jostled him like a twig in the current. He didn't care. He would do well on the test because he enjoyed biology and what it taught him about animals, like in zoology in the afternoon, right after phys ed. But he couldn't take the pushing, and he didn't want the shoving, and he almost panicked when he felt his breakfast moving again. With a lurch he stumbled into the nearest boy's room, found an empty stall, and sat with his head cradled in his palms. Belching. Tasting sour milk. Spitting dryly and wishing he would either throw up and be done with it, or calm down and get on with it.

The bell rang.

He jumped, dropped his books, scooped them up, and ran down the hall. Mr. Falcone was just closing the door.

"Ah, Donald," he said, "I'm glad you could make it."

He managed a pained smile and headed for his seat, as in all his other classes as far toward the back as his teachers would permit. Then he dropped his books on the floor and waited as Falcone passed out the test sheet while giving instructions. The young instructor, he saw, was in a casual mood today—no jacket or tie, just sleek pants, with an open shirt under a light sweater. His hair was barely combed, the tight curls damp as if he'd just taken a shower. Face and body of a Mediterranean cast that many of the girls lusted for and some of the boys coveted.

Finally he reached Don's seat, held out the paper, and wouldn't release it when Don took hold. Instead, he continued to talk, letting the class know this was probably the most important test of the semester, since it was going to be worth a full third of their final grade; failing this would make the exam in January much too important.

Then he let go, and smiled.

"Do you understand, Mr. Boyd?"

He did, but he didn't know why he'd been singled out.

Falcone leaned over, pushed the test to the center of the desk, and added quietly, "You'd better be perfect today, Boyd. You're going to need it."

It was a full minute before he was able to focus on the questions. Falcone was in front, leaning against the blackboard rail, arms folded at his chest, eyes half-closed. The clock over the door jumped once. Fleet was staring intently at his wrist, Tar was scribbling, Brian was staring out the window at the football field. Don blinked and rubbed his eyes. He couldn't believe what he had heard, and refused to believe it was some kind of threat. He couldn't fail. He knew the work, and he knew the teacher. He checked the first question, answered it almost blindly, answered all the others just as the bell rang.

It couldn't have been a threat.

The paper went onto a pile on the desk, the books tumbled into his locker, and he grabbed his brown paper lunch bag and left the building by one of the rear exits. Despite the morning frost the sun was warm, and he crossed a broad concrete walk that ended at a six-foot wall in which there were regularly spaced gaps. He picked one, passed through, and was on the top row of the stadium's seats, the field below, the much lower wooden visitors' bleachers across the way. The seats were nothing more than steprows of concrete, and it occurred to him suddenly that half the school and its grounds seemed made of the stuff, maybe once white and clean, now grey and brown with use and the pummeling of the weather.

The ham sandwich he had made for himself tasted lousy.

It couldn't have been a threat.

"If you kill yourself, they'll never get the blood up."

He jumped and dropped the sandwich, recovered it gracelessly, and squinted up.

"It seeps in, you know? Right into the cement. They'll be scrubbing it for days and they'll hate your guts. It's a rotten way to get sympathy, take my word for it."

He smiled and moved over.

Tracey Quintero sat beside him and shook her head. "Are you really that depressed?"

She was dark from hair to skin, her oversize sweater more dazzlingly white as a result, and her pleated skirt somewhat out of style. Her features were more angles than curves, and he thought her nice but not all that pretty, except when she smiled and showed all those teeth. Spanish; and he wondered at times what she would look like in those tight colorful dresses the flamenco dancers wore.

"I guess."

"Biology that bad?" She had Falcone after lunch, but she wasn't fishing for answers.

"Yeah. No. I guess not."

"How'd you do?"

"Okay, I guess." He bit into the sandwich and tasted grit from its fall. "Harder than usual."

She nodded, unconcerned, leaning forward to rest her arms on her legs, and they watched two gym classes make an attempt to run around the seven-lane red-stained cinder track that outlined the football field. Laughter drifted toward them, a sharp whistle, and a sudden scent of lilac that confused him for a moment until he turned and sniffed, and knew it was her.

She pointed down to a lanky redhead sweeping effortlessly around the far turn. "Is that why they call him Fleet? Because he's so fast?"

Making polite conversation, that's what they call it, he thought; boy, I even have to be made conversation to today.

"Yeah," he said.

"He should be on track, then, not football," she said with a slight lisp in her voice.

"Football scholarships are bigger money."

"Whoa," she said, staring at him intently. "My goodness, but that sounded bitter."

He shrugged. "It's the truth. Fleet needs the scholarship to go to school, and he'll get it with football. He's the best wide receiver in the county."

"I thought Tar was."

A crumb of bread stuck to his lips, and he sought it with a finger, stared at it, ate it. "Tar's a running back." He frowned. "You know that."

She leaned back, her books huddling against her formless chest. "I forgot." A glance behind him, up at the school. "Hey, Don?"

"Huh?"

"Do you know what your father's going to do about the strike?"

He watched Fleet, who waved and blew Tracey a kiss. "I don't know. I'm not his political advisor."

Tracey ignored the sarcasm. "I hope he does something. God, I mean, we're seniors! If our grades are screwed up because of a strike . . . god!'' She traced circles on the back of one of her books. ''My father will shoot them all, you know. He will.''

Her father was a policeman. Don believed he would do it.

''I don't know what's gonna happen, honest.''

''Oh. Okay.'' A check of her watch. ''Bell's gonna ring soon.''

''You know what I wish?'' he said, suddenly not wanting her to leave. ''I wish I had the nerve to cut classes just once before I graduate. Just once.''

''Your father would kill you,'' she said quickly.

''No kidding.'' His grin was mischievous. ''But it would be a lotta fun, I bet.''

She studied his face, his eyes, and finally gave him a broad smile. ''You haven't got the nerve. I know you better than that.''

''Right,'' he said, mischief gone. ''I'm too predictable.''

''Reliable,'' she corrected. ''You're reliable, that's what you are.''

The gym classes began filing off the field, Fleet trailing with an arm around a ponytailed girl.

''Wonderful. They can put that on my tombstone. I'll sound like somebody's grandfather's old watch.''

Her expression soured. ''Hey, you are in a mood, aren't you. Jeez.''

When she stood, he rose with her, dropped his lunch bag, and had to lunge after it to keep the breeze from taking it down the steps. Then he stumbled after her, catching up barely in time to open the heavy glass-and-metal door. She gave him a wink and a mock curtsy and slipped in, and they stood at the landing just as the bell rang. There were footsteps on the iron-tipped stairs, thunder in the halls.

''You want to go to a movie or something tomorrow night?''

She seemed as surprised to hear the question as he was

astonished he had asked it. Christ, he thought, Brian's gonna
kill me.

The stairs filled and they were separated, but before she
was gone she mouthed an *I'll call you tonight*, which was
sort of an answer and no answer at all. God, he thought as he
headed down for the gym, you are an idiot, Boyd. Boy, are
you an idiot.

When he reached the locker room and started changing,
Fleet was still there and Tar was just coming in, running a
monster comb through incredibly black hair. The gossip dealt
primarily with the game with North over Ashford Day weekend, the Howler, and the strike that was going to set them all
free until long after Christmas.

"Hey, Donny," Tar yelled as he laced up his sneakers,
"you tell your old man to stop farting around, huh? I need
that vacation now!"

"Aw, shit," said Fleet, racing by naked, his towel over
his shoulder, "he don't care about us poor peons, Tar baby.
Don't you know he's his daddy's spy in the ranks? Secret
Agent Man of the senior class."

Though Tar was only teasing, Don's face tightened. He
stood and made his way along the crowded aisle. A handful
of the guys tried to kid him about his father and the strike,
but he shook them off angrily. He was sick of hearing about
it, sick of being labeled a spy—from some of them, seriously—
sick of being called Donny Duck, sick of being treated
special when they pretended he wasn't.

He stepped out onto the gym's polished floor, hands on his
hips.

Brian shouted, "Hey Duck, duck!" and a basketball hit
him square on the nose.

FOUR

Images floating through a red-tinted haze: a bobcat lurking high in the trees, fangs gleaming, snarls like thunder, claws like steel blades hunting for someone's throat; a leopard stalking through the high grass of the broiling summer veldt, closing in on its kill, shoulder muscles and haunches rippling with tension; a hawk snatching a rabbit from the ground; a black horse causing the ground to tremble as it charged down the road, fire from its nostrils scorching the earth black.

Images that made his fists clench, his nails create craters in his palms, his chest rise and fall in barely contained rage.

Images: the basketball in slow motion smashing into his face, his knees buckling, tears leaping from his eyes, blood spotting the gym floor; the roar of surprise, the sudden silence, the laughter. Laughter until the gym teacher saw the blood, laughter in the hall as they half-carried him to the first floor, a grin from Falcone as he stood outside his door flirting with Chris.

Only the nurse didn't laugh.

Images: the basketball, the leopard, the gym, the hawk, the corridor, the stairs, the horse waiting in shadow.

He swallowed a moan, rolled his head to the other side, and lay on the nurse's hard cot for fifteen minutes more before he couldn't stand it any longer. His nostrils were plugged with cotton, and a throbbing tenderness spread across his right cheek. When he sat up at last and looked into the mirror over the basin, he saw the beginnings of a beautifully grotesque black eye.

"Hell," he said.

Grabbing a paper towel from the wall dispenser, he cleaned the dried blood off his face and combed his hair with his fingers. The nurse was gone. He looked back, peered closer, and gingerly plucked the cotton out. A sniff, and he tasted blood; another sniff and a daubing with a wet towel, and he waited with held breath until he was positive he wouldn't start bleeding again. Then he found a permission slip on the desk, filled it out, and signed it himself. A check on the clock told him he'd still be able to make the last class, zoology, on the third floor. The corridor was empty and he hurried without running, slipped into the stairwell and took the steps two at a time, head down, breathing heavily through his mouth.

Someone, more than one, came down from above.

He ignored them, averted his head so they wouldn't see the ignominious damage, and only whispered a curse when they bumped hard into his arm, spinning him around and shoving something into his hand. He yelled a protest and grabbed for the iron banister, and managed to end up sitting on the top step. Dizziness made him nauseated, and he clenched his teeth until it passed. Another minute to regain his composure and he hauled himself up; as he reached for the door, Mr. Hedley bulled through.

"So!" the teacher said angrily.

He frowned. "Sir?"

Hedley held out a palm, waited, then grabbed his arm and pulled him into the hall, took something from his hand, and held it accusingly in his face.

"You've never seen this before, right, Boyd?"

It was an unstoppered vial, and as the heavyset man waved it in his face he realized that part of his nausea came from the stench drifting out of its mouth. He gagged and turned his head.

"Don't like the tables turned, do you, boy?"

"I . . . what?" He looked over the man's shoulder and saw a dozen students in the hall. Some were leaning against the wall and talking softly, others had handkerchiefs pressed over their noses. A few saw him and grinned; the rest saw him and glared.

"It was a stupid thing to do, Boyd."

"Do what?" His nose hurt. He had a headache that reached to the back of his neck. He pointed at the vial. "That? I didn't do that."

"Then who did? The ghost of Samuel Ashford?"

His head hurt; god, his head hurt.

"Well, Boyd?"

He tried to explain about his accident, about how he'd been running up the stairs when someone—two or three of them, he didn't know for sure, he didn't see—when someone ran past him and put that bottle in his hand.

Hedley tilted his head back and cocked it to one side.

"But I didn't do anything!"

"Mr. Boyd, keep your voice down."

"But I didn't do it!"

Hedley grabbed his arm again, and Don shook him off.

"I didn't do it, damnit," he said sullenly.

Hedley was about to reach again when a murmuring made him turn and see Norman Boyd striding through his class. The principal paused to speak to several students and send them on their way, presumably to the nurse, with a pat on the shoulder. When he was close enough, Hedley explained over Don's silent protest that someone had opened the lab door in the middle of a test and dumped a bottle of hydrogen sulfide onto the floor.

"From this," he said, displaying the vial with a dramatic flourish, "which I found in your son's possession, over there in the stairwell."

Boyd cleared his throat and lifted an eyebrow.

Don told him, words clipped, attitude defensive, and when he was done, he dared his father with a look not to believe him.

Boyd took the vial, sniffed, and grimaced. "My office."

"But Dad—"

"Do as you're told! Go down to my office."

Don looked to the chemistry teacher, who was smiling smugly, looked to the kids still in the hall, whispering and grinning. The odor of rotten eggs was making him sick. Boyd stoppered the vial with his handkerchief and gave the order a third time.

"Yeah," he muttered, turned, and walked away.

"Hey, Don," someone called as he went through the door, "tell him the giant crow did it!"

Norman slouched in his chair, a hand on one cheek, one eye closed as if sighting an invisible weapon. There was a stack of reports to be filed when he found the time to read them, the in basket was crowded with letters to respond to, the out basket held more files he hadn't bothered to look over, and in the middle of the blotter was Adam Hedley's vial with the handkerchief still dangling from the top.

A finger reached out to touch it, poke at it, shift it around, before the hand drew back and covered his other cheek.

Norm boy, he thought, for an intelligent man, you are one very stupid sonofabitch.

A chill settled on the back of his neck and he shuddered

violently to banish it, and glanced up to see that the office
was dark. A look behind and out the window, and he groaned;
the sun had gone down, the streetlamps were on, and the
traffic on School Street was mainly people coming home
from shopping and work.

He was virtually alone, then, in the building. Just him in
his office, and the custodial staff sweeping the hallways and
auditorium, washing the blackboards, and probably stealing
him blind from the supply room in the basement.

"Stupid," he muttered, staring at the vial. "Stupid, and
dumb, and you ought to be shot."

Jesus, how could he believe Don had really tossed that
bottle into Hedley's room? How could he believe it? Or was
he trying too hard to believe the boy was really normal,
doing normal things like any normal kid.

That was the problem—thinking Don was special. He
wasn't. He was perfectly, sometimes unnervingly fine, with
quirks like any other kid to set him apart. And there was
Norman Boyd, forgetting who they both were and playing
King of the Mountain, Lord of the Hill, laying down the law
as if he were Moses.

As if he were his own father.

For the first time in ages he wished Joyce were here, to
remind him that he wasn't Wallace Boyd still working the
mills, that Don wasn't Norman struggling out of the gutter.
He recalled with a silent groan the day Joyce had told him
she was pregnant the first time. He had sworn on everything
he held dear that he would do better, that he would be
there—a harbor for childhood storms, a rock to hang on to
when the winds grew too strong. A father; nothing more,
nothing less.

He covered his face with his hands and took a deep breath.

It was the pressure, that's what it was. After Sam had
died, the pressure had begun; he didn't know how, and he
wasn't sure why, but it was there. Waiting for him. Whisper-

ing to him that Donald had to be protected at all costs. And when he recognized the futility of it, and the unreason, he hadn't realized how far in the opposite direction he had gone with the boy's life.

It was the pressure.

What he needed was a respite. What he needed was for Falcone and his teachers to cave in and stop the strike. Then they'd be off his back, and the board would be off his back, and the press and the mayor and the whole damned world would leave him alone to reacquaint himself with his son.

Twice he had blown it—first, Don's announcement about being a veterinarian, and now this afternoon.

Twice, and suddenly he was very afraid.

His wife was falling out of love with him.

What would happen if his son did the same?

. . . and so the crow saw how bad the little boy was feeling, and he flew out of the tree and into the night . . .

The park was deserted. A breeze crept through the branches and shook loose a few leaves, spiraling them down through the dark, through the falls of white light, to the ground, to the paths, to the pond where they spun in lazy turns, creating islands that floated just below the surface.

No one walked.

The traffic's noise was smothered.

. . . and found the evil king alone in his bedroom, and he flew in through the window, and before the evil king could wake up and defend himself, the giant crow had plucked out both his eyes!

The only concentrated light was set around the oval. A dim light, and there was no warmth to it, no weight, as he sat on a bench and stared at the water, rolling his shoulders to drive off the cold.

His eyes were closed.

His lips moved so slightly they might have been trembling.

And then the giant crow flew through the castle until he found the evil king's brother, who was just as evil and just as mean, and the giant crow tore out his throat with one swipe of his giant talons.

The houses that faced the park were hidden by the trees and the width of the land, and the boulevard that ran past it on the south was too far away to matter. He was alone; no one would bother him unless he stayed until dawn, and on a night like this not even a tramp would try to make a bed on the redwood benches. He was alone. His hands were clasped tightly between his knees, and his jacket was too light for the sudden temperature drop, turning the air brittle and the leaves to brown glass.

A noise in his throat; his shoulders slumped a little more.

He had waited nearly an hour in his father's office before the man finally walked in. Don had jumped to his feet and was ordered down again. A fussing with papers, instructions not to interrupt him, and he was lectured forever on the image both of them had to project—to the faculty as well as to the student body. Norman brandished the vial as if he were going to throw it. Don explained for the second time how the kid—he was sure now it was Pratt—shoved the bottle into his hand on the way down the stairs. His face hurt as he talked, and he kept touching the side of his face to be sure it hadn't bloated. His father saw the situation, sympathized for the injury, but refused the whole pardon while relenting to the degree that he supposed Brian was capable of such a trick.

"I didn't say it was him." Don had retreated, suddenly

fearful his father would call the boy in and unknowingly start a war. "I just think it was."

Norman seemed doubting, and Don didn't understand. In all his life he'd never done anything like that; he had been told often enough that he was neither to take advantage of his position—whatever that was—nor pretend he was only one of the boys. He wasn't. He was, by fate, special, with special problems to handle. And Norman expected more of him than to have it end up like this.

"End up like what?" He sprang to his feet and approached the desk. "Dad, why don't you listen to me? I didn't do it!"

Norman stared and said nothing.

"All right, I left the nurse's office when I shouldn't have, I guess, and I wrote out my own pass. All right, that's wrong. Okay. But I did not throw that crap in Mr. Hedley's room!"

"Donald," his father said in perfect control, "I will not have you speak to me that way, especially not in here."

"Oh, Jesus." And he turned away.

"And you will not swear at me. Ever."

Don surrendered. Suspended between belief and suspicion, bullied off the subject by time-worn and weary pronouncements, he surrendered, he didn't care, and he didn't argue when he was given six days detention, beginning the next day.

"You should count yourself lucky," Norman said as he escorted him out the door just as the last bell rang. "Most other kids would have been suspended."

"Then suspend me!" he said, surprised to hear himself on the verge of begging. "Please, suspend me."

"Don't be smart, son, or I will."

Don pulled away from the hand that guided him around the counter, ignored the curious looks the five secretaries gave him. "You don't get it," he said as he walked out the door. "You just don't get it."

He fetched his books and went home. His mother wouldn't

be in for at least another hour, and his father would stay at South until just before dinner. That gave him time to unload his gear and change into his jeans, fix himself a peanut butter sandwich and go for a walk.

Shortly before dark he walked into the park.

. . . and then the crow . . .

He stopped, and cocked his head.

He could not see far beyond the lights that ringed the oval, but he was positive he had heard someone approaching out there. Listening, his hands gripping his knees, he guessed it was his mother, come to take him home and scold him and make him eat a bowl of soup or drink a cup of watery cocoa. And when the noise didn't sound again, he convinced himself it wasn't really a footstep he had heard.

He heard it again.

To his left, out there in the dark.

A single sound, sharp on the pavement, like iron striking iron as gently as it could.

Without looking away he zipped his jacket closed and stood, slowly, sidling toward the pond for an angle to let him see through the light.

Again. Sharp. Iron striking iron.

Not his mother at all; someone else.

"Hey, Jeff, that you?" he called, jamming his hands into his pockets.

Iron striking iron. Hollow.

"Jeff?"

The breeze husked, scattering leaves at his feet and making him duck away with his eyes tightly shut. The pond rippled, and a twig snapped, and something small and light scurried up a trunk.

Swallowing, and looking once toward the exit, he walked around the oval and a few steps up the path. With the light now behind him his shadow crept ahead, reaching for the next lamppost fifteen yards away. And between there and here he

saw nothing that could have made the sound that he'd heard.
A frown, more at his own nervousness than at the puzzle, and
he walked on, cautiously, keeping to one side and wincing
each time his elbow brushed against a shrub.

Iron striking iron, hollow, an echo.

He started to call again, changed his mind, and made a
clumsy about-face. Whatever it was, it didn't want to be
seen, and that was all right with him; more than all right, it
was perfect. He hurried, shoulders hunched, cheeks burning
as the wind worked earnestly to push him faster, the tips of
his ears beginning to sting. His own shoes were loud, slapping back from the trees, and his shadow had grown faint,
even under the lamps. He looked back only once, but all he
could see was the pond reflecting the globes, freezing them
in ice, turning the oval into a glaring white stage.

Iron. Striking iron.

He ran the last few yards, skidded onto the sidewalk and
gaped at the traffic on the boulevard. The air was warmer,
and he took a deep breath as he chided himself for being so
foolish.

Then he turned to check one last time.

And heard iron striking iron, muffled and slow, and not
once could he see what was back there in the dark.

Tanker cowered in the bushes, covering his face with his
hands and praying that the moon would keep him hidden
from whatever was walking out there in the dark.

At first it had been perfect. He had been feeling the
familiar pressure all day, building in his chest and making it
swell, building in his head and making it ache. He had
ignored it when it started, thinking it was because he was
hungry for people-food; so he had scrounged through some
garbage cans, panhandled four bucks in front of the movie
theater on the main street and had filled himself with ham-
burgers and dollar wine. But the pressure wouldn't go away,

and his hands shook with anticipation when he could no longer deny it—it was going to be soon, no question about it. Maybe tonight, and that kid was going to help him.

Slowly, using every skill he had left and a few he hadn't learned from the babyfucks in the army, he had made his way through the underbrush toward the oval once he had heard the lone voice telling itself a story. It was too good to be true, but when he peered through the bushes, he almost shouted. It was the punk from the other night, the one who had been dressed in black and talked about a giant crow. And there he was, looking like he'd just lost his best girl, and for god's sake, would you believe it, telling himself a stupid story.

It was perfect.

Then the punk turned his head sharply, and Tanker had looked back into the park.

Iron striking iron.

There was absolutely no reason for it, but the sound terrified him, loosened his bowels, poured acid into his stomach, and he couldn't help it—he whimpered softly and covered his face with his hands. Listening. Trying to make himself invisible. Hearing the punk walk away and swearing in a cold sweat that he couldn't follow and get him.

The sound grew louder and Tanker dropped to the ground, shifted his hands to the back of his head and waited, holding his breath, listening as whatever it was moved in front of him, as if following the boy.

And stopped.

The breeze died; there was no traffic noise, no footsteps.

He swallowed and turned his head to expose one eye. Through the shrubs he could see pieces of the pavement, the dark on the other side, and nothing else. A puzzled frown. His hands sliding off his hair to press on the grass and lift him up. Slowly. Bloodshot yellowed eyes darting side to side, taking in as much of the path as they could before his head rose over the top, before his knees straightened, before his arms spread outward to balance for flight, to lunge for a fight.

But there was nothing there.

The path was empty, the punk gone, and when he pushed through to the oval and checked both directions, he realized he was alone.

Alone with the pressure, and nobody to kill.

Then he heard it again.

Iron striking iron, muffled, slow cadence; and when he whirled around to meet it his eyes opened, his mouth gaped, and he couldn't stop the denying shake of his head.

He was alone.

He could hear something large moving toward him, but he was completely alone.

The booze, he thought; it's the goddamned booze. He rushed back into the trees, zigzagging to lose whatever was out there, then made his way to the westside wall. His lungs were aching and his hands were trembling, and when he tried to swallow, his throat felt coated with sharp pebbles. He listened, hard, and sagged with relief when he heard nothing but the wind.

Then the pressure came again, in his head, in his chest. A deep solemn throbbing as he looked up at the moon.

It was time, then, no stalling, and he vaulted the wall nimbly, keeping to the shadows as he hurried to his right. The houses facing the park were large and lighted, but he couldn't hear a television, a radio, or any voices through open windows.

All he could hear was that noise from the park, and it goaded him to the corner, where he slumped against a telephone pole and checked the street up and down, panting slightly while his fingers flexed and his forehead creased.

Five minutes later Tanker saw him.

He was walking on the same side of the street, fingers snapping, hips and feet moving. Tanker frowned, thinking the punk was drunk, until he saw the earphones, and the radio clipped to his belt.

A great way to die, he thought, grinning, and angled back around the wall's corner. A great way to die—smiling, listening to your favorite music, a nip in the air and on your way home.

He chuckled, and it sounded like a growl.

He followed the kid's progress carefully, poked his head out, and saw him tap the top of the wall in time to his listening, once spinning around and snapping those fingers high over his head.

When he spun around a second time, Tanker was there, smiling. Taking the kid's throat and pitching him effortlessly into the park. Before the kid landed, Tanker was kneeling beside him.

Before the song ended, Tanker was howling.

"Don the Barbarian sees the slime-covered trolls at the end of the witch's tunnel," he whispered as he moved slowly out of the kitchen, half in a crouch, his left arm braced across his chest for a shield, his right extended to hold his anxious pal, Crow. "The sexy maiden is chained to a burning rock, and only Don has the strength to break the magic chains and save her from a fate worse than death." He looked to his right. "Crow, what's a fate worse than death?" His pal didn't answer, and when he tripped over the fringed edge of the hall rug and slammed into the wall, the telephone rang.

"Got it!" he shouted, wincing at the pain. His parents were in the back, in what used to be his father's study and was now the television room. There was a championship fight on some cable channel, and he could hear his father cursing while his mother told the underdog's manager what he could do with his fighter and all his fighter's family.

Despite the language it was a good sound, a normal sound that hadn't been heard in the house for several weeks. They were laughing, cheering together, and it sounded so right, he wished they would make up their minds how they felt about each other.

On the other hand, maybe they already had. Maybe they had made up and it was going to be all right.

The telephone rang again on the low table by the entrance to the living room. He snatched up the handset, winked a good-bye at Crow, who was off to save the maiden from whatever her fate, and leaned against the doorframe.

It was Tracey. He had completely forgotten she had said she would call.

"Sorry I'm late," she said, her voice muffled as though she were cupping her hand around the mouthpiece.

"No problem. I was out walking anyway."

"Oh, yeah? Anybody I know?"

"Nope. Just me." But he was pleased she had asked.

"Oh, yourself, huh? Not much company, Boyd."

"I wouldn't say that. If you must know, I happen to be very sophisticated when the mood strikes me."

She giggled, and he looked blindly toward the ceiling.

"How's the eye?"

He tested the side of his face. "Still there, I think."

"Bummer about the detention."

Christ, he thought, bad news travels fast.

"I don't care," he said. "My grades haven't been all that good this year. I could use the time to study."

"Senior slump," she said. "You get complacent, y'know?"

Depressed is what you get, he thought, but he only grunted.

"Well, listen, Vet, about tomorrow night."

His stomach filled with insects too crawly to be butterflies; he could hear it in her tone—she was going to say she already had a date with Brian. "Yeah?"

"I can't make it."

He decided to slit his throat; then he decided he was glad

because now he wouldn't have to face Brian. But first he would slit his throat.

"My father's got the weekend off and we have to go see my grandmother on Long Island. We're gonna leave right after school, he says."

"Oh. Well, okay."

"But look, we can go next Friday, if that's okay with you. Next Friday would be great. If you still want to, I mean."

He didn't say anything. His throat healed, the ceiling abruptly came into focus, and he could see her up there, floating, smiling, her dark hair in a wisp over her eyes.

"Vet, you still there?"

"Yeah, sure," he said, shaking himself.

"Okay." Subdued now. "I thought you were mad about tomorrow. Or about me calling you Vet."

"I don't mind. Really." The cord had twisted itself around his wrist and he couldn't get it off without taking away the earpiece and losing what she might say. "Really, no kidding."

And he didn't. She thought it was great that he was going to be so close to animals for the rest of his life. The day he had let it slip, she had immediately fantasized his working out in the country, traveling from village to village, farm to farm, making sure all his charges were in perfect health.

She had been serious.

Brian and Tar thought it was too perfect to be true—Duck, off to treat the ducks. For nearly a week afterward, every time they saw him they quacked and flapped their arms and told him they had hernias and had to swim standing up.

"So," she said, "I thought you told me that bio test was a snap."

They talked then the way they usually did, the preliminaries over and his heart slowly finding its way back into place. His mother walked by once with a sandwich and a beer, looked a question, and he smiled and pointed at her.

A girl? she asked silently.

He nodded.

Chris Snowden?

He shook his head and mumbled a reply to something Tracey said.

His mother shrugged—*it doesn't matter, dear, as long as it's female and she doesn't want to marry you before you go off to college*—and moved on after checking on the status of his black eye, hip-swinging through the living room and back to the TV set. It was the long way around, and they both knew it.

"Don, damnit, are you listening to me?"

"It was my mother," he said in a near whisper, checking to be sure the coast was clear. "Spying on me."

"Oh. Well, my folks don't care as long as he wears pants, combs his hair, and is rich. Dad figures I should be married a year after graduation."

"I thought you were going to school."

"I am. He just doesn't believe it yet. God, the man lives in the last century, I swear."

"Boy, tell me about it."

"Yeah, for sure." She yelled something at her older sister, and he could hear her mother fussing in the background. A deep voice chimed in—her father venturing an opinion about the family going to hell.

"So," he said, "what were you saying?"

"The walk. Where did you go?"

"Out. The park."

"Wow!" A pause, more whispering. "Wow, Don, don't you ever listen to the news?"

He looked back toward the kitchen, at his mother's radio on the counter. "Nope. Don't have time."

"Well, you better," she told him, her voice low. "Somebody was killed in there tonight. A couple of hours ago. My father just came in and—" She stopped. "Jesus, you were there then!"

He put a hand to his cheek and scratched lightly. "I didn't see anything. I didn't hear anything." The hand pressed a bit harder. "What happened?"

"I don't know. My father isn't talking. The radio said that this kid, from North, he was walking home from work, and he got it. They said . . . they guessed it was the Howler. Gross."

"Yeah."

Iron striking iron.

"Boy, you could be a witness or something."

"But I didn't see anything, Tracey! Jesus, don't tell your father."

"Okay, okay." Her mother interrupted, and she snapped at her, groaning about how great it must be to be an only child. "Hey, Vet? What's your favorite animal?"

He sniffed, combed his hair with one hand while he drew on his imagination to put images in the air before him. "I never thought about it, you know that? Gee, that's funny but I never thought about it." His bedroom came to mind and he sorted through the posters and prints and figurines he had. "Horses, I guess. I don't know. Leopards and panthers."

She laughed, and someone in the background laughingly mocked her. "I didn't know you rode."

"Panthers? You don't ride panthers."

"No, stupid, horses. I didn't know you rode horses."

"I don't."

There was a pause, and a man's voice began grumbling.

"Then why horses?"

"I don't know." He saw the poster, the horse, and shrugged to the empty foyer. "They look . . . I don't know, they look so big and powerful, y'know? Like they could run right over you and not even notice."

"A horse?"

"Sure."

"But they're stupid."

"I guess."

"I mean, they're—" The man's voice was louder, and she covered the mouthpiece. He tried to make out the words but all he heard sounded like an argument. "Don, I have to go."

"Okay, sure."

"See you tomorrow?"

"Sure! Sure. I'll—"

She hung up and he stood in the middle of the floor and stared at the front door until his father walked by on his way upstairs and reminded him gently that he started detention the next day.

Don nodded.

Norman, halfway up the stairs, looked down and frowned, started to say something, and changed his mind.

Don didn't notice.

He was looking at the door, at the black horse imposed on it, with Tracey Quintero riding on its back.

Five minutes later Joyce pinched his rump as she walked by and he jumped, blushed at her laugh, and nodded when she asked him to check the lights and lock up. As he did, he thought about Tracey, and about the kid who had been killed. It could be that what he had heard was the murderer himself, thinking there had been a witness and coming to kill him. He felt cold, and he stayed to one side when he drew the draperies and double-checked to make sure the bolts on the front and back doors were turned over. Then he ran upstairs and into his room, considered telling his parents, and changed his mind. Mom would only get excited and demand they call the police; and Dad would tell them both there was nothing to worry about, the boy is all right, and since he didn't actually see anything, there was no sense their getting involved.

And he would be right; there would be no sense at all.

A wash, then, and a careful scrutiny to be sure his face hadn't broken out since that morning and that his eye wasn't getting any worse. Then he closed his door and sat crosslegged on the bed. He was in nothing but his underwear, and he looked around him—at the panther, the bobcat, the elephants, rejecting each one silently until he came to the poster over the desk.

There, he thought; there's what I need.

"Hey, look," he said to the barely visible horse, "I hope you don't mind if I don't give you a name. I mean, I suppose I could, but all the good ones are already taken, and half of them sound like you're in the movies or something anyway. Besides," he added with a look to the panther lying in the jungle over his bed, "I don't want to make the other guys mad."

He grinned, and rolled his eyes, muffling a laugh in a palm.

"But you don't need one anyway, right? You're too tough for a stupid name. What you want to know is, how come you and not the black cat over there, right? Well, because you're big, and you're strong, and . . . just because. Besides, Tracey likes horses, and you're a horse, and she'll like you, and if she likes you she'll like me and then we'll all be pals, right? Right. And boy would you scare the shit outta that kid with the dumbass hat."

He grinned again and rocked back, struck his head against the wall and didn't feel a thing.

He didn't think his other pals would mind, him singling out just one, just this once. They would understand. They always had, and they would this time.

"So listen up, old fella," he said, looking to the ceiling where Tracey floated on a cloud, "you're gonna have to teach me a few things, y'know, because I figure you've been around, if you know what I mean. Give me some hints and stuff, okay? And if you take care of me, I'll take care of you. That's what pals are for, right? Right."

And he slipped off the bed, kissed the tips of his fingers, and placed his hand on the horse's head.

"Pals," he said. "Pals."

*   *   *

"He's talking to those animals again," Norm complained while Joyce was brushing her teeth. She mumbled something, and he shook his head, pointing to his ear.

"I said," she told him after spitting out the toothpaste, "kids talk to themselves all the time. It's like thinking out loud. You should hear my classroom sometimes."

"Yeah, but you teach flakes."

"Budding artists are flakes?"

"Look in the mirror."

She threw her hairbrush at him, launched herself after it, and they wrestled on the bed until he had her pinned under him.

"Norm?" she said, putting a hand on the hand that was covering her breast.

"What?"

The willow at the corner of the house scratched lightly at the window, and he could hear the cooing of the grey doves that nested in the eaves of the garage.

"It's terrible, but did you ever wish we'd never had any kids? So when something like this comes up, I mean, we could walk away without worrying about tender psyches and trauma and warping the kid's mind? Did you ever think about that, Norm?"

He tried to see her face in the dark. "Are we being honest?"

"Yes."

"Then . . . yes. Yes, it has crossed my mind now and then." But he didn't tell her about the guilt he felt when it did.

"That doesn't mean we don't love him," she said anxiously, begging for belief. "And god, I still miss my little Sam."

"I know."

"But it would be so much easier, you know what I mean?"

"Yeah."

The alarm clock buzzed softly. The wind blew over the roof. They could hear, faintly, two cars racing down the street.

"Don was in the park tonight."

"So?"

"Didn't you listen to the news after the fight?"

"Oh." He shifted but didn't release her. "Yeah. I guess I'd better have a talk with him. At least until they catch that guy."

"Maybe he saw something."

"No. If he did, he would have told us." He kissed her right ear and made her squirm.

"Norm?"

Wearily: "Yes?"

"Don's grades are going down. Not a lot, but it worries me. You should talk to him about that too. He spends too much time fixing up those animals of his, and making new ones."

"I will," he promised. "Maybe we should tell him to get rid of the beasts."

"That would be cruel."

"He wouldn't waste time on them." As she agreed, he nipped an earlobe.

"Norm?"

"Jesus, now what?"

"I want to work things out, really I do."

"Good," he said, rolling her breast beneath his palm.

"No, I mean it, Norman. I really do want to work at it."

"So do I," he said, almost believing. His head shifted to the hollow of her shoulder. "So do I, love."

"Norm, it's late," she whispered, her eyes half closed, "and you know how tired you get lately after this. Besides, I have a committee meeting first thing tomorrow. We have to decide on the fireworks."

"Good for you. Make them loud as hell."

"Norman!"

"Joyce," he said, "if you really want to work things out, you'd better shut up."

FIVE

On Saturday afternoon Don returned with his mother from a shopping expedition for new clothes during which she cited dubious, sometimes outlandish statistics which contrasted the annual before- and after-taxes incomes of veterinarians and surgeons, suggesting jokingly that spending the day shoving your hand up animals' rectums and down their throats was about as glamorous and status-marking as his late grandfather's working for the cloth mills here in town. Don laughed and almost told her what he was really planning.

When they arrived home, he found his father in his room, looking at his pets.

"Aren't you a little old for these?" Norm asked, and left without an answer.

In the middle of the hall on Monday Don grabbed Jeff's arm and nearly spilled the books he was carrying.

"Jeff, you got a minute?"

"Hey, it's the Detention Kid. What's up? The bell's gonna ring. Jesus, that eye looks like hell!"

"Thanks a lot, pal. It feels better, sort of. Look, I want to ask you about Tracey Quintero."

"What's to ask? You know her as well as I do."

"I want to know if she's with Brian."

"Brian? Brian the Prick Pratt? That Brian?"

"Stop kidding, Jeff, I gotta know."

"Jesus, where the hell've you been? And she isn't. Hey, you know that kid that got offed in the park last week? It was the Howler, they said. Chewed the poor bastard up like he was dog meat or something. That guy's a real pervert, you know it? Killed five kids in New York. Like us, I mean, not little kids."

"Jeff, I don't care about some freak, I am talking about Tracey."

"And I told you she's not with Brian, okay?"

"But the other night at the park, after the concert . . ."

"You mean all that talk about her boobs?"

"Well . . ."

"Boyd, are you really that dense?"

"I don't know what you mean."

"Brian sees boobs on anything that even faintly looks like a female. And if you listen real close, you'd think he's laid every damn one of them."

"Then she isn't."

"His? Hell, no."

"Jeez. Oh . . . jeez."

"You gonna tell me what this is all about or am I gonna have to read it in the paper?"

"Can't, Jeff. The bell's rung. We're late."

That afternoon Detective Sergeant Thomas Verona walked into Norm's office, Patrol Sergeant Luis Quintero at his side. After a few minutes of small talk, Quintero left to have a word with the secretaries in the outer office, and Verona asked the principal if he had heard anything, rumors or otherwise, about a stranger hanging around the school. Norm insisted he hadn't, but if the police wanted to ask either students or teachers during school time, it would have to be cleared with the board first. He himself didn't mind, though he didn't quite understand why they were interested if the man was already gone. That, he said when the policeman looked at him oddly, was the usual pattern as he understood it: the Howler would strike, then move on to another town. Verona, whose father had worked the mills and had known Norman since they were kids, told him off the record that if the guy had actually approached any of the students, or if he had gotten wind of the Ashford Day activities, there was a fair chance he'd stick around because there were going to be a lot of people on the streets starting the middle of next week, and safety in numbers was apparently something he counted on. When Norm asked why the man hadn't yet been caught, Verona, again off the record, told him there wasn't a picture, not a fingerprint, nor a scrap of cloth or drop of blood to build even the skimpiest physical profile. They couldn't begin to guess at his appearance, though they didn't have to guess at his strength. Norman didn't ask for more details, but he did promise to keep his ears open and to have a quiet word with the faculty to the effect that it would probably not be a good idea to keep kids very long after school for a while. Verona appreciated the cooperation and suggested they stop being strangers after so many years and have a beer together sometime soon. Verona's wife was on the committee with Joyce, and the detective allowed as how he was tired of being an Ashford Day widower. Norman laughed, but he didn't think it was very funny.

After gym Don managed to get next to Fleet under the last nozzle, for the first time forgetting his embarrassment at seeing another guy naked. It took him a moment, too, to stop staring at the clouds of freckles that covered Fleet's body.

"Hey, Fleet, is Trace . . . you know, is she Brian's girl?"

"Trace? Gimme the soap, man, I smell like horseshit. Trace Quintero, the cop's kid?"

"Yeah."

"Nah. Last I heard she wasn't with nobody."

"No kidding."

"Man, will you look at that gorgeous eye! You put a steak or something on that, or you'll go blind, sure as shit. Jesus, Brian can be . . . never mind. Hey, you interested in Trace?"

"I don't know. Hey, Fleet, c'mon, that's my soap! Don't pass it around."

"Y'know, you'd do better with somebody like Chrissy Snowden, man. Don't you dare tell Amanda I said this, she'll cut my ass off, but that's one hell of a woman, if you catch my drift."

"I guess."

"You guess? Jesus, Don, you mean you ain't once whacked off just thinking about that fox?"

"I—"

"Donny, you are truly hopeless. You are an excellent human being, but you are truly hopeless."

"I suppose."

"A good thing you didn't meet up with that dude that stomped that kid. You probably would've asked him home for dinner. You're a good man, Don, but you need a little spunk, you know what I mean? A little of the old intestinal fortitude when it comes to dealing with the real world."

"I do all right, and gimme back my soap, damnit."

"What I think you'd best do is tell everyone you got that eye in a fight. You get a little respect and you get all the women you need, if you know what I mean."

"It's a little late for that."

"It's never too late to lie through your teeth, if you know what I mean."

"Yeah, I know."

"Besides, from what I hear, under all them sweaters Tracey's a carpenter's dream—flat as a board."

Don wasn't sure if it was a nightmare or a dream. He walked through the rest of the week with a slight smile on his face, a good word for everyone including Brian Pratt, and he didn't even blush when Chris came up to him in the hall and touched a finger to his cheek, wincing at the purpled blotch around his eye and hoping in a soft and high voice that he wasn't hurting too badly; when he sputtered nonsense for an answer, she didn't laugh, she only smiled and winked as she left. On the other hand, he didn't hear a thing any of his teachers said, and twice he was reprimanded for daydreaming in class. Falcone's announcement that the test papers wouldn't be ready until the following week didn't faze him; Hedley's glare in the hall didn't register until an hour later; when his detention supervisors snapped at him for staring, he didn't know what they were talking about, and they told him he was rude and would let the front office know; and when Tar Boston jammed his locker with a pen on Thursday, he only shrugged and walked away without his books.

It wasn't right. He was acting like a fool, knew it, and couldn't do anything about it. He was beginning to regret his rash invitation; yet between classes he loitered near the doors as long as he dared, trying to get a glimpse of Tracey, just nod to her casually, give her a knowing smile, and remind her with a look of their date this week.

He didn't see her.

By Friday noon he hadn't seen her once close enough to give the signal and he became convinced she was avoiding him, ashamed because she couldn't think of a decent excuse to get out of their date. He knew, beyond question, there would be a message for him when he got home—she had a headache, she had to do her hair, she had to go back to her grandmother's on Long Island and they were leaving again right after school. By the end of his last class he was ready to believe that Brian had put her up to accepting, another classic gag on the stupid Duck, and since he was who he was, it didn't make any difference if his feelings were hurt.

As he stowed his books in his locker, he almost cried; as he started for the side exit and a run around the track, he almost screamed Tracey's name. But he didn't. That was a rule too—it was all right for his mother to shout, to cry, but it wasn't all right for him. Or his father. Hold it in and work it out, his father had told him; hold it in and work it out. That's what a man does.

Hold it in.

Work it out.

And it wasn't until he was halfway down the steps to the gym that he remembered today was the last day of his detention.

The hell with it; he wasn't going to go. There was no way he was going to sit one more day in a stuffy room staring at the ceiling while his whole life was slipping away between his fingers. He gripped the railing and continued down, slower now, listening to his heels crack on the iron tips of the steps. No; he had to run. He had to think. And to think, he had to run.

"Don?"

His father was on the bottom landing with Gabby D'Amato, the head custodian. He glanced at his watch, then raised an eyebrow over a faintly amused look.

"You forget something?"

His face grew hot, and he almost told his father to shove it, to take the detention and cram it because it wasn't deserved and he didn't do it and who the hell was he to play God with his life?

Why the hell, he wanted to shout, didn't the old man get the hell off his back and put the pressure on someone else for a change.

He wanted to.

He almost did.

Until he thought about what it would be like when he got home, what his mother would say, how his father would treat him.

Hold it in; work it out.

Shit, he thought; oh, shit.

So he gave his father a sheepish smile and headed back to his locker to get something to read. Below, he heard the two men talking, laughing quietly, Norman's slap of the hunkered old man's shoulder. If the black horse were here, he thought as he pushed into the hall, he'd smash them into the wall without a second thought.

Dinner was almost like the good old days. His father was in a great mood, his mother chatted excitedly about the committee meeting at the high school that night, and he managed not to tell them about what had happened after detention.

First it had been Tar and Brian.

They were on their way to practice and had wedged him into a corner, slapping his shoulder and punching him lightly on the arm.

"Hey, fucker," Tar said, his mood as black as his hair, "you trying to get us in trouble?"

"What?"

Brian, who thought that his rugged playing-field-bashed face and close-cropped blond hair made him look like a marine, took hold of his belt and yanked him closer. "Your daddy had a talk with us, sonny. He said we shouldn't do things like stink up Hedley's room anymore."

Oh, Christ, Don thought; oh, Christ.

"Now, he didn't do nothing," Tar said, grinning to show Don a mouth filled with nicotined teeth, "but he did say he'd keep an eye on us, didn't he, Brian?"

"Damn right."

"Now look, guys," Don said, and gasped when a stiff finger jabbed into his stomach.

"No," Brian said. "*You* look, Duck. You look good, because Tar baby and me, we don't forget. And we sure as shit don't forgive."

They grinned and stepped away, and as they moved toward the door, Brian looked over his shoulder. "Watch your back, Duck. I'm gonna bust it, and I ain't telling you when."

After they left, Falcone came up to him, frowning. "You having trouble with the boys, Donald?"

"No, sir."

"Oh, good." And he handed him his test paper and said with a smile, "For you, Boyd, just for you." A look at his grade and he groaned—passing, but just barely.

The red had come then.

The familiar red that took him when he started to lose his temper (hold it in), the red cloud that whirled around him and threatened to suck the ground from under his feet and left only when he forced himself to remember the rule (work it out). But this time it was hard. Hedley and Mrs. Klass had been lecturing him all week during detention on his responsibilities, on his daydreaming, on the slip of his grades. And now this.

It lasted only a moment, and when the red left, he was leaning against the wall, trembling, and Falcone was gone.

Now dinner was fun, and he didn't mention that test paper for fear he'd be grounded for the rest of his life. Nor did he say anything about Brian and Tar. Norman would only tell him he'd simply handed them a friendly warning; he wouldn't believe that one of these days Don was going to pay for his father's big mouth.

He showered after dessert, washed his hair, and nearly cried when he couldn't locate a clear pair of jeans right away. A quick whisper to the horse about the girl he was seeing—

and a wish that he not make a complete fool of himself—and he touched the animal's nose for luck. A shirt with a pullover sweater, shoes generally worn on Sundays, and he was finally in the foyer checking his wallet when his father came out of the kitchen munching on an apple.

"Out with the boys, huh?" Norman said.

"No," his mother called gaily from the kitchen. "I think he has a date."

"He does? No kidding."

"No," his mother said. "Really."

Don felt as if he had been rendered invisible and shifted to recapture his father's attention. "Yeah," he said, stepping back for approval. "Going to a movie. Maybe to Beacher's for something after. I don't know. She has to be back by midnight."

"Ah, Cinderella," his mother said, laughing, and he wondered how her hearing had gotten suddenly so acute.

"Who is it?" Norman asked, his hand magically holding a ten-dollar bill when Don turned back from the coat closet with his windbreaker in hand. "An advance on your allowance," he explained when Don hesitated. "Hell, why not. Anyone I know?"

"Probably," he said, slipping on the coat and opening the door. "Tracey Quintero."

"Quintero?" Norman frowned for a moment. "Oh! Oh, yes, yes. Little Italian girl. In your class. A senior."

"Spanish, Dad. She's Spanish. Her father's from Madrid. He's a cop."

"Oh. Well."

"Remind him about tonight, Norm," Joyce called over the rush of water from the faucet.

Don waited, smiling, while his father rolled his eyes to the ceiling. "You remember the meeting, right?"

"Right." He grinned. "And I know—if I'm home before

you are, the key's in the garage if I've lost mine, and I'd better be home before you are or I'll be in deep . . . trouble."

Norman grinned and slapped his arm. "Just watch it, okay? Don't give your mother hysterics by being too late."

Joyce called out something else, but it was drowned in a louder roar from the garbage disposal, and he nodded quickly to his father, was answered with a wink, and left as fast as he dared. He knew that look on the man's face—it came when Norman thought it was time to have a man-to-man talk, usually when one or the other had only five minutes to get where they were going. And usually it was aborted before the first sentence was done.

God, that was close, he thought, shook himself dramatically and waved to his mother, who was standing in the living room window drying her hands, Norman at her side. They always did that, waiting as if he were going off to war; and if he didn't get back first, they would be there when he returned, slightly drunk from the bourbons they'd had while watching TV.

Waiting for their baby.

But tonight, if he were lucky, they would have had a good meeting—teachers, public officials, and the Ashford Day committee—and won't be stiff from a fight.

Can it, he ordered then. This wasn't the time to be thinking about them when he had himself to worry about—what to say, how to say it, how to impress Tracey without tripping over his tongue. His usual dates weren't really dates at all but a gathering of forces down at Beacher's Diner next to the theater. It might have been a real diner once, but now it was more like a restaurant with a counter in front. Weeknights it closed at nine; weekends it catered to the movie crowd and the teens, and more often than not six or seven of them would troop into the theater together.

On the other hand, when he was alone with a girl he was lucky if he could think of a dozen coherent words to say between the time he picked her up and the time he brought her home.

He checked his watch under a streetlight and broke into a lazy trot. Tracey lived seven blocks down and two over, and he didn't want to be late. He only hoped that her father was on night shift this time; the man scared him to death. He was short, built like a concrete barrel, and if he ever had a good word to say about anyone under forty, Don had yet to hear it.

Please, God, he pleaded as he turned into her block; please don't let Sergeant Quintero be there.

And as he walked up to the door, he checked to be sure his fingernails were clean.

"I swear to god," Brian said, his voice overriding the others sitting at the counter with him. "I mean, they were out to here!" He stretched out his arms, curved his hands back, and flexed his fingers. "To frigging here, for god's sake."

There were a few sniggers, some groans, and Joe Beacher in his stained apron and squashed chef's cap scowled until Pratt shrugged an apology for the language.

The front section of the diner was a long counter with eighteen stools and five jukebox terminals, and nine small tables arranged in front of the wall-long window; there was only one waitress and Joe Beacher himself, who knew he belonged in front, rough-dressed, and not in back wearing a suit. The decor was Formica and aluminum, with a round-faced clock on the wall beside the door, above an array of posters announcing upcoming charitable events, rummage sales, and the Ashford Little Theater's latest program. A wide passage straight from the entrance ran past the cash register to the larger dining room in back, where the walls were paneled in pine and had watercolor landscapes depicting each of the seasons. The tables were larger, were wood, and the menus were tucked into red leather binders; three waitresses here, and Joe's brother-in-law in a black suit that passed for gentility and a bit of class. Just now the room was nearly filled as families and high-spending seniors hurried to finish their meals in time for the nine-fifteen show; and despite the Jekyll-and-Hyde appearance, the food was about the best in town.

Don stood just over the threshold, Tracey behind him, and he hesitated until she poked his back. A quick smile and he stepped aside, let her pass, and followed her to a small round table in the center of the diner's front window. When he held the chair for her, there were whistles from the counter; when he sat, Pratt cupped his hands around his mouth and made a loud farting noise.

Don winced and there was laughter, and more when his cheeks flushed a faint pink.

"Damn," he muttered under his breath, and Tracey smiled at him, telling him silently to ignore it as she handed him a plastic-coated single-page menu from behind the napkin dispenser. He inhaled slowly and nodded, and scanned the offerings though he knew them by heart.

"Hey, Don," said Tar Boston, spinning around on his stool, "a good flick or what?"

He didn't know, though he said it was all right, nothing great, lots of blood, shooting, stuff like that. He didn't know because he had been too busy sneaking sideways looks at Tracey, debating whether to try to hold her hand, or put his arm around her shoulder, or even to steal a kiss. He had known her for years but had never been out with her alone; he had confided in her as a friend ever since junior high, but when she slipped off her jacket and he saw that she had, under all those clothes, an honest-to-god figure, he didn't know what to do. This wasn't Tracey the friend any longer; this was Tracey the woman, and suddenly he didn't know which rules to follow.

The realization that things had changed without his knowing it made him miserable throughout the film, seeing nothing, hearing little, though he could have told anyone who asked exactly how many lines there were at the corner of her right eye, how high the white collar of her shirt reached toward her ear, how the intricate twirls and tucks of her hair related to each other as they brushed back toward her nape.

Brian hummed the school song mockingly, loudly, then leapt from his stool and stretched as he announced it was time for the real men to head next door, to see how Dirty Harry compared unfavorably with the Pratt. Groans again, and only Tar strutted with him to the door, their dates hustling out behind them. Fleet and his girl, Amanda, stopped by the table and asked again about the film.

"Boring," Tracey said. Then she winked at Amanda. "Unless you're into Eastwood."

Amanda clung to Fleet's arm and feigned a swoon, and was rewarded with a slap to her rump for her troubles.

Don laughed and relaxed a bit, and wondered aloud what the coach would think of his three top players staying out so late the night before a game.

"The man," Fleet said, "just doesn't realize that an athlete who is so smooth and graceful like myself needs a bit of relaxation and stimulation before the impending onslaught in the trenches." He grinned. "How 'bout them words, huh? Mandy makes me do crossword puzzles in bed."

Amanda slapped his back, hard, and a brief scowl crossed his face before he laughed with the others and made his way to the door. As it hissed shut behind him, he stuck his head back in and winked broadly at Don, circling thumb and forefinger and making a fist with his free hand.

Don grinned back, and sobered as soon as Robinson was gone. This was a disaster, and for the first time in ages he wished the guys had stuck around. Even the teasing he'd get would be better than sitting here like a dummy, playing with the salt shaker, rearranging the silverware and paper place mat, finally folding his hands on the table as if doing penance in the third grade.

"Are you all right?" Tracey asked. "You've been awfully quiet since we left the house."

He ducked his head and shook it. "Fine. I'm okay, no problem."

"It was a lousy movie."

"Yeah."

"My father scared you, didn't he?"

He looked up without raising his head and was pleasantly surprised to see the distress in her eyes. He couldn't deny it, however; Luis Quintero had scared the shit out of him, standing there, in uniform, in the middle of the living room and reading him, quietly, the that's-my-baby-and-don't-you-forget-it riot act: do not mess with her, do not corrupt her, do not get her drunk, do not bring her back a second late, do not show yourself in this house again if you as much as breathe on a single hair of her head. Then he had shaken Don's hand solemnly and walked out of the room, leaving him to wonder what the hell had happened to make the man so unpleasant.

Tracey told him it was the Howler. It had taken her an hour to convince him Don wasn't the killer, that his father was the principal, for crying out loud, and that she wasn't going to have to enter a convent just because she went out with a boy.

"Does . . . does he do that all the time?" he asked finally.

She sighed, and nodded. "If he's home when I go out, yes. Mother just stands there and holds her hands like she's going to cry any minute. If they had their way, my Aunt Theresa would be my duenna, for heaven's sake."

He didn't know whether to say he was sorry or not, but she saw the sympathy and covered his hand with hers, squeezed it, and drew it back slowly.

"So," she said explosively, "what'll we talk about?"

He didn't know, but they must have talked about something because the waitress and the food came and went, and the next thing he knew he was standing in front of her house, holding her hand and wishing she didn't have to visit her grandmother again the next day. Then they could keep on walking, from one end of town to the other, laughing at the displays in the shop windows, making words from the three letters on the license plates they could catch, and trading notes on teachers they had in common. He said nothing about the biology grade. She mentioned the Howler only once, when they passed a corner bar and saw a pair of dingy men sitting with their backs against its wall, brown bags in hand. One was snoring, the other watching them intently, sneering as they walked by. They saw a third derelict at the next corner, but he ignored them, being too busy scrubbing his grizzled face dryly with his hands.

Tracey had guessed that any one of them could be the kid killer, and he thought they were too weak-looking; this guy, this nut, had to be massive to do what he did to his victims.

"My father," she said, "is shorter than you, and he can break the handle of a shovel over his knee when he's mad enough."

That's when she had taken his hand, and that's when the fun and the conversation had stopped.

"Well," she said, looking at the small house separated from its neighbors by paved alleyways leading to postage-stamp backyards.

"Yeah."

She stood in front of him and looked up. Shadows drifted over her face and made it soft, smooth, and he couldn't help but touch a finger to her cheek.

God, her skin was soft.

"Have a good time tomorrow," was the only thing he could say.

She pouted. "Yeah, great. I'd rather go to the game."

He shrugged.

She leaned closer, stared at him, then raised herself up and kissed him. "See you Monday."

She was up the stairs and through the door before he could think to kiss her in return, and he walked with his hands in his pockets and the tip of his tongue flicking out to test each part of his lips, to taste her, to remember, and finally to realize that she hadn't promised to call him, or perhaps see him on Sunday.

See you Monday was what she had said.

In spite of the kiss the translation was easy: *don't call me, I'll call you, and don't hold your breath.*

"Shit," he said. "Shit, boy, you sure screwed that up."

He scored himself all the way home, not noticing until the door had closed hard behind him that his parents were already there, sitting in the living room and watching him.

"Hi," he said with a wave, and stopped before he ran up the stairs. There was something wrong. His mother wasn't looking at him, and his father was drumming a tattoo on a knee. "What's up? Good meeting?"

"A very good meeting," Norman said. "Until it was over and I had a word with Mr. Falcone."

His eyes closed slowly. A moment later they snapped open, and he pointed and said, "Wait a minute," and was up the stairs and into his room before they could stop him. He snatched up his notebook and pawed through it until he found the test, ran down and stood in front of his father, pressing the page to his chest to smooth out the wrinkles.

"Don—"

"Wait," he said, he held it out. "Just look at it, Dad. Just take a look."

"Donald," Joyce started, and stopped when he pleaded her patience with a glance.

Norman looked up, looked at the paper and read through it, his lips moving slightly. When he was finished, he passed it to Joyce, sighed, and sagged back in his chair.

"Well?"

"Don . . ." Norman closed one eye, pulled at his lower lip; he was hunting for the right word. "It does seem a bit harsh, I have to be honest."

"Harsh?" He sputtered, trying to control his voice before it broke into falsetto. "Harsh? It's more than harsh, it's wrong, Dad! He took points off he never would have for somebody else. He deliberately marked it earlier than the rest of them, and he deliberately picked on me. He . . . he said before the test that I would need all the luck I could get. He said that, Dad, I swear to god."

Norman dropped the paper into his lap and set a knuckle to his cheek, ran it down to his jaw, and stared at the fireplace. "I can't believe that, Don."

"Dad—"

"Damnit, you just listen to me, boy, and stop interrupting. For all the fighting that man and I are doing now, he is still a professional and you'd better remember it. I cannot believe he would deliberately single you out. It's too obvious, don't you see that? Christ, all I'd have to do is compare this with another paper from the same class and I'd see right away if he was picking on you."

"But he is! Wait until Monday, I can get a hundred—"

"No," Norman said forcefully, without raising his voice. "I won't. He's a damned fine teacher, Don, and I won't insult him that way."

"You're grounded," his mother said behind him.

He whirled, unable to take it in, unable to speak.

"Donald," she said, near to tears, "if you're going to college, you simply cannot afford to let your grades slip the way they have. This is the last straw. Colleges look at things like that, they check to see if you let your grades go down just because your school is almost over. You're obviously distracted from your work by . . . a number of things.

S—Donald, you're grounded until you can prove you're doing better."

Tears brimmed into his eyes, and he felt as if he had stumbled into a dream, someone else's dream, and he was lost and didn't know how to find his way out, back to his own bed, his own family. There was a roaring in his ears, and a constriction that prevented the air from passing his throat. He swallowed, hoping to find his voice again, fighting not to break the rule in front of his father; he looked to Norman, who was still staring at the hearth.

He had a headache, and he knew his skull would split in half if he didn't leave the room immediately.

He reached out, and Norman handed the test back.

He looked at his mother blankly, and turned.

There was a hint of red floating in the foyer.

Behind him they shifted uncomfortably; punishment meted and neither felt right though they knew it was the right thing.

He walked away. Slowly. So slowly a cramp began building in his left calf and he had to grab the banister to keep from racing upstairs.

The roaring increased, to a winter's storm trapped in a seashell.

The red danced, and he told himself to remember the Rules.

Then he opened his door, and nearly screamed.

The shelves were empty except for his books, his desk was clean except for a pencil neatly centered, and the posters and prints were gone from the walls.

He was alone.

The door closed behind him and he walked to the bed, sat on the edge, and stared at nothing.

They were gone, his friends gone, and he was alone.

The red darkened, then faded.

"Donald," he whispered after five minutes had passed. "My name is Donald, goddamnit. Goddamned Sam is dead!"

X

Defiance: it was terrifying.

And the power implicit in it even more so because he knew it was there and didn't know exactly what it would do or how he should use it. All he knew was he couldn't stand it any longer in the prison cell of his room, couldn't stand the stench of decay and betrayal that had filled the empty shelves and spilled into his dreams. It had been an oasis once, a place where he could do his homework, read his books, dream his future as he wanted it to be. Now it had been devastated. Corrupted. His mother had walked in without his permission, and without his permission had taken away everything that had been able to give him some peace.

So he had waited until they'd left the house in the middle of Sunday afternoon, for still another meeting with still another committee determined to celebrate the birthday of a two-bit town that didn't matter to anyone except the people who wanted their pictures in the paper; they had left, not saying a word to him because he was still in the ruins of his room, assuming he would be there when they returned. He heard them at the front door, his mother laughing at his father's good-natured grumbling about not being able to attend the game because of the meeting, and how important it was that he at least show his face before the final gun sounded. There was a response, Norman laughed loudly, and the door had slammed shut.

And in the abrupt silence he hadn't been able to stand it any longer. He grabbed his jacket and left, cursing them, fighting so hard not to cry that he gave himself the hiccoughs. A small and still reasonable part of him continued to insist that they weren't being malicious, that they truly believed they had done the right thing because they loved him and didn't want to see him hurt. But what the hell did they know about hurt? What the hell did they know about what it was like to have to memorize all the rules and do your damnedest to follow them, only to have someone sneak in behind your back and change a word here and there, change a rule, change the way things were supposed to be.

What the goddamned hell did they know about how he felt inside?

I was young once, though you probably don't believe it, his father had said on more than one occasion; but if he did know, what did he think he was doing, going along with Joyce, standing aside and letting her strip him of his pets, of practically everything he owned, without even having the goddamned decency to let him know before he walked into the room and saw it—the rape. What the hell had he been thinking of, telling Brian and Tar about Don's thinking they had been the ones who'd dumped the vial into that classroom? Jesus, didn't he have eyes? Didn't he see what was going on?

He may have been young once; he wasn't young anymore. He may think he remembers what goes on in a kid's head, but all he knows is what he's read in those damned books, what he hears in the office, what he's told by the Board of Education, who are only a bunch of stupid men and women who think they remember what it was like to be young and what it was like to be in school and what it was like to have your parents rape you without laying a finger on your arm.

Just like Norman and Joyce, they think they know kids, but they goddamned don't know him.

And the worst part, the absolute worst and most horrible part of it was, because he didn't know what to do or how to teach them a lesson or show them he wasn't their goddamned dead son or their puppet or their pet . . . the worst part of it was, he was frightened to death because he wanted to kill them.

He walked aimlessly, first near the school, where he heard the crowd cheering and the blaring discord of the band, then toward the center of town, not realizing where he was heading until he passed Tracey's house and paused at the front walk, staring at the closed curtains, the empty curb, sighing and moving on and wondering if maybe he wasn't being too hard on himself, that she had after all given him a kiss, and her reputation was that such kisses were not granted lightly. Nevertheless, she hadn't encouraged him, nor had she been dragged screaming into the house before she could tell him when they'd meet again.

What he needed to do was think.

This wasn't the place to do it, and the track was out until the game was over.

So he moved on, shoulders slumped, feet barely lifting off the pavement, until he reached Parkside Boulevard and walked west toward the far end of town, watching pedestrians pass him without recognition, watching the traffic pass from one invisible place to another. There were garish signs in most of the shops, announcing sales in honor of the celebration beginning on Wednesday; there were workmen on lampposts and telephone poles, clinging to ladders or safely standing in the baskets of cherry pickers, hanging up large oval medallions that featured the town's crest and the years of its incorporation; there were double-parked vans making deliveries, and a fair number of men putting the finishing touches on new paint jobs and storefront repairs, filling potholes on the side streets and trimming dead matter from the trees at the curbs.

In spite of his mood he was impressed by the effort, and within the hour his depression had changed from black to grey. What happened to him when he got home he would deal with later; right now he just wanted to find a place that would make him forget. Even for an hour it would be nice to forget so he could figure out what had gone so suddenly wrong.

By four-thirty he was having a hamburger at Beacher's and not answering Joe's questions about why he wasn't at the game. When he heard the triumphant horns in the street, he knew the game was over and the home team had won. Within minutes, then, the place would be swarming and he would have to listen to the stories, the laughter, see the girls and the players and suffer the replays of the game. It took him only a moment to conclude this was not what he needed while he thought things out. He slid off the stool without finishing his food, dropped a bill beside the register, and walked outside, saw Brian's car aiming for the curb and turned immediately to his left and bought a ticket to the shoppers' special early show at the theater. It was the same film he'd seen with Tracey, and he didn't see it again, sitting in the front row with his legs outstretched and his hands clasped across his stomach and his eyes blank on the center of the screen.

Until the first gunshot made him blink and he saw a dark-suited man fall through a window with blood on his face and fear in his eyes.

He shifted uncomfortably, thinking of that morning when he had wanted his folks dead. Thinking, too, of the power one had to have not just to kill another human being, because anyone could do that if anyone had a mind to, but to cause the terror that came just before it.

Another man was slammed against a wall from a shotgun blast, and he marveled at the effects they used to make it all seem so real and at the same time so gigglingly funny.

He closed his eyes.

He pictured Joyce sprawled on the kitchen floor, blood seeping from a wound in her back, her left hand gripping the table leg as though she were trying to pull herself up.

It frightened him even more to think: *serves the bitch right*.

When the film was over, he walked to the park's boulevard entrance and leaned against the wall. Hands in his pockets. Gaze on the curb. A car passed and honked, and he smiled quickly when Tar waved from the backseat of Chris Snowden's convertible. She was driving, and they were heading toward New York, and she gave him a big grin and a wave before a bus cut between them.

Football players, he thought, have all the luck. Then he felt his legs tighten, and he realized what he should be doing instead of feeling sorry for himself. The game was long over. The stands were empty. And the sun wasn't quite ready yet to set behind the town.

He hurried, trotted, put on the brakes when he felt himself straining to break into a full run; and ten minutes later, windbreaker on the ground and shirt open to the waist, he was alone on the track.

There wasn't anyone in the world who could keep up with him when his legs were moving and his arms were pumping and his lungs were taking in that fresh cold air.

No one.

His sneakers crunched on the finely ground cinder, the

wind pushed back his hair, and there was a not unpleasant ache settling into his left side.

He was alone on the track, and it was his world, no one else's.

His world, where there were no ambushes, no snipers, no battles for his soul.

For one brief moment he had wanted to kill his parents, and at that moment he had forgotten the Rule: never take your anger out on someone else, not even your enemies.

In place of striking out in anger, giving vent to his temper, there were words. Sticks and stones may break my bones, but words will never hurt me.

Christ, how wrong that was. How pious, and how wrong!

Words were how his folks did their fighting—hissing quietly, bitterly, venomously. Using time-honed razors instead of clubs to bleed each other to death. He hadn't seen that until recently, and yet one couldn't hit the other. It just wasn't done.

Well, maybe that was one of the Rules, he thought as he began his second quarter mile, but it was a damned dumb one. Sometimes he knew, he simply *knew* how great it would feel to land a punch on Brian Pratt's face.

The trouble was, you had to know what to do if you were doing to get into a fight, and he didn't. The second Saturday he had lived in Ashford, when he was nine, Brian had come over with a bunch of his friends. Don was in the front yard playing soldier by himself, and Pratt jumped him. There was no introduction, no posturing, no threats. Pratt jumped him, forced him onto the ground, and punched his back solidly a dozen or so times. Then he got back onto his bike, and rode off. Don cried because he hurt, and because he was confused, but he hadn't gone to his father because he knew what he'd hear: *you have to stand up for yourself, son, you have to show them you're better than they are.*

Sure. But don't act like you're better because the new Rule

was—you weren't. You were the same as everyone else. You were the principal's kid, but you were the same. Sure.

Goddamn rules. They're never the same from one day to the next.

How was he supposed to act when they kept changing the Rules?

His legs were loose now, and his breathing regular. The air was no longer cool, the track no longer too hard to run on. He stretched out, picking up speed, letting his mind wander because that was the best way to keep the laps from beating you in the end. Pay no attention to them and you've got it all firmly in the palm of your hand.

The sky turned darker, and a pale ghost of a moon settled over the town.

He ran alone, alone in the stadium, thinking about Tracey, about Hedley and Falcone, Pratt and Tar Boston, and his parents. If life was like this forever, he decided he would stay in school until he was an old man.

Into his second mile, panting a bit, but his legs were holding up.

He liked running.

He liked the solitude, the way he was able to work out his problems just by sending his brain out ahead of him. Some days he caught up, some days he didn't, and some days it just didn't matter at all. But there was no one faster than he, not when he was alone and the wind was blowing in his face and the stadium was filled with cheering crowds that waved red handkerchiefs as he passed. He saw the finish line and knew that given a little luck and one extra push, he would break the world's record. In one more turn of the track he would become the fastest man on earth.

The crowd was on its feet.

He felt himself breathing through his mouth and knew it was a bad sign, but there was a reserve somewhere down in the middle of his chest, and he called on it now. Grunting as he kicked his legs out for the bell lap. The crowd screaming, horns blaring, television cameras tight on the grimace frozen to his face like the scream of a clown.

Hedley was standing in the middle of the track, twirling his mustache and combing his red fringe, and Don ran right over him without breaking stride.

Pratt and Boston were down in a two-point, ready to block him into the next town, and he leapt, soared, came down lightly on the other side while they stood and gaped and scratched their heads like monkeys.

Tracey threw him a kiss.

Chrissy tore off her clothes and wet her lips when he passed.

Mom and Dad shook their heads and turned to help little Sam, who was having trouble tying his shoelaces.

The finish was ahead now, around that last turn.

The crowd was in a frenzy, pressing against the police line that tried to keep them back, though the cops were just as excited as the people they were holding.

He could hear his heart, and it was doing fine; he could hear his feet in perfect rhythm with the swing of his arms and the tilt of his head; he could hear his name being called over and over again, like the beating of a drum, like the slam of a fist hard against cement, like the march of an army across a treeless plain.

He ran harder, sobbing now because he knew he had to break the record so they would know who they were dealing with here. So they would know he wasn't a goddamned kid anymore.

He ran harder and thrust out his chest, and broke through the ribbon just as pandemonium broke loose and smothered him, washed him, rose in awe of him while he staggered across the grass and dropped onto his back, arms outspread, legs wide, eyes staring straight up at the goalpost's crossbar.

The crowd left, the cameras, the police, the sighing women.

But he wasn't alone.

The field stretched ahead of him, longer now from down here, and at the far end, in the ten-foot tunnel in the thick brick wall whose heavy wooden gates were still open at both ends, he could see something standing there. Deep in the shadows. Watching him. Waiting. Not moving a muscle.

There was no light behind it though the streetlamps were on; it cast no shadow darker than itself.

But it was there. He could see it.

And it was watching him. Waiting.

Not making a sound.

He blinked the sweat from his eyes, wiped his face with a forearm, and looked again.

It was gone.

The stadium was empty, and he was lying on the grass.

He puffed his cheeks and blew out, blinked again rapidly, and stared at the tunnel. "Oxygen, kid," he told himself as he stumbled to his feet. "You need a little of the old O_2, if you know what I mean."

His jacket was gone.

He looked down on the spot at the fifty-yard line where he had dropped it, stared with a perplexed frown, and finally looked up to scan the field. Then he turned and scanned the stands. It was gone. He knew he had left it right here; he could feel it leaving his hands and could hear it striking the ground. And now it was gone. He waited a moment for someone to start laughing, waited until he was sure it was not a joke. And when he was sure, when he knew he wasn't even safe on his track anymore, he put his hands into his pockets and started for home.

This, Tracey thought, is the pits.

She sat alone on a crumbling stoop in front of a crumbling brownstone, one of a whole block that could just as easily have been in any of the city's boroughs. The curbs were lined with cars, the pavement packed with children, and there wasn't a single face she recognized, not a single voice she knew.

The pits.

This was supposed to be Long Island—trees and beaches and elegant houses and developments, a place you visited to get away from it all. But even Ashford was better than this, for god's sake. At least it had the football game she was supposed to be playing the flute for right now; it had her books and her stuffed animals and the seclusion of her room; Ashford had Don Boyd.

She squirmed, thinking of the way she had kissed him before she'd known what she was doing. He'd looked as if she'd punched him in the stomach; she felt as if she'd been punched herself, and had run straight to her room without giving her mother the usual minute-by-minute account of her time out of the house. She must have been blushing, though, because her sisters began a teasing that hadn't let up, not even on the trip over, until her father had finally laid down the law—no talking, he was driving, he needed to concentrate on the idiots who were on the road with him.

She clasped her hands between her knees, watching a game of stick ball grow dangerously close to a brawl, suddenly thinking of the Howler and what he could do to these kids. A shudder. A swallow. A look over her shoulder to the windows above, to the window where she saw her father's face looking down. She smiled at him, waved, and sighed when he gestured her off the steps and into the building.

Damn, she thought. If he's such a *macho* cop, why the hell can't he get the old lady to move? At least to a place that had trees instead of garbage cans.

Long Island was the pits.

At the doorway she stopped and turned, and a sour smile parted her lips. Good-bye, twentieth century, she said to the noisy street. I'm going in my time machine now. Fasten your chastity belts, please, it's going to be a rough, boring ride.

The house's original porch had been torn down long before Don and his family had moved in, the previous owner claiming the wood had been rotted, and he didn't want anyone hurt in case a board or the steps gave way. It had been replaced by one that barely reached to either side of the door, and its roof was peaked, the railing up the steps twisted black wrought iron. It was the only house on the block with a porch like that, and Norman had once insisted he was going to restore the old one; that was before Sam had died. Now he said nothing beyond a grumbling that what was there did little to protect him from the rain or the snow.

Don sat on the top step. He had been inside only long enough to towel himself off and fetch a sweater, had intended on going back to his room, when he saw that his parents hadn't yet returned. They would never know he was gone. They would assume they had been obeyed. He had actually sat down on the bed and stared at the blank wall where the stallion had been; then he felt the weight of the empty shelves, and the hollow sound his breathing made, and the chill that seemed to drift from the white-painted walls. He looked into his parents' room, into Sam's room, then opened the attic door and went up.

They were there. Piled on cartons, helter-skelter on the dusty floor, dropped on a trunk that belonged to his grandfather. He had swallowed, stood, and finally picked up the poster and brought him back down. Taped him up over the desk and stared at him, wondering.

He saw little save the withdrawing of the light.

He heard only the leaves, and the shadows, and the silence of the house rising behind him.

An automobile or two had sped past, but he paid them no heed; a flock of kids shrieked through the twilight, but he didn't smile at their greetings; a red convertible crawled down the street, radio on full, and it wasn't until he realized it had pulled into a driveway a few houses down that he turned his head slowly, as if it were too heavy to move.

The driver's door slammed.

Chris. He blinked. It was Chris Snowden, and she wasn't with Tar. She was still in her dark cheerleader's sweater, still had on her saddle shoes, but her pleated skirt had been replaced by a pair of faded-to-white jeans.

And she wasn't going into her house; she was walking across the intervening yards directly toward him.

He cleared his throat and wondered what she had planned for him—a bit of teasing, a little temptation, a breathless request for his zoology homework.

He could wait; and he did, until she stopped at the foot of the stairs, leaned on the railing and crossed one foot over the other, toe down.

"Hi!"

Her pale hair was parted down the center and gathered in two braids that flopped over her chest. Her face was flushed, her eyes wide and of a blue so dark they seemed nearly black.

Warily he smiled a greeting. He recalled her brief show of solicitude when she'd seen the damage done to his eye, saw it again as she examined his face closely, a half smile at her lips.

"Looks better," she said.

"I barely feel it," he admitted, unconsciously poking around the discoloration. She turned to look at the empty street; he couldn't take his eyes from her profile. "I, uh, saw you and Tar before. I figured you guys were going to the city."

A shrug, and a sideways look of disgust. "He got sick. Brian had some beer in his car, and after the game they had a

he-man chugging contest. Tar lost.'' She pointed down the
street. ''So did my car.''

''Gross.''

''The creep wouldn't even help me clean it out. Last time I
saw him he was falling into the park.'' A grin—full of
humor, touched with malice. ''If there's a god, he'll end up
in the pond.''

He chuckled and shook his head at the foolishness of kids,
and did his best to not to stare when she turned back to him
and leaned forward on the railing, folding her arms on it and
putting her chin on a wrist. This wasn't happening, he knew;
this was something his mind had dreamed up to punish him
for thinking he could somehow rule the world and make it
fair again.

''Were you at the game?''

''No. I had . . . other things to do.''

An eyebrow lifted. ''We won.''

''We always win.''

''Really?''

''Every year,'' he said, making it clear there was a book
somewhere filled with things he thought more important, or
less boring. ''Especially since Brian and Tar got on the
team.''

''Oh?'' Her eyes drifted closed. ''You gonna be down at
Beacher's later?''

''I don't know. Maybe. It depends on my folks.''

She pushed abruptly upright and he almost gasped, thinking he had said something to make her mad. The expression
on her face was a dark one, the lines stabbing from the
corners of her eyes deeper and longer, giving her age, turned
her soft white-blonde hair into a hag's wig, her softly pointed
chin into a boney dagger. The transformation startled him,
and he leaned away from it slightly, could not meet her gaze.
Instead, he turned to the right where he saw in dismay the
station wagon approaching.

Aw shit, he thought; not now!

"You're in trouble, huh?" she said sympathetically.

He couldn't help himself—he nodded.

"Shit. So am I."

"Huh? You?"

"Oh sure," she said with venomous disgust, each word the swing and crack of a bullwhip. "It happens all the time, I'm getting used to it. They say get to know the kids, go to the parties, join the clubs. You're gonna need it, Christine, on your college applications. You're gonna need all that stuff." She snorted and managed a patently false smile as the station wagon pulled slowly into the drive. "Y'know, Don, no offense but there's a lot of scuz in your school."

"No offense. There is."

The smile, when she turned it on him, was genuine just long enough for him to notice; then it faded as Norman and Joyce opened their doors and got out, Norman pointing stiff-armed to Don, then to the grocery bags in back.

"A girl," she said quietly, "can't even get a decent lay around here."

He wanted to laugh, to grab her, to find someplace dark and deep where he could hide and start this conversation over. He wanted to tell her he knew exactly how she felt. What he did was stand meekly and murmur a good-bye when his father gestured again for help with the bags. Chris touched his arm in farewell, smiled again and introduced herself to the Boyds as she headed for home. Norman watched her; Don grabbed the two heaviest bags and grunted back to the house where his mother had the door open and waiting.

In the kitchen he lowered them onto the counter and backed into a corner while he waited for the storm.

Norman dropped his load solidly on the table, Joyce did the same, and they proceeded to move awkwardly about the room, putting things in their places and not looking at him save for a flat glance or two.

"I thought you were to stay in the house," his father said.

"Chris seems like a very nice girl," his mother said with an anxious smile.

"She is," Don told her. Guess what, Ma, she wants to get laid and I'm still a goddamn virgin.

"You're grounded," Norman reminded him.

"Well, maybe you should get to know her a little better, what do you think?"

Back and forth. Figurines on a clock.

"I guess, Mom. I don't know."

"Her father is a surgeon, you know. He works in New York. A fairly important man from all I hear."

"How come he lives here then?" he said, flinching when Norman opened a cupboard next to his head and gave him a look that demanded a response.

"I don't know," Joyce said, frowning over a box of cake mix, weighing it in her hand before putting it aside. "From what I'm told, he isn't lacking for the old green. And it certainly isn't because this is the perfect suburb. There is, I gather, something about the mother that—"

Norman slammed a can of soup on the table and faced his son. "I want to know what you were doing outside, Donald, when you were specifically told not to leave the house."

He lowered his gaze to his shoetops and swallowed the burrs that climbed into his throat. His left hand began thumping lightly against the wall. There was heat in his chest, and heat on his neck, and he could feel the seconds skip by like rocks dropped into a puddle. Without seeing her he could sense his mother shifting toward the doorway, fussing meaninglessly with something, staying because she had to, wanting to leave because she knew what was coming.

That was the Rule: the family never ran out on a discussion.

"I'm grounded," he said. "That doesn't mean I can't sit on the dumb porch, does it?"

"You know damned well what it means," Norman said.

"No," Donald said, "I don't know damned well what it means because you never told me before because I was never damned well grounded before."

Joyce put a hand to her mouth; Norman took hold of the table's edge and for a moment Don thought he was going to tip it over and come for his throat.

Don looked past him to his mother. "Mom, why are my things in the attic?"

"Things?"

"From my shelves. The animals. You took them away, remember? I'd like to know why they're in the attic. Am I ever going to get them back?"

"Go to your room," Norman said before she could answer. "Go to your room and don't come down until you have a civil tongue in your head."

"Sam," Joyce said.

There was no time then; no sound; no air.

Don raised a fist, and Norman looked at his wife in shock and disgust.

"Oh," she whispered, and ran out of the room.

There was red, briefly, before Don became aware of what he was thinking. He lowered the fist, forced the fingers to open, and headed for the staircase, his father behind him. At the landing he looked down.

"What if I'm not sorry?" he said flatly.

Norman swallowed and came up a step.

He knew it then—he knew as surely as he could see the red gathering in the corners that if his father lifted his foot one more time, one more step, there was going to be a fight. He was going to hit his father, or his father was going to throw the first punch. He had seen it in the movies and thought it stupid, that it never happened in real life. But he hadn't been able to feel it until now, until he saw this stranger looking up at him, not even the courtesy of hatred in his eyes, this stranger fighting with himself because all the rules said you can't hit your son when he's almost eighteen.

"Do as I tell you," Norman said tightly.

"I'll go," he answered, not conceding a thing.

He sat cross-legged on the bed, his back against the wall, his hands in his lap.

He deliberately avoided looking at the shelves, the neat desktop, the window, the floor.

He looked at the stallion, forever charging through the forest, and he thought.

First he thought about what it would be like to be an orphan and how he might accomplish the fact without leaving school to take a job;

He thought about Tracey and why she hadn't said anything to him about going out again, or seeing him at school, or even seeing him around;

He thought about Brian and Tar and the not-always-rotten Fleet, and why he had to be known as Donny Duck when he wasn't the only Don in the school, when there were others who had worse and funnier names, when there were others who were clearly meant to be the butt of stupid jokes;

He thought about Chris, thought about what she was like under that sweater, and wondered how many there were who knew exactly what was there and why did she have to talk to him and ruin everything about her;

He thought about the Rules.

He thought about how he could get all these people off his back before it broke in half and he was left lying in bed, crippled and dying.

Finally he thought about nothing.

At midnight he stirred.

There was nothing left in his mind he could cling to for more than a few seconds, but he smiled when he felt a curious settling inside. He looked down at his chest and was amazed to see how wet his clothes were; he touched his hair and it was matted to his scalp; he touched the bed and it was unpleasantly damp. But he didn't move because he still felt himself settling. It was the only way he could describe it to himself—a mass of something light piled high on a plain that had nothing but horizon, something that shifted and settled and eventually became a small something else, a nugget, compact and incredibly hard.

He reached without moving his arms, and he touched it, and it was hot, and it was red, and it was perfectly fitted to the palm of his hand when he picked it up and stared, and knew what it was.

There was a moment as he watched it—all the rage, all the frustration—when fear hovered over him, a storm cloud rumbling before the first clap of thunder. Yet despite the heat, the red, the hardness it had, it was more than anything something comforting, something familiar.

It was his, and it was him.

A smile, just barely.

He shifted to the edge of the bed, let his feet touch the floor, let his hands grip the mattress.

He switched on the light over the headboard and turned away from the bulb until his eyes adjusted. Eagerly he leaned forward, ready to explain to his friend what he thought had just happened.

But he couldn't.

He could only open his mouth in a scream that was never more than silent.

The poster was still there, taped over his desk.

The forest, the road, the darkening sky.

The poster was there.

But someone had tried to destroy the black horse. It was streaked, barely visible, as if a knife or a pen had attempted to scrape the picture off and leave only the background.

poem, eyes closed and distracted, being pulled in her wake by their son, his chum, and yet their happy prince.

The mother had dreaded the trip to the sffir breakfast, had balked tonight, for their son had walked out and she grew cold.

She hadn't cared to hear him as "If

Thank God, I hope...

<hr>

SEVEN

<hr>

Sunday's dawn never showed the sun; there was rain instead, a driving downpour that filled the gutters swiftly and washed driveways into black rivers. Leaves dropped sodden into the streets and onto the pavement, the Ashford Day medallions on the boulevard lampposts were twisted on their wires in the wind that followed. The park was deserted. A handful of pedestrians ran from shop doorway to shop doorway, heading for the bakeries and their hot cross buns, their dinner cakes and breakfast rolls. Cars hissed. Buses sprayed the shoulders. Headlamps were weak in the not-quite-daylight.

And when the downpour was over, the drizzle remained. Colder somehow, more touched with gloom. It prevented the puddles from holding clear reflections, prevented the windows from seeing clearly outside; the wind was gone, but collars were kept up and umbrellas stayed unfurled, and when a church bell tolled on the far side of town, it sounded like a buoy heralding the fog.

In Don's room the light was grey but he didn't notice it at all. He sat against the wall, on his bed, and stared at the poster, eyes puffed and bloodshot, hands palsied at his sides. He wore only his shorts, and his chest barely moved.

His mother had checked on him shortly after breakfast, and he had stared at her until she had backed out and closed the door.

His father hadn't come to see him at all.

He didn't mind.

He was working on a new set of Rules.

The telephone rang.

Tracey bolted from the couch and raced for the kitchen, but by the time she got there her mother had already answered. An aunt, by the sound of it, and she waited until she knew it would be one of those long, Sunday conversations that mixed with the aromas of Sunday dinner and the quiet of Sunday afternoons, when the house was ordered peaceful, a fiat from her father.

Later, she thought; I'll call Don later.

Brian was worried about the size of his neck. Several times before he left the house he checked himself in the hall mirror to see if it was getting too bulky, too thick. He didn't want to end up like Tar or Fleet, with necks sticking out to the ends of their shoulders, looking like goofballs and sounding like they had cotton shoved halfway down their throats. He wanted to look as normal as possible. A thick neck meant you were dim-witted and stupid to those assholes out there, and he wasn't kidding himself—once his professional career on the field was over he would have to make it in a real job, and you don't get real jobs if you look stupid, or bloated, or like your face had been stomped on by a herd of elephants.

Now he adjusted the rearview mirror and pulled at the top of the sweater, just to be sure nothing had changed in the past five minutes.

"Jesus Christ!" Tar yelled, cringing back in his seat. "Will you for Christ's sake look where you're going?"

A bus horn blared. Brian yanked the wheel hard to the right, back to the left, and grinned as the car held on the rain-slick blacktop. "No sweat."

"No sweat, fuck you, pal," Tar said. He wriggled lower until he could prop his knees up on the dashboard, his head barely rising above the edge of the door.

"Chicken?" Brian asked with a grin.

"Careful."

He laughed, shook his head, and swerved off the boulevard onto a street that took a sudden plunge down halfway along the block. They were headed for the flat below the school, and after checking his neck once again, Brian glanced into the backseat to make sure they had everything.

"I still think," Tar muttered, "we should've made Fleet come, y'know? Hell, it was practically his stupid idea in the first place."

Brian shrugged. He didn't give a damn. Fleet Robinson had sort of dropped out anyway, ever since he picked up Amanda Adler and got into her pants. Not, he thought with a palm rubbing over his chest, that he wouldn't mind it either. She wasn't all that bad, considering she didn't have much in the tits-and-ass department. He guessed Fleet was into something different, like that ass-long ponytail of hers. Maybe she whips him with it or something. He grinned. Maybe she does.

Tar was right though. The creep oughta be here, with them, driving into a place that looked like God forgot to clean up. The houses were ancient and falling apart; there was silt over everything now that it had rained, from the factories whose smokestacks rose glumly above the trees. You could hardly tell it was the same town, and he wondered why all the girls who came from down here had the best bodies.

"Jesus, what a dump," Tar said, his chin hard on his chest. His hair was short, dark, cropped high over his ears; his face was pale in the late afternoon's dim light. He sniffed, and fumbled in his shirt pocket for a cigarette, lit it, and rolled the window down to let out the smoke. Brian hated smoke.

Another right, and Brian slowed to not much faster than a brisk walk. Since they'd left the boulevard they hadn't seen a single car or a single person. Early dinner for the rubes, he thought. He snapped his fingers, and Tar groaned as he unfolded himself, reached into the backseat and pulled the two plastic garbage bags to the front. He stuffed them carefully into the well between his legs, and rolled the window down a bit more. Despite the ties that held the bags closed, he could still smell the crap, and he wiped his hands on his jeans.

"Beautiful," Brian said.

"Fleet oughta be here."

"Jesus, will you give it a rest, Boston? He ain't, and that's that, and besides, he'll regret it when he sees the look on the Tube's face tomorrow morning."

Tar considered it and decided Brian was right. As usual. Even when he was wrong.

A left, a right, and Brian pulled to the curb on a deserted street, the homes here in considerably better shape than the ones they had passed. They were still old, and still looked as if their owners made less than a buck an hour, but the tiny lawns were well kept, the houses clean and painted, and no rusted hulks cluttered the road.

Water dipped from the leaves onto the roof, loudly.

Brian rubbed his hands together and leaned over the steering wheel to peer through the windshield. "There," he said, pointing. "The green one, two in from the corner."

Tar followed the finger's direction and nodded. Then he checked the neighborhood again. "What the hell is he doing living down here, man? The way he talks you think he lived in fucking Scarsdale or something." He peered at the nearest house. "Maybe we got the wrong address."

"No," Brian said, though he'd been thinking the same thing. "He probably lives in the same house he was born in. Too fucking lazy to move out."

"Maybe he's got a secret lab in the cellar, where he experiments on women."

"The Tube? You gotta be kidding. If you were a girl, would you want that thing on top of you?"

Tar shuddered, and laughed, and took a deep breath. "Y'know, our ass is doomed if we get caught."

"Shut up, Boston, okay? We're not getting caught, and besides, we voted the fucker deserved it, right?"

Tar didn't need to think about that one. "Right. But I still don't get why we don't just bash the Duck's face in. That black eye of his would be the best thing left on his body."

"Because," Brian said, wondering why Tar had to think so much all the time.

"Because why?"

"Jesus, are you stupid or what?"

"I ain't stupid. I just think—"

"Look," Brian said, his hands kneading the wheel, "we bash up the Duck and everyone knows who did it, right? His old man comes down on us like we were killers or something, and we won't see graduation from the ass end of a warden. But we do this, Tar baby, and the Duck gets creamed. His old man creams him, Hedley creams him, and maybe even if we get lucky the frigging cops cream him too. So what the hell's the bitch?"

Tar didn't know. He supposed it made sense. "All right," he said. "But if we sit here much longer, someone's gonna call the cops on us, not the Duck."

Brian grunted his agreement and checked the green house again. "Okay. We'll go around the corner. I'll keep the engine running, and for Christ's sake, don't forget the other thing, all right?''

As Brian pulled away from the curb, Tar scrubbed a fist over a nose that been broken three times since he was a freshman. "I could use some help. That's why Fleet was supposed to be here, in case you didn't know."

"I know, I know, okay?"

"So help."

"So you run faster than me, okay?"

"Not that much faster," Tar muttered as they rounded the corner and parked on the left, facing traffic.

There was no time for further argument. As soon as the car stopped, he was out with the bags and running hunched over back to the green house. He sprinted up the walk, turned once in a circle, and heaved them both against the front door. He was already back on the pavement when they hit, when they burst open, when they spilled dogshit and rotten eggs and vinegar onto the porch. There was a low hedge in front of the property, and just as he veered onto the sidewalk he dropped Don Boyd's windbreaker onto it, dragging a sleeve until he was sure it had caught. Then he was back in the car, Brain pulling away before the door shut. He didn't drive so fast as to leave rubber, but fast enough to have them out of sight by the time Adam Hedley responded to the thumps upstairs and left his basement, his plaid robe tied tightly around him, his nose already wrinkling in disgust before he took hold of the knob and pulled the door to him.

Brian didn't laugh as he headed back up the hill. He just looked at Tar with a grin that never reached his eyes.

"Mission," he said, "accomplished."

Something moved in the rain.

It passed across streets without making a sound; it passed under streetlamps without leaving a shadow; it walked through a puddle and the water remained still; it brushed by a hedge and the branches didn't move.

A dog on the porch next to Adam Hedley's home began yapping, pulling at the leash that held it to the door, howling once, snarling, then cowering with a whimper against the welcome mat when it moved up the walk and fixed the terrier with a stare, turned around, and moved away; and the dog began trembling, snapping at its legs, growling at its tail, urinating on the mat and foaming slightly at the mouth.

Something moved in the rain, without making a sound.

The room was large and perfect. The furniture was new enough to keep its shine and already old enough to be comfortable when used: the bed was canopied just the way Chris liked it, the desk and chair were straight from Regent Street in London, the soft rainbow rug from India, the loveseat under the window from a little shop in SoHo she had discovered two years ago. The walls were papered in white and flocked gold, the ceiling freshly plastered, the alabaster lamps with just the right touch of frills but not so feminine that it looked like a room belonging to a girl who wanted only a husband and two kids to complete her life. In the far corner was an upright piano, sheet music piled on the bench and ready to fall.

Next to the desk was an open door leading into her private bathroom. It had been one of the requirements for her agreeing to leave Manhattan—that she have as much a private environment as possible to keep the rest of the house out of her affairs, if not out of her life; had she thought it possible she would have lobbied for a private entrance as well, but that would have been pushing it. Her father, indulgent to the point of easy manipulation, would have balked, no question about it, and might possibly have sent her to that damned fancy school in Vermont where all she'd have to look at were other girls, some trees, and herds of stupid cows.

Her mother didn't care one way or the other; she spent most of her time writing ten-page letters to her two older children in Yale and Vassar, and flying down to Florida to visit her own mother.

It was, then, as perfect as she could have it, and whatever complaints she had she kept to herself.

She brushed her hair at the bathroom mirror, turning side to side, scowling at the thought of having to wash it again. She hated it—the washing, the drying, the constant brushing to keep it gleaming. She wished she could cut it off and dye her scalp blue like the Picts did for the Romans. But if she cut it off, she would look like a freak, and looking like a freak was not part of the plan.

The bath towel began slipping off her chest and she grabbed for it with an oath, held it while she flicked off the lights and walked into the dark bedroom. A reach for the wall switch was pulled back. Not yet, she thought. She wanted to stay in the dark a while longer, listening to the rain run down her window, listening to the blessed silence that meant she was alone. A sigh, contented, and she padded across the warm rug to the cushioned window seat, sat, and pulled her legs up so she could hug them and look out. There wasn't all that much to see, not while it was raining, not after sunset, but the lights in the houses beyond the yard were still visible, and growing brighter as the leaves were pounded from their branches.

The towel slipped a bit more; she didn't touch it.

She put a palm against a pane and shivered at the cold, pressed her head beside it, and tried to see the Boyds' backyard. It was too far away and blocked by too many trees, but she saw it, and she saw Don, and she saw his father.

She wondered if either of them would understand what she was doing, if Don would be very hurt if he knew he was included. Norman, she thought, wouldn't be any trouble. Certainly not from the way he looked at her yesterday when she was walking away from his son, or the way he smiled at her whenever she could think of an excuse to talk to him in his office.

He wasn't stupid. She damned well knew he knew the plan. He understood why she was going to stay in this damned dirty town until she graduated from its mediocre high school with the highest grades she could get, no matter how she got them; he sure as hell understood that a flower in a drab garden was brighter than a flower among her sisters, especially when the flower had the pick of the men who tended that garden—in a place like this, she was a god-damned champion orchid.

Her mother had chosen to be a shadow, and she had paid; her friends were too busy turning every job and love offer into political statements.

Chris, on the other hand, knew she was in a war, and only assholes and bitches didn't use their best weapons.

Norman understood, she could see it in his eyes; Don would, eventually, but not before. Not before she was ready.

A shadow down in the yard.

She peered, wiped the pane, and peered again.

And sighed.

It wasn't Don, and Norman wasn't that stupid.

It was a cat, and she grinned at it while she stretched and purred and thought about how the next phase should open.

Something moved in the rain, and Sergeant Quintero in his patrol car heard it in an alley. He was waiting for Verona to get out of the john in the bar, declining to go in himself and wait because he knew he would see women there. On Sunday. Even on Sunday there would be a woman on a stool, having a drink, talking with the barkeep, waiting for her date to show up and take her home. It made him sick, and he refused to go in when Tom had decided he'd had enough of the car's useless shocks. Jarred his kidneys, he said as he slid out and walked away; Quintero only grunted, and rolled down the window to breathe the fresh air.

And heard it in the alley.

He stared for a moment, figuring it was a rummy looking for a place to sleep, looked at the rain, and decided to leave the bum alone.

Then he heard it again, moving away, slowly.

It sounded like someone thumping soft dirt with a shovel.

He glanced at the bar's closed door, then shrugged and pulled his jacket collar up over his neck. He climbed out and touched a hand to his left side to be sure the gun was there, then scowled at the drizzle and moved to the mouth of the alley.

It was dark.

At the back, he knew from rousting Saturday night drunks, was a broken-down wooden fence that led to a backyard. A kid could squeeze through; a grown man would have to swear and climb over.

Wood splintered then, echoing like gunshots, and reflex had him running, revolver in hand, eyes squinting through the mist. But despite the faint light from the street behind and the homes ahead, he could see nothing, not even when he reached the fence and saw the gaping hole.

A tank, he thought; someone's driven a tank through it.

He searched for a culprit, in the alley and the adjoining backyard, and decided it was a drunk in a stumbling hurry to get home.

Another five minutes before he holstered his weapon and headed back toward the car.

And behind him, softly, something moved in the rain.

"It's like going to the same funeral twice a month," Tracey said to Jeff as they walked down the stadium steps to have lunch. "She lives in this really creepy apartment, a fourth-floor walkup in the middle of a block that looks like it's been bombed. My father's been trying to get her to move out since Grandfather died two years ago, but she says all her friends are still there and she just won't budge.''

Jeff pushed a forefinger against his glasses to shove them back along his nose, and grinned as they sat, opening their lunch bags and taking out the food. They had bought cartons of milk in the cafeteria, and oranges for dessert, and when they didn't see Don there, they thought he might be outside. Sunday's rain was gone though the clouds had stayed behind, and the temperature had risen as if the sun were shining.

He sighed as he scanned the seats, still dark with moisture. ''Don't see him.''

''Well, he was in math.''

''Did he say anything?''

She shook her head, and a wide fall of hair slipped from behind her ear to cover her eye. ''He looked like hell though. He looked like he hadn't slept all weekend.''

They ate in silence, not close enough to touch, but close enough to sense they were alone out here.

''Trace?''

She looked at him absently, and wondered why he didn't have a girlfriend. He wasn't bad-looking in spite of the thick glasses, he kept his outdated long hair gleaming like a girl's, and when he wanted to be, he was pretty funny in a sarcastic sort of way. She supposed it was because he was third string on the football team, which didn't make him anywhere near a hero, and something less than the fans who crowded the stands at home games. A bad spot, she imagined, and a little silly too.

''Hey,'' he said, rapping knuckles on her forehead. ''Hey, are you in there?''

She laughed. ''Yeah.''

''Thinking about Don?''

She shrugged; not a lie, not the truth.

"You going to the concert Wednesday if it doesn't rain?"

"I think so."

"He ask you yet?"

That's what her mother had asked her that morning, and yesterday night, and yesterday afternoon. But she wouldn't let Tracey call him. It was not the way, she was told sternly; the proper way is for the boy to call first. Only, Maria Quintero didn't know Donald Boyd. Tracey knew he had enjoyed their date as much as she had, and she knew, too, she should have said something to him when he had walked her home. But then there had been the kiss, and the running away.

And as soon as she had realized her mistake, up there in her room, she'd started out again, to stop him from leaving, and her father had walked in from the kitchen. He had been dressed in street clothes, explaining quickly he was working double shifts from now on with Detective Verona, hoping to keep the Howler from striking again in this town.

He hadn't permitted her to leave.

She'd protested tearfully and was promptly ordered straight to her room; it was late, the boy was already gone, and there was the visit to *abuela* Quintero the following day.

What could she do? The last time she had defied him openly he had taken the strap to her and confined her upstairs for an entire weekend. Her mother, bless her, had snuck food up, and comfort, but could do nothing to gain her release. Luis Quintero had made up his mind.

"He hasn't said boo to me all day," she told Jeff sadly. "I don't know if he's mad or what."

Jeff grinned. "I think he's scared."

"Scared? Of what?"

He pointed at her.

"You're crazy."

Jeff debated only a minute before telling her about Don's asking practically the whole school about her relationship with Brian Pratt. When she protested that there was none, never had been, and as long as there was a breath in her body never would be, Jeff assured her that that's what everyone had told him.

"He was a total loon, you should have seen him." He chuckled, and drained the rest of his milk in a gulp. "Put that on top of the detention he had and he was a Space Cadet the whole day." His head shook in amazement. "I never saw him like that before. Never."

"Really?" She didn't bother to feign indifference. Jeff knew her too well. "Then I don't get it."

"What's to get? I told you—he's scared shitless."

"Oh great."

"Hey, don't sweat it, Trace. By the end of the day, if you wink at him or something, he'll carry your books home in one arm and you in the other."

She laughed, and felt a blush working on her cheeks. A swallow to get rid of it, a touch to her hair to hide it, and she jumped when the late bell sounded over the seats. Two minutes later she was in the hallway, on her way to Hedley's lab, when she saw Don slumped against the wall outside his history class. She slowed, hoping he'd turn and see her, slowed even more, and finally walked right up to him and jabbed him in the arm. Startled, he pushed away and backed off a pace, his eyes wide, almost panicked, until he recognized her face.

"Hi!" she said brightly.

"Hi," he replied, not meeting her gaze.

"You're, uh, late for class."

"Yeah. You too."

"You going home right after school?"

He lifted a hand. "I . . . I think I'm going to run a little."

A man's voice called her name, and Don turned away, heading for the staircase.

"I'll see you," she called softly, and kicked herself when she saw the faces of the class as she rushed to her seat. They knew. She must have it written all over her, from her forehead to her knees. They whispered, someone giggled, and she felt the blush rise again; she cursed then for a full three minutes before the pressure left her chest and her cheeks felt cool again.

The class was endless. And her last class made her feel as if it were Friday and not Monday, and she was almost to the exit with her books cradled against her sweater when she stopped, turned, and collided with Chris Snowden.

Chris smiled and laid a hand on her shoulder. "Take it easy," she said quietly, her head inclined for privacy. "I saw him heading down for the gym."

Tracey could only mutter her thanks and rush off, tears of embarrassment filling her eyes. My god, it was that obvious. And if Chris, who didn't know if she were alive or dead, if Chris could see it, then the whole school knew it. And if the whole school knew it, then her freshman sister would too. Oh, god. Dinner tonight was going to be hell.

At the ground floor she was tempted to forget it and go home. This was ridiculous. She had never in her life chased a boy before; it was humiliating, and she had seen the blank look in his eyes when she caught him outside class—there was neither delight nor fear nor even a polite smile. There was nothing. She might as well have been a tree, or one of the wall tiles.

She stepped out of the stairwell and into the corridor. It was deserted, the lights already dim and made dimmer by the lack of windows, the drab paint, and the absence of doors. The gym and the stadium exits were on the other side. He said he was going to run, Chris's comment confirmed it, so she walked slowly toward the doors that seemed a hundred miles away. Somewhere, a group of boys laughed raucously, probably the football team getting ready for practice. A higher voice trilled, choked, blew into laughter; the girl's basketball team heading for the small gym opposite the main one.

And her footsteps on the hard floor, as if there were taps on her heels.

She hurried, feeling nervous, her shoulders lifting a little, her chin bringing her face down.

And behind her, when she slowed again to be sure this was really what she wanted, something followed.

Uneven steps, sounding hollow, sounding loud.

She glanced over her shoulder and saw nothing, looked back and moved on. A boy, maybe one of the coaches, Gabby D'Amato dragging one of his brooms.

The idea that the grizzly custodian might be following her gave her the shivers and she moved faster. She didn't like the old man; none of the girls did. They suspected he spent more time in their locker room than that of the boys, and they knew damned well he spent hours every day standing in the girls' gym doorway, watching them in their shorts and T-shirts, intently.

Behind her. The footsteps.

She was thirty feet from the exit, and there was no other sound on the floor but her shoes, and her breathing, and the slow trailing footsteps that were hollow, and loud, and moving closer all the time.

Don't look, she told herself; just get to the door and get outside, and get hold of Don and shake an invitation out of him even if you have to chop him in the throat.

Steadily, moving closer—the deep hollow sound of slapping against wood.

Don't look, idiot; and she turned around at the corner.

The corridor was empty.

But she could still hear the footsteps.

And she could see a huge shadow spilling across the far wall.

It wasn't a man; she was sure it wasn't a man, because if it was, he was stumbling, drunkenly careening off the tiles, off the lockers. But there was no sound of anything like a shoulder striking metal, no sound of panting, no sound at all but the steady wooden thump of something moving down there.

Something much larger than a boy, or a man.

She blinked once, the books crushing her breasts, her mouth and throat dry, her lips quivering for a scream.

Then it started around the corner and she did scream, and spun through the door and raced up the steps, shouldering open the upper exit and running for the seats. She was halfway down to the field when she realized the stadium was empty. Don wasn't there. No one was. She was alone.

The school loomed above her, and she hurried down to the track.

What was it?

She didn't know. And she wasn't going to be dumb enough to stick around just to satisfy her curiosity. It might have been a trick of the light, and it might have been her nerves gearing up to face Don, but whatever had started around that corner wasn't human; it couldn't be, unless, she thought so suddenly she stopped, it was the Howler looking for someone to kill.

She ran, then, and didn't stop until she reached home.

The office door was closed, the secretaries dismissed early, and Norman stood at his window, frowning when he saw the Quintero girl race across the street as if a rapist were after her. He leaned forward to see if there was, in fact, anyone following, saw no one and grunted, and sat back at his desk.

"It's a bitch," he said, pulling his tie loose and unbuttoning his collar.

Harry Falcone was in the leather chair opposite, his legs crossed, his sport jacket open. "You can say that again."

"Okay. It's a bitch."

They grinned, but not for long.

Norman picked up a pencil, turned it, tapped it on the blotter. "You can't do it, you know. You'll have every paper on your ass, and the board will just tighten theirs, and the parents of the seniors will be out for your heads."

Falcone made a noise that might have been a grunt, or a groan, and leaned back until he was staring at the ceiling. "What choice do we have, Norman?"

"Accept the offer that's on the table, for one."

Falcone laughed sharply.

"Then what about binding arbitration?"

Another laugh; this one bitter.

"Well, then, what, for god's sake?"

"Walk," Falcone said without looking at him. "We're going to walk. If the vote's right tonight, we'll walk on Wednesday after the last bell unless someone hands us a contract we can live with and live on."

"Insane."

"That," said Falcone, finally sitting up, "is your opinion."

Norman swiveled around quickly, looked out at the lawn, and ordered himself to relax.

"Do you have a statement you want me to read to the faculty tonight?"

"Read the last one," he said sourly. "I've got nothing else to say."

"Christ, Norm, you're an ass, you know that? You're a real jackass. You could be setting yourself up for life, you could be a hero and every teacher in this school would kill for you, but instead you're insisting on cutting your own throat."

You son of a bitch, he thought; you smug little son of a bitch.

He swung the chair back around, dropped the pencil, and leaned his forearms on the desk. Falcone was smiling.

He picked up Don's test paper.

The teacher's smile didn't waver.

"I know what you're doing," Norm said evenly. "And it isn't going to work. God knows, you're not going to get to me through Joyce, and you're not going to get to me through Donald either. It isn't going to work, so lay off, Falcone. Lay the fuck off my son."

"Oh, my," the man said, rising, smoothing his lapels as he headed for the door. "Is that a threat, Mr. Principal?"

Norman considered a mild retraction, a half-hearted apology. He knew what the man would do if he didn't—a statement to the faculty about the principal's accusation, perhaps a judicious leak to the press. Norman becomes the instant villain, the board's henchman in the streets. Norman is losing his cool because he's lost control of his school, and would you want a man like that running this city?

"Harry," he said, slamming the paper to the blotter, his fist planted atop it, "let me put it to you this way—I'll kick your balls into your fucking mouth if you pull this stunt again. Trust me, Harry. I'll ream your fucking ass."

Falcone hesitated before he crossed the threshold, turned only slightly and stared back, not frowning. "I concede you the kid," he said, just barely loud enough to hear. "But I'll be damned, Mr. Boyd, if I know why you're dragging your lovely wife into this."

The door closed.

Norm was on his feet, ready to charge, when a restraining hand gripped his shoulder and pulled him back. There was no one there, but he felt it just the same, and began trembling when he realized how close he had come to throttling the man. He bit down on his lower lip, to feel the pain, to shock himself back, and when he did he muttered, "It isn't fair. It just is not fair."

Then he cleared his throat loudly, and decided he wasn't going to bring any work home, the hell with the reports. He smiled, stood, and plucked his coat from the small closet on the far side of the room. Habit took him out the private door directly into the corridor, where he turned right and headed for the main entrance. And when he pushed out onto the concrete plaza and saw Gabby taking the flag down from the pole, he paused for a moment as if part of a ceremony, gave the custodian a two-fingered salute, and started walking.

Adam Hedley's car sped past.

Norman watched it, praying the chemistry teacher wouldn't spot him, stop, and demand to know if anything had been done about the windbreaker found caught on his hedge yesterday. The jacket Don had claimed he'd lost two days ago.

"I have not called the police," Hedley had told him piously that morning. "The school certainly has enough trouble these days with that maniac on the loose. Not to mention the horrid scandal it would cause at the celebrations this week."

"I appreciate that, Adam," he'd replied, too stunned by the evidence in hand to say anything more.

"I'm sure you do." Hedley had shaken his hand then, and had held it just a second too long. "I only want your assurance that you will take care of this, Norman. It wouldn't do to have it get out. It would be rather disastrous, wouldn't you think?"

Norman had agreed mutely. He knew exactly what the man meant, what Falcone could do with something like this—that the principal couldn't even manage his own son, and the teachers were expected to manage an entire school of kids like him.

He knew. And he still refused to believe, despite the jacket, that Don had done such a stupid thing.

But there was the vial in his top drawer, and the coat, and there was Don's recent, increasingly odd behavior.

Maybe, he thought, I'll have a word with him tonight.

And maybe not. Maybe tomorrow.

He thought: rope—give him enough rope and he'll hang himself and I won't have to be the accuser.

"Jesus," he muttered, "you're a bastard, Boyd."

But he didn't change his mind.

When he reached his corner, he paused and glanced over his shoulder. The street was empty, the sun dropping rapidly and filling the spaces under the trees with twilight. A look to his house, then, hidden back there under the trees and shadows, and it struck him with a twinge of guilt that he didn't want to go home. If Joyce wasn't there, waiting to talk, Don would be, hiding in his room.

He had seen the boy only twice during the day; once in the corridors before lunch, looking like hell and walking like a zombie, and then again just before the final bell, heading for his locker. Norman had almost called him into the office, but changed his mind when he saw Fleet Robinson stop, whisper something into his ear, and slap his back heartily. Don had turned and grinned, nodded once, and moved on. But he still looked like hell, and it wasn't just that damnable black eye; it was the way he looked at people—blankly, as if he were little more than a shell, his body making the rounds through habit. It was the way he had been most of yesterday, according to Joyce. He still smarted from the boy's backtalk and wasn't about to yield just yet. The kid had to learn that breaking the rules meant taking the consequences.

And if he had anything to do with that nonsense at Hedley's, he was going to pay much more than he thought.

A breeze kicked at the leaves piling up in the gutter, and he hurried, hands deep in his coat pockets, head down, skin feeling damp. As he passed the Snowden home, Chris backed out of the driveway in her car, the top down in spite of the weather; she smiled and waved when he looked up at the sound of the racing engine. He mouthed a hello, she winked and drove away, and he stood there a moment, watching her hair fight with the wind.

She wants to go to bed with you, old fella.

He swallowed, looked quickly side to side before realizing the leering voice he had heard was his own, and silent.

But it was true, no question about it. He had been in the business long enough to know the difference between a harmless flirtation and one designed to produce better grades. Chris was definitely the willing type, and as calculating as any he had ever met. He hastened, then, to pat himself on the back for not once having fallen into the ultimate trap. Returning a flirtation was nothing; it was painless, and no one much cared. And it was a kick to do it knowing full well he wasn't about to grant an A just because the girl had a fine figure or a lovely smile or a pair of eyes that made him restless at night.

This, on the other hand, could be serious. He suspected that if she didn't get him compromised on the mattress, she would somehow find a way to compromise him by implication. Either way, he was going to have to be careful with that one.

A laugh, bright and genuine, put a bounce in his step as he headed for the front door. Calculated or not, it was still nice to know he wasn't considered too disgustingly old for her to make the effort. In a backhanded way it was rather flattering.

A second laugh, that was strangled when he stepped over a puddle on the walk and turned around sharply.

The water lying on the sagging brick was clear and unrippled, and along one edge was a shadow that was neither the tree in the yard nor the eaves nor himself crossing over.

He stared at it, drawing out a hand to hold the coat's collar closed around his neck.

The shadow didn't move.

It suggested something much larger, much darker, than he had first imagined, but when he examined the street, the sidewalk, the yard, the stoop behind him, he saw nothing.

The shadow was still there, and when he kicked at the

water to rough it and scatter it onto the grass, it remained
unmoved.

"Jesus," he said.

It grew larger.

Darker.

He stamped a foot into the puddle and watched the shadow
slip over his toes.

The shoe yanked back and he looked up quickly, then
sighed his relief aloud. A cloud. It was a black patch of cloud
in the overcast made unnervingly substantial by the failing
light below. Nothing more, Norman, nothing more.

He had his hand on the doorknob then when he heard the
noise behind him.

Soft. Hollow. Slightly uneven, stones dropping lightly
onto a damp hollow log.

It was coming up the walk.

He did not turn around. Deliberately he turned the knob,
pushed open the door and stepped inside. He closed it behind
him without looking over his shoulder and stood in the empty
foyer for several long seconds before taking off his coat.

He was listening while a silent whisper irrationally insisted
the cloud hadn't made that shadow.

A shuffling, and Don appeared at the top of the stairs.

A muffled hollow sound, and something thudded heavily
against the door at his back, just before the door slammed
open.

EIGHT

Joyce scowled as she pushed inside, grocery sacks unwieldly in her arms and her purse starting to slip maddeningly off her shoulder. But instead of the stinging remark that came to mind, she blinked when she saw the look on her husband's face. He was pale, and moving away from her as if she were a corpse newly risen from the grave.

"God," she said, "I hope to hell I don't look that bad."

Norm managed a wan smile after wiping his face with a palm, and quickly relieved her of one of the bags. Trailing after her into the kitchen, he asked about her day, helped her place cans and boxes in the cupboards, and finally wondered aloud what was eating their son.

"So ask him," she said, snatching a saucepan from under the sink. "You speak the language of the young, the last I heard."

"Hey, touchy today, aren't you," he said, but without his usual bitterness.

She watched him drop into a chair, light a cigarette, and stare at the smoke until it had vanished. "My day was shitty, but yours must have been hell."

"To put it mildly," he said.

And as she prepared them a quick meal, something they could eat in five minutes and have no complaints about not feeling full, she listened while he told her about Hedley's bitching about a prank someone had pulled at his place over the weekend, about the coaches whining about the teachers who were in a conspiracy to hold back their best players and ruin the Big Game coming up Friday night against Ashford North, and about the teachers themselves and that sonofabitch Falcone and his threat to take the faculty out for a walk in only two days.

She said nothing because a single wrong word would set off his temper. The signs were there. And she knew he had deliberately held back the news about Harry until he'd reached the end of his weary tirade. Maybe he'd thought to catch her off guard; maybe he thought she would fly to the man's defense and reveal herself as his not-so-secret lover.

And maybe he didn't think anything of the sort and was only rambling, hoping to get this day off his chest before he could relax and start thinking about tomorrow.

Three cigarettes later he was done, and the silence made her nervous. She turned from the stove, and he was staring at her.

"Sorry about dinner," she said, waving toward the soup and sandwiches. "There's a—"

"Committee meeting tonight," he finished for her. "I know."

"Well, there is," she insisted without wanting to. "My god, things start on Wednesday, you know."

"I know."

"And as long as you're here, I might as well tell you that that so-called bandmaster of yours is being a real prick, Norm. He acts like he's in charge of the New York Philharmonic, for Christ's sake. It's not like we're asking for his blood, for crying out loud. And he's even talking about extra pay!"

"I know."

She slapped at the counter. "Will you please stop saying that? If you know so damned much, why the hell don't you talk to him like I've asked you a hundred times already?"

"Three hundred, but who's counting," he said.

"Jesus."

She put her back to him and stirred the soup, her free hand pulling her ponytail over her shoulder to stroke it, to calm her, to figure out a way to get him to talk to Donald—right, Joyce, his name is Donald. She couldn't do it herself. When she'd looked in on him on Sunday and he had looked at her that way, she knew she couldn't have a decent conversation with him without running from the room.

It was horrible.

It was unnatural.

But after seeing him like that, not sick but something else, she was ashamed to admit that she was afraid of him.

"Did you talk to Don?" she asked at last, her voice sounding too small, making her clear her throat and ask the question again.

"No. I just walked in the door when you came."

"Then will you?"

"When I'm ready."

The spoon clanged against the side of the pot.

"If you want to know the truth," he said, sounding less angry but no less tired, "I think the kid needs a spanking, but he's too big for it. If I tried it, he'd probably bash in my teeth."

Last year, last month, last week, she would have turned on him furiously for even suggesting such a thing; tonight, however, she only nodded without letting him see her expression.

"Actually, I think he's in love."

She lifted the spoon from the soup, tested for warmth, and returned to her stirring. "You think so?"

"Yep. I think he has the hots for the Quintero girl. The cop's kid."

"Norman, I wish you wouldn't talk like that."

"Like what?" Perfectly innocent, and uncaring.

"Like saying Don has the hots for someone. If he's in love, he's in love, and it doesn't necessarily have anything to do with having sex with the child."

But he isn't in love, she thought, half-hoping he would read her mind. He isn't. I know. I'm his mother, and I know.

"Well, maybe," he conceded. "And another thing."

"What?"

"If you don't let up on that spoon, we're going to have butter for supper."

It wasn't all that funny, but she laughed anyway as she went to the foyer and called up to her son, telling him supper was ready and he'd best get down here before it got cold. There was no response. She called again and wished he had turned out more like Sam, who had never had to be called twice, never got into trouble.

"Donald!"

She heard the door open, heard his footsteps in the hall, and smiled as well as she could when he appeared on the landing.

"I'm not really hungry, Mother," he said.

"Well, you'd better come down and eat what you can. It can't hurt, and I don't want you sick for all the fun this week."

"Yeah," he said, looked back up toward his room, and started down. Slowly. His hand dusting the banister until he was less than a foot from her. The smile held, but she could see his eyes now, could see the look in them, the dark look that made her feel as if she were an ant to be stepped on, or not, at the whim of a perfectly ordinary and inexplicably terrifying young man.

"Come on," she said brusquely and walked away. He followed and she walked faster, and barely suppressed a relieved sigh when she saw Norm still at the table. Even a fight, now, would be better than nothing.

But Norm only nodded, and Don only nodded back, and during the meal they exchanged words so polite, so noncommittal, so infuriatingly inane that she wished for the first time that Harry were here. He would know what to do. He was, despite his dress and his manner with his students, an old-fashioned type when it came to dealing with children, and he would know how to handle this stranger who was her son.

And when the meal was over and she was piling the dishes in the sink, Don said, "Are you two getting a divorce?"

She spun around, a bowl clattering to the floor unbroken. "My god, Donald, what a thing to say!"

"Go to your room," Norman ordered in a strained voice.

"Just asking," Don said with a shrug. Then he rose, folded his paper napkin, and walked out.

"Jesus," Norm said, pulling a beer from the refrigerator.

"Norm, what are we going to do?"

He looked at her, drank, and forced himself to belch. "Seems to me," he said as he headed for the TV room, "that's your problem. You're the one who doesn't think I love you, remember?"

"But—"

And she was alone, hands tangled in a dishtowel, lips moving soundlessly, her dream of running away with Harry for some remote paradise suddenly more the dream of an old woman still a spinster.

Then she saw the clock and knew she was going to be late. Oh, shit, she thought, threw the towel on the floor, stomped to the doorway, and said, "I'm going. I'll be back around eleven."

"I'll be here."

"Talk to Don, okay?"

He lifted a hand—maybe, maybe not.

Damn you, she thought, and managed to get behind the wheel before she started to cry. Not long, and not loud. Just enough to prove she could still do it, and still cared enough to want to in spite of the daydreams and in spite of Falcone. It wasn't easy; she had admitted weeks ago he meant nothing to her, not even as a port in her private storm. He meant, if she were going to be honest, even less than that lawyer she'd taken up with shortly after Sam had died. That episode had been a search for meaning, or so she claimed, and so Norman said he believed in his forgiving; this was a search for something else, something she couldn't define and was growing weary of trying. What it probably was, she thought bitterly, was a woman on the verge of menopause, looking for her teenaged self in a mirror that lied.

She snorted a laugh at the image and backed out into the street, driving off with the resolve to get home as soon as possible. Maybe then they could talk, the three of them, about what was going on, and what they could do, and how much they really loved each other. They had to. Don's question tonight proved it.

Something moved in the shadows.

"You know my father's gonna kill me," Tracey said, walking as fast as she could, her shoulders lifted against the cold that had come with Monday's dark.

"God, you're not that late," Amanda told her. Her long black hair was tied back with a black ribbon, her school jacket open to the night's chill. "God, you'd think he was your keeper or something."

"Sometimes he thinks he is," she said, though with a smile that made Amanda frown and shake her head. "It's just a pain how old-fashioned he is sometimes, you know? But . . . well, he's just afraid for me, that's all. Because of the Howler."

"Well, for god's sake, that slime's probably a million miles away by now. He can't be stupid enough to hang around, right? Christ, he's probably all the way to Ohio or someplace." She giggled. "Damned fuzz can't find the lint on their shoulders."

"Hey," Tracey said softly.

"Oh. Sorry." Without regret, only a shrug and a lengthening of her stride.

"Sure."

"No, I mean it."

Tracey waved off the weak apology and readjusted the notebooks she carried in her hand.

Amanda began humming, and cut herself short. "I wonder if old Tube's gonna be up all night again."

"Again?"

"Yeah, sure. Didn't you hear Brian today? He said the old fart was up all night yesterday scrubbing his porch. He had one light, a flashlight, and when Brian drove by, he turned it off. I guess he didn't want anyone to see what he was doing. I'll bet he used some of that crap from his lab, y'know? Homemade bleach." She giggled and mimed a scientist pouring a solution from one beaker to another. "Maybe he drank some of it. Maybe he thinks it'll give him more hair."

"All night, huh? No kidding?"

"I'll tell you," Amanda said, moving closer and lowering her voice. "I'm glad Fleet wasn't there. With his luck they would have been caught, suspended, and thrown in jail." She sniffed and looked behind her. "The old fart had it coming though. He's been busting our asses since school started. I don't think he wants us to graduate." A laugh, and a slap at Tracey's arm. "He really hates it that Fleet's getting straight A's, y'know? He thinks Fleet oughta be dumb just because he plays football. Maybe he has the hots for him, y'know?" She laughed again, harder, when Tracey looked away, embarrassed.

The boulevard was empty of everything but its streetlamps and shadows, and it wasn't hard for Amanda to hear footsteps behind her. She looked, and saw nothing.

Tracey saw the move. "Me too," she said, and they moved closer to the curb, ready to dash across to the other side should they need to run.

"Dumb."

"What?"

"This," Amanda said, nodding to the way they were almost tightroping the curb. "He's a million miles from here."

"Sure," Tracey agreed.

"Besides, I'd kick his balls in if he tried anything with me."

Tracey nodded, patting the purse she held close to her side. "I've got a piece of pipe in here. I'd bash his brains in."

"Pipe?" Amanda was impressed. "No shit?"

"Dad makes me carry it."

"Well, hell, sure he does. He's a cop."

"I don't know if I could use it though."

"What?" Amanda stopped, staring her disbelief. "You're nuts, Trace. You're . . . nuts! Of course you can use it! You think you're gonna die, you'll bite the bastard back if you have to."

Tracey considered, then nodded. "I guess."

Another block, and the chill deepened, sharpening the sound of their feet on the sidewalk, giving the light from the streetlamps a sharp, shimmering edge.

They walked arm to arm.

The boulevard was still empty.

"You know what?" Amanda whispered.

"What?"

She looked around and lifted her head. "The fucker is dumb, that's what!" she said loudly.

"Dumber!" Tracey yelled.

"Dumber than shit!" Amanda screamed.

"Dumbshit!" Tracey shouted, and broke into a fit of giggling that soon had her choking.

And Tanker laughed with them silently, watching as they rushed along the pavement, almost running as they headed toward the park and the shops' lights beyond and keeping themselves brave by daring the dark. He knew that method well, had used it himself a number of times when he was tramping through enemy territory and didn't want to die.

The difference here was simple—

He hadn't died.

And they were going to.

He kept to the treed islands in the middle of the wide avenue, staying almost directly opposite them, herding them with his presense though he didn't show himself, didn't make a sound, only curling a lip when they almost broke into a headlong dash once the shorter girl stopped choking.

It was tempting, taking two whores on at once, and the shakes were on him bad enough to make his legs cramp and his hair feel as if it were being torn from his scalp. It hadn't been this bad in a long time, and he was glad the clouds had thinned a little, to let out the moon; he was glad, too, of the rain over the weekend. It had kept his friend hidden while he was in that pissant jail, him and a handful of other men, bums picked up on Saturday night by two cops in plain clothes, one of whom, a dark little creep who looked like a snotty spic, actually looked more frightened than stern. Tanker hadn't tried to run away though, because they didn't know what he looked like, didn't know who he was, didn't know what he had done. He had gone along, acting like he was weak and smaller than he was, saying "sir" every time he spoke, giving them a phony name, sleeping on their damned cots and eating their damned food, which wasn't all that bad, all things considered.

But this morning he had been released, and cautioned not very gently not to hang around anymore, not at the food joints, or the movie house, or the park, or even the goddamned churches. Babyfuck reasons to run him out of town. Two of the other guys headed directly for the city limits, one for the nearest bar, and Tanker had smoothed and combed and neatened himself up as best he could and stood at the bus stop right in front of the station. He knew they were watching him, and he gave them a little wave when he stepped into the bus and let it take him as far as the park.

Shitheads didn't even check to see where he had gone.

It was close. God, how he'd wanted to howl when he walked out the station door, to see them shit in their pants at what they had missed.

But he had been strong because the shakes were coming on, and he needed to do it, and he figured they figured he was halfway to California by now, just like those assholes in Yonkers, and New York, and Binghamton had figured he was someplace else when he was right there all the time.

Idiots. True and real idiots, and he had helped them get that way.

One of the whores laughed again, nervously, and finally he couldn't take it anymore. They were exactly where he wanted them to be, and so he drew himself up and ran out into the middle of the deserted street.

The shorter bitch saw him first, screamed, and started to run, her notebooks falling onto the sidewalk; one popped open, pages tumbling toward the gutter. The other one turned and gaped at him, heard her friend's frantic call and began to run a few seconds later.

But she was too far behind, and Tanker angled to position himself in front of her, pushing her closer to the park wall, closer, grinning as he loped until she shrieked a name and darted through the open gates.

The first whore stopped when she saw Tanker race for the opening, but a feint and snarl had her off again, her voice shrill and laced with tears. He didn't care. By the time she got help the shakes would be gone.

He ran. Easily. Up on his toes. Silently. Ducking into the brush as soon as he was through the gates, following the babyfuck whore by the sound of her shoes and the sound of her breathing and the sound of her tremulous prayers for someone to hear her.

At the oval pond he broke out and grabbed her.

She screamed so loudly he winced, and before he could stop her she had raked the side of his face with her nails. Shrieking. Kicking, aiming for his groin. Screeching when he slapped her, and clawing at him again until he grabbed her wrists and pulled her forward, spun around once and dumped her into the water.

She gasped as she struggled back to the surface and stood, water dripping from her eyebrows, from her jaw, backing away as he stepped calmly in to join her.

"No," she said.

He only grinned and moved in.

Amanda leapt for the apron and fell when her wet soles slipped out from under her. Tanker was on her back before she could regain her balance, and with a sad shake of his head he slammed her face into the concrete.

"Whore," he said, baring his teeth.

Amanda groaned and coughed blood.

He drove her facedown again, his hands snarled in her wet hair, one knee jammed in the small of her back.

"Whore."

She groaned again, and fell silent.

"Whore," he said a third time, and dragged her by the hair into the bushes. Then he tore off her jacket and tossed it aside, rolled her onto her back and stood over her. He was right, as usual—a whore. He could tell by the way the sweater clung to her breasts, the way the tiny gold cross on the fine gold chain around her neck mocked the religion she supposedly believed in; he could tell by the way she bled from the gouges in her forehead and chin.

She was a whore, and Tanker was hungry, and with a grateful look to the unseen moon he dropped beside her, put a hand to her cheek, and licked his lips twice before tearing out her throat.

NINE

The stadium held over fourteen hundred people in the concrete stands alone; the wooden bleachers on the opposite side added three hundred more. Don imagined every seat filled now with people in black, weeping for the loss of the butchered Amanda Adler.

Weeping. Wailing. Demanding retribution.

But as he ran, the cool wind stinging his eyes into infrequent tears, there was only the sound of his soles on the cinder track, and in the stands there were only about two hundred students and less than a handful of teachers. He had counted them, or tried to, but each time he made a new circuit someone had moved, or new faces appeared and old ones vanished. Some of the kids just sat there, staring at nothing; others milled about, talking softly, tugging at arms, shrugging at leaving.

It had happened just after third period—an announcement by his father over the P.A. system. Amanda Adler was dead, murdered in the park, and the school would close now in her memory and would remain closed tomorrow so that her friends might pay their respects in their own private ways.

After a respectful pause he added that the Ashford Day park concert tomorrow night would not be canceled as rumored, but would be considered a memorial for the two students who had recently lost their lives so senselessly and violently. Then he asked the teachers to end classes and dismiss their charges as soon as possible.

Brian Pratt had said, "All right! Freedom!" and Tar Boston had punched him in the stomach;

Adam Hedley sat with Harry Falcone in the faculty lounge and groused about the closing, obviously one done not in sincerity but with a clear political eye out for preventing a teacher's strike from getting much play in the papers. It was, he claimed, a cynical and effective move for which Boyd ought to be given credit; and one that might be countered. When Harry asked for an explanation, Hedley told him about the jacket;

Jeff Lichter cleaned his glasses fifteen times in ten minutes, trying to get rid of the elusive blur on the lenses;

Fleet Robinson was absent;

After shutting down the P.A. system, Norman sat behind his desk, and stared out the window, thinking that Harry was going to be pissed, Joyce was going to be understandably upset at the solemnization of her opening celebration, and the newspapers would probably cut his statement in half and make him look like just another politician—all in all, a hell of a day;

Don immediately put his books into his locker and headed for the track. On the way he met Chris, who flung her arms around him and mumbled something about just talking to Amanda the other day. He was stunned and stroked her back absently while trying not to seem embarrassed as students passed around them, trying not to feel the soft tickle of her hair against his chin. No one seemed to notice. Then she stepped away, smiled, kissed his cheek, and thanked him. It was several minutes before he was able to move on, not bothering to change, needing the fresh air and the quiet, and something else to think about, except that even with the feel of Chris's thin blouse on his palms he couldn't think about a thing except Amanda, with the long black hair, hanging on Fleet's hip and taking his crude macho teasing with remarkable good grace.

He had already known about the killing.

Last night, Sergeant Verona had called just after Joyce had returned from her meeting. Don overheard the Boyd end of the conversation, and was prepared when his father told him what had happened. Then the phone rang again, and continued to ring for hours while reporters and god knew who else asked the principal for his official, his private, his off-the-cuff reactions. Norman handled it well, Don thought, and Joyce was right there, drafting a quick statement at the kitchen table for him to read or expand from after the first twenty minutes.

During a pause Norman had turned to him and asked if he'd known her, if she was a good friend. He had only nodded and had gone unhindered to his room.

He was angry because he wanted to do more than just nod his head. He wanted to say that it didn't make any difference whether she was a friend or not. She was seventeen and he was seventeen-and-a-half, and now she was dead and in some goddamn morgue lying under a dirty sheet. She was dead, and nobody else was. This wasn't some poor unknown sucker from another school; this was Amanda, Mandy, Fleet's beautiful dark-haired lady, and he knew her and she was dead and she was only seventeen and strangers may die even younger, but not Amanda because Don knew her and people he knew just didn't die. And they sure didn't die because some maniac was out there, getting away with murder while kids were damned dying on the damned streets and who the hell cared if he knew her or not; she was dead, and she was only seventeen.

That morning he had promised not to say a word until the official announcement had been made. It didn't matter, since most of them knew it anyway through the macabre reach of the grapevine, and those who didn't were soon filled in after school closed and a quiet had sifted over the grounds.

But he had kept the promise, and when classes were dismissed, he took off for the track.

Seeing the same faces move about, seeing different ones take different places, seeing some of the kids smiling because of the time off, and some of them grim and staring blindly at the grass that rippled as the wind came up.

There was no one in the bleachers.

On his third lap he saw a flickering under the wooden seats, and he slowed, peered into the shadows, and sped up again. It was nothing. A trick of the light. A trick of the sky and the sun that didn't give a damn that a seventeen-year-old girl had been mangled because the cops couldn't catch one lousy killer.

And that, he decided, would be part of the new order he had devised: no one, not even adults, would die at the hands of a crazy bastard who obviously thought he was some kind of animal.

He walked the next lap, head down, arms limp at his sides. His shirt was stained with perspiration, his trousers damp and clinging. Tracey wasn't in school. He didn't blame her. From the garbled story he'd heard last night, she had practically been killed herself, and the first thing he was going to do when he got home was forgive her for not getting in touch, and call her.

Someone called his name.

He ignored it and started around the front turn, heading for the bleachers again. Once there, he would take one more lap, then go home and shower. After that he would call. And after that he would try to figure out what had happened to his best friend.

On Sunday, when he was finally able to examine the poster more closely, he realized that in one respect he had been wrong, that no one had attempted to mutilate the picture—a finger touched the paper and he saw that the flaw was in the picture itself. There were no raised edges, no indentations. Just a static screen of white lines that made no sense at all. Flaws like that didn't come with time.

Someone called his name.

He scowled and looked around, saw Jeff at the railing at the bottom of the stands. A glance to the bleachers, a brief wondering what he had seen there, and he decided he had had enough. With one hand massaging the back of his neck he walked over to the nearest steps and hauled himself up, dropped onto a seat and waited for Jeff.

"Hey," Lichter said without much enthusiasm.

"Yeah," he said, passing a sleeve over his mouth.

"What a bitch."

Don rested his forearms on his knees and leaned over, still trying to get his wind back. Thinking about Amanda. A drop of sweat landed on his shoe.

"I mean, they don't even know what this dude looks like, for god's sake! What the hell kind of thing is that? This makes what, seven? And they don't even know what he looks like!" He took off his glasses and pulled out a shirttail to clean them. "Tracey's practically ready to move in with her grandmother, and I tell you, Don, I don't blame her."

He covered his face with his hands, drew them down an inch at a time, and looked up at the sky. "What do you mean?"

"I mean, she and Mandy were walking back from the library, minding their own business, and all of a sudden this crazy guy runs out at them, and the next thing Tracey knows, Mandy and this guy are gone into the park. She—Trace, I mean—she screamed so much she's hoarse, and she ran all the way to Beacher's to use the phone. Her old man was there, but she says she could hardly talk she was so scared. Some doctor was supposed to go over to their place and give her something so she could sleep." He replaced the glasses, pushed back his hair. "I bet she didn't though. I bet she didn't sleep a wink."

Don pushed back on the seat until he could lean his elbows on the one behind. Then he squinted at Jeff. "She called you?"

"Yeah."

He nodded, and felt a wall begin to crack somewhere inside him, a fissure splitting the wall in half.

"She cried a lot, believe it."

The wall fell to dry, colorless dust. "She called you."

"Yeah, I said she did." Jeff started to smile, then found something to look at intently on the gridiron. "She said she had to talk to someone, and your line was busy. She said she tried for nearly an hour, but she had to talk to someone, and when she couldn't get you, she tried me."

"You were home."

Jeff's laugh sounded almost genuine. "Sure! You think my father would let me out that late on a school night?"

"Well, it just goes to show you," Don said, rising and dusting at his trousers.

"Hey, Don, I told you she tried to call."

"I know, I know."

"But your line was busy."

"My father," he said. "Reporters and all, and the police."

"Oh. Well, look, you oughta call her when you get home, you know? I mean, it was you she wanted to talk to, not me."

"Sure." He started for the stairs; he had to run again in spite of the stitch that lingered in his side.

"Hey, Don, damnit," Jeff called.

He didn't look around.

"Hey, it ain't my fault."

He started to run.

"Well, fuck you too, pal."

And when he came around again, Jeff was gone.

The burning in his left eye he blamed on the wind, and he lowered his head so his vision would clear, and so he could watch the out-and-back rhythm of his feet gliding over the track.

Out. Back. The cinder so smooth he imagined he wasn't moving at all.

He felt it then—the slipping away, letting anger stiffen his muscles and labor his breath, color his mind until he couldn't think, could barely see, made him stop, panting, hands hard on his hips while he gulped at the sky for air to calm him.

He was back at the bleachers, blinking the tears away and trying not to scream Jeff's name at the sky. Trying not to chase after his friend, slam him against a wall and demand to know what he thought he was doing, talking to Don's girl when it was Don Tracey wanted, Don she had tried to call and could not reach because his goddamned parents were too busy trying to lessen the blow of Mandy's death. Not soften. They were hunting for ways to let life go on with a minimum of disruption: the school and the celebration. Ashford. One hundred and fifty years. And Mandy was only seventeen and he was only seventeen-and-a-half and he would be damned if he was going to let it happen to him.

He bent over and let his arms hang loose. His hands shook wildly but the tension wouldn't drain; his knees felt like buckling, and he was ready to give in, to collapse and try to make sense of this new thing when, from his right, he heard a noise.

A shuffling, a sniffing, something moving under the seats.

He turned his head and peered into the shadows. A dog, probably. That's what he had seen before—a glow from its eyes, or something in its mouth. A claw, or the color of its fur.

He listened, and heard nothing.

He stared back at the track, shaking himself all over to loosen up and drive the red from his eyes. When he was finished, he took several deep breaths he released explosively, then walked over and leaned down, supporting himself on his palms while he looked between the seats.

He overcame an initial rush of surprise and said, "Hey, who are you?"

But the man cowering against the brick wall only lifted a filthy hand to wave him away. A man of indeterminate age, in fatigue pants and tweed jacket, with grime on his face and dark stains on his fingers and unshaven chin. A man who pushed himself back against the wall and waved him away a second time, a third, without saying a word.

"Are you all right, mister?"

Again the dismissal.

"Hey, if you need help or something . . ."

The man glowered and Don backed off, looked to the stands for someone to call, looked back and blinked. Once. Slowly.

The red vanished, and he could see again with a clarity that hurt his eyes. But he felt nothing. He only returned to the bleachers and smiled at the man hiding under the seats.

"Fuck off, kid," the man said.

Don continued to smile, but there was no mirth, no humor, just a grim, silent message that he knew who the man was; he *knew*, and he didn't approve.

"Damnit, fuck off you punk creep," the man snarled.

He nodded and walked away, across the grass and up the steps and around the side of the school toward home.

Fantastic, he thought; this is fantastic.

If he wanted to, he could be a hero. He could go right into the kitchen and call the police and tell them that he knew where the Howler was. And if the killer had fled by the time they arrived, he would be able to give them more than just one lousy clue, he could give them a complete description. The first one. The only one. And the Howler wouldn't be so safe anymore.

But when he came into the foyer, he saw his jacket draped over the newel post. He poked at it, then hooked a finger under the collar and flung it over his shoulder.

Boy, he thought, this is a great day. My jacket's back and I could be a hero if I wanted.

He went to the kitchen to get a can of soda and stopped in the doorway. His father was at the table, scribbling on a yellow legal pad, looking harried and tired, and not at all pleased.

"Found your missing jacket, I see," Norman said after a glance up.

"Yeah. Who brought it back?" He opened the refrigerator, got his drink, and hook-shot the pull tab into the garbage.

"Mr. Hedley."

"Who?"

Norman dropped his pen onto the pad and leaned back. "Mr. Hedley. You remember him, the teacher? He brought the jacket to my office yesterday morning."

He didn't understand, and stared at the man until, at last, he began to see.

"You think I did it, huh?"

Norman shook his head. "No, not really."

Red again, this time like a wave.

"What do you mean, not really? I didn't do it, if you want to know." He slammed the can on the counter, ignoring the soda foaming over the sides. "Jeez!"

Norman puffed his cheeks and blew out. "Donald, I don't have time to argue. You say you didn't dump that crap on his porch, but he did find the coat on his hedge. And he does think you emptied that bottle in his classroom. He puts two and two together and decides to be a nice guy and come to me first, not to the police."

"Okay," he said. "Okay."

"And you say you didn't do it. Even after all the grief, and the detentions, you still didn't do it."

"My god!" he exploded. "What do you want from me, a written confession? You want me to take a lie detector test?"

"Donald, that's enough."

Don almost told him that they were father and son, and there ought to be a little trust in a guy's word now and then.

But he didn't.

He said, "You're right, Dad. It's enough."

He walked stiffly to the foot of the stairs, hesitated until he was sure he wouldn't be chased, then hurried up to the bathroom. He filled the basin with cold water and splashed it over his face, soaked a washcloth and ran it around his neck.

But the red wouldn't go away.

It spread across the mirror and faded to a pink pale enough for him to see his reflection; it thumped through his chest until he thought he would explode; it poured into his ears with a roaring like the ocean just after a storm; it swirled around him, drew him in, spun him out and vanished so suddenly he had to grab the edge of the sink before he fell to his knees.

He was sweating, and he was cold, and he draped a towel around his neck and went into his room, closed the door, and stood in front of the poster.

The trees were still there, and the ground fog, and the road.

And the stallion was still partially hidden behind a screen of white lines.

"What's going on?" he whispered nervously, reaching out a cold hand to touch the space where the stallion was fading. "What's going on?"

Then he sat on the bed and clamped his hands to his face. Quite suddenly he was afraid. Not of what was happening to the horse, but of the madness that must be taking hold of him to make him think it was slowly disappearing. That had to be it. He had to be going crazy. There wasn't a poster in the world that had a picture that disappeared by stages, and there wasn't another kid in the world who talked to a stupid photograph and called it his friend and told it his secrets and asked for its advice. There wasn't anyone like him at all because he was going crazy, and he couldn't even tell Tracey because she had called Jeff and not him.

Jeff was scared.

There was some maniac running around town killing off the people he knew, there was a feeling deep inside him in a place he couldn't find that he'd lost his chance to have Tracey, and there was a madman, an unknown person or thing or something else that was taking over the body of who used to be his best friend.

As soon as Don had walked away from him at the stadium, he'd stomped up the steps and back into the school. For a while he stood helplessly in the team locker room, knowing there'd be no practice, but not knowing where else to go. Home was out of the question because his dad was at work; Beacher's was out because he didn't have any money.

What he wanted to do was go to Tracey's. What he wanted was someone to talk to. What he wanted was someone to tell him—as she would, he just knew it—that it was all right to cry when a friend of yours dies.

And he did.

And when Tar Boston came in, whistling, he wiped his face without taking off his glasses.

"Christ Almighty," Boston said, "she wasn't your damned sister, you know."

Jeff turned away.

"Fuck," Boston said, and kicked at the wall. "It ain't right, you know? It ain't right."

Jeff waited, heard nothing more, and snapped his lock shut

and headed for the door. As he reached for the knob, he thought he heard a sniffling behind him. A muffled sobbing.

Jesus, he thought, and turned around.

Tar was leaning against the wall, grinning while he made the sounds of weeping. "Four-eyes," he said, "you ain't half bad, but you sure ain't a man."

Jeff walked over to him, and Boston laughed, lifting his hands to ward off the expected blow. He laughed so hard he didn't see Jeff shift his weight to his left foot, and he didn't have time to duck when Jeff kicked him in the balls.

The yell was strangled, and strangled with it were threats that made him smile as he left, striding across the gym to a martial tune in his head. He was going to pay for that. Boy, was he ever going to pay for it. But the look on the bastard's face was worth every broken bone he was going to get.

Worth it, in spades.

So why the hell, he thought then, couldn't he get the same courage up to ask Tracey out?

The smile widened. Well . . . maybe he could. Maybe he really could. And then maybe he could walk over to Don's and find out what the hell was wrong with the guy's head.

Don heard his mother drive up, heard the front door close, heard muffled voices in the kitchen. The telephone rang. Someone answered. He shifted to lie on his back, hands behind his head. He sniffed, made himself shudder, and heard footsteps outside his door. A soft knocking. The door opened.

"Darling," Joyce said, "are you all right?"

She was beautiful, her hair unbound and flowing over her shoulders, a brightly colored blouse unbuttoned at the throat, a skirt not quite matching and not quite snug around her hips.

He nodded, but only once.

She gave him a tentative smile and sat at the foot of the bed. "It's been rough. I guess, huh?"

He nodded.

She laid a sympathetic hand on his leg and rubbed it absently, looking around the room at the empty shelves, the neat desk. She said nothing about the poster. "It isn't easy, I know. You know someone, and they have to . . . to die like that. It isn't easy, believe me."

He knew she meant Sam, and while Sam was his brother, he was only a kid. Mandy wasn't really his friend, but she was seventeen and he knew her better than he'd ever known his little brother.

Joyce cleared her throat, and her smile was sad, then brave, then gone altogether.

He watched her, and felt sand in his throat. "Mom," he said before he could think and stop himself, "there's something I have to tell you. Over at the school this afternoon I saw a—"

"In a minute, dear, please," she interrupted in the way she had that told him she wasn't listening at all. "That was Tracey Quintero on the phone before." She patted his knee, rose, and went to the door.

"What?" He sat up, hands splayed to the sides to give him balance. "Tracey? Why didn't you tell me?"

"Well, dear, this is kind of hard for you to understand, but she needs someone to talk to, and I think it best she talk to her parents first, don't you?"

"What?" he said, so softly she didn't hear him.

"Grown-ups, they have experience, and they know, most of the time, how someone your age is feeling, like about . . . well, like something like this." The smile returned, briefly. "I think, right now, Mr. Quintero will help her more than her friends."

He dropped back again. "What did you tell her?"

"I told her you were sleeping. That you were disturbed by what had happened, and you were sleeping."

"Thanks," he said tonelessly.

Joyce winked at him and left, closing the door behind her.

The room filled with a silence that breathed, in and out, over the beating of his heart, the muffled creak of the bed-springs, the voices that slipped uninvited under the door.

What, he thought to the afterimage of his mother, do you know about what I need, huh? What the hell do you know about Tracey? Jesus, you didn't even know she was Spanish, for god's sake.

"Oh, hell," he moaned, "oh hell, oh hell."

And the hell with them, then. He had given them a chance to help him be a hero, and maybe save some kid's life, but they didn't care. They didn't care at all. One thought he was an asshole who dumped shit on people's porches, and the other thought he didn't know how to help his own friends feel better.

They looked at him and they saw baby Sam.

The hell with them then.

He closed his eyes and felt the nugget still buried in his chest. Warm, red, and every inch of it his.

If they didn't want to help him, if they didn't trust him, then he would do it on his own. He was the one who knew what the Howler looked like; he was the one who could put the killer behind bars for the rest of his life; he was the one who knew it all, and they could all go to hell for all he cared.

How, something asked him then, do you know he's the Howler?

For the space of a heartbeat he blinked in confusion, and for the space of a long breath he didn't know the answer.

Then his eyes narrowed, and his breathing came easy, and it didn't bother him at all when he thought: *birds of a feather*.

Because in a way it was true. That creep under the bleachers worked under his own rules, and Don had written some new rules of his own. He couldn't speak them aloud, but he knew them just the same—they were written on that nugget, in red, just waiting.

He rolled onto his side, head propped on one hand.

He looked at the poster, and a sigh changed to a whimper. He was on his feet, across the room, gripping the edge of the desk and staring through a fall of perspiration from his brow.

The black horse was gone.

The static scratches had vanished, but the stallion was gone.

He touched the paper, traced the boles of the trees, the swirl of the fog, ran his palm over it, pressed his forehead to it, lifted a corner to check behind it.

The road was empty.

It was gone.

A panicked step took him halfway to the door, but he heard movement outside and ran to the window. The yard was dark and fringed by moonlight, and in the middle of the grass was a shadow. At first he thought it was Chris, coming the back way to see him for some unknown reason; then he squinted and pressed his palms to the pane and felt the glass. It wasn't—it was the same visitor he had seen last week when he'd run, the one who had watched him from the tunnel in the stadium wall. Unformed. Black. And watching him as surely as if it had a perfect set of eyes.

A drop of ice touched his nape.

His head whipped around and he looked at the poster.

The horse was still gone.

When he looked back, the shadow was gone too.

Suddenly, inexplicably weeping, he backed away from the window, from the poster, and fell onto the bed. He tried to swallow, and couldn't; he tried to call for help, and couldn't; he tried to tell himself that he wasn't crazy, not really crazy, but posters didn't change and black ghosts didn't walk across his backyard at night.

"Help," he whispered. "Somebody. Help."

TEN

*B*irds of a feather.

He waited until well past eleven, until he was positive the boards in the hallway wouldn't betray him. Then he dressed in his black denims and crept downstairs, took a flashlight from the hall closet and left the house by the back door.

The night had turned winter cold, and his breath gusted greyly from his lips, wafted back into his eyes. He stood with his hand on the metal knob until his vision adjusted, then moved in a low crouch toward the middle of the yard, the rod of white light bleaching the grass. He searched for depressions, disturbances, something dropped by whoever had been there before, whoever had been watching him through his window. He criss-crossed the yard twice and found nothing, did it twice again and decided to try the front, where the moonlight and the streetlamps would give him some aid.

Going back inside was out of the question.

He wanted desperately to convince himself that he hadn't gone crazy. He wanted to find tangible evidence of a prowler—maybe Brian and Tar up to another prank they were going to blame on him—which he could then show to his parents, to

161

prove he hadn't lost his mind when he told them about the poster. Because he was going to have to. If he didn't, and didn't do it soon, one of them was going to notice and think he'd done something to it and make it too late to protest.

The street was quiet, empty, and even as he watched, many of the lights upstairs and down were switched off to yank the houses back into darkness.

Birds of a feather.

He zipped his jacket closed to his neck and sat on the front stoop, the flashlight on the step beside him. Dampness seeped through his jeans to his buttocks, and he shifted, stood, and walked down to the sidewalk.

This is crazy, he thought, and grinned at the word. Of course it is, because you are, jackass. The poster, the shadow, and thinking you're the same as some murdering bum. Three strikes. Third out. Sanity retired and the ball game's over.

Unless it was true.

Unless he and the Howler were closer than he could ever possibly imagine and somehow his subconscious had tuned in to that fact. And if so, he had to find the man, find out where he hid during the dark hours and bring the cops to him. Be the hero, just like he planned, and then dare his father to ground him again, doubt him, and look at him with those pitying eyes. Dare him to yell because he'd left the house without permission.

Crazy.

He hurried toward the park.

Crazy.

He slipped his hands into his pants pockets, thumbs hanging out, and tried not to come down too hard on his heels. He had to look casual, just out for a late night stroll, in case a patrol car came around and wanted to know what he was doing on the streets when there was a madman on the loose. He couldn't tell them then. He couldn't say that he knew the Howler, because they wouldn't believe him. He had to find him, and his den, and only then would he be able to bring in the troops.

Halfway to the corner a car pulled over to the curb and the passenger door opened. He slowed and glanced in, and caught his breath when he saw Tar.

"Hey, Duck, does your mommy know you're out?"

"Lay off," he said glumly.

"Aw, poor Ducky. Hey, Brian, the Duck says to lay off." Pratt leaned over from the steering wheel and grinned. "Okay, Mr. Duck. Whatever you say."

Don glared and moved on, and the car followed him slowly.

"Hey, Boyd," Tar said in a loud whisper, "glad to see you found your jacket. Looks good. How'd you get the shit off?"

Don stopped, turned, but Brian drove on, his and Tar's laughter filling the night.

He wanted to raise a fist, but it would have done no good and he would have only gotten into a fight. But it was them, and he groaned because his father would never believe it.

At the corner he stopped again, waited in shadow for a bus to pass, and in waiting considered heading down to Tracey's. She'd be in bed but a pebble against her window might bring her out before her father woke up. He would talk to her. He would tell her. He would . . .

"Shit," he muttered, and dashed across the boulevard, reached the park wall at full speed, and vaulted over without pausing.

A minute passed, and five before he got up from his knees and made his way to the central path. The park was so much his, he knew right away there was no one nearby, no one to overhear and question him, and take him back to the house.

He was alone.

And as he approached the oval and its curtain of white light he knew he was wrong.

There was something out there, out there in the dark.

Something familiar.

He slowed; he stopped; he sidestepped just before the trees fell away, and he squinted into the light.

There, he thought, craning his neck. It was over there, on the other side, not moving, only watching, and when his left hand reached around behind him he realized with a silent curse he had forgotten to bring the flashlight—he had nothing now he could use as a weapon.

Brian and Tar; it had to be them, back to make sure he understood their position. Beating the shit out of him; and when the police came, they would be sleeping soundly in bed and he would have to explain what he was doing in the park.

He backed away.

A hand rubbed at his mouth.

Crazy; if he wasn't crazy before, he was sure crazy now for thinking of this stunt. The poster obviously had an explanation, the shadows were his nerves because of Pratt and his hatred, but this was complete madness.

A swift search of the nearest brush rewarded him with a four-foot length of dead branch. He hefted it, tapped it against his palm, and prayed frantically that he wouldn't have to use it, though against what or who he didn't know.

Then a voice behind him said, "Babyfuck," and a hand grabbed his throat.

Don screamed without making a sound as his hand spasmed and the branch fell from his hand, and before he could attempt to break free, an arm banded hard across his chest, pinning his own to his sides. Brian! he yelled silently; Tar, for god's sake, get the hell off me! But his head was forced back, and when he lowered his gaze from the spin of the treetops, he saw the tweed sleeve, the dried blood, and he knew.

Panic flared and made him hollow. But he was not going to die. Amanda was dead, and Sam was dead, and he was not going to die because he was not anyone else, not just a name on the news; he was Don Boyd, and Don Boyd didn't die. Not yet. God, not yet.

The Howler was too strong to fight, and he had no choice but to let himself be dragged around the rim of the pond, his neck close to breaking, his breathing harsh and shallow, the back of his head hot from the breath that came from the monster's mouth.

"Babyfuck," said Tanker Falwick. "You sure are one stupid babyfuck, boy."

Don swung one leg around and braced a heel against the concrete. The man grunted, and Don whimpered at the pain that blossomed along his spine, but progress toward the dark was momentarily halted.

Falwick whispered, "You wanna bath? Like the whore? You wanna bath, punk?"

A vicious kick to a calf, and Don went down, the fingers whipping away from his throat to grab a patch of hair. His eyes watered, and his left arm was taken by the wrist and bent up along his back.

"Look, you punk!" the man gasped in his ear. "Stop fucking around and look! See that dark shit there? That's blood, pal. Blood. From the whore. Beautiful, ain't it? Must be a gallon of blood there, at least a goddamned gallon. And you know something, punk? They can try for a hundred years, they ain't never gonna get that whore's blood outta there." A cackling laugh, and Don's face was pressed closer to the ground. "Hungry, boy? You wanna lick it, punk? You wanna—"

"Please," Don managed.

"Oh, my, listen to that."

He swallowed phlegm and acid, blinked away the tears, and wondered why he couldn't have been built like Fleet or Tar so he could leap out of the man's grasp, turn, and beat him to a bloody mess where Amanda had died.

Tanker forced his face even closer to the ground, and when his nose touched the cold cement, he shut his eyes tightly.

"Please," he said, less pleading now than commanding.

"Aw, babyfuck, you getting mad at the old sarge? You getting mad at me, punk?"

He was. He didn't understand it, but he was. He was terrified of what was coming, and enraged at his helplessness, and he didn't want to die and there wasn't a damned thing he could do about it, not a thing, just like always.

"I—I won't say anything, honest I won't."

"Aw, the punk's begging. Ain't that nice. They all do, y'know, punk. They all beg at the end. They think they're hot shit, but they all beg at the end."

Not the end, he thought, suddenly contorting his body in hopes of breaking the hold. But his head shrieked at the pull of hair, and his thigh burst into flame when a heel jammed into it, and his jacket and shirt where the man had gripped them from behind closed around his chest and restricted his lungs.

"They all beg, the little whores, and it don't do any good. Say good-bye, punk. You little white trash shit."

Don gagged as his head was pulled back; his eyes opened and stared, and then he lashed his right hand around and caught Falwick on the biceps with an elbow. The man grunted his surprise, dropped the hold on his hair, and Don jabbed again swiftly, scissoring his legs until he was over on his back, his left arm still behind him but pinning Falwick's arm there as well.

And he saw the man's face.

The same hard-lined face, the same grubby man he had seen under the bleachers.

Falwick spit at him, clubbed the side of his head with a fist, and rose, dragging him up, releasing the bent arm and spinning him around. Laughing. Coughing. Four times around until he let go with a squeal and Don pinwheeled into the pond, landed sitting up and shaking water from his eyes.

A mistake! he thought jubilantly; and I can outrun him.

But first he had to outmaneuver him or distract him, and the man in the tweed jacket and fatigue pants was standing right there on the edge, watching him smugly, licking his lips and lightly rubbing his arm.

"You gonna run?" Falwick asked with a sneer. "You gonna try for it, boy? If you are, you better get up, or I'm gonna cut you where you sit."

It was unreal.

It was something happening to someone else in a dream.

It was like . . . and Don saw himself on the movie theater screen, rising vengefully from the cold water and lunging to the apron, whirling to plant a foot solidly in the man's chest. A bone snapped. Blood gouted from the man's scabbed lips. Another foot to the stomach, a lethal fist to the chin, and the Howler fell backward, rigid and unconscious, into the pond.

On the screen.

"Goddamn punk," the Howler said in disgust. "You're all the same, you fucking little punks. All the goddamned same. You ain't got no guts. You're babyfucks, you don't deserve to live."

Don eased himself along until he felt the apron press against his back.

"Good," Falwick said, nodding. "Very good. You're trying for a head start."

A car horn sounded shrilly on the boulevard. The screech of panicked brakes, the prolonged, sickening crunch of metal slamming into metal.

"Well, shit," Falwick said.

Don looked over his shoulder, not daring to believe it. An accident. The police. He stumbled to his feet, cupped his hands around his mouth, and shouted. Scrambled to the apron and started to run.

Falwick was in front of him, arms spread, fingers waggling at him to try it.

Don made a feint to the left, to the right, but the Howler only stood there, his hands up and out now, showing him the nails that had grown into claws.

A cry and a wild turn, and he was racing up the path toward the ball field, head high and arms pumping, trying to ignore the agony in his neck and thigh, trying not to listen to the man chasing him and closing ground, wheezing a laugh and snarling like a dog let loose from its leash.

Out of the trees and across the grass, heading for the north exit. There were houses there. He could yell. He could break a window. He would get somebody to come to the door, see what was happening and call the police. He could still be a hero; he could still get home and still be alive, and jesus please don't let me die I don't wanna die not like Amanda.

The Howler appeared at his side, pacing him easily and grinning. "Hey, punk, this the best you can do?"

He faltered, and the man bellowed and snapped a clubbed fist into his chest. He fell forward, still running, feeling the fire around his heart while he scrabbled on hands and knees before his elbows gave out and he slammed to the ground. Panting. Crying. Furious at himself for being such an idiot, furious at the Howler for not letting him live, furious at the whole fucking world for all their goddamned rules!

He tensed, waiting for the blow.

He looked up, grass and dirt stuck to his cheeks, and saw the Howler standing over him, hands on his hips.

"You done, punk?"

He sagged, curled, and felt his mouth open slowly.

"Little bastard."

The Howler looked up at the sky, at the moon, and cocked his head as though listening to instructions from the night. Then he reached down to grab the jacket, and Don wriggled away, twisting until he was crab-walking on his buttocks.

"Christ," the Howler muttered, reached again, and froze.

The kid's eyes were open in terror, but he wasn't looking at him.

Falwick snorted, reached again, and froze again when he heard it behind him—

Iron striking iron. Hollow. Slow.

"What the fuck?"

Don felt his lips begin to quiver, felt the cold from the ground travel up through his clothes to cling to his skin, but he could neither move away from the man who was turning aside nor could he look somewhere else, to see something, anything, that proved he wasn't crazy at all.

Iron. Striking iron.

Stones on a hollow log.

Wood against wood.

The hooves of a black horse clopping softly on the earth.

Falwick shook his head, rubbed his eyes, shook his head again and lifted his hands. "What the hell is this?"

The stallion was on the far side of the diamond, more shadow than substance, its sides gleaming black, its mane untouched by the wind that rose from the light of the moon. It moved without moving its head, gliding across the basepath, across the pitcher's mound, across the grass, and stopping.

Falwick tried to look behind it, to see where the owner was and if he would have to kill more than once tonight; Don pushed himself backward, not daring to believe it.

"Fuck off," Falwick said then, and turned back to his prey with a *this is it, pal* grin.

The horse snorted and pawed the ground.

Falwick looked over his shoulder, and Don saw the blood drain from his grimy face.

The horse, moving again, deliberately, more slowly, was half again as big as any Don had ever seen. Its muscles rolled and flexed like black waves over black water; its tail was arched and twitching, its forelock blown back between ears that lay flat along the sides of its massive head; and the eyes were large and slanted, and a dark glowing green.

"You?" the boy whispered.

It paused, and looked at him, and he saw from his vision's corner the Howler backing away.

"You?"

The horse waited.

Don looked to Tanker Falwick, closed his eyes, and saw Amanda.

I could be a hero, he thought, and who would believe me?

His eyes shut more tightly and saw his empty room, heard his mother call him Sam, heard his father as much as call him a liar. Teachers pushing him. Tracey not calling. Brian and Tar and Fleet and all the others. The rainbow lights behind his eyelids stung like dull needles; his fading black eye felt as if it were bleeding at the edges; and then he saw himself on the park grass, his eyes open and blind, his throat torn and bleeding.

The horse waited.

His eyes opened again, the stinging gone, the images gone, and the animal was still there.

I'm crazy, he thought; and suddenly the nugget in his chest expanded, exploded . . . and he felt nothing at all.

"Yes," he said flatly. "Yes. Do it."

The animal waited a moment longer, then headed straight for the Howler, its gaze fixed on the man's chest, its legs lifting higher, coming down harder, and striking green sparks from the earth beneath its hooves.

When it was ten yards away, Falwick groaned in terror and whirled to his left, bolting for the trees, and the stallion rose against the moon, forelegs snapping out, mane billowing now as steam flowed like dark smoke from its nostrils.

Then it ran.

And the ground was silent except for the slap of the Howler's shoes, silent except for the sparks snapping into the dark, green and trailing and dying before landing.

Don rolled to his knees, his right hand closing unconsciously over the branch he'd dropped earlier, and he watched as the Howler veered to the left, swerved to the right, and spun around just as the horse reached him and reared.

Don shouted.

Falwick screamed.

And the stallion came down on him, sparks streaking to green fire.

ELEVEN

Don sat up suddenly, eyes wide, mouth open in a scream that never passed his lips. His arms were rigid at his sides, and his head jerked in clockwork degrees side to side until he felt pressure on his right shoulder. His head snapped around. His mouth remained open. There was a woman's hand, long fingers pale as it tried to ease him back. His gaze traced it warily, found the wrist, found the arm, found his mother's face puffed and wan.

"Don, it's all right."

He saw the lips move (the stallion rearing), heard the words (the Howler shrieking), and after several seconds he let himself be levered back while a dark figure at the foot of the bed cranked up the mattress until he was almost sitting again.

"Don, it's all right, honey."

The echoless scream died at last, the tunnel collapsed in upon itself, and once his vision cleared, he didn't have to ask to know he was in a hospital room.

A nurse at his left side took his pulse; a doctor whose face was familiar entered and picked up the chart, read it, nodded, edged the nurse aside and pulled up a stool. His face was lean and creased with too many summers under the sun, his hair a thicket of unruly grey.

"How are you feeling, son?" Large hands moved—his brow, his chest, pressed through his hair and lightly squeezed his scalp. "No aches, no pains? Your back is probably sore though, right?"

"How'd you know?" Don asked hoarsely, still trying to bring himself back out of the park.

The doctor gave him a smile. "In bed this long without moving, it's bound to be."

"Can he go home now, Jerry?"

"Later this afternoon, I think," Dr. Naugle said. He looked to Don. "Just to be sure, son, okay? I doubt we've missed anything, but just to be sure." He looked across the bed to Joyce. "Suppertime." A jerk of his head toward the IV stand and the fluid dripping into Don's arm. "After what we've been feeding him since midnight, he'll be starving." A satisfied sigh, and he rose to his feet. "I guess that'll be okay with you, son, right?"

Before Don could answer, he was gone, his mother hastening after him, the nurse behind. The dark figure finally moved out of the shadows.

"Dad?"

Norman tried to speak, then licked his lips and grinned as he took Joyce's chair. He patted Don's shoulder, his leg, stared blankly at the IV tubing and the tape on the boy's arm. His hair was uncombed and appeared greyer in the dawnlight that slotted through the window's venetian blinds; his eyes were bloodshot, the nose faintly red, the one visible hand jumping every few seconds.

Don was shocked—his father had been crying.

"Boy," he said too eagerly, "I could drink a whole lake I'm so thirsty."

Norman grabbed gratefully for the water pitcher on the bed table, poured a glass, and finally a second.

"How do you feel?"

"Terrible. No; just lousy." He shifted, and felt the bruise on his thigh and the circle of hurt where the Howler's knees had jammed into his spine.

Norman stood and walked toward the door and walked back to the chair. "Sergeant Verona will be here in a few minutes, I guess. He's been waiting for you to . . . for you to wake up."

"The police?"

Green sparks green fire

"They want to know what happened out there." He clearly wanted to ask, and was just as clearly afraid to. "The reporters too."

Don rolled his head to stare at the ceiling. "Reporters."

"Well, you're a hero, son. It's already on the radio."

He felt panic, and it was cold. "Dad, listen, I've got to—"

The door swung open and Verona walked in. His suit jacket was rumpled, his tie gone, a blade of wet grass clung to one elbow. Joyce was right behind him, and she protested when he suggested that the Boyds leave him and the boy alone. Norm took her arm; she glared at him, then blew Don a kiss on the way out. The door closed without a sound. The window light brightened.

He felt the panic again, but it subsided when Verona shook his hand warmly while taking the chair.

"That," he said, nodding to their clasped hands, "is for now. Later, I'll probably be cursing you from here to Sunday for what you did. Not that I don't like you," he added with a crooked smile, "but the papers are going to wonder how a teenage kid could dispose of the Howler when the police in two states couldn't even find a clue."

Don shrugged, and his stomach growled.

there was blood, lots of blood, and the sound of trampling hooves

"So. Do you want to tell me what happened?"

Tell him, Don thought; and told him that he had been unable to sleep, that he had gone for a walk to do some thinking and had ended up at the park. That's where the man grabbed him, and that's where he'd gotten away.

Verona didn't take notes or have a tape recorder with him. He nodded. He listened. He asked more questions, and in the asking told Don what he needed to know.

It was the Howler. That grizzled old man was the man who killed Amanda. Tissue samples from the body matched those found under the girl's fingernails, and his name was Falwick, an ex-army sergeant who evidently couldn't fit into the system. They had been able to retrace most of Don's struggles, but they still wondered about a few things. It couldn't be a pleasant memory, Verona acknowledged as he mopped his face with a handkerchief, momentarily hiding his eyes, but they did need to know. Just a few things. Then he'd leave Don alone for some well-deserved rest. He would even keep the reporters off his back for a while. Just—why did Don beat the man so severely? So savagely?

Don didn't know. "I was afraid. He was going to kill me."

Verona made a clucking sound. Jerry Naugle, Don's doctor, had suggested it was an hysteria-induced defense and certainly not uncommon. Instead of running away, Don had found the branch and used it to protect himself. He had known Amanda. Fear and anger, and perhaps a lucky blow, had knocked Falwick down. That's when hysteria took over. Adrenaline fueled it. Luis Quintero had been at the scene of the accident on the boulevard and had heard someone shouting in the park. He found Don kneeling a few feet from the body, the branch still in hand, blood on it and the boy's clothes. He was in deep shock and didn't even answer to his name.

"I guess," Don said. "Yeah. I guess."

And it could have been, he thought. It must have been. If there had been a horse, they would have said so; if the horse had been real, someone would have seen him. It could have been him, because he remembered the rage.

Verona shook his hand again, and Don's eyes blurred with tears when his parents returned.

Must have been. Hysteria, and shock, and maybe he wasn't crazy after all. His friend had been summoned because of the fear, but Don had done it all on his own. He had blacked out and done it himself. No magic. No giant stallion. He had killed a man. All on his own.

He wept for nearly half an hour—loudly, then noiselessly, soaking his mother's blouse while she stroked his hair and kissed his cheek and his father held his hand so tightly the knuckles cracked. He wept until Dr. Naugle returned and hustled the room clear, saying Don needed his rest if he wanted to go home to get something decent to eat. Norman was reluctant, but he went; Joyce embraced him once more and whispered, "I know you're not Sam, dear. You're my Donny, and I love you."

Without a pill he slept soundly until well after noon.

When he woke the IV was gone and the nurse was there with a tray of food he ate without tasting. When he begged for more, she laughed and told him there'd be plenty when he got home; when he wondered about his parents, they were there and told him there was a mob of kids down in the waiting room eager to see him. A group of reporters too. It was, his father said in quiet excitement, as if the President were in town. Don was pleased and tried not to show it, embarrassed because the image of the stallion still darted through his vision, and anxious because suddenly all he wanted to do was go home and take a close look at the poster on his wall.

Maybe he wasn't crazy, but he still had to know.

"And do you know what else?" his mother said. "Are you ready for this? The mayor wants to give you a medal at the concert tonight. A medal! Can you believe it?"

"Me? Me, a medal?"

A look to his father brought a proud nod; a look to his mother brought him another kiss.

"I can't," he said, fingers digging into the stiff sheet. "I can't, Mom."

"We'll talk about it later, when you get home, dear," she said quickly and softly. "We'll send up the kids now, while I get you some clean clothes."

greensparks
greenfire

Don didn't understand why Tracey was wearing jeans and an old jacket until he remembered that school was closed today, because of Amanda. Nor did he understand why Lichter had to come with her.

Tracey, after exchanging glances with Jeff, took the chair while he sat on the bed and grabbed for Don's hand.

"The Detention Kid strikes again," he said heartily. "Man, are you nuts or something?"

"Shut up, Jeff," Tracey ordered gently, and leaned over to kiss Don's cheek. Her hand found his and held it. "Are you all right?"

"I think so," he said. "I didn't get hurt or anything. Your father—hey, easy on the merchandise," he protested to Jeff, pulling free his hand and wincing in false pain. "I'm a black belt, remember?"

"I remember you're crazy, that's what I remember."

"It takes one to know one."

"Very funny."

"Don," Tracey said, "Brian says—"

"Shit on Brian," Jeff mumbled.

"—my father was the one who did it, not you. He's saying all kinds of crazy things, like he chased you home last night before you even got to the park." Concern was then replaced by a smile. "But nobody's listening."

"Did they ever?" he asked without much humor, then swallowed the sour moment with an effort that made him grunt.

"You okay?" Jeff said quickly.

"Gas," he said, patting his stomach. "It's the food. Almost as bad as Beacher's."

Jeff laughed, slapped the mattress and looked to Tracey. She giggled, shook her head, and he told her to go ahead.

"What?" Don said, not liking the intimacy. "What?"

"Beacher," Tracey started, then burst out laughing, shook her head and her hand and inhaled deeply to choke off the fit. "He's named a sandwich after you."

"He did what?"

Jeff nodded. "He named a sandwich after you and he's serving it to all the reporters! God, can you believe it?"

"What is it, raw hamburger?"

"No. It's . . ." Jeff stood and leaned against the wall to keep from falling down. "It's grilled cheese and bacon, with lettuce and onions."

"What?" Don yelled. "I don't even like grilled cheese. What the hell does that have to do with anything?"

"Who the hell knows? But if you go in and ask for a Don Boyd Special, that's what you get."

It was prairie fire laughter that spread from one to the other, dying down, then roaring again, until his sides ached and his cheeks felt ready to split and his lungs refused to give him enough air. Jeff crumpled to the floor with his hands locked over his stomach. Tracey rolled in her chair until it slammed back against the wall and nearly skidded out from under her. The nurse looked in once, and saw them and grinned and winked at them to quiet down; Dr. Naugle came by and suggested loudly they calm down before they were all put in straitjackets.

Don sobered first, blinking away the tears and moaning while the ache faded from his ribs.

The nurse reappeared, arms folded over her chest, one eyebrow lifted to signal the end if the visit.

"Shit," Jeff whispered, and shook his hand again, averting his eyes when Don saw the question there—did you really kill him with your own two hands?

"See you later," Tracey told him before the question could be asked. "Take care of yourself, hero, okay? We'll see you later, maybe tonight."

She kissed him on the lips, once and quickly, so quickly he couldn't taste it. When they were through the door, he watched as Tracey went left, as Jeff grabbed her hand and pulled her to the right. She giggled; he hushed her with his head close to hers.

A sandwich, he thought; Jesus Christ, a sandwich!

greensparks and greenfire
and the stallion's silhouette against the white of the moon

"I wouldn't let him come up," Chris said, perching on the mattress by his hip. "He's acting like an asshole. Would you believe, even Tar thinks he's acting like a jerk?"

Gratefully, and somewhat embarrassed, he turned his cheek toward her oncoming lips, and was nonplussed when she cupped his face in her hands, turned it back, and gave him a kiss he knew the doctor wouldn't approve of. She didn't seem to notice his bewilderment, only leaned away and slumped so that her man's white shirt bagged over her breasts under the fall of her hair.

"I think he's jealous."

"Brian?" That he could not believe. "You're kidding."

"Well," she said, one hand leaning on his waist, "he's been drinking already. Smells like a brewery, and he can't figure out why the reporters won't talk to him anymore." A finger toyed with the sheet. "He said . . ." A look without looking up. "He said something about Donny Duck to them, y'know?"

"Wonderful," he said.

"Oh, don't worry about it. Nobody cares. My god, you're a genuine hero, you know that? I mean, you're the kind of man that craphead only dreams about."

"Jesus, Chris." He looked to the window and wished she'd go away. No, he thought in a panic. No; just lay off the bullshit.

"No, really."

"God, knock if off, huh?"

"Man can't take a compliment," she said to the wall.

"Well . . ."

She laughed silently and pushed her hair back behind her ears, the movement half-turning her toward him so he could see, if he wanted, the flat of her chest where the shirt was creased back.

"I guess you're all right though."

The finger waltzed aimlessly, over the sheet, and he couldn't help looking at it without seeming to, watching it, mesmerized by it, and finally squeezing his legs together because of where it was heading. When he cleared his throat and pushed himself into a higher sitting position, the finger only paused before dancing on.

"Yes, thanks."

"I hear they're going to make a big deal at the concert."

"Yeah, so I heard too."

She smiled at him and winked. "Brian and Tar aren't going. He says you'll make him puke."

"If that's true, I'll be there early."

Her lower lip vanished briefly between her teeth before she leaned over again and kissed him, hard, surprising him so much he let her tongue in before he knew she was doing it, astounded him so much he opened his eyes and saw her staring at him. She laughed without pulling away, and the laugh was deep in his mouth, and he prayed neither of his parents would walk in, not now.

She broke the kiss, but didn't move away. "Listen, after the concert?"

He waited.

"If your folks let you—I mean, you being in the hospital and all, they may not even think it's a good thing for you to go—but if they do let you, maybe we can go to Beacher's after."

He laughed. "And try the Don Boyd Special?"

"You know?" And she laughed, rocking slowly as her finger moved to his groin, traced the bulge there, and retreated. "All right! The Don Boyd Special it is!"

All he could was nod, and swallow, and watch the play of her buttocks beneath the skin of her jeans.

Jesus, he thought; oh Jesus.

someone was screaming and there was blood on his hands

He closed his eyes and saw Jeff take Tracey's hand, and saw the promise in Chris's eyes, and felt someone in the room, watching him and not moving.

Please, no, he thought, and opened his eyes with a soundless gasp.

Fleet stood at the foot of the bed. His face was lined, his eyes red-rimmed, and his hands gripped the metal footboard while he examined Don's face.

"God, you scared me," Don said, smiling.

Fleet nodded.

"Hey, you okay?"

"I'm supposed to ask you that, m'man," Robinson answered, his smile only a pulling back of his lips. "Shit, you done it good, didn't you?"

He shrugged. "I guess."

"You guess?"

"I don't . . . I don't remember everything, exactly."

"No shit?"

"No shit."

Fleet pushed away from the bed, and the light from the window put half his face in shadow.

"Thanks," he said then, in a voice barely heard. "Thanks. For Mandy."

Don didn't know what to say, nor did he know what to do when Fleet came suddenly around the bed and leaned close enough to touch. "I wanted that dude, Donny boy," he said, the words scraped out of his throat. "I wanted that fucker myself, can you understand that?"

Don nodded, afraid that Robinson was going to hit him.

Fleet nodded back as if a point had been made, straightened, and walked out without saying another word.

Dr. Naugle came in, Joyce and Norman behind, and before Don could ask anything, there were reporters in the room. They were quiet but eager, and they had apparently agreed before hand on the rotation of questions. He did the best he could with some help from his father who sat on his one side while his mother sat on the other, and he tried not to squint in the glare of the lights or lose his temper when one of them suggested offhandedly that Brian's story was somewhat closer to the actual fact than the police report; he made a few self-deprecating jokes they laughed at politely, and just as politely he refused when a photographer wanted him to hold a bat like a club; a woman reporter asked about girlfriends and his running; a man in a tweed suit made his throat freeze up; and when someone asked how he felt about the medal, he said in a quiet voice he was pleased and didn't deserve it.

They left without a fuss when Dr. Naugle called time.

His parents left him alone to dress in the clothes they had brought.

And when he was tucking in his shirt, the nurse returned with a wheelchair.

"Do I have to use that?" he said, pointing with one hand while the other hurried to zip his fly and buckle his belt. "I can walk."

"If you don't, I'll have to carry you."

He grinned and took the seat.

And there were more pictures at the hospital entrance, and while he was getting into the station wagon, and while the wagon pulled away slowly from the curb. He wanted his father to hurry, and didn't want to think that the smile on the man's face was meant for more than him.

When they arrived home, there was a police car at the curb and Sergeant Quintero on the sidewalk. He opened the door for Joyce and took Don's hand when he climbed out weakly. The moment was awkward because he knew the man wanted to say something about the Howler, about Tracey, and he was rescued by Joyce, who hustled him inside after a quick invitation to the patrolman to come in when he could and have a cup of coffee.

In the foyer he glanced up the stairwell and let himself be led into the living room, where he was put in on the sofa. A fussing over him he enjoyed and didn't care for, and with apologetic smiles his parents left him alone.

He looked around, thinking things should be different, realizing with a start he hadn't been gone for even a full day. It unsettled him. Time shouldn't have stretched so far, shouldn't have had so much crammed in, yet his father's chair hadn't moved, and there was an empty cup on the floor beside it, folders on the couch, magazines on the end table. Nothing had changed, and suddenly he was convinced that somehow, this time it should have.

They returned with steaming coffee, and a can of soda for him. He grinned as his father sagged loudly into the chair and kicked off his shoes, squirmed when his mother dumped the folders on the floor and knelt on the cushion beside him. She kept looking at her watch.

"Well!" Norman said explosively, and took a sip of his drink.

Joyce hugged him quickly and gave him an impish grin.

"Are you all right, son?" Norman asked solemnly. "I mean, really all right?"

"I think so," he answered truthfully. "A little shaky, but I think I'm okay."

"Good," his mother said, retreating to her corner. Then there were tears. "God, I was so frightened!"

"We both were," his father said when Don reached out a hand to touch Joyce's leg. "From the moment we found you gone, we were scared to death something had happened to you."

The tone in the man's voice made him turn. "Oh," he said then. "Oh, shit."

"Right," Norman said, sternly but not unkindly. "I got up to get a glass of water and I saw your door open. You were gone, Donald. It was almost midnight and you were gone. You can't imagine what we thought."

"You ran away," his mother said. "I mean, that's what we thought—that you'd run away or something." Her smile was one-sided and her laugh was abrupt. "I was going to call the police, can you believe it?"

"I couldn't imagine," Norman said tightly, "where you had gone. We took the car and started to look for you. We drove around the whole neighborhood trying to figure out what the hell you were doing to us, why you'd do something stupid like this."

Don swallowed. "I couldn't sleep," he explained. "I went for a walk."

"Without telling us?"

"You were asleep. I didn't want to wake you."

"You drove your mother crazy, you know that, don't you?"

I'm a hero, he thought then; I'm a hero, don't you remember?

Norman slumped back in his chair and covered his face with his hands, rubbed, pulled, then shook his head. "You could have been killed."

Joyce started to cry.

"But Dad—"

"You could have been goddamned killed!" Norman said, his hands flat on the armrests. "We could have gotten a phone call in the middle of the night, and we would have had to tell the police we didn't even know you were gone. In our own house, our own son, and we didn't even know you were gone! Jesus Christ, Don, if you ever do that again, I'll break your neck!"

Don struggled to understand—they were mad because they were afraid for him, afraid because he was their son; yet he couldn't help the rise of his own temper when he saw the expression on his father's face, a hard and murderous look untempered by compassion or relief. A glance to his mother— she was drying her face with the backs of her hands, bravely smiling to show him he was right, and this was only their after-the-fact reaction.

Then her eye caught the hands of the clock on the mantel and she uncurled with a loving pat to his knee. "I've got to get dinner," she announced. "There's only a couple of hours before the concert and . . . oh, Lord, I'll never be ready in time. Never. Norm, would you mind peeling the potatoes. I've got to start—" She took a step toward her husband, looked at the clock again and rushed out of the room. "Lord!"

she called. "Please, just three or four more hands, what do you say?"

Norman laughed indulgently and winked at his son. "It's a big night for her, you know," he said. "For all of us."

"Oh, god," Don whispered. "Oh, god, do I have to go?"

"Do you feel up to it?"

"I don't know."

"Well, if you don't, we'll understand." His fingers tented under his chin. "It would be nice, though. There are a lot of people grateful to you for what you did last night." The fingers folded into a double fist. "You know," he said thoughtfully, "I would have thought, to be honest, you didn't have it in you." He glared then to keep Don from responding. "You scared the shit out of me, son. Don't you ever do that again."

"Dad, I'm sorry."

He stood, shook off an instant of dizziness, and watched as Norman pushed himself out of the chair. They faced each other for several seconds, and Don waited for the hug.

"The potatoes," Norman said with an uneasy laugh. "Your mother'll have my hide. C'mon, give me a hand."

Don followered him into the foyer, but veered off to the stairs instead of the kitchen. When his father turned, he said, "I need to clean up, Dad." He wrinkled his nose. "I smell like disinfectant, you know? I'll be down in time for supper, don't worry I just . . ."

He gestured vaguely toward the second floor and Norman nodded, gave him a big smile, and went off, whistling.

They were afraid for you, he told himself as he took the stairs slowly; they really are proud of you, really they are.

In the hallway he hesitated, then turned into his room and stopped. Gasped. Held on to the jamb and felt his jaw working.

"I went up to the attic after we saw you this morning," Joyce said behind him, her voice small.

He didn't jump. He only nodded. And he walked slowly in with a grin on his face, giving silent greetings to his pets back on their shelves, to the panther on the wall over his headboard, and the elephants that once again flanked his door. There was a bit of dust on the bobcat, and a cobweb on hawk, but he didn't care as long as they were back where they belonged.

"Don, I'm sorry."

She hadn't come into the room, waiting in the hall as if for an invitation. He turned and smiled at her, ducked his head and shrugged. She was expectant, her hands twisting around her hairbrush, waiting for his reaction, waiting for absolution.

Then he looked to the desk and the empty space above it.

"Where is it?" he asked, more sharply than he'd intended. "I had a poster up there too. Where is it, Mom?"

"What?" Joyce came in, looked, and nodded. "Oh. Well, I wasn't sure about that one, so I took it down and put it in the hall closet. I'll get it if you want."

"But why?" he said plaintively as she started up the hall.

She stopped, returned and swept an arm through the air. "Well, with all these animals and things around, I . . . well, I didn't think you really wanted a picture of just some trees."

TWELVE

Dinner was a hasty affair. Joyce spent more time waving her hands about and babbling than eating, Norman lost his temper more than once in an effort to be patient, and Don ate everything on his plate, had seconds, and seriously considered third helpings to satisfy his sudden, ravenous appetite. Yet his stomach bubbled acid, and a tic refused to leave the corner of his left eye. It was nerves, he decided, aggravated by his mother's self-propelled ascent into near hysteria over her participation in the opening ceremonies at the park tonight, and goaded by the return of his father's waspish tongue. The closer the time for leaving came, the more surly Norman grew, until Don finally excused himself and rushed upstairs to dress.

With the door closed behind him he switched on the light and forced himself to look at the poster retrieved from the closet and returned to its place.

The running horse was gone.

He checked it only once, could not look at it again without seeing the stallion charging across the ball field, green eyes, green sparks, heading for Falwick because Don had commanded.

When he looked out the window, he saw only the night.

"Don," his mother called as she sped past the door. "Hurry up, dear, or we're going to be late."

His fingers refused to work his buttons, tie his laces, do anything with his hair; his lips quivered as he warded off a sensation of wintercold that stiffened his arms and made bending over a chore; and his eyes were pocked with grains of harsh dust that sent stabs of white fire into his skull, fire that swirled and coalesced and formed a flame-figure of a horse.

A dash into the bathroom emptied his meal into the toilet.

Kneeling on the carpeted floor, hands gripping the porcelain sides, he heard Joyce bleating in the hall about something spilled on her dress, heard Norman complaining that the photographers would make him look like a corpse if he wore, as she insisted, his good black suit.

Another surge of bile, and the acid tears that came with it before he gulped for air, flushed the toilet, and grabbed for a towel. From his position on the floor he dumped the terry cloth into the sink and turned on the cold water, waited, pulled the towel out and slapped it over his face. His shirt was soaked, but the shock was a comfort; his throat was raw, but when he staggered to his feet and scooped a palmful of water into his mouth, the expected reaction didn't happen. The water went down, stayed down, and he smiled sardonically at his reflection, his face and hair dripping, and his eyes turning bloodshot.

"Big hero," he mumbled. "You look like Tar after a three-day drunk."

He dried himself quickly, brushed his teeth, and combed his hair; back in his room he changed his shirt and slacks, found a sports jacket he could wear, and hurried downstairs to wait, standing in the living room and looking out the window.

The street was dark, and a light wind taunted the last leaves on the trees. A couple passing by huddled close to-

gether though they weren't wearing heavy coats. Mr. Delfield
from across the road argued with his dachshund, who didn't
want the leash, and when the dog slipped its collar, the old
man shambled after it, one hand raised in a doom-laden fist
while the other whipped the leash angrily against the sidewalk.
The red convertible sped past, the top up and music blaring.
The wind gusted, and there was movement in the gutters, an
acorn rolled along the walk and dropped into shadow.

Where are you? he thought, feeling the cold through the
pane.

There was no answer, and he had no time to ask the
question again. Joyce was in the foyer, rattling the car keys
and calling up to Norman, telling Don to leave on one light
so they wouldn't break a leg when they got home, and
wondering aloud what she had forgotten, what would go
wrong, what people would think if the celebrations began
with a thud, not a bang.

He followed them out, and took a deep breath, saw Mr.
Delfield rushing back to his house with his dog wriggling
under his arm, and took the backseat without any prompting.

He watched the street as they drove over and parked on
the north side because there were no ready openings on the
boulevard, Joyce complaining because they should have started
earlier to get a decent spot.

At the gates—similar pillars of stone that marked the other
entrance—he hesitated and listened, and could hear nothing
but the murmuring of a patiently waiting crowd, the slam of a
car door, the heels of his mother's shoes cracking on the
path.

Folding chairs had been placed in orderly half-moon rows
facing the bandstand. The lights were bright and focused on
the orchestra that took its place to a smattering of applause
that grew, swelled, had people on their feet with smiles and
whistles and proud looks for their children. A television news
crew was off to one side amid a clutch of newsmen who

scanned the front rows, discounting the mayor and the community leaders who couldn't keep from glancing surreptitiously at the cameras.

Don sat between his parents, not liking the way he was looked at, pointed at, highlighted by smiles that claimed him as their own. The Quinteros sat behind him, and he spent as much time as he could whispering to Tracey about how silly this all was as he returned a nod or a wave when it came in his direction.

The bandmaster climbed to his stand, and the audience settled down; he turned to the microphone set up to his left and cleared his throat, causing a squeal to rip through the clearing. He laughed nervously; the audience laughed with him. He thanked them for coming, and introduced Mayor Garziana, who spent fifteen minutes orating Ashford's history in such a way that the back rows began squirming and the front rows froze their smiles.

A moment, then, in dramatic pause before he introduced each of the Ashford Day Committee members, the principals of the two high schools, and a dozen others who had worked to bring the town together for its birthday.

Norman and Joyce stood together, and Don winced when his father turned to the crowd and waved.

Then the mayor paused again, spoke again in a voice so soft no one dared sneeze for missing a word. He alluded to the Howler, and introduced Don.

Don didn't move though the applause was loud.

"Go on," Joyce urged him with a hugging grip on his arm.

He couldn't. The cameras were watching, and the mayor was beaming, and the police chief in his dress uniform had climbed to the bandstand with a package in his hand.

"Go, Donald," Norman hissed, poking his ribs harshly.

He couldn't.

Where are you?

Tracey leaned forward and pulled a strand of his hair. "Go for it, Vet," she said into his ear.

He grinned, shook his hair loose and stood. Hand smoothed his jacket, his throat went dry, and the walk across the infield through the flare of the spotlights was long and slow and filled with the sound of his soles striking the ground.

Hollow. Booming. Iron striking iron.

The applause started again when he positioned himself between the police chief and the mayor, and he smiled shyly, unable to see anything beyond the wall of white light.

The mayor said something—Don heard Amanda's name and heard the silence that followed—and said something else before shaking his hand vigorously; and suddenly there were people right in front of him, kneeling, crouching, cameras working, flashbulbs exploding, mouths working as they ordered this pose and that, bumping into one another, crowding together, a hydra with white fire-eyes that made his own water.

The police chief said something, and handed him the package. His medal, and a certificate, and the grateful thanks of a town he had saved from further grief.

The applause punched his ears, the mayor slapped his back, and the chief pumped his hand without once seeing his face.

Then he was standing in front of the mike, and it was quiet. Only the whirr of a camera forwarding its film, only the scuffle of feet on the grass and the creak of a few chairs.

It was quiet, and it took him a moment to realize they wanted him to speak. Say a word. Tell them all how a kid had beaten a murderer to death.

A voice broke through the white wall from somewhere in the dark: "Hey, Duck, tell them the giant crow did it!"

He looked up sharply, searching for the voice and the derisive laughter that followed.

"I . . ."

He wasn't close enough to the mike, and only the mayor heard him start; but the laughter was still there, and spreading through the crowd, feeding on his nervousness, sympathetic at his plight and trying to tell him there was only good cheer out there and the gratitude hadn't died.

But they laughed, a few of them, and Don held the velvet-covered box close to his chest.

The mayor patted the back of his head and pushed him closer; the bandmaster cleared his throat. The laughter settled, and died, and there was quiet again.

Except for the wind that waited in the trees.

He looked down and saw his parents—Joyce was brushing a tear from her eye, and Norman was scowling; behind them, he could see Tracey holding tightly to her father's arm as if holding him in his seat.

"Thank you," he said at last and clearly, and stepped off the platform before anyone could stop him.

The applause was swift and short, and by the time he reached his seat, the bandmaster was already rapping his baton.

The police station was deserted except for the desk sergeant and dispatcher and, in a second floor office that faced the main street, Thomas Verona. His shift was over at twelve, but he felt as if he'd already strung three of them together—his eyes were bleary, his hands unsteady, and whenever he tried to concentrate on anything for more than a few moments at a time, the world began a slow spinning that forced him to shut his eyes tightly before he lost his balance.

Three fingers massaged one cheek as he stared out the window. There were few pedestrians, and the cars that stopped at the light on the corner were more than likely from adjoining towns, passing through, going home. He shifted his ministrations to the other cheek and imagined he could hear the concert in the park. Susan was there, sitting with the

Quinteros, and he wished he could have joined them. But he couldn't. It was Luis's night, not his—Luis had found the boy and had taken care of him until the ambulance had arrived, Luis, who also managed to clear up the accident between a bus and car that had jumped a boulevard island.

Luis Quintero deserved what attention he could garner; he, on the other hand, was needed to fill in when one of his colleagues was taken ill.

Still, it would have been nice, sitting beside Susan and holding her hand. A hell of a lot better than sitting in here.

"Shit," he muttered, and turned away from the window, laid his palms on the cluttered desk, and stared at the file folder spread open before him. Test results on Falwick's injuries. Test results on Amanda Adler and the Howler's other victims. Test results on the blood found on Boyd's clothes and hands. A preliminary autopsy report made just around noon, precedence over others because of the case's notoriety. He poked at them with a finger and frowned. By necessity, most of what he looked at was initial findings only, though certainly conclusive enough for him to shut the folder, file it away, and move on to the next thing.

But he couldn't.

He kept seeing the slender figure of that boy lying in the hospital bed, seeing the fear in his eyes, in the way he spoke without really answering questions. It wasn't right. He would have surmised through visual evidence that Boyd was hiding something, covering up for a gang that had almost torn the retired sergeant to shreds—and he had, until the first results came in and he saw he was wrong, another theory shot to hell like hundreds before it and the ancestor of hundreds more.

One kid. One victim.

Footsteps in the hall and he looked up in time to see a white-jacketed man stride past his open doorway.

"Hey, Ice!"

The footsteps hesitated and returned. A short man with

wispy hair atop a constantly wistful face leaned against the doorframe and grinned. "Such devotion, I can't stand it," he said.

Verona lifted his middle finger, smiled over it, then used it to stab at a sheet of green paper. "This thing here."

Ice Ronson stretched without leaving his place. "Right, Tom. It's a piece of paper."

"The Boyd thing."

"Okay. It's a piece of paper about the Boyd thing." He snatched a stick of gum from his breast pocket and folded it into his mouth. Blew a bubble he sucked back before it broke. "So?"

"So who did most of the work? I don't recognize the signature here." He turned the sheet around and waited until Ronson crossed the room to stare. "Christ, you guys can't even write your own names except on checks."

"Hey, man, it's tough down there in the trenches," Ronson said, taking a pair of wire-rimmed glasses from the same pocket as his gum. "We deal in volatile chemicals, delicate measurements, knowing all the time a man's life may hang in the—shit, this is impossible! Why the hell don't you get a decent lamp, huh? A man could go blind." He held the paper up toward the fluorescent light in the ceiling. "Oh, yeah, it's Adam. He did this stuff."

"Adam?"

Ronson sighed for the ignorance of the people he had to work with. "Adam Hedley, don't you know him? Incredibly brilliant chemist wasting his time teaching high school. He likes police work, does this part-time when he ain't baby-sitting the brats. Y'know, he could get three, four times what he's making now and he doesn't? Stupid, if you ask me. The guy's a genius."

Verona nodded. "Nice for him. But even Einstein was wrong once in a while."

"Name three."

"Ice, look, this isn't right, okay?"

Ronson spread his hands. "Tom, I said Adam did it."

"Then he did it wrong."

Ronson perched on the edge of the desk and shook his head. "*I* may do it wrong, boss, but not Adam. He's a maniac. Every test gets done a zillion times, and he still wants us to send samples to the FBI, just in case he's goofed."

Verona leaned back. "Well, he's goofed this time."

Ronson shook his head; Veron a was declaring the impossible.

The detective sighed, took out a handkerchief and mopped his face. "Ice, read it."

Ronson shook his head; Verona was declaring the impossible. when he was done, he closed the folder. "Interesting."

"Interesting, shit!"

The lab man shook his head and took off his glasses, added another stick of gum to the first, and blew another bubble as he moved out into the hallway. Then he locked an arm around the frame and leaned back to peer in. "I think," he said, "if Adam's right, and he probably is, you've got a problem, Dick Tracy."

"The same to you, fella," Verona said without smiling, and swiveled his chair back to the window, three fingers to his cheek, trying to imagine Susan listening to the music, hoping she was missing him as much as he missed her.

Then he glowered at the dim reflection in the pane and stood, took his coat down from the rack and walked out. He would take a car, ride around with the window down to clear his head, and maybe he would come up with a reason why there were no particles of wood found on Falwick's corpse. And why there were no chips or gouges or strips missing from the club the Boyd kid had used.

Just before he reached the entrance he stopped, considered, and took the stairs down into the basement, to the room at the back, where the evidence was kept.

He unlocked the heavy iron door, locked it behind him, and moved through the stacks like library shelves. When he found the Boyd case he took down the cardboard carton and sat on the floor with the box between his legs. There wasn't much—shards of clothing in plastic bags, bits of grass and dirt, the branch with bags tied at both ends. The light was dim, only a single bulb overhead, but he held the branch close to his eyes and stared, shaking his head at the streaks of dark on the grey bark, at the heft of it, swinging it once and knowing that two or three collisions with a man's skull or shoulder would have shattered it.

But the Howler was dead, case closed, decreed by a relieved and gleeful chief who reported to a mayor whose first reaction was to wonder if he could declare a national holiday.

He stood, swung the club like a bat once more, and replaced it, replaced the box, and unlocked the door before switching off the light.

The kid didn't do it.

Goddamnit, that kid didn't do it.

Then he heard it—footsteps in the hall that curved away from him to the right. To his left it curved again, a circular corridor in whose center core was the boiler room. He waited, listening to the steam heat gurgling and hissing through the pipes bracketed to the low ceiling.

"Ice?"

The footsteps moved closer, slow, steady, and Verona felt his hand moving toward the gun holstered under his arm. He chided himself for the reflex, but didn't stop it when he saw the shadow growing on the wall.

It was indistinct and dark, and spread to the ceiling, bled onto the floor.

"Ronson, goddamnit, stop playing games!"

The footsteps halted, the shadow remained.

Verona felt behind him with his free hand and turned the

heavy knob on the evidence room door. Forty-three is too old
to be having hallucinations in the stationhouse, but he knew
damned well that what he saw wasn't a man.

The footsteps began again, hollow and soft.

The shadow darkened, spread farther, form hidden in the
dust that floated in the cold air.

The gun was out, the door was open, and any thought he
had of running for the stairwell was erased when the shadow
made a sound like an animal snorting, the footsteps grew
louder, and the lights went out.

Verona whirled into the room, slammed the door and
locked it; the gun was still in his hand when he pressed an ear
to the iron, knowing he wouldn't hear anything, hoping he
would be able to feel the vibrations should the intruder
attempt to break in.

He backed away when he sensed something stopped on the
other side, jumping when his shoulder struck a shelf, swearing when something pounded softly on the door.

There was no other exit, no windows, no air or heating
ducts; no place else to go but stand against the back wall and
listen to the pounding, listen to his heart, and feel the gun in
his hand become slippery and warm.

Norman was talking with a reporter, Joyce was conferring
with the mayor, and Don sat rigid in his seat, wishing they
would all go away.

It seemed that no one could wait until the last note of the
last piece had drifted into the sky before they were on him,
wanting to shake his hand, kid him, or just stand by him so
they could be in one of the pictures. He had squirmed around
the first chance he got, but the Quinteros were already gone,
and when he asked his father about Beacher's, he was told
that it would be a better idea to get a good night's sleep.
Don't try too much, Joyce had cautioned, not so soon after.

Don had agreed without more than token argument; a

cloud had enveloped him, soporific, making it difficult for him to keep his eyes open, to keep his lips in a smile. At one point, just when he thought he was going to bolt through the crowd and head for home on his own, he caught Chris's eye as she walked by with a portly florid-faced man he assumed was her father. She smiled in anticipation, but he mugged a sorrowful expression, signaling with a jerk of his head and a shrug that he was trapped into going home. She grinned, and mimed holding up a noose around her neck, her eyes popping, her tongue hanging out, and walked on, with a single glance over her shoulder before the crowd closed in again and she was lost.

Finally, when a buzzing began deep in one ear, he shoved himself to his feet and took hold of his father's arm. Norman tried to brush him off without looking, then turned and saw the boy's face. A wavering that Don wanted to slap from his face before he said one last word into the mike held toward his lips. A smile, a shake of hands, and Don felt himself being led toward his mother. The mayor was long gone, a handful of men and women in his place; one of them was Harry Falcone.

"Joyce," Norman said with a brusque nod to the teacher, "we have to be getting home."

She balked and the others groaned at his unsociable behavior until he took her arm and pointed at Don. "Oh, god, I'm sorry," she said, was flustering in her farewells and did not object when Falcone congratulated Don with a handshake, Norman with one as well, and kissed Joyce's cheek with both hands on her shoulders.

In the station wagon Joyce kicked off her shoes and whooped. "Keerist, did you *see* them?" she yelled as they pulled away from the curb. "Jesus, I had them eating out of my damned hand!"

"What about the other committee members?" Norman

asked, taking a corner too quickly and squealing the tires, braking too abruptly and almost sliding her into the well.

"Hell, they had their glory, too, don't worry," she grumbled. "God, a woman can't even have a moment in the sun around here."

"You did a great job, Mom," Don said hastily from the backseat, his medal beside him, the box still unopened.

"Thank you, darling."

"He's right," Norman agreed with an expansive show of good humor. "Great job, Mrs. Boyd. If you run for mayor, I want to be dogcatcher."

"You got it," she said.

"It was still a great job."

She grunted, "Damn right," and less than five minutes later they were in the driveway, and the wind picked up before they reached the door; it bellowed down the street ahead of a cloud of dust and leaves and clattered branches together, caught one house's shutters and banged it hard against the wall. A garbage can tipped over and rolled into the gutter, a dog howled, and somewhere near the corner someone's window was smashed.

They tumbled laughing into the foyer, brushing back hair and staggering toward the kitchen, Joyce declaring a moratorium on coffee in favor of their best brandy.

"What timing," she yelled from the den while Norman fetched three glasses. She peered through the back door curtains, twirled on her toes and presented the bottle to her husband, who poured. "Fantastic! One more encore and we would have been drenched."

Don was about to tell her it wasn't raining yet when he heard it begin in a lull of the wind, slapping the windows, hissing in the grass. A downpour that wouldn't last more than ten minutes, but she was right—the timing was so perfect, she must have a divine guardian somewhere. Then he blinked when his father pressed a warm glass into his hand.

"It's okay," Norman said laughingly to his surprise. "It's a special occasion. I'm not trying to corrupt you." He cleared his throat and took hold of a narrow lapel. "I think . . . to us."

"Damn right," Joyce said, grinning, and emptied her glass at a swallow.

Don was cautious, sniffing the liquid first and wrinkling his nose, swallowing hard against the burning when he took his first sip. He didn't see what all the fuss was about, but he wasn't going to spoil anything by refusing the drink; by the time his glass was empty, the fire in his stomach had been reduced to gentle embers, a furnace in winter that would warm him until dawn.

He yawned.

The telephone rang, and Joyce answered, indicated with a thumb it was for her and disappeared into the living room, the cord trailing behind.

He yawned again as the brief storm ended and Norman poured himself another glass.

"You'd better go to bed," his father suggested while he toed off his shoes and sat at the table. "School tomorrow."

"Jeez, don't I even get a day off for good behavior?" He made himself laugh to prove it was a joke. "Besides, Dr. Naugle said I should rest, remember?"

To his astonishment, his father considered the idea seriously and compromised by telling him they'd discuss it in the morning. He didn't push it; he headed straight for the stairs, blew a loud kiss to his mother, who blew one back absently, and ran up two steps at a time, kicked into his room and dropped onto the bed.

The velvet box was still in his hand. He switched on the light over the headboard, winked at the panther still licking its paw, and pulled up the hinged lid.

"God," he said. "Hot damn."

It was as big around as his palm, heavy and gold, elaborately embossed with the words For Public Service, Donald Boyd. He read them aloud for his friends to hear, then placed the box on his desk. Deliberately not looking at the wall, he turned around and unbuttoned his shirt, kicked off his shoes and trousers, and yanked back the coverlet. He could feel the poster behind him, could feel the emptiness, the fog, the weight of the trees.

When he switched off the light, he could feel the dark at the window.

He yawned so hard his jaw hurt; he stretched so hard his leg muscles ached; he closed his eyes, rolled onto his side and punched at the pillow, sighed as a signal for sleep to get a move on, rolled onto his stomach and felt the pillowcase cool against the flush on his cheek. His feet tangled in the sheets.

The blanket was too warm; the sheet alone not warm enough.

He went into the bathroom and brushed the brandy's taste from his mouth.

He stood at the head of the stairs and listened to his parents talking in the kitchen; he listened for almost half an hour and not once heard his name.

"Way to go," he said quietly as he returned to his room. "Good job, son, we're really proud of you, you know."

The lamp was still out, and he stood at the window, watching the wind toss the neighborhood under glimpses of the moon that found cracks in the clouds.

I'm feeling sorry for myself, aren't I? he asked the night sky. Mom worked hard for all this; she doesn't want me to take it away.

But it was only a gesture, this attempt at understanding, and he knew it, and knew he should feel worse for it. He didn't. He felt as if something had been taken away before he could make it his own, as if something uniquely his had been lost from the moment he had heard Brian's voice sneering in the park.

He stretched out his right hand, and his fingers caressed the head of the bobcat; up a shelf, to follow the lines of a leopard. His breath condensed on the pane. The clouds reclosed, and there was only a glow from a house a block over, and the dark against dark of the grass and the trees.

If you're real, he thought then, where are you? Where are you?

And he didn't move at all when he saw the slanted green eyes that opened slowly, and looked up.

THIRTEEN

*H*e slept until well past noon, scarcely moving, not dreaming, waking only once—when Dr. Naugle came by on his way home from the hospital to check on what he called his celebrity patient. A soft nervous laugh—his mother standing in the doorway, a light coat over her arms as if she were ready to go out, to get back to the business of celebrating the town. Don's mind was fuzzy, disconnected, and he barely heard the man recommend that another day in bed wouldn't hurt to regain the strength he had lost, more emotional than physical.

Joyce agreed, and Donald didn't argue—he didn't like the weakness that had infiltrated his muscles, and he didn't like thinking what would happen if he should show up at school and have a fainting spell or require someone's help to walk before the day was out.

And he didn't like thinking what would happen should he inadvertently mention the horse.

He slept, then, and this time came the dreams.

Of the bedroom, whose walls expanded slowly outward, leaving his bed in the center of a cavern with caves in the dark walls, and in one of the caves he could see a shadow, drawing him in, beckoning, calling his name soundlessly and telling him over and over and over again that everything at last was going to be all right;

Of the bedroom, through whose window he could see the world from a hawk's lazy perspective, refocus, plunge, and see Ashford, refocus again and see the horse waiting patiently under the maple tree in the backyard, watching his window, waiting for the signal, telling him by his stance that he never need fear again, not anyone, not anything—all he had to do was call and his friend would be there;

And of the bedroom at the last, and on his desk the remnants of the nugget that had exploded in his chest. He walked over to it and felt nothing on his soles, blew on the ebony dust and watched it leap into a dervish, a tornado, a tower of black that snapped around him before he could duck away, insinuated itself behind his eyes and showed him the faces of the people at the concert, their eyes bright with laughter, their mouths open like clowns, fingers pointing, heads wagging, elbows nudging neighbors, and feet stamping the ground; it showed him the flushed face of Brian Pratt at the back, hands cupped around his mouth—*tell them the giant crow did it!*—and grinning malevolently at Tar Boston who lifted both his middle fingers—*hey donald the duck*—and turned to Fleet Robinson, who stared sullenly at the one who had stolen his revenge; and it showed him the story of a giant crow, told by a clown who wore black denim.

He woke at ten minutes to three, sweat covering his face, and he watched the ceiling trap shadows shrinking away from the sun.

Norman sat in his office, doing little more than going through the motions, waiting, expecting that every time the door opened, Harry would slink in to tell him that the teachers' strike that should have been called the day before had been called for that afternoon. But Falcone had apparently been made aware of the principal's mood and stayed away, for which small favor Norman mentally sacrificed his wife's heart to the heavens.

Falcone had kissed her. In front of hundreds of people the sonofabitch had laid his hands on her and had kissed her.

"Jesus," he said. "Jesus."

The telephone calls were being screened by the secretaries, but enough filtered through to finally lighten his mood by the time the last class had begun. A few reporters from out of town, several board members, enough well-wishers to finally have him smiling.

Shortly afterward, the mayor called to suggest they not waste any more time but meet as soon as was politically feasible to discuss the man's successor. Anthony Garziana was preparing to retire; he had run Ashford for a dozen years and was tired, looking hungrily toward the day when he could pack up his young wife and family and flee to his carefully built estate on the Gulf of Mexico, outside Tampa. He was unimpressed with the deputy mayor; he liked Boyd's style and the way he had glossed Donald's day with a sheen of his own. That took guts, Garziana had said; Don, Norman told him, had a medal and could be generous.

Splendid, he thought as he rose to stretch his legs. Jesus, wait until Joyce hears this. She'll be hysterical; she'll have the mayor's house redecorated before the end of the year.

He grinned and decided to take a walk around his school, left by the private door, and almost immediately collided with Tracey Quintero. She babbled an apology, he took her shoulder and calmed her down, and told her sotto voce how proud he was of her.

Tracey was flustered. "Me? I didn't do anything."

"You called the police the night . . . that night."

Her face darkened. "I was too late."

"But you panicked the man, Tracey, you panicked him.

You forced him into a mistake, and he paid for it. For that, a lot of us parents are very very grateful.''

Her expression doubted the sentiment, but not by much. She blushed prettily and hurried on, her hands with nothing better to do smoothing her shirt over her stomach, her hips, until she reached the girls' room and pushed in.

She was alone, and she stood in front of the wall-long mirror and checked her hair, her hem, then turned on the cold water and let it run over her wrists. She should have been in zoology, but a slow-building dizziness made her ask for a hall pass, granted on the condition she return before the bell. It was silly, but she accepted, and after her odd meeting with Don's father, she was more confused than ever.

Last night she had wanted to remain in the park after the concert, but her father insisted she return home with him. He was embarrassed by all the attention he was getting, and insisted that Thomas Verona should be complimented as well. No one listened. Luis had been at the scene while Verona had been on patrol; Luis had discovered what Donald had done.

On the night of the Howler's death, she had asked him directly what it was he had seen. There were only rumors, and there was no way to break through the constant busy signals at the Boyds' home telephone. She wanted to know. He wouldn't tell her. She reminded him cruelly that Amanda could have been her if she had tripped, or had turned to use the length of pipe she carried; she could have been the one the school had closed for. He grew angry, but he relented.

And she didn't believe him.

Even now, while she straightened her clothes that were fine the way they were, she could not imagine Don clubbing a man to death, not the way her father had described it. A bash over the head, yes; a good smack or two to the temple, sure; but not so hard that the man looked trampled. And when she heard the television newscasters talk about adren-

aline rushes and hysterical rage, she still didn't believe it. To
do otherwise would turn Don into someone she didn't know.

Jeff had said Don was changing; and maybe she was too.
How could she not, when every night she had the dream—the
race down the boulevard, the Howler in pursuit, Amanda
spinning as if trapped in an invisible web that held her until
the killer dragged her into the park . . . while Tracey watched,
and screamed, and woke up feeling as if someone had kicked
her in the groin.

Tonight, she resolved. Tonight she would call him, and if
she couldn't get through, then she would go over there. No
matter what her father ordered, she would go over there and
talk to him. She didn't know why, only knew she must, and
that more than anything was the root of her confusion.

"A mess, Quintero," she told her reflection. "*Es verdad*,
you're a mess."

With a pinch to her cheeks to bring back some color she
hurried back into the hall, looked both ways and entered the
stairwell. On the first landing she paused, debating whether it
was worth returning to class or not, shrugged and hurried up,
stepped into the upstairs hall and turned right just as Brian
Pratt leapt out at her from the bank of lockers in the corner.

"Hey!" he said, taking her arm as she made to pass by
him.

"Brian, I've got to get to class, okay?"

"God," he said, "you could at least say hello."

"Hello." She shook the hand off and hurried away, glancing back once at him, frowning and thinking that if South
won the night game tomorrow and he had anything to do with
it, he would be even more insufferable than he already was.
Then she remembered Jeff telling her about Don, how he had
asked everyone he'd known if she was going with Brian. The
thought warmed her, and she rubbed the back of her neck
self-consciously, grinned to herself, and turned abruptly at
the classroom door.

Brian was still there, shaking his head.

She couldn't resist—she blew him a kiss before going inside.

Brian grinned stupidly and started toward her, stopped when she ducked into the classroom, and shrugged. It didn't matter. She was smitten, another conquest for the Pratt; and this one all the sweeter because word was she was the Duck's girl.

The Duck.

Christ, he was going to puke the next time he heard someone mention that queer's name. All goddamn day it had been Don did this and Don did that and Don made the world in seven fucking days and the next thing he was going to do was walk on fucking water.

One lucky hit on a crazy old man and the Duck was God.

A shame, man, he thought, because they could've been friends. If the little faggot had only stood up to him that first day, taken one swing at him, they could have been friends. But no, the creep had cried, run crying into the house just like a baby. And Brian had no use for babies. All this bullshit he was reading about sensitive men was just that—bullshit.

Crying never got anyone into the National Football League.

Yeah, he decided; it was time he made a move on Tracey, and soon. He didn't give a shit that she didn't have any tits; she was after the Duck, and that's all the reason he needed.

His eyes narrowed and he made an about-face, deciding that his good mood was ruined and there was no sense going to chemistry now. Besides, the Tube was busy piling on the homework, and if he wasn't there, he couldn't get the assignment, and if he couldn't get the assignment he couldn't be held responsible for it. Right now there were more important things to work on—like figuring out how to ace Fleet and Tar out of the glory tomorrow. Ashford North was known in the conference for its defense against the run, which meant in an ordinary game that Boston and Robinson were going to have a field day while Brian was used solely to decoy the opposition.

But not this time.

Tomorrow night he was going to show them what he was really made of, and the scouts he knew were in town from the Big Ten were going to get an exhibition of ball handling and running they'd never seen in their lives. With any kind of luck at all he would be beating them and their contracts off with a baseball bat before the first half was over.

A fist thumped his chest as he took the stairs down two at a time, three at a time, until he was on the ground floor and heading for the weight room on the other side of the gym. Coach might be there, but he wouldn't mind. Brian would tell him Hedley had agreed to his missing class this once, and Coach would believe him whether he believed him or not. Brian was his star. Brian does his job. Get Brian sulking, lose a game or two, and Coach would be teaching kindergarten someplace in Kansas.

The sharp echo of his mirthless laugh rebounded from the walls, and he swung around the corner, whistling and marching, and stopping dead in his tracks when he saw Mr. Hedley lounging against the gym entrance.

"Were you by any chance lost, Mr. Pratt?" the short man asked without moving away.

"Hadda ask Coach something," Brian said easily, trying to contain his impatience.

"You can ask him after class."

"He won't be here."

Hedley's upper lip pulled back. "He won't be here? You mean, he's skipping practice today? The day before the big game, Mr. Pratt?" The man shook his head. "I cannot credit that, Mr. Pratt. And I suggest, if you want credit for the course and a diploma in June, you head back upstairs."

Brian worked hard to keep his hands from curling into fists. One punch. One punch and the little shit would fall apart. And one punch, caution reminded him, would lose him his graduation, entrance into the Big Ten, and his professional career. Hedley, by his expression, knew that as well, and it made him angrier to know he could do nothing about it.

"Two minutes, Mr. Pratt, or I'll turn in a cut slip."

"Aw, jeez, Mr. Hedley," he said, spreading his hands in appeal, "have a heart, huh?"

Hedley stared at him so intently Brian thought for a moment the prick had finally figured out who had dumped the shit on his porch, and was already preparing an alibi. For himself. Tar, the little coward, would have to take care of himself.

"Two minutes," Hedley repeated and walked off, arms swinging like a sergeant major leading a parade.

"Little prick," Brian muttered. "Fucking little prick."

Hedley heard but didn't turn, didn't lose a step. He continued to the stairwell and headed up for his class. A mistake leaving them alone and he knew it; there were too many legal and ethical ramifications. But Pratt had been getting away with too much for too long, and seeing him in the hallway talking with that little Quintero girl had made him furious. A swift order for questions to be completed in the workbook, and he was gone, racing down the center stairs, barely able to control his heavy breathing before the bastard came around the corner.

Bastard, he thought, and nodded. A fair choice of words. The mother lived alone, most of the time, and there was no telling who could claim fatherhood for that monster. A mental note to see if he could get Candy to reveal the truth, and a wince at the idea that anyone, most of all her, could be named after a confection.

He grinned, then, and stroked his mustache. What, he wondered, would Brian think if he knew that his flabby little prick of a chemistry teacher was regularly manhandling his mother; what, he wondered further, would the thick-necked grunt do if he knew that among Hedley's collection of glossies in his cellar was a choice set of color photos unmistakably starring her.

Probably try to wring my neck, he decided, or cut off my balls.

"Mr. Hedley?"

He cleared his mind of the image of Brian Pratt frothing at the mouth and replaced it with the more realistic and far more pleasant one of Chris Snowden, standing in front of his door with a pile of books in her arms.

"Mr. Hedley, you wanted these from the library?"

He was about to deny it, suddenly remembered the bit of research he'd wanted to do for tomorrow's truncated classes, and nodded, snatched the volumes from her with a curt nod of thanks, and swung open his door as if daring the class to be misbehaving.

Chris stared at his back, and told him silently to go to hell before she wheeled about and headed back for the library on the other side of the building. Though it was excruciatingly boring shifting books from one shelf to another, catering to creeps who needed this author and that reference work, it at least kept her away from teachers for forty-five minutes, kept the males from trying to unclothe her without lifting a finger, kept the females from consigning her to that airhead category all attractive blondes seemed doomed to inhabit from birth.

It also gave her furtive opportunities to do her homework before she left for home, thus enabling her to work full-time on her plan once school was out.

Today she was testing excuses to see which would work the best when she dropped in on the Boyds. She'd thought to learn what assignments Don had missed by staying home, then play the Samaritan by dropping them off—but with classes shortened tomorrow because of the end-of-the-day pep rally that would lead up to the game, most of the faculty wasn't bothering. Then she had wondered if there wasn't something she could manage from the front office, something she hadn't yet been able to figure out.

In a way the idea of seeing Don was beginning to turn her on. She had heard several graphic versions of what he'd done to the Howler, and even taking it all with a pound of salt, it must have been one awesome battle; and to look at him, you wouldn't think he could step on Brian's shadow without breaking a leg.

Appearances, she thought; it's all in appearances, the one subject she knew better than anyone else.

Probably the simplest thing would be just to go, to say truthfully she was concerned and wondering how Don was feeling, could she see him for a minute, and bring him some false greetings from his friends.

Sometimes, Chris, she thought, you try too hard, you know it? You just try too damned hard.

She pushed, then, on the swinging door, heard a thud and a grunt, and looked up through the narrow wire-embedded glass pane.

Oh, Christ! And her eyes closed briefly when Mr. Boyd pulled on the handle and let himself out.

"Gee, I'm sorry," she said, putting an unthinking hand on his arm. "I'm really sorry, Mr. Boyd, honestly. I wasn't looking. I didn't mean it."

He smiled and rubbed his shoulder ruefully. "I think I'll live, Chris. Don't worry about it."

"Honest to god, I didn't mean it, really."

"All right, take it easy," he told her, laughing easily at her distress that bordered on the comic. "I'm not mortally wounded. I'll survive. Just keep your head up from now on, okay? I'd like to last through the year if you don't mind."

His touch on her shoulder was more a brief caress than a pat, and he was gone, leaving her swearing at herself for botching the first chance she'd had to make some points with the old man. She could have pretended a temporary injury, or fallen against him; and now, when the opportunity almost literally knocked her off her feet, she had blown it.

"Shit!"

"Miss Snowden!" the librarian scolded from behind her desk.

Fuck off, you old bitch, she said silently; at least I've been screwed more than once in the last twenty years.

She stalked to the back of the room, grabbed a cart of books, and set about trying to put them all back before the last bell rang. She would have to stop home first to change her clothes, make them easier to discard should the occasion arise, or at least make them seem as if they were ready for stripping. And the more she thought about it, the warmer she felt, the more electric grew the feeling that circled her breasts and centered below her stomach. It was crazy, but she was going to do something stupid if she didn't get out of here, and do it right now.

A book slammed into position. A second one, four more. Up and down the rows, not caring about the glares she received because she was making too much noise. Not caring about the bindings or the bent pages of the squeaks the wheels on the damned cart was making.

She couldn't get out. She had to stay and be a good girl, and confound her classmates until she had everyone who counted right where she wanted.

"Hey, watch what you're doing!"

She looked up and saw Fleet Robinson's freckled hand in the space where she'd almost tried to jam a history book.

"Sorry."

"No problem, okay?" Fleet winked at her through the gap in the books. "You going to the concert tonight?"

She looked sideways at the librarian. "Hell, no."

"Neither am I. You wanna see a flick?"

"Hell, no."

He shrugged, but she backed away in a hurry. The invitation had been given pleasantly enough, but she could see Mandy's ghost still lingering in his eyes. That's all he'd talk about, she knew it, and she wasn't about to waste an evening playing earth mother confessor to a jockstrap in mourning.

She backed up another step, saw Fleet's eyes widen in warning, but it was too late. A look around and down as she moved, and she stepped on Norman Boyd's toes.

"Oh god," she groaned.

Norman creased his brow. "It's an assassination attempt, is that right, Miss Snowden?"

"Mr. Boyd . . ." She lifted her hands, shook her head, and he touched her shoulder again before taking the book he wanted from the shelf and walking out, this time glancing back to see her watching him, ready to cry. A grin, and he strolled on to his office, not bothering with the fiction of scolding himself this time—he had done it deliberately so he could see her reactions, so he could feel the silk against his fingers. All perfectly legitimate, unless she was smarter than the credit he gave her.

Trouble, Norm, he cautioned as he entered through the private door; there's trouble in them thar hills if you ain't careful.

The telephone rang, and in a moment he was on the line with Tom Verona, explaining that his son was home on doctor's orders but seemed, all things considered, almost back to normal. No, the boy hadn't said anything about the Howler, nor had he mentioned any nightmares—though, he added, Tom didn't sound very good himself. Verona told him he'd had a restless night. Boyd asked about the beer they had promised themselves, and Verona agreed readily, suggesting tomorrow night after the game, and vowing he'd find the principal somewhere in the stadium when Norm said it sounded good to him. When they hung up without good-byes, Norm frowned at the phone. The man sounded godawful, and he instantly regretted the invitation—it may well be he was in for a night of listening to another man's series of marital problems.

Wonderful, he thought; just what I need when I can't handle my own.

Then the bell rang, and the school emptied, and once all was done and the last letter signed and dropped on his secretary's desk, he headed for home.

The sun was nearly below the treetops, skeletal shadows cracking the pavement before him, and he supposed there was no way he could get out of going to North after dinner to listen to the program of the schools' vocal programs. He'd much rather put his feet up in the den and watch a football game, or a movie on cable, or go across the street to see John Delfield and tease that stupid dachshund and play a hand or four of cribbage.

Or call up Chris and tell her to come on over and get fucked.

He stopped at the foot of the walk, rubbed the back of a hand over his nose, and saw the first of the night's stars pale above the house.

Trouble, he warned again, and didn't quite not run when he heard the noise behind him, something large and slow coming down the tarmac. It sounded like a horse, but he wasn't going to look; for one reason, it was impossible; and for another, it reminded him of the shadow in the puddle he had seen the other day.

Neither one of them belonged; and neither one was friendly.

Adam Hedley stared at the photocopies of the lab reports he had typed himself yesterday morning, and realized with a groan that filled the house that he had made an error. An inexcusable error. A careless error. In his entire life he had never made such a stupid misstep in procedure.

He held the page up, letting the flickering beam from the projector fall on the police form, ignoring for the moment the writhings and moans from the screen he'd erected in his cellar and concentrated on the precise language he had chosen for describing the condition of the club Donald Boyd had used to end a madman's mad life.

After he had read it a fourth time, he slapped off the projector and hurried up the stairs. There was no way around it; he would have to go to the station and see if he could find Ronson or Verona, see if either would permit him to run the tests again.

Buttoning a salt-and-pepper overcoat to his neck, he stood on his porch and wrinkled his nose before heading for his car. The stench was gone, but he still smelled it, still felt it, and thought perhaps it was time to find another home.

He would have to call the coroner's office too. If he'd made a mistake, they had as well.

Then he slid in behind the wheel, turned on the ignition, and looked down the street for signs of oncoming traffic.

What he saw was something standing in the middle of the road, down at the far corner, just beyond the reach of the only streetlamp the local hooligans hadn't shattered.

It stood there, and it waited, and for no good reason he could think of, Hedley made a U-turn in the middle of the block and sped off the other way.

After practice Brian lifted weights with Tar, Fleet, and a half-dozen others from the team until long after the dinner hour, took a shower knowing Gabby D'Amato was watching, and sprinted home because something was behind him, pacing him silently and staying hidden in the dark.

Fleet rode home in Tar's battered sedan, looking through the rear window so often, Boston almost threw him out.

Jeff made excuses for the weight session that afternoon. He knew Tar must have said something to Brian about the other day, and he didn't want an Indian club smacked between his legs. He did his homework, cleaned his room, and each time he passed a window he couldn't help looking out, looking for something he knew was out there, wondering if he should call Tracey and afraid to pick up the phone.

His father called and told him he'd be working late at the office, so he made his own supper, with his back to the kitchen window.

And when the dishes were done, he looked at the telephone and wiped his hands on his jeans, took off his glasses and wiped them on his shirt.

It was dumb.

But he knew that if he lifted the receiver now, nothing would be there, not even a dial tone.

Not even static.

Only a dead spot, like the dead black he saw in the street, something more than shadow, something less than the night.

After supper Tracey tried to call Don. The line was busy, and at a stern reminder of the promise to herself, she set her mouth and shoulders and went downstairs to fetch her coat from the closet. Her mother asked where she was going, and Tracey told her; her father never stirred from his nap on the couch.

"Please," her mother said with a fearful look to the sleeping man, "wait until he wakes up."

"I have to go, Mother. It's something about school. Don has something I need." She took her mother's wrist and smiled. "I need it for tomorrow. Don't worry, I'll be all right."

"I don't know. Maybe you should—"

"Mother, the man is dead. Donald killed him. He's dead. I'll be all right, honest."

She left before the pleading escalated to a command, and

took the first three blocks at a run in case her mother changed her mind. Then she stopped and leaned against a tree, breathed deeply a half-dozen times, and shook her head to clear it of the vertigo she felt.

There wasn't much traffic though it was only just seven, yet it felt like past midnight. The air had a feel to it, as if it were weary and hoping the sun would soon give it warmth; the sidewalk felt crisp, with a veneer of ice that cracked and shifted as she walked; and the streetlights were sparkling on their way to the ground, white flecks of whirling mica that made her blink her eyes and look away.

It was cold; and it was silent.

Except for the movement behind her.

He's dead, she told herself as she quickened her pace; he's dead and Don killed him and there's nobody back there.

She looked suddenly; there wasn't.

Four blocks to go and she would pretend to have a headache and Mr. Boyd or Don would give her a ride home.

Dumb, she thought as she stepped into the street; dumb, dumb, dumb. Why don't you just go home and try to call him again? What are you gonna say, you were just passing by? Seven blocks out of your way, and you were just passing by? Gee, Don, I was wondering who you were going to the game with tomorrow. Jeff's already asked me to wait for him after, but he understands if you ask and I go with you. Just passing by, that's all.

She angled to her left, toward the center of the block, intending to turn right at the next corner and save herself a walk past the high school.

And when she reached the center line, she heard the movement behind her again. And the breathing—heavy, slow, something larger than a man moving slowly up on her shadow.

It was the school again, the same thing she had seen down in the lower hall. She felt it without looking, and without looking began to run, mouth open to take the air, arms pumping to propel her while she leapt over the curb and raced down the sidewalk, listening to it follow her though it stayed in the street.

Rhythmic, pounding, sounding so much like a horse that she had to chance it and take a peek, and saw nothing but a huge shadow moving toward her along the road. A gasp—it's a car without headlights, Trace, don't be an idiot—and she whimpered, ran faster and heard the animal—it's a car! —match her speed.

A second look and she stumbled.

Above the black, in the black, there were two specks of green.

And below it, and moving with it, a flare of green sparks.

Her balance was regained by windmilling her arms and lifting her knees, and the corner was too far away by fifty yards. She was going to be caught. Whoever was chasing her was going to catch her, and she was going to die now because she didn't die the other night.

She was going to be murdered by a shadow with green eyes.

A sob, please don't panic, and something sent her streaking across a lawn toward an illuminated white door. Up three brick steps, and her finger found the bell, slipped off, and found it again, pressed hard and long until the door swung open and she bulled Jeff aside.

"Shut it!" she demanded, and when he didn't move fast enough, she grabbed it and slammed it and leaned against it, and closed her eyes.

"Trace?"

There were narrow windows on either side of the frame. Jeff pulled aside a white curtain, looked out, and frowned.

"Trace, what's wrong? Was somebody chasing you?"

FOURTEEN

Don set his desk chair so that he could look out the window, angled it so he could appear to be studying in case someone came in. Not that anyone would. Norman and Joyce were at the concert, and their return would be loud enough to forewarn him should he need it. Now all he had to do was sit and wait, and he got up only once, when the room's lamp turned the pane black and all he could see was his ghost staring back. He hurried downstairs and switched on the light over the back door, hurried back up and dropped a towel over the lampshade. The backyard was white now, the grass seeming flat, the trees like ragged gaps torn out of the night; there was a wind blowing, a storm coming, and the houses on the next block were infrequently silhouetted by distant flashes of lightning.

He waited, and pondered the dreams, latching on to an image, turning it, poking at it, casting it away for another until, shortly before nine, he concluded there was nothing he could do about it—the horse was real. And not real. A creation out of something he didn't understand, though he

223

knew that because of what it had done to the Howler it was there to protect him.

Real. And not real.

He looked at his other friends, now tinted in orange from the towel over the bulb, and back to the window.

The horse was not going to let anyone hurt him.

The how and the why of it would come later; right now he had to learn more. Real or not, the horse was an animal, and he had to know more about what that animal was, and what control, if any, he had over it, how it would fit into the new Rules he was making.

His lips moved in something less than a smile, and the doorbell rang. He jumped, a hand flat on his chest. A swallow, an embarrassed glance around, and he rushed downstairs, waited for the bell to ring again before pulling open the door.

It was Sergeant Verona, hat in hand and an odd smile, asking to come in.

"Sure," Don said, stepping back and pointing to the living room. "Have a seat."

There were questions, and Don told him he was fine, still a little shaky but planning on going back to school tomorrow. The press hadn't bothered him all night, though he admitted that while it was kind of unsettling seeing himself on television, it was also kind of nice.

"I don't look like a freak," he said, taking his father's chair.

"You think that? That you look like a freak?" Verona was on the couch, the hat turning over slowly.

"No, not really. Maybe I look like a movie star."

"Just don't get used to it, son," the man said kindly. "Tomorrow there'll be another murder someplace, or a factory fire, and they'll forget all about you."

"Good," he said. And: good, he thought, that's real good.

"My mother and father are over at—"

"I know. It's you I wanted to see anyway, if you don't mind. You're not studying or anything?"

"A little. It can wait."

"The branch," Verona said.

Don was puzzled. "The branch?"

"The one you hit Falwick with."

Verona stopped playing with the hat, looked down at one foot tapping on the rug, looked up at Don. His hand slipped a handkerchief from his jacket pocket and wiped it over his face, but Don saw the eyes—they never left him, never blinked.

"This is hard," the man confessed. "I don't know how to say this right, so I'm just going to say it, okay?"

"Sure." Don didn't care; he didn't know what the cop was talking about.

"I keep thinking maybe you didn't do it," the man said rapidly, each word a snap followed by a stare to measure his reaction. "I've had a chance to take a look at the reports, and there's something wrong there, Don. Something wrong I have to get right in my own mind or it's gonna drive me up the wall. You've had that, I'll bet. Something bugs you, and you don't understand it, so you work at it and worry at it until it makes some kind of sense. Do you know what I'm talking about?"

Don did, and didn't; he knew the sensation, was emmeshed in it now, but didn't know the reference.

"Falwick," Verona said. "I'm thinking you didn't hit him with that stick."

Don frowned. "But I did," he said.

Verona nodded as if expecting the answer. "What I'm thinking, you see, is that you were there, all right. I mean, everything points to it, there's no question about it. But I don't think you were alone."

Don gripped the armrests tightly. "I was," he insisted politely. "There was no one else, just me."

"No friends?"

"No friends."

"I wonder, see, if a few of you got together after your friend was killed and decided to take matters into your own hands. It wouldn't be the first time." Verona smiled guilelessly. "It's possible you were sent out there as bait, and when Falwick jumped you, the others came out of the trees."

"No," Don whispered.

"It's possible that after it was done, after you had beaten that old man to death and saw what it looked like, they left you to take the rap, or the credit."

"No."

Verona mopped his face again and put the handkerchief away, picked up his hat, and flipped it several times as if flipping a coin.

"It's good to protect your friends, Don. But," he said louder, when Don leaned forward to protest, "it's not good to do what you did. It's murder, Don. Planning and executing a scheme like that is murder in the first degree no matter how old you are. That's the law. You're a good kid, a great kid, and there's not a damned thing I can do about it now but tell you that I'm thinking you're a murderer, you and your friends."

"I'll tell my father," was all he could think of to say.

"Do that," Verona said, standing and waving Don back in his seat. "Maybe it'll reopen the case and we'll find out the truth."

He left quickly, quietly, leaving Don in the chair staring at the fireplace, tapping a foot on the floor. He thought maybe he was in trouble, but he didn't know what kind. There was no evidence to implicate anyone else, certainly not the stallion, and he would be laughed into the loony bin if he tried to explain what really had happened.

His eyes fluttered and closed.

There was a sour taste in his mouth.

Then his hands raised in fists high over his head and he slammed them down on his legs, on the armrests, against his forehead and staggered to the hearth where he kicked at the bricks.

They were doing it again.

Jesus Christ, now even the police were trying to take away something that belonged to him. He whirled, his hands grasping for something to throw, found nothing, and jammed into his pockets instead. Stiff-legged, he stalked across the room, heading for the stairs as he tried to decide if it was worth crying over or not. He certainly felt like it, and stabbed the back of his hand against his eyes while he cautioned that he was feeling sorry for himself again. Nobody was going to take anything away from anybody. Verona sure wasn't, because he had nothing but a stupid suspicion that something smelled wrong about the death of a killer. And Don wasn't stupid—he hadn't been so blinded by the attention that he hadn't noticed how relieved everyone was that Falwick was dead. They wouldn't want to resurrect him, not even his memory, just because a detective didn't like being upstaged.

The telephone rang as he hit the first step.

He stared at it, wondering if it was a reporter, or someone for his parents. It didn't occur to him until it rang a fourth time that it might be for him.

It was.

It was Tracey.

"Are you okay?" was the first thing she said after he'd said hello.

"Sure." He sat crosslegged on the floor, facing the kitchen door. "Why?"

"You sound terrible."

"Thanks, I needed that." A voice in the background made him frown. "Is that Jeff?" he asked flatly. "Is Jeff at your house?"

"No," she said. "I'm here. At his place, I mean."

"Oh."

"Oh," she echoed in quite a different tone. "Why . . . why, Donald Boyd, are you jealous?"

The frown became a squint. "Who, me?"

She laughed. "My god, I don't believe it."

He didn't speak. He supposed she was right, and the way she laughed hinted that perhaps he had nothing to be jealous about; but that still didn't explain why she was over there and not over here. When he asked her, there was a pause and he squinted again, at the door.

Then he blinked slowly. Through the dark in the kitchen he thought he saw faint pinpricks of green light.

Tracey said something. He blinked again and asked her to repeat it.

"Someone was after me," she said at last.

"What?" He sat up, nearly pulling the cord straight.

"If you want to know the truth, Vet, I was on my way over to your house, when someone started to chase me. I don't who it was, but he scared the hell out of me, and Jeff's was the first place I came to."

Through the panes in the door—a faint glow of white.

"Who was it?" he demanded, hoping he sounded as concerned as he felt as he slowly moved to his knees and stared down the hall.

White light, shifting like fog.

"I told you, I don't know. Jeff went out to look around, but he didn't see anyone." She paused. "I don't know. Maybe it was my imagination."

"Probably." Oh, my god, he thought. "Who else is out there but Pratt, y'know?"

Her laugh this time was a bit forced. "I suppose. He's really pissed at you, you know."

"So I heard."

A muffled *thump* on the door.

"Really?"

"Sure." His voice sounded as if he were speaking from the moon; he was amazed she hadn't noticed. "Chris told me when she came to the hospital."

"Oh?"

Now it was his turn, and he wondered what he had done that rewarded him with two girls at the same time.

Then her voice softened, and he had to strain to hear her say, "I'm proud of you, Don. I wanted to tell you, but I couldn't get the chance at the park."

"Yeah, well . . ."

Another *thump*, and in the white glow two green slanted eyes.

"I'd still like to come over, if I can."

"What?" He was on his feet, teeth worrying his lower lip. "I'm sorry, Trace, what did you say."

"Don, I want to come over. I . . . I need you."

White light green eyes

"I'd like that too," he stammered. "But it'll have to wait, okay? The dragons just came home. I'm supposed to be resting."

"What? Are you all right?"

"I told you I was. I'm just . . ." He thought about it then, the chance to talk to someone about what he had seen, what he was believing, what he was hoping wasn't the slipping of his mind.

The door trembled, and he closed his eyes and silently begged Tracey to forgive him.

"Look," he said, "can I see you in school tomorrow?"

"Sure. Lunch?"

"Okay."

"Jeff wants to know if you're going to the game."

Off, he thought then; get the hell off the phone!

"I don't know. I guess so. It depends on my mother, I think. I have to—" He saw the light fading, the green disappear. "Shit, here they come. I gotta go."

"Lunch," she said, and he slammed down the receiver before she could say good-bye, and raced into the kitchen.

He wanted to throw open the door, to step out boldly, but he hesitated, hands rubbing his legs, his teeth still at his lip. To go out there, now, would mean he really was crazy; to look into an empty yard would mean . . .

His eyes shut. His hands clenched. His breath came in shallow gulps.

And he opened the door.

"Oh Jesus," he whispered. "Oh . . . Jesus."

It stood back under the maple tree, mottled by shadow, outlined now and again by the distant flare of lightning. But he couldn't see the whole of it, couldn't see it in detail—it was blacker than the night around it, and only portions of its skin gleamed and rippled when it moved.

He pressed a hand to his head as if checking for a fever, then stepped down off the stoop.

The horse bobbed its head, green eyes watching.

He could barely breathe; the air was too still, and his legs felt ready to collapse as he moved across the grass.

Green eyes. Watching.

He wanted to smile then, or to scream, but he only held out his hand, palm up, as he walked, hoping the stallion wouldn't smell his fear, would know instead his wonder at the size of it, the breadth of it, the way it turned its head and looked at him with a single flaring eye.

"I—"

It backed away, snorting, and sending plumes of grey about its head.

"It's me," he said softly. "It's me, fella, it's me."

The horse shifted, and there was greenfire curling around the maple's trunk, greenfire that crackled and scorched a black ribbon in the bark.

Don stopped, swallowed, reached his hand out again and

took a single step forward. He was less than five feet from its
nose, and he wanted desperately to feel the velvet, feel the
flesh and the bone. But when he moved another foot, it
tossed its head and in its throat started a low sustained
rumbling.

"All right," he said calmly. "All right, take it easy."

Please, God, he thought; please, God, am I crazy?

The horse watched him carefully, greysmoke and greenfire
for almost a full minute, then lowered its great head and
pushed at Don's arm, pushed him back and followed until
Don could reach up and stroke the silk of its mane, the black
satin of its neck. Real flesh warm and cold at the same time;
muscles jumping, a foreleg shifting, and he wasn't ashamed
when he felt the tears building, felt them spilling, heard them
splashing though he knew it couldn't be.

He hadn't killed the Howler; this creature had, this beast
that was his friend.

"Why?" he whispered then. "Why are they like that?"

The horse retreated again, and left him standing alone.

He sniffed, and wiped his eyes with a sleeve that felt like
coarse burlap on his skin.

"They won't stop, y'know? They keep coming at me, they
won't leave me alone. I'm not Sam, I'm not special. I'm just
me, and they won't . . ." He stopped, bowed his head,
wiped his eyes again. "I just wish I knew what I'm doing
wrong, you know? If they'd only tell me what I'm doing
wrong, maybe the Rules wouldn't change so much, maybe I'd
know then what was going on."

He felt it then, out there in the cold—the stallion was
listening—every word he said, every tear he shed was marked
by the emerald eyes and the pricking of its ears.

He wanted to ask why they wouldn't even let him be a
hero, just this once; he wanted to ask why he couldn't cry,
why he couldn't get mad, why the Rules said he had to be
like stone or wood; and he wanted to ask why they couldn't

make up their minds to let him be a kid, or a man. But he didn't, because he knew that the horse already understood, and that he was right—it was there, really there, and it was going to protect him.

He grinned through his tears.

The stallion snorted and buried them in grey smoke, snorted again, and blew the smoke away.

"It's true," he said in the midst of a loud sigh. "It's true, you're my friend." He laughed once, softly. "Oh god, it's really true!"

He stretched out a hand to stroke its muzzle, to seal the bargain, and froze when the animal began its throated rumbling. It backed away. He started to follow, and nearly bolted for the house when it reared under the tree, snapping branches, casting dead leaves, greenfire and greeneyes and slashing hooves at the air.

Headlights flared around the corner of the house.

Oh shit, he thought; damnit, they're home.

The horse lowered its head, eyes dark now, its tail slapping its legs.

"All right," he said nervously. "All right, I gotta go now."

The horse didn't move.

He backed toward the kitchen door, wanting to laugh, wanting to shout, wanting to race around to the driveway and drag his father back, to show him, to *show* him what his son could do.

With one hand on the doorknob he looked over his shoulder, couldn't find his friend until he found the green eyes. "Please," he said. "Please." And ran inside, skidding to a halt in the foyer just as he heard a key rattle in the lock and could hear his parents on the porch, talking loudly, not quite arguing. He turned toward the stairs to make it seem as if he were just going up, when his mother stormed in, slamming the door back against the wall as she charged past him toward the kitchen. His father was right behind her, slower, his jacket over one shoulder and his face pale.

"What are you doing up?" he snapped, and didn't wait for an answer. He jabbed a commanding finger toward the stairwell and followed his wife.

I'm fine, Don thought as he started up the stairs; thanks for asking, I'm fine.

"I will not have it!" Joyce said loudly, and he stopped on the landing.

"Keep your voice down! The boy'll hear."

A laugh, short and bitter. "Hear what? I'm not an animal and I'm not stuffed. What makes you think he'll hear me?"

"Jesus, you're crazy, you know that?"

She laughed again, and Don squatted, one hand on the banister in case he had to move fast.

Cupboard doors slammed, cups cracked into saucers, the faucet ran so long she could have filled the bathtub. When the water was shut off, his father was laughing.

"Honest to Christ, you're something else, you know that? You really are something else."

"Well, really," Joyce said. "All they did was ask you to stand up and take a bow, and you were waving your arms like a goddamned politician! Christ, I thought you were going to kiss babies next."

"Wouldn't have been a bad idea."

A chair scraped; another was slammed down on the floor.

"All right," Norman said wearily. "All right, I'm sorry."

"Sorry is too late. You and the boy have been upstaging and hassling me since this thing began, and I've had it! I worked my ass off so you'd look good, and this is the thanks I get."

"Me?" A muffled sound—Norman either laughing into a hand or trying not to choke. "God, the next thing is you'll be accusing me of sending Don out there myself to kill that crazy bastard."

"I wouldn't put it past you."

The silence was cold, and Don wrapped his free arm over his chest.

"That was a shitty thing to say, Joyce."

The silence again.

"I know," she said at last, but without apology in her voice. "I . . ." She began to cry and Norman cursed, and the water began running again.

Don didn't wait to hear any more. He climbed slowly up the rest of the stairs, shuffled down the hall, and pushed open his bedroom door. He yanked the towel off the lampshade and dropped it on his desk. His shoes were kicked under the bed, shirt dropped onto the floor. For a moment he stood at the window, looking down at the tree. There was nothing there, the horse was gone, but he no longer questioned the state of his mind.

When he finally dropped onto the mattress, he deliberately fell back so his head would hit the wall. Maybe they'll hear it, he thought; maybe they'll think I've had a relapse or something, and they'll come running up and see what's wrong.

Or, he thought, they'll call the papers first, and then come up to see if I'm dead.

And maybe, he thought with a cold, mirthless grin, I'll take them both outside and show them my new pet.

He lay there for nearly an hour before he blinked and saw his father standing in the doorway.

"You okay, son?"

"Sure. Just thinking."

"You'd better turn out the light. School isn't going to be exactly normal for you tomorrow."

He nodded and swung his feet over the side. "Dad?"

Norman stiffened, and raised his eyebrows.

"Do you think—"

A sudden, faint shattering of glass stopped him, had him

on his feet and beside his father in the hallway. Joyce came out of their bedroom, a robe wrapped loosely around her.

"What?" she said nervously.

Another shattering, and the sound of heavy blows on something metal.

"Damn, the car!" Norman said, and ran for the stairs, Don just behind though his mother called to him to stay where he was. The front door was locked, and Norman fumbled with the bolt before flinging it open and switching on the porch light. Don crowded out past him, not feeling the snap of cold air on his bare chest. The bulb was directly over his head, and he shaded his eyes, scanning the lawn before looking to the driveway.

"Oh, god," he whispered.

Norman shoved him aside and leapt over the stairs, hit the walk at a run, and didn't stop until he came up against the station wagon's front fender. The windshield was smashed, there was a dent in the hood, and lying on the blacktop just under the bumper was Don's bike—the handlebars twisted out of place, the front wheel broken, half of its spokes wavering like antennae where they'd been snapped from their places along the rim.

Norman whirled and raced around the side of the house, but Don only stumbled to the driveway and knelt beside the bike, one hand reaching out to touch it, withdraw, touch it again and follow the lines of its destruction. When he shifted and leaned over to stare at the back wheel the glint of metal made him pause, made him reach out and pull a red leather key case wedged beneath the battered frame.

"Don?" his mother called from the doorway. "Are you all right?"

"Fine," he said dully, slipped the case into his pocket, and heard her gasp when she saw the damage.

"Oh Jesus, my god, look at that," she said just as Norman appeared around the far side of the house, panting heavily, one palm massaging hard at his side. She held out a trembling hand, and he took it, pulled her to him and glared at the empty street. "Who?" she asked.

"How the hell should I know?" he said. "Damn, that's going to cost a fortune to fix."

Joyce took a step to one side, the glass crunched under her slipper. "I'll get a broom," she said. "We can't have that stuff lying around. It's dangerous. Someone'll get hurt."

"Sure."

"Look, you'd better call the police. Don? Get the broom from the garage, will you? Help me here."

Don looked over his shoulder. Neither of them were looking at him—Norman was staring at the depression in the hood and absently rubbing his wife's back; Joyce was trying to smooth the hair from her eyes. And when she finally saw him looking, she pointed to the garage, then turned Norman around and pushed him gently toward the house.

Don rose, dusted off his jeans, and reached down to grab the handlebars, to drag the bike away.

"Leave it," Joyce said. "There might be fingerprints or something."

He straightened and fetched the broom, handed it to her and returned inside, where he listened to his father explaining to the police what had happened. When he rang off, he told Don to put on a shirt before the cops arrived. You never know, he said. There might still be some reporters hanging around, and when they got wind of this, it would be circus time again.

"Damn," he said as he headed out the door. "With my luck, it'll probably rain tomorrow."

The police came and went in less than an hour. They made a decent show of searching the yard, but they found nothing, not a clue, and explained to the Boyds that in cases like this there was nothing much they'd be able to do if no one saw anything or offered information. No one came out to watch because the patrol car had arrived without its lights spinning; no one overheard the conversations because Joyce kept them speaking low, or whispering. And they asked Don nothing at all when Norman told them the boy was with him, inside, when the incident occurred.

After they left, Don dragged the bicycle into a corner of the garage and stared out at the street, at his father using a small brush to get the glass from the front seat. Joyce was inside, making coffee.

A press of a button and the garage door lowered. Norman looked up and gave his son a rueful smile. "You win some, you lose some, right?" he said. "Sorry about the bike."

"Yeah."

Don shivered at a gust of wind and turned to go inside, and stopped when he saw something white fluttering in the shrubs that fronted the house and ended at the drive. He leaned close, closer, and picked a feather from a branch.

"Dad?"

Norman grunted.

He found another one at the bush's side, two more on the ground. "Hey, Dad?"

"In a minute, okay? I don't want to slice my thumb off on this stuff."

He parted the branches, and his mouth opened in a silent gasp.

There, on the ground under the bush was the body of a bird, its neck twisted around, its eyes closed, its feathers covered with blood.

"Dad, look!"

Norman pushed him aside with a hip and knelt down, gagged when he saw the mutilation, and poked at it with his toe.

"Jesus," he said. "It's a goddamned duck."

FIFTEEN

Beautiful, thought Tar as he watched Mr. Boyd shovel the remains of the dead bird and dump them with his face averted into a plastic garbage bag. Don was in the driveway, hands in his pockets and staring out at the street. For a moment Tar thought the Duck had seen him, but no alarm was given. He heard the rattle of a garbage can lid being slammed into place, then the principal came out of the garage and put his arm around the Duck's shoulders. They went into the house like that, the door slammed, and the porch light went out.

"Excellent," Tar whispered, crouched low and bouncing on the balls of his feet. "Beautiful."

He had run behind the empty tool shed in old man Delfield's backyard when the cops finally came around, wedging himself between a stack of empty orange crates and the rear wall. They weren't looking very hard, missed him, and after he was sure they weren't coming back, he snuck around the side of the house and dropped into the corner of the front yard, protected by the hedges and a twisted oak at the curb. From there he had been able to watch everything, sorry only that he couldn't hear what the two bastards were saying.

He waited another five minutes, licking his lips and grinning, before bulling through the hedge into the adjoining driveway. He walked slowly in case someone was watching, the baseball bat held tight against his leg, his football jacket turned inside out. As soon as he reached the corner, he slipped the bat into the storm drain and reversed the coat, then broke into a high-stepping run, mouth open in a silent laugh. He couldn't wait to get home and call Brian, couldn't wait to let the asshole know that Tar Boston was not just a stupid jock.

School Street was empty, and the pavement sounded like thin ice beneath his sneakers. By the time he reached the next corner he could feel the cut of the night air against his cheeks and in his lungs, and he sniffed to keep his nose from running. Now he wished he had the car, the ten-year-old junkpile his old man had bought for him on his last birthday. It barely ran, when it bothered to run at all, but the heater still worked and he could use it now.

Or the relative luxury of Pratt's automobile.

He slowed and scowled. Stupid jock—that's what Pratt had called him at practice today—stupid jock, get the fuck outta my way before I run you down. There was a bug up his ass, that's for sure, because he hardly said two words to him and Fleet the whole time, even when they were doing weights after the coach had left. Like he was mad or something, and Tar hadn't been able to get him to tell him what was the matter.

Fleet was almost as bad, but different. That jerk acted like he was running from the cops or something, the way he kept looking around on the way home. Tar had gotten so damned nervous he almost sideswiped a bus.

But Fleet wouldn't say anything either.

And it wasn't until Tar was home and eating supper that he had the idea that would even the score between himself and the Duck for accusing him and Pratt of dumping that shit on

Hedley's porch. A truly fantastic idea. A blow at the fucking principal and at the Duck at the same time. Stunning. And it would shut Pratt up about how Tar must've blown it when the Duck didn't get the blame the way it was planned. The idea for the dead bird came as he passed a butcher shop on the way home and saw a goose in the window. From there it was a simple matter of stopping at a friend's house, a friend who had two little brothers who kept four ducks in a pen in the backyard. He didn't even have to look at the bird; he'd clobbered it with a stick while it struggled in the burlap bag he'd dropped over its head; then he'd wrung its neck. Not a speck of blood on him. Even when he dropped it into the bushes he didn't look. Didn't have to. Didn't even care if the Boyds found it that night or the next morning.

He picked up the pace, racing for the goal line with Pratt the jerk blocking in front of him.

The hard part was getting the car. He knew he would have time for only a few good blows before somebody heard him, and after he'd taken care of the bike, he took them standing on the hood. He pretended the windshield was Boyd's face, that the hood was the Duck's chest, and it had been beautiful! And a shame that Brian couldn't be there. But he was acting like an asshole, like the minute after the game the pros were going to carry him away to the Super Bowl on their goddamned shoulders, for Christ's sake.

He rounded another corner and headed for home, taking in air in deep, satisfying gulps. It was going to be like this tomorrow night. He was going to take North apart, and those fuckers wouldn't know what hit them. It was going to be excellent, and Brian was going to have to show him respect. Absolutely.

Something moved behind him.

He turned and walked backward a few steps, seeing nothing but the empty sidewalk, the porch lights hazed in the crisp air, the cars at the curb silent and black. He turned again and groaned when he saw a battered pickup in the driveway, blocking his own car—his old man was home early from the factory tonight. That meant he was going to have to put up with the back-slapping and the jabbing and the reminders of how the old fart had been a star in his day, the best quarterback in the state and don't you forget it, boy, when I give you the best goddamned advice you ever had in your life. The trouble was, it's been twenty years since they played the way his old man did, and the jerk didn't know it. He didn't know why his mother put up with it, and him, all these years. He sure as hell wasn't going to. As soon as he had that diploma in hand, he was gone. Out of that house and out of this town and out of this whole goddamned state if he could.

Something moved.

Shit, he thought, angry at the way his good mood could be shattered by the simple thought of his father. Shit!

He looked over his shoulder, his expression daring anyone to say something, to do something, even to breathe wrong tonight. And he walked past his house with his head down and averted, spitting at the pickup, zipping up his jacket and jamming his hands into his pockets. Fuck it, he would walk over to Brian's instead of calling. The story would be better anyway, with him doing the telling in person.

Something . . .

He stopped at the boulevard, looked up and down the avenue, and then whirled around, fists at the ready.

There was nothing there.

But something was moving.

"Yo!" he said loudly.

A porch light blinked out, and he could see his breath feathering out of his mouth.

With his head tilted slightly to one side, he stepped off the curb and looked curiously down the block, under the trees that reached over the blacktop and created a tunnel almost solidly black. He tried to bring to mind a picture of Don's stricken face when he found the dead bird, when he discovered the bike, because suddenly and inexplicably anything would be better than seeing into that dark. But all he could see was the broken and faded white line stretching into the night, and something in the middle moving toward him without a sound.

"Yo, stupid!" he called.

Only one streetlamp worked, and his gaze kept moving toward its light where it caught the front end of a car and the lip of a driveway.

"Asshole," he muttered, and turned away, but didn't move. He was suddenly indecisive. Beacher's was already closed, and the idea of going to Brian's didn't seem as much fun as he'd thought. But he couldn't go home. Not yet. Not until his old man had had his beers and was asleep on the couch and his mother had already finished the dishes. Then he'd be able to kiss her goodnight and go to bed, get some sleep. Tomorrow, as the coach kept reminding them, was the Big Day, as if they didn't know it, and he supposed he might as well get all the rest he could.

Tomorrow, he was going to be a hero, and the hell with Brian Pratt.

Then he heard something move and he whirled again, and took a deep breath, holding it until John Delfield's fat dachshund waddled into the light.

Don stood in the shower, oblivious to the hot water turning his skin pink. Slowly he pulled the plastic curtain aside and stared again at the jeans lying beside the wicker laundry basket. A bit of red leather poked out from one pocket. His hand released the curtain and it rattled closed, and the steam rose to cover his face while he tried to understand what was going on. He knew who the keys belonged to. He knew what he should have done the second he had found them. Yet he'd put them in his pocket and had said nothing, hadn't heard a word his father had said about whoever had committed that atrocity, hadn't felt a thing except a slow roll of nausea he only just managed to keep down.

Norman had suggested they not mention it to his mother; she was upset enough about the car, and they needn't bother her with this. He hinted about Brian, about Tar, even about Fleet, and there was something in his voice that made Don stare at him for a second—a realization that Norman didn't like kids.

It wasn't just the troublemakers, the snobs, the ones with influential parents who made being a principal a vicious sort of hell—it was kids, period. And he remembered his father saying once that he wished all children could be born adults, without the parents having to do anything but show them the front door. Don had thought it a joke then; now he knew, perhaps more than Norman did, that it wasn't a joke at all.

That, more than anything, had stopped him from fixing the blame. His father, in the mood he was in now, would have gone over to the Bostons and had Tar arrested—after he had slammed him a few times into a wall.

Because of the car; *you win some, you lose some* was the only epitaph for the bike.

He backed out of the spray and wiped the water from his face, sat on the cool edge of the tub with his hands dangling between his knees. Tracey was right; but it wasn't just Brian who was jealous, it was Tar as well. He doubted that Pratt had put his friend up to it tonight, because it wasn't Brian's style. But he guessed that Brian had said something today to give Tar the idea that something had to be done to put Don in his place, retaliation for being called into his father's office.

He moved the curtain again and looked at the key case, and he smiled. There was power of some kind in that bit of cheap dime store leather. He knew it, and now all he had to do was figure out how to use it.

The simplest thing would be to threaten to show it to his father. And if that didn't work, he could bring it to the police. Tar would protest, of course, and claim that he'd lost it or something, but there'd be enough hassle, enough problems, that—

"He'll beat the shit out of you."

The words were soft in the room's steamy fog, but harsh enough to make him sigh.

Someone rapped on the door, and he turned off the shower, grabbed a towel and wrapped it around his waist. His mother called, and he yelled back, telling her he'd be only a few minutes more. And when he was dry, he held the jeans to his waist and slipped into the hall. A light was still on in his parents' room. The downstairs was dark. Shivering at the shock of cool air on his skin, he hurried into his own room and closed the door behind him, dropped the jeans where he stood and dropped onto the bed.

A few minutes later he stirred, stood, and padded to the window.

The backyard was empty.

All right, he thought to his friend in the dark, now that I know you're there, what do we do next?

"Stupid mutt," Tar said. He approached the dog with one hand out and waving. The fat old thing had gotten out again, probably through the flap Delfield had put in the back door of his house. Sometimes the old man forgot to latch it at night, and the dog would spend hours roaming the neighborhood, getting at garbage cans, digging up flower beds, until someone spotted it and brought it back. Tar had always ignored it before. The last time, however, he'd been pissed on beer and grabbed it up and took it back himself before he knew what he was doing. Delfield had given him ten bucks for the trouble. Crazy. Just like the dog.

But hell, he thought as he bent into a crouch, ten bucks is ten bucks.

"C'mon, stupid," he said in a pleasant voice. "C'mon to Tar or I'll cut your head off."

The dachshund recognized his voice and stopped in the middle of the streetlamp's fall, its rat's tail wagging furiously, its tongue lolling from the side of its mouth.

"C'mon, baby, come to Tar."

The dog sat on its haunches.

"Ah, Jesus."

He straightened and took a step forward, and stopped when he saw a shadow on the other side of the light.

The dog yipped once and jumped to its feet, its head down now, its tail snaking contritely between its legs.

Tar squinted and moved to his right toward the middle of the road, snapping his fingers in an effort to bring the dog to him while he tried to make out who was standing there in the road.

The wind rose.

A trailer truck coughed and thundered down the boulevard behind him.

Then a hand swooped into the light and snatched up the dog, and John Delfield followed, shaking the animal lightly before hugging it to his side.

"Foolish beast," he said with a slight German accent, and smiled at Tar. "You try to catch him for me?"

Tar nodded, wondering what in hell was wrong with his heart that it wouldn't stop pounding. Hell, it was only old man Delfield and who the hell was scared of him?

The dachshund squirmed in the man's grasp, but Delfield managed to reach into a hip pocket and pull out his wallet, finger out a bill. "Take it," he insisted when Tar protested with a wave. "You try. That's good as doing."

Tar accepted the money with a nod and a smile, and watched him waddle off around the corner. Crazy, he thought;

the two of them are goddamn crazy. Then he raked a hand through his hair and decided to drive over to Pratt's anyway. Walking now was out of the question. He reached for his keys, and couldn't find them.

"What the . . . ?"

He slapped at his pockets, turned them all out, then rolled his eyes skyward and slammed the heel of his hand against a temple. "Fuck. Jesus . . . fuck!"

They must have fallen out at Boyd's while he was doing the station wagon. Christ, all he needed now was for someone to pick them up and his ass was grass. Damn, he had to go back and find those stupid keys. He started for the curb, and stopped again.

Down at the end of the block, barely lit by the streetlamps on School Street, something was standing. And watching.

Delfield, he thought; the stupid dog must've gotten away again and the old man was out prowling.

It moved, then, out of the light, into the dark, and Tar heard the distinct sound of something breathing. Something large, and breathing heavily.

He half-turned toward the boulevard, and swiveled his head back slowly.

He was mistaken; it wasn't Delfield and it wasn't his imagination.

It was there, and it was darker than the shadows, moving slowly toward him straight down the white line. He could hear it breathing, snorting once, and could hear the sound of something hard striking the blacktop, rhythmically, steadily, and unless he was as crazy as Delfield, it sounded just like a horse.

He blinked and took a side-step toward the avenue.

He shuddered, unable to shake the feeling that whatever it was, it was coming for him, not toward him. That was stupid. It was all stupid. There were no horses in Ashford, and it was only Delfield for god's sake looking for his stupid fat dog.

Closer to the light, and he saw a glint of dark green hovering in the air; two of them now, and a long second passed before he realized they were eyes. Green eyes. Large, and slanted, and staring right at him.

The streetlight didn't reach to the middle of the blacktop, but when it passed the white on the ground, Tar could see a massive black flank, and the side of a massive head. One green eye flaring. A flash of long white teeth.

And steam, maybe smoke, drifting from its nostrils.

"Shit," he said, and started to trot away. He didn't know what it was, but he wasn't going to hang around long enough to find out. He'd go somewhere else. Maybe Brian would know.

The sound picked up speed, and when he reached the middle of the empty boulevard, he looked over his shoulder and saw it.

Running, forelegs high, hooves casting greenfire and greeneyes dark with hate.

The hope it might have been some sort of joke, Don getting back at him for the dead bird and the bike, faded to an ember. And something inside told him he was dying.

Running, galloping, and seemingly moving in slow motion.

He broke into a panicked sprint, slanting across the avenue toward the inlands in the center, leaping the curb and ducking around the trees, the bushes, toward the center of town. Sooner or later he'd see a car, the cops, and everything would be all right.

Don't look; and he did.

It was pacing him ten yards behind, fully visible now and terrifyingly huge. Green eyes staring, greenfire snapping, the steam from its nostrils raising a cloud that it moved through, an ebony ghost flying through the boiling fog.

Tar whimpered and ran harder, leaping over a fallen branch,

plowing through a bush he couldn't swerve around in time. He stumbled and grabbed a tree trunk, spun around, and ran again.

Hooves on the blacktop, iron striking iron.

A U-turn break in the island surprised him, and he fell shouting to the street, the skin on his palms scraping onto the tarmac, one cheek slamming down and bringing tears to his eyes. He lay for several seconds gulping air, wondering where all the traffic was, the people, why couldn't anyone see what was going on? He swallowed and tasted blood; he pushed himself to his knees and staggered to his feet.

A snorting; he spun around, and it was standing right behind him.

Tar screamed for his father.

And the stallion reared in a cloud of greenfire and white.

The telephone rang, and Tracey hurried into the kitchen to grab it before it woke her mother or one of her nosey sisters. She hadn't been able to sleep, had come downstairs to do some studying, which she knew would make her tired sooner or later. A knee banged against a chair and she swore as she yanked the handset off the cradle, taking a moment before saying hello.

"Trace?"

"Don?" She fumbled for the chair and sat down in the dark.

"You awake?"

"Yeah, sure." She tried to see the wall clock in the dark, but there was only enough light from the front room to tell her it was close to midnight; how close she couldn't tell.

"No, you weren't. I woke you. I'm sorry."

"I wasn't asleep, Vet," she said almost angrily. "I was studying." She inhaled slowly and rubbed a knuckle across her eyes. "What's the matter, something wrong?"

"Why should anything be wrong?"

"Well, it's nearly twelve on a school night for one thing. And you're whispering for another."

"So are you."

"I don't want to get killed."

"Neither do I."

She pushed the chair closer to the doorway so she could see the front door. Her father was due back from his shift any minute now, and she didn't want him catching her on the phone. After wriggling back on the seat, she brought up her legs to sit Indian fashion, holding on to one ankle with her free hand. "Don, what's up? You want me to elope or something?"

He laughed, and she was glad to hear it; she hadn't heard much of that lately and it made her feel good. "C'mon, hero, what's the occasion?"

She listened without comment then as he told her about the car, and the dead bird mangled in his front yard. And when he told her about finding Boston's car keys under the bike's wheel, she groaned. "What a jerk," she said. "What a stupid jerk." When Don agreed, she asked what he was going to do.

"I don't know. I thought I was going to let him know I knew and maybe he'd get off my case. But I figure he'd deny it, then rearrange my face for the parade."

"God, what a mess."

He said nothing, and her eyes narrowed. This wasn't it, she thought; this isn't why he's calling.

"Tracey?"

"Still here, hero."

A pause. "I like 'Vet' better."

She frowned now. "Sure. Okay."

"Trace, this may sound dumb, but have you ever made a wish?"

Have I ever, she thought, and what's wrong with you, Don?

"Sure I have," she said. "Every year on my birthday I blow my lungs out for a zillion bucks and a mansion in Beverly Hills. Doesn't everybody?"

"You ever wish on a star?"

"What is this? Hey, are you trying to get me to do a term paper for you or something? Is that what this is? Are you taking a survey?"

"Tracey, please."

She heard it then, and she didn't believe it. Because they were both whispering, it had been difficult to tell, but the moment she recognized it, she knew it was true—Don was afraid of something, and it wasn't Tar Boston.

"Okay," she said slowly. "Yeah, I do now and then." She laughed. "Silly, isn't it?"

"Do they ever come true? Your wishes, I mean."

"Don . . . no. I mean, I don't think they do. Not like they were magic, anyway. You wish for something hard enough and it comes true? No. You work at it and make the wishes come true yourself, if you know what I mean."

"God."

"Hey, Vet, would you please tell me what this is all about?"

"Tracey—"

A key rattled in the front door, and Tracey quickly told Don her father was home, she'd see him tomorrow in school. She hung up and had the chair back in place just as her father walked in the door. When he demanded to know why she was up so late, she pointed to her books in the living room and explained that she hadn't been able to sleep and, she added when she saw the expression on his face, what was wrong, was he hurt?

"No," he said wearily. "A hit-and-run just before I left."

"Oh, god, no." A closer look, then, and she bit down on her lower lip. "It was somebody I know, wasn't it?"

He shrugged. "I don't know."

"Father."

He made his way toward the kitchen, but she stopped him with a hand on his arm.

"Father?"

"Please, child, go to bed."

"What?" she insisted.

"It was as if someone had run him down, then kept backing over him. Again and again. He's so mangled we don't know who he is yet."

SIXTEEN

*T*he day wasn't as bad as he feared it would be. With all classes cut by twenty minutes, the lessons were either uselessly short or not given at all. He spent then as much time as he could looking for Tracey, but the only time he saw her, martial and uncomfortable in her red-and-black band uniform, she was with a group of her girlfriends. When she spotted him, she mouthed an incomprehensible message to which he shrugged his ignorance and moved on before the late bell rang.

Brian stayed away, once deliberately ducking into the wrong classroom just to avoid him. Don saw it and grinned, thinking some good might come of this medal stuff after all.

But study hall was strange. He sat in his usual place and flipped through his zoology textbook, trying to discover what the stallion had in common with the real world. After five minutes, however, he felt someone watching him. By then he had almost grown used to it—the students in the hall inspecting him slyly, some outright staring, some of them hesitant as if they wanted to reach out and squeeze his muscles or take off his shirt, anything to discover the secret of the strength that had pummeled the Howler into the ground.

But this was different. From the others he could feel envy and disbelief and a fair dose of new respect; from this there was something he couldn't name at all.

He looked up and around. The rest were either reading or talking softly among themselves. None of the football team were there; they were down in the gym getting ready for the rally. Then his gaze took in the front of the room.

It was Mr. Hedley. He was sitting behind the desk with his fingers folded under his chin, and he was staring at him. Boldly. Without apology.

Don looked down quickly and turned a page, another, and glanced up without raising his head.

Hedley was still watching, and suddenly Don felt as if he were squeezed into one of the teacher's test tubes, forever floating in a solution, forever exposed for inspection before being dumped down the drain.

He swallowed, flipped back a few pages, flipped them forward, and forced himself to read paragraphs at random, none of the words filtering through, none of the illustrations registering. And when he looked up a third time and saw the man still watching, the skin across the back of his shoulders began to tighten and he found it increasingly difficult to breathe.

He knows, Don thought, and blinked the idea.

No. Nobody knows. He can't know.

He squirmed and turned to look out the high windows at the clouds massing on the horizon, seeming blacker and higher because of the intense clarity of the near sky still untouched by the coming storm. It made the roofs of the houses below the stadium more sharp-edged and less dingy, made the gridiron more brilliant, and added vibrancy to the colors of everything he saw. It was odd, that light, as if it were artificial; he focused on the stadium's rear wall and the first houses behind it, thinking they could have been razor-cut from stone and polished with diamonds. In a way it was beautiful; and in a way it was so unreal, it was almost frightening.

Hedley's voice was quiet: "Mr. Boyd, you have nothing to do?"

No one laughed.

Don half-lifted his book and looked down at the page.

"One should never waste time, Mr. Boyd, even the few minutes we have here. In some countries, in the old days, that was a criminal offense. Just as wasting someone else's time is just as criminal."

Don didn't understand, but he was positive the man was trying to send him a message.

He knows.

he can't know

And the bell rang.

He filed out behind the others, feeling Hedley watching him all the way to the door. He wanted to turn and demand to know the reason, and refused to find the courage. Whatever the man's problem was, it couldn't have anything to do with what happened. Maybe he was pissed because he still thought Don had vandalized his house.

He hurried for the stairwell and headed down for gym, was reaching for the door when someone grabbed his arm and yanked him out of the crowd into the landing's corner.

"Hey, what . . ."

It was Chris. She was in her cheerleader's outfit, the short Indian-style skirt exposing her long legs, the white sweater with the school name exposing even more because it was so snug. Her hair was in two braids that dangled over her breasts, and she wore a beaded headband she kept pushing up with a thumb.

"Hey," she said quietly, her eyes on the students who passed through the door.

"Hey," he said, and waited.

She smiled so beautifully he had to smile back, and had to resist the urge to put a hand to her cheek.

"You seen Tar?"

He shook his head.

"The jackass didn't come in yet, can you believe it?" She pulled at the headband, adjusting it with a grimace. "He wants to make some kind of grand entrance, I bet."

"I don't know," he said. "That's not him, y'know?"

She shrugged; she didn't give a shit whether it was him or not. "It's still dumb. If he does do it, Brian's gonna take off his head." A quick laugh he could barely hear, and she leaned closer. "Are you okay? I mean, I was gonna call or come over, but I figured . . . you know."

"I'm okay, yeah. Thanks for asking."

"Well, listen, I gotta get up to the library before the Dragon chews me up for being late stacking her precious books, but listen . . ." She looked at him then, took his arm and maneuvered him unprotesting until his back was flat against the wall and hers was to the staircase. "So listen, are you going to the game?"

"Sure, I guess so."

He could see a few faces turn toward him, look away—none of them was Brian's.

"What about after?"

Tracey, he thought. "I don't know. Beacher's, I guess. I hadn't thought about it. I suppose it depends on whether we win or not."

Before he could stop her, she took his hand and pressed it briefly to her breast, leaned into it and away, and released him with a smile.

"After," she whispered. "Win or lose." And she was gone.

His face burned, his hand burned, but he didn't dare touch one to the other for fear of losing the sensation that lingered on his palm. He wondered if anyone had seen; it had happened so fast he wasn't sure now it had happened at all. He pushed through the door with his eyes down, and when no one said anything, he broke into a slow trot and veered into the gym.

The classes were sitting by the walls from which wrestling and gymnastic pads were hanging. The teachers were in the middle of the basketball court, leaning over their roll books, checking the room and every so often barking out a name to which a "yo!" or a "here" was shouted back. Don stood by the double doors, not knowing where to go, until someone spotted him and called out his name. He waved blindly and lowered himself into a crouch, trying not to hear the silence that washed over the gym, not to feel the eyes that examined him frankly. He studied the polished floor between his shoes. He sat on his books and studied the floor again, until a pair of cleated black shoes stepped in.

He looked up; it was Brian Pratt in his football pants and shoulder pads. Pratt hunkered down, stared at him, and shook his head. "I don't get it."

Don lips moved into a smile he didn't feel. "Get what?"

"How you did it?"

"Just leave it, all right?"

Pratt shook his head again. "My old man was right, you know," he said. "It's always the assholes of the world who step in it and come out smelling like roses."

Don's forearms were resting on his knees, his hands between them clasped now and white-knuckled. "Leave it, huh?"

"Oh, my. Hey, you gonna get tough with me now, Duck?"

He looked up, expressionless. "Just get off it, all right?"

Pratt jabbed a stiff finger into his shin. "Just don't get tough with me, Duck, you hear? Don't you believe for a minute I'm like that farting old man." He stood without effort. "And stay away from Chrissy or I'll fuck you over so bad your own mother won't recognize you."

He walked away, arrogant, cleats smacking on the hardwood floor until one of the teachers ordered him off to the side. Pratt nodded and did as he was told, and left by the far door without once looking back.

The eyes were on him again; he could feel them, and he prayed for the bell to ring so he could go back to his locker, get his jacket and books, and head for the stadium and the day-ending pep rally. He prayed for Brian's head to fall off as soon as he walked onto the field. He prayed for a tornado to rip through the school and carry him away, to a place he never heard of and whose people never heard of him.

When the bell did ring, he was the first out the door, the first to the stairs, and had just started working his combination when the word spread about Tar Boston.

The band marched raggedly onto the field, a fanfare of hard-edged drums leading the way—the Ashford Braves on the warpath. It formed an A across the fifty-yard line and played the school song, the "Star-Spangled Banner," and two marches. The students cheered, whistled, and clapped as the band marched off again and took its place in the first four rows in the concrete seats' center. Ashford Day banners had been strung between the goalposts and hung from the top windows; a handful of workers adjusted the banks of lights that would illuminate the field that evening for the game; a portable platform was carried out to the field, microphones and chairs set up, and Don's father, the head cheerleaders, and the coach hurried into place. All very efficient and over in no time.

Don sat in the top row and did nothing but watch Tracey playing her flute and holding her music in one hand. Snippets of their conversation last night kept drifting back to him, and he was sure he had not mistaken the concern in her voice, or the caring. By the time his father began to speak, he had made up his mind to meet her after school and tell her everything.

Including the fact that he had probably murdered Tar.

It had to be. Even discounting exaggeration as rumors and fact danced around each other and merged, it was clear that the condition of Tar's body was the same as the Howler's. It was also clear that no hit-and-run driver would be stupid enough to return to the scene and race back and forth over a body he had just created, just for fun, or because he was crazy.

It was the stallion.

And he was frightened in a way he'd never been before. Not because of what had been done, but because he didn't feel the same as he had when Amanda had died at the Howler's hands. Then he was angered; now he was . . . glad.

And it made him sick.

A person was dead. A human being. Someone he knew. And he was glad Tar was dead because the stupid asshole couldn't torment him anymore, couldn't hang on Brian's every command, couldn't murder birds and smash bikes and pretend he was a king in a land without royalty. Dead. Smashed beyond recognition until the dental work had been run through whatever tests they do.

Now that I know you're here, what do we do next?

He needed to talk, and he needed to be alone, and he applauded absently as the coach was introduced, as the players were introduced and ran onto the field between two lines of cheerleaders waving their pompons and leaping into the air, as the band played marches and another speech was made, and reminders were given about the parade.

He applauded and heard nothing, saw nothing until he realized the others were filing out. Chattering excitedly, making plans for the night, for the next day. Ignoring him because he was a hero on Wednesday and time marches on, like the band marching swiftly to the end of the field to sloppy drumwork, out of step, finally falling apart and heading for the exits.

Quickly he made his way against the crowd to the bottom of the stands, vaulted the iron railing down to the track, and ran toward Tracey. He called out. She didn't hear him. He called again and dodged around a handful of team members who laughed when Brian in their midst made a loud quacking noise.

Don't mess with me, Brian, he said silently as he glowered back; don't mess with me, man, or I'll have you dead.

He stopped then and swallowed.

Oh Jesus. Oh God.

"Y'know, I'm beginning to think I'm a jinx."

He stepped back quickly, just able to avoid colliding with Tracey who was trying to juggle her music, disassemble her flute, and open its case at the same time. When he looked blankly at her, she gave him a sour grin and forced the sheets of narrow paper into his hands, put the instrument away and took the music back. Her cap was off and her hair was taken by the afternoon's breeze across her forehead, over her eyes. The uniform's tunic was unbuttoned at the top and he could see the hollow of her throat, the top of her chest.

"Sorry," he mumbled.

Her head tilted. "You looking for me, Vet?"

"Yes. I . . . do you need . . ." He bit down on his lower lip.

"You want to walk me home?"

"Please," he said, and she took his arm and led them to the open tunnel in the wall. Others hurried past, and the growling of engines in the street competed with shouts, with laughter, with a few of the band members blaring their trumpets and tubas, the whole sounding less like school just over than a game just ended. No one spoke to them and for that he was glad. He was too busy playing the blind man to Tracey's guide dog, trying desperately to force what he'd thought at Brian out of his mind.

Once through the tunnel they turned up toward School Street, closer now against the press of students, so close that she finally slipped her hand into his.

"So what?" she said, looking at him sideways. "Tar?"

He nodded.

"God, it was horrible, huh? You should've seen my father when he came home last night. If he'd known I knew him, he would have made me stay home. My nerves. He thinks I'm pale and weak and suffer from the vapors every time I cut my finger, and you're not listening to a word I'm saying, Donald Boyd."

"Huh?"

"See?"

He squeezed her hand and shoved them through the dispersing crowd onto the school's front lawn. As they walked toward the plaza, he made several attempts to explain what was going on inside his head, and each time he had to stop because he didn't want her to think he was crazy and didn't want her to say that he should talk to his parents.

Finally he just gave up and accepted her silence as patience for his fumbling.

The flagpole was surrounded by a raised brick wall into which had been dumped earth for a planter. The blossoms were gone, but the frost over the past two weeks hadn't yet killed the stems and broad leaves. Don sat on the edge and Tracey sat beside him, dumping her instrument case and books from her arms, then twisting so she could see him.

They were alone.

The sun was already behind the building and the plaza was coated in chilly shadow. There was no movement in the windows, and the flag above them snapped at the air like cynical hands clapping.

"He wasn't your friend, you know," she said, one finger skating over the top of the bricks, following the riverbed of mortar that held them together. "It's not like it was with Mandy, I mean."

"Yeah, I know."

"I mean, he couldn't stand you, Don, and you probably hated his guts. Especially after last night. So I don't get it. I don't get it."

He looked toward the school, the steps, the lawn, the street. "I killed him."

She slapped his arm, hard. "That isn't funny."

"I know." At the plaza, his thighs, the sky, the trees.

"I . . . you didn't, you know. I know you didn't. Even after what he did, I know you didn't take a bat and lure him out into the street and bash out his brains. You—"

A hand butterflied to her lips to silence herself, and he knew she was remembering the Howler and how he died.

Then he heard cleats on the concrete and he stiffened, drew his lips tight, and closed his eyes when a hand took his right arm.

"How do I look?"

"Like a sports store dummy, dummy," Tracey said lightly.

Don looked at the hand, the face, and grinned at Jeff, who was still in uniform and holding his helmet under his arm.

"Coach says we have to wear this crap the rest of the day." Jeff drew himself up and gave them his profile, slightly marred because of the droop of his glasses. "For inspiration to ourselves and others. So that the Ashford North Rebels will tremble when they see us and never forget the demolition they will suffer." He stuck out his tongue. "That is a quote, I swear to god. You going?"

"Sure," Don said. "You playing?"

Jeff's expression turned sour. "Are you kidding? Coach wants to win this one. Why should he play me when he has Brian, Fleet, and . . . and the rest of the guys." He looked at

Tracey, saw her sad smile, and slumped against the wall, bouncing the helmet lightly on his lap.

"You know, huh?" Tracey said.

"Yeah. Coach gave us the Gipper speech. It sounds lousy when you say 'Win one for the Tar.' "

Don said nothing; Tracey laughed nervously.

More cleats, and Fleet passed them. When it was obvious he wasn't going to stop, Jeff called to him, called a second time and shrugged. When Fleet reached the sidewalk, however, he paused and looked over his shoulder. It was clear he was looking at Don, and just as clear he was wondering.

God, Don thought, and only nodded when Jeff stood with a show of puffing his chest and stamping his feet, announcing he had to get home before the men in the white suits dropped their net over his head. A wave, a look to Tracey, and he trotted away.

Sounding, Don thought, just like a running horse.

Tracey looked at her watch.

The school's shadow deepened.

"Don, I have to go. You—"

"No," he said. "Look, Trace, I'm sorry I said anything, okay? I think . . . I think I just want to be alone for a while."

Her eyes were hurt though her mouth worked at a small smile. "Sure. And look, I'll give—why don't you call me later, okay? I have to be back here at six, but call me before, all right?"

"Yes," he said, and snapped his head around to look at her. "Yes, I will. It's just that . . ." and he waved his hand in the direction Jeff and Fleet had gone.

"It's okay, Vet, don't worry about it. Just don't give me any of that crap about . . . you know, all right?" Then, her eyes wide with surprise at herself, she leaned over and kissed him, harder than she thought, clearly not as long as she wanted. "Call, or I'll break your legs."

He grinned as she hurried away, juggling sheet music, books, and case in her arms. But the moment she was on the other side of the street and around the corner, the grin faded by degrees until he felt the pull of skin as his lips turned down.

What in hell was he thinking of, telling her right out like that that he killed Tar? If she didn't think he was crazy, she was as crazy as he was; and if she believed him, she sure as hell wouldn't belieye the part about the horse.

He brought a fist down on his leg.

Damn Jeff, anyway! And Fleet! It was his own fault for stopping here. He should have taken her somewhere else, maybe the park, where he could work it all out so it wouldn't sound so stupid, so she wouldn't be afraid to be with him because she was afraid he'd kill her because he was . . . oh shit. Shit. Because this and because that and when the hell did it all turn so damned complicated?

He struck his leg again and gathered up his books. There was a moment, as he faced the school, when he was tempted to go inside and talk to his father. Then Falcone came out and took the steps two at a time. He nodded as he passed, jacket tails flapping and a briefcase in one hand, and half-walked half-ran over the plaza. Don turned toward home, taking a shortcut across the grass, kicking the ground once in a while and only half turning his head when a car raced past.

A book fell. He knelt to retrieve it, but he didn't take his eyes from the car. It was Falcone's, and his mother was driving.

She was wearing dark glasses and there was a dark kerchief around her hair, but he knew it was her.

A panicked look toward his father's office; there was no one in the window.

A stunned look back to the street; the car was gone.

Without thinking he hurried around the corner of the building and down the steep slope to the wall gates. They were still open, and he ran through, dropping his books at the edge of the grass and falling into a rhythm as he began to take a lap. Eyes blinking rapidly. Mouth open. Feet flat. Arms nearly motionless at his side. By the time he was into the first turn, he had recovered enough to bring his knees and arms up, to correct his breathing, to pace himself for a session he knew would last a long time.

The stands were empty.

A white ghost of sheet music flapped across the field like a broken-winged bird.

A glance at the school, and he saw a face in a window on the third floor.

"Fuck you, Hedley," he said between clenched teeth. "Fuck you too, and leave me alone!"

Adam Hedley worked a forefinger across his mustache and turned away from the window with a puzzled grunt. He had intended on staying at school, working on a few papers so he would have nothing to take home over the weekend. There was no sense in leaving since he had to be back by five-thirty in order to take tickets, and he'd already conned sandwiches from the cafeteria to pass for supper until he could get something better after the game.

Boyd changed that, however.

Watching the kid moving like a drunken zombie around the track reminded him of the tests he had run a second time at the station's limited facilities. And the results, which were the same as he'd gotten the first time around. The moment he'd finished, he had hurried to Verona's office, but the man was gone, and Ronson had left town on an extended weekend. He thought of calling the coroner, but discarded the notion almost immediately; he and that prissy little sonofabitch never did get along, and he would be damned if he was going to hand the man his own head, especially on a platter he had made himself. Instead, he had decided to wait until he could speak alone with the detective, to give him his findings and, frankly, pass the buck.

Now he wasn't so sure the buck ought to be passed.

Now he wondered if there wasn't something in there he could use against Norman, especially after the talk about Tarkington Boston's death—remarkably like Falwick's if half the stories were true.

It took him half an hour to clean up the lab to his liking, cursing all the while the students who couldn't read labels and didn't give a damn when they could. He locked the storeroom, the cupboards, and his desk; he switched off the lights and was startled to realize how dark it had become. A check of the windows showed him the clouds that had moved nearer since the rally, obscuring the sun and bringing a false dusk to the roofs of the town.

A gust of wind slapped at the panes, found a crack somewhere and rustled the shades.

He locked the door and dropped his keys into his jacket pocket, ran his palms back along his fringe of red hair, over his bald scalp, and started for the staircase, squinting because there seemed to be something wrong with the fluorescent lights in the ceiling. Dimmer; one of them down there flickering a little. He would have to speak to that cretin, D'Amato, about it. If he wasn't careful, he would trip and break a leg.

A smile flared and vanished.

That wouldn't be so bad. Then he could sue Boyd and retire on his winnings.

The second floor was dark.

When he emerged on the first, he took two steps toward the main office when a door banged open somewhere ahead of him. He paused, listening for the footsteps of a colleague leaving late, or Norman Boyd's voice calling him to join him.

Echoes of the door meeting wall, hollow against the tiles, booming around the deserted corridor.

A look to his left. The back hall was dark, and the one ceiling light burning made the side hall seem as if it were swirling with fog.

A shrug with his eyebrows, and he headed for the main entrance, passed the office, and wondered at the lack of lights in there. Usually, at least the secretaries' area was illuminated all night for the police to check on when they cruised by. Shoddy, he thought as he took the corner into the foyer. Shoddy procedure, and not the way I'd take care of things.

A noise behind him made him stop—a shifting of weight more felt than heard.

He looked and didn't like what he saw.

Opposite the foyer were three sets of double doors leading into the auditorium. One of the center doors was swinging shut.

"D'Amato?" he said loudly.

No answer.

The door closed, hissing.

It certainly wasn't any of his affair, but indecision kept him from leaving. Only last year, after a particularly unruly homecoming rally, he had on a hunch used the upstairs doors and stepped into the balcony, and had discovered two students screwing their brainless heads off in the front row. No alarm was raised; he just sidled into the shadows and watched, excited not by the scene but by the spontaneity of what he saw—most of his films at home he could replay in his sleep without missing a frame.

It was possible, then, that after today's emotional charging, someone had gotten a similar idea.

He checked the front—there was no one in the plaza, no car waiting at the curb.

Then, on his toes and breathing shallowly through his mouth, he hurried to the door, took the handle, and pulled it slowly to him, just enough to permit him to slip inside.

Someone was there.

He could barely see across the rows of dark upholstered seats, and the stage lit by a single bulb in its center was perfectly bare save for an old battered couch against the rear curtain-draped wall.

But years of keeping his eyes on classes with his back turned had given him, he knew, a certain honing of a sixth sense, and he knew beyond doubt he wasn't alone in the dark-walled cavern.

Carefully he slipped on tiptoe down the center aisle, stopping at every row to check its length on both sides, ears almost pricked to catch the slightest hint of panting, of clothes rustling, of moans smothered by kisses.

By the time he was ten rows down, he was out from under the balcony's overhang, and he looked to see if perhaps the culprits were up there.

Looked back and saw it standing at the door.

"Jesus," he said, and his voice echoed in the empty auditorium, and came back to him, whispering, almost like a prayer.

Greeneyes, staring.

There was no curiosity about what it was, where it came from, what it was doing here. He turned and ran down the rest of the aisle, swearing at the weight he carried when he swerved to the right and slammed into a chair, stumbled forward, and had to grab the back of the next one to keep from falling. As he did, he was turned around, and the stallion was coming toward him. One step at a time.

Greenfire, flaring.

I'm going to die, he thought, and he didn't know why.

The fear that sent a warm wetness down his legs didn't keep him from running again, not stopping until he came up against the stage apron with a jarring, wind-stealing collision. He swallowed bile, shook perspiration from his eyes, and lifted a leg to hoist himself up. He failed once and whimpered, tried a second time and made it, rolling onto his back, spread-eagled for a moment while the stallion kept walking, out of the dark.

"Jesus, Mary, and Joseph."

He looked wildly to the wings as he scrambled to his feet, hoping that D'Amato hadn't locked the doors leading to the halls beyond. Squinted at the balcony in case the custodian was there, then looked at the creature that had stopped in the aisle's center.

Its ears were back, its eyes narrow and watching, and there was no chance at all it was a joke and he knew it.

It ran.

One moment it was there, a foreleg pawing the aisle's carpet into green flame, the next its muscles rippled and launched it into a full gallop.

Adam gaped, momentarily frozen.

The stallion filled the air with smoke and flame.

For a reason he never knew, Adam looked up at the bulb that formed his own spotlight, and when he looked down he was partially blinded.

But not blinded enough not to see the stallion in the air, leaping easily from the floor to the stage, gliding, glowing, its mouth opened and teeth bared as its head lunged for his throat.

Adam screamed.

The bulb shattered.

And greenfire in the dark that here and there shone on red.

SEVENTEEN

Norman was sitting on the porch steps when Don came home. The clouds were still ponderously gathering and the yard was already nearly dark, the streetlamps already on and laying dull silver over the grass and blacktop. The porchlight was glowing a faint yellow as he turned onto the walk hesitantly, unsure why his father should be out here like this—without a coat, his tie off, an empty glass in his hand.

"Hi," Norman said, and patted the step beside him.

"Hi." Don sat, holding his books snugly in his lap. He hoped this wasn't going to be an attempt at a father-and-son night. If it was, he might blurt out what he knew, and then he would learn what his father really thought about him.

"What did you think of the pep rally?"

"It was okay, I guess."

"Roused the troops' blood, I think."

"I suppose."

"Gonna smash North's face in tonight, I bet. Brian looked like he was ready to kill anything that moved."

Don hadn't noticed.

"A shame about Tar. Kid could've been a real star some-

271

day. Pratt hasn't got a chance; his head's too big. Boston knew his limitations. You gotta know that to make it big in the world.''

"Tar's dead," Don said flatly.

"Yeah. What a bitch." He shifted, belched, ran his hands over his hair. "Cheerleaders have nice legs, you ever notice that? I mean, when you're not talking to the animals, you ever notice that cheerleaders have interesting legs, son?''

Don didn't know what to say, and so said nothing.

Norman took out a handkerchief and blew his nose. "You're probably wondering what I'm doing out here, right? I'll probably catch pneumonia and miss the game which, considering the relative importance of this week, is not the proper thing to do.''

The smell of bourbon was not quite a stench, his father's hair not quite untidily mussed over his forehead.

"Well, I'll tell you, son. I'm waiting for your mother."

Don winced, but Norman didn't see it; he was staring at the lawn and turning the glass around and around between his fingers. Finally he lifted his chest as if taking in a sigh.

"You remember that goddamned rude question you asked us a few days ago? You remember that, Donald?''

He did. With a clarity that made him take the inside of his cheek with his teeth and bite down, hard.

"Well, I suppose you deserve an answer. After all, you are my sole surviving heir. You are soon to launch yourself upon the unsuspecting world and start your own goddamned life.'' He lay a hand on Don's knee and gripped it, massaged it, pulled the hand away. "You know, your grandfather used to tell me, when he was busting his hump down there in the mills and getting nothing for it but a kick in the ass, even when he became foreman, he used to say that you ought never to plan for your own future because that road you're walking is made of shit. Some of it hard enough to go over, some of it soft enough to drop you in up to your ass. But it's still shit. He said you should make a future for your kids, like he was doing for me. He said it's the only way people are going to remember you.

"He was right, you know, so don't look so shocked. It's all shit, Donald, and I'm telling you that like my father told me. Of course, some of it, you learn to live with it, if you know what I mean. And some of it can actually do you some good, you know?

"Like Falcone. He's shit. He wants to take his dumbass teachers out on strike and he would have done it first thing Monday morning, but you know what that stupid ginzo did? Aside from pulling that stunt with your grades, do you have any idea what that jackass did?"

Don looked away, hoping that by swallowing hard enough he wouldn't have to cry. He was beginning to understand why he thought the bourbon smelled sour.

"Oh," Norman said. "Oh, you saw them."

He nodded.

"Dumbest thing I ever saw." Norman laughed sharply. "He actually ran out of the school and into his car. His car, mind. And there she was, all dressed up like Greta Garbo, like nobody would know who the hell she was. The mystery woman in Harry Falcone's life, you see what I mean? Well, that was dumb, Donald. Dumb. Because now he can whistle Dixie naked on the boulevard and he ain't gonna get one teacher to follow his ass.

"Good shit for me, bad shit for him."

"Dad, please."

Norman set the glass on the edge of the step between them; Don grabbed it before it could fall and put it on the porch.

"Yes," Norman said.

Don looked at him.

"The answer to your question is yes. I probably knew that the day Sam died and your mother blamed me because we went camping instead of farting around at the shore like she wanted. At the shore they had hospitals. Camping has trees, and if your mother thinks I don't miss him, she's dumber than I think.''

Don stood, but Norman froze him with a sideways look.

"You don't like to hear me talk about your mother that way, and to tell you the truth, I don't like to hear me say it. She's a hell of a woman, Don, a hell of a woman. So when she gets back from wherever the hell she went with that slick, greasy idiot, I'm going to put it to her—make a choice, Joyce. You either got to stick with your family, or stick with him." He shook his head slowly and sucked at his teeth. "I think it was my news that made her do it though. I got to give her that. Up until now she was keeping it all quiet and careful. My fault, I guess."

"What news?" Don whispered.

"I'm going to quit at the end of the year."

"What?"

"Don't shout, boy. I'm your father."

"Quit? You mean . . . quit school? Your job?"

You're drunk, he thought; you're drunk, you're drunk!

"Damn right. Told her this afternoon. Falcone, the board, they can take the school and every kid inside and shove it where the sun don't shine, you'd better believe I'm quitting."

"But why?"

"My father told me that the only way you can make it in this world, walking on shit the whole time, is by making money. And he was right. You can't live like a human being unless you have money. Lots of money. I sure as hell ain't gonna make it as a principal, now am I? No way in hell."

Don tried to find a way to breathe and leaned hard against the railing. "What are you going to do then?"

"Ah, you haven't been listening to your mother, son. You haven't been watching the way Garziana's been treating me lately."

"Garziana? Mayor Garziana?" Punch drunk; somehow he

was punch drunk; he had to be, or else he wouldn't feel like laughing.

Norman nodded, looking at his hands as if expecting the glass to still be there. "I'm going to run next fall, Don. Your mother thought I was kidding when I told her the first time. But I've been thinking about it, thinking hard, and I've been taking a look around to see what Garziana has for himself. He has it good, son. He has it damned good for a little shittown like this."

Don took hold of the railing and pulled himself to the porch.

"She thinks I'm crazy. She made a good point though— that the real money won't start coming until I've been in office a few years. Means a little sacrifice here and there; the job itself doesn't pay shit, but it'll be worth it in the long run, no question about it. I got it straight from the horse's mouth."

"School," Don said hoarsely. "What about . . ."

"You got any prospects for scholarships?"

"Oh, no, please, Dad. No, please."

"Y'know, I think . . . I wouldn't be surprised if she thought I clobbered that poor kid last night for what he did to my car."

Don looked wildly to the front door, looked back and saw his father watching him. "You were in my room!" he accused, not caring how drunk Norman was.

"Damn right I was. I got nosey. It's my goddamned house and I wanted a closer look at all your little buddies in there, try to figure out where the hell your head is at. I got to admit I still don't know, but I do know you're not very smart, Don. You shouldn't have left those keys on your desk." He turned slightly and leaned an elbow on the top step. "I'm not stupid, Donald. Don't you ever think I'm stupid. I don't know what you were thinking of when you didn't tell me about Tar, but I know you thought I was going to kill that little sonofabitch. Why did you do it? Were you going to do it yourself?''

Don turned away from the laughter that began as a chuckle and ended in choking. He opened the door, dizzy and wanting to run for the bathroom.

"Were you?" Norman persisted. "Jesus, I hope you aren't starting to believe all that crap about being a hero. You know as well I do you didn't do it."

He gasped, but didn't look back.

"Nope," Norman said. "That wasn't you. That was a crazy kid, not my kid. Five seconds of crazy doesn't make you a hero."

Don wanted to faint, to get away into the dark.

"You go on in," Norman said kindly, thinking the pause was a wait for him. "I'm going to sit here and sober up a bit. Can't go to the big game like this, right? It'd make a bad impression. Folks don't like their mayors drunk in public. Besides, maybe your mother will come home. Maybe not. Personally I hope she—"

"Shut up!" Don yelled. He whirled around, his books scattering in the foyer, ripples of faint red at the corners of his vision. "You shut up!"

"No, you grow up!" Norman yelled back. "It's about time you grew up, boy, and stopped thinking that your daydreams are going to make things better around here." A finger pointed spearlike at his chest. "I'll tell you something, son—if you don't break out into the real world real soon, you're going to be in serious trouble. All that crap about taking care of those poor helpless animals, all that wailing like a two-year-old just because your mother cleaned some baby toys out of your room—you better grow up, Donald. You better open your eyes and learn a few things about what it's really like, out here in the real world."

Don slammed the door. He kicked aside a book that nearly tripped him and plunged up the steps, slipping twice, falling onto the landing and yanked himself up into the hall. He leaned against the wall and stared down it at his parents' room, at his room, looked over his shoulder at Sam's room, and he sobbed.

"Don?" Norman called from the bottom of the steps.

"Leave me alone!" he shouted. "Just leave me alone!"

"I just wanted you to know there's sandwiches on the counter in case you want to eat before you leave for the game."

"Jesus Christ," he screamed, "will you leave me alone!"

He fell into his bedroom and picked up the desk chair, held it over his shoulder while the tears drenched his cheeks, threw it against the wall while his knees grew rigid.

"Leave me alone!" he said loudly.

An arm swept books and pencils off the desk.

"Leave me alone," he whispered.

He grabbed a stuffed hawk from a shelf and tried to wring off its head, then hurled it at the window and winced when the pane cracked and the bird bounced back to rock slowly in the middle of the floor.

"Leave me alone. Just . . . leave me alone."

Footsteps in the hall that neither faltered nor paused. The shower drummed. The toilet flushed. Something made of glass shattered on the bathroom floor.

Ten minutes later the front door slammed, and Don jumped up from the bed and ran into his parents' room, pulled aside the drapes, and looked down at the street. Norman, in slacks, sweater, and sport jacket, was turning onto the sidewalk. He didn't look back, didn't look up, and stopped with hands out when Chris backed the red convertible out of her garage. They exchanged words. Norman shook his head politely. Another exchange with Chris flashing her best smile. When he shrugged, she waved briskly at him and grabbed her pompons from the front seat, dropped them in back and leaned over to open the passenger door. Another wave, and Norman shrugged, walked around the back of the car, and slid into the passenger seat. When they drove off toward the stadium, Chris had both hands on the wheel and his father was staring off to his right.

Don backed away from the sill and returned to his own room, picked up the hawk and laid him gently on the bed.

"I'm sorry," he said.

Downstairs it was dark. After switching on the living room lamps and the small chandelier in the foyer, he saw the note tacked to the inside of the front door.

Don, don't forget to eat something before you leave. And I drank too much. Stupid and drunk. Sorry if I hurt you. Don't forget your key.

He reached out to touch the piece of paper, pulled his hand back, then grabbed the note and tore it in half, in half again and tossed the pieces on the floor.

"Sorry doesn't cut it, Father," he said as he walked into the living room and stared at Norman's chair.

A string of cars drove past the house, horns sounding, music loud and tuneless.

He looked to the ceiling. "Why?" he asked, his throat raw and burning. "What did I do wrong?"

In the kitchen he poured himself a large glass of milk and took the sandwiches one of them had made. After standing at the table making sure he hadn't forgotten anything, he sat, and he ate, and he stared at his transparent reflection in the back door, half expecting to see his mother walk through and shake out her hair, give him a smile and her cheek to kiss, then walk to the sink and fill it with hot water, dump in the dishes, and stand back to inspect it as if what she'd done was a work of fine art.

When he was finished, he rinsed out his glass, cleaned his plate, and turned off the light. At the table in the downstairs hall he stopped and watched his fingers curl around the handset. He dialed Tracey's number and held his breath.

She answered, and he sagged to the floor, unable to speak until she let loose with a harsh string of Spanish that startled him into saying "What?"

"Don, is that you? Hey, I thought it was an obscene phone call."

"Yeah, it's me. God, what did all that mean?"

She giggled. "You don't want to know, but it sounded good, didn't it?"

"Scared the hell out of me."

"It was supposed to. One of my father's bright ideas." Her mother yelled shrilly at her sister, and her father yelled at them all. "What's up? Oh, lord, something else happened?"

He nodded, then said, "Yes."

"I ought to be a priest, you know."

"Huh?"

"A priest. The last few days everybody's been finding a place on my shoulder. I'm getting pretty good at it. I should get paid, what do you think?"

He stared at the mouthpiece.

"Don," she said solemnly, "that was a joke."

"Oh. I'm sorry."

"Don't worry. Hey, look, I'm going to be late. And if I'm late, I'll have to turn in my flute and they'll strip my epaulets off." She paused. "That was a joke too."

"Yeah. I know."

Her father shouted something in Spanish, and her sister shouted back; a second later he heard the unmistakable sounds of a slap and someone crying.

"Don—"

"I heard."

She whispered, "I'm sorry. It really was a joke. See you later?"

Before he could answer she hung up, and he twisted the

cord around both palms and pulled it taut. Now, he thought; I need you now, Tracey, goddamnit.

He sat on the couch and tried to guess the time, every few minutes going into the kitchen to check his accuracy with the clock. He was wrong. Every time. And every time he left the room he knew his mother wouldn't be back before he left. If he left. He wasn't sure he would go. All those people, all those faces, all that noise keeping him from thinking.

He went upstairs and into Sam's room.

His mother's sewing machine was on the floor next to Sam's single bed with the Winnie-the-Pooh sheets; in the far corner she had put a small table where her art supplies were piled when she wasn't using them; the wallpaper was dusty, columns of cowboys and Indians and cactus and stagecoaches. The shade was down. There was no pillow on the mattress.

He looked around and tried to remember what his brother looked like, what his brother had said and done to make his mother remember him so clearly.

"Sam," he said, "you're a bastard, you know that? You're a goddamned bastard."

Tracey hurried down the hill toward the stadium's street entrance, feeling like a jerk in her uniform when all the kids she passed were dressed for a good time, a warm time, and wouldn't have to go home to change once the game was over. Besides, she didn't care about the game, or the music, or how she looked on the field—she was worried about Donald, about what was happening to him, and why, when she spoke with him earlier, the sound of his voice hadn't caused her to tremble the way it used to.

Then someone called her name, and she turned just in time to see Jeff rushing after her. She smiled, and waited, and laughed when his cleats skidded on the pavement and he tumbled onto the grass.

"Nice," she said, walking over to help him up. "That's the secret play, huh?"

He stared at her morosely, sighed loudly, and reached down to retrieve his helmet. "I tried to call," he said as they walked toward the entrance, "but the line was busy."

"I was talking to Don."

He said nothing.

She looked at him, and looked away, and felt a constriction in her chest that had nothing to do with the rapidly cooling air.

Inside the short tunnel his cleats were loud, and echoing.

"Trace?"

They stopped on the track. There were already people in the stands, and the band was off to the left, listening to last minute instructions from their leader. On the far side she could see members of the team slowly filtering into the low concrete clubhouse.

"There's something the matter with him," she said quietly.

He took her hand and squeezed it, and didn't let go.

"I don't know." A trumpet blared, and the bandmaster shouted an order. She looked over, then looked quickly at Jeff. "He scares me," she admitted, to him and to herself. "I don't know what's the matter with him, and he scares me."

And the look then on his face almost made her kiss him—concern, and anger, and frustration merged and dark.

"Look," he said at last, "why don't we meet later, okay? After the game? I'll walk you home or something, and we can—"

"I can't," she said. "I'm going to see Don."

"Oh."

"He needs to talk, and I guess I'm—"

"But you're afraid of him, Trace. You just said you were afraid of him."

"I know. But he's a friend, too, you know?"

Then she squeezed his hand and released it, waved him on and watched him break into a trot around the track toward the clubhouse. Poor Jeff, she thought, and frowned at the way the words suddenly confused her. It was Don she was supposed to feel sorry for, not Jeff; it was Don she had kissed the other day. But it was Jeff she wanted to kiss now, or hold onto, or just stand beside and listen to his mocking deflation of the game his father had forced him into.

Jeff. Don.

And she wondered if maybe she shouldn't see Don after all. At least not alone.

She hadn't been lying—he scared her.

The telephone rang.

He took his time getting down the stairs, thinking that if he hurried, it might be his mother and he wouldn't know what to say to her except come home, please come home.

It was Sergeant Verona.

Don hung up without answering a single question and took his jacket from the closet.

He couldn't stay now. If he did, the cops would be around, asking him about Tar, asking him about the Howler, not letting go when they knew it was all over. Staring at him like Hedley, seeing into his soul and knowing what he was like, and what he had become since the nugget exploded. They wouldn't give a damn that his parents were splitting up and he was going to be alone.

He stood on the porch and locked the door; he left the light on in case his mother needed it.

At the end of the drive he looked toward the park, thinking maybe he should go there first and calm himself down before he showed up at the school. His hands were jittery, and he couldn't breathe without panting, and no matter how many times he wiped his face, it was still masked in perspiration.

Maybe his friend would come and let him touch him again.

A car stopped, and a woman he didn't know leaned out her window. "Are you Donald Boyd?" She giggled and turned to someone sitting beside her. "I sound like a jerk, don't I? God, I sound like a real jerk." Back to Don. "So. Are you that boy I saw on television, the one that killed the killer?"

He nodded dumbly.

"Thought so," she said with a sharp nod. "Told you it was him," she said to her companion. "The minute I saw him I knew it was him."

She drove away with an I-told-you-so, nearly sideswiping another car that was trying to get around her. Horns blared angrily, curses were passed, and someone from the second car yelled at Don to hurry or he'd missed the opening kick-off, or was he too big to care? Leave me alone, he told them with a glare he knew they couldn't see, leave me the hell alone.

He stopped in front of Chris's house and traced with his eyes the way she had picked up his father, followed with his mind the way they had driven off, sitting so far apart they might have been strangers. His palm itched where it had been pressed against her breast, and he rubbed it hard against his jacket until it started to burn.

Delfield's dog started barking.

Shut up, he thought.

In his chest there was a tension that constricted his lungs; in his spine there was a rod that refused to let him bend; in his arms there were cramps that kept his fists closed.

A police siren wailed; *leave me alone*; a gang of teenagers raced by on School Street, jeering at passing cars and shrieking at pedestrians on the other side of the road; someone exploded a string of firecrackers; *leave me alone*; tires squealed; *leave me*; Tar's body sprawled in the middle of the street, more blood than flesh, the blood running to the gutter.

His head ached.

A trio of school buses sped past, turning him in their wake

as North supporters taunted him from open windows, blowing air horns and bugles, a beer can rolled into the gutter.

Jesus, leave

From the last bus someone tossed a beer can that landed on
his shoes, spilling half its contents over the bottoms of his
slacks. "Christ!" he bellowed. "Christ, leave me alone!"

Five steps later he heard all the screams pouring over the
stadium walls and he started to run, saying "I didn't mean it,
I didn't mean it" until he reached the entrance gate and the
screams grew even louder.

EIGHTEEN

Don almost leapt over the turnstile in his panic to get in and see what he had done, what the stallion was doing to the spectators and the team. But there was a cop, and he was staring glum-faced at the latecomers, and Don fumbled for the ticket in his shirt, handed it to a red-faced woman in the cubbyhole that passed for a ticket booth at the games, and pushed the metal arm until it clicked.

And he was in—watching the stands filled with faces, with open mouths, with hands in the air waving and voices shrieking on both sides of the field, the lights glaring and turning the grass a rich green, giving a luster to the uniforms that chased each other down the gridiron after the opening kickoff.

That's what it was, he thought in relief, and sagged against the brick wall; that's all it was, I didn't do a thing.

He slumped to the ground and sat there for ten minutes, seeing little more than legs hustling by, hearing nothing but the continuous screaming that merged into a roar that didn't stop, didn't end, made him groan and cover his ears and wonder why so many were getting so excited by a lousy high school football game. Didn't they know Tar was dead? Didn't they know that the guy running patterns with Brian was a lousy substitute, not the real thing?

He breathed deeply and fast until his head cleared and his hands stopped shaking.

Sure they knew. But this wasn't murder. This was a tragic accident and no classes would be canceled and no concert would be dedicated to Tar Boston's memory.

When the ground became too damp to sit on, he groaned to his feet and made his way toward the stands. Amazingly they were filled, and as he followed the iron railing, he couldn't see a single space large enough for him to squeeze into, save for the open section where the band was filing in now after playing the national anthem. He tried to catch Tracey's eye when he saw her, but she was chatting with her neighbors and trying to keep the wind from taking off her beret.

A strong wind that snapped at the pennants flying from the goal posts, that took more than a few hats and sailed them over the far wall to the houses behind. There were no stars when he looked up, only a solid shifting black, and he realized that most of the people there had brought umbrellas and ponchos and blankets for cover when the rains finally came and turned the game into a mud show.

He circled the field slowly, avoiding loud roving gangs of youngsters who were showing off for their girls, seeing Jeff on the bench and giving him a victory fist, not seeing his father but seeing Chris on the field, cheering and dancing through a dozen routines.

When he reached the main gate again, it was well into the second quarter. There was no score, and the fans on both sides were getting a little restless.

Jostled, sworn at, he stood in the middle of the track and watched the game from behind the snow fence that followed the edge of the field from one end of the goal line to the other. There were cops there, and a few photographers, and a bunch of little kids trying to see through the red slats.

North's quarterback fumbled. His own team's center fumbled it right back.

The electronic scoreboard at the far end counted the time in amber lights and kept the scores at zero.

He moved to the fragile fence and crossed his arms over the top. One minute to go before the first half was over. The screaming was subdued, the cheering half-hearted. Nobody liked a good defensive battle when they had to sit in the cold and wait for the rain.

Suddenly he was watching Brian racing toward him, looking back, following the spiraled flight of an impossibly high pass as it arced over the tops of the secondary and seemed to hesitate before settling perfectly into his arms.

The screams began again, but Don only watched Brian, watched the way he dodged a potential tackle and stiff-armed another and trotted across the goal line five yards ahead of the nearest Rebel pursuit.

The stands erupted, the band blared discordantly, and Brian was grinning when he came up against the fence and saw him.

"Hey, quacker, you wanna see it again?" he said, and was immediately swarmed under by the rest of the team, practically carried away to the bench, where the coach shook his hand.

Don was pushed aside by the photographers, by the little kids, and was warned by a cop to find a seat and sit down before he was told to leave. He almost argued as he felt the tension rise again, felt a sheen of warmth begin to spread over his cheeks. But he swallowed it down and turned away, a part of him thinking, they don't know who I am anymore, a part of him realizing that leave me alone was not a plea now, it was a threat.

That for all his aching, that might be the only Rule there was.

He found a place, a narrow place, at the end of the first

row at the near end of the stands. He couldn't see much, not during half time when the home team band went out to strut its stuff, and not when the Braves' defense scored the second touchdown with a run from the second half kickoff. He didn't much care. If he went home, he might see his mother; but if he stayed, he'd be able to talk to Tracey after the game. Maybe she'd be able to tell him what to do next.

By the middle of the third quarter he was unable to contain his restlessness. He jumped down to the track and started walking again, passed by the band and this time saw Tracey. She grinned and waved; he pointed to the scoreboard clock, to his watchless wrist, and then to his chest. She frowned puzzlement, then brightened and nodded quickly. His smile was only a small part of his relief, and it clung there when his gaze drifted to the spectators behind and caught his father sitting with the mayor and the mayor's wife. Joyce was beside Mrs. Garziana, the kerchief still around her hair, the dark glasses gone.

Don looked to Norman, back to his mother, who saw him and waved—a weak and apologetic wave in front of a smile so forced he thought her face would shatter with the effort. A polite smile. A public smile, not for him but for those around her.

He waved back and moved on, for the first time realizing that sooner or later he was going to have to make a choice— stay with his father, stay with his mother, either way losing out on a dream to help heal his friends.

The crowd roared to its feet.

Ignoring the field, he looked up to the scoreboard and saw another touchdown recorded and Brian's number flash. Before he reached the far end zone it happened again; and as he passed in front of the Rebels' wooden bleachers he felt the antagonism and defeat, the growing rowdiness that comes with losing frustration.

He walked around a second time and the Rebels made their first score.

The third time, he stopped in front of the band, bracing himself against the people who were crowding around the Braves' bench, spilling onto the track, paying no attention to the police and security guards who were trying to keep a semblance of order and still watch the game.

He stared at Tracey, and felt his father staring back, in peripheral vision saw his mother laughing at something the mayor's wife said. His eyes narrowed, but she seemed not to understand that this wasn't a time for laughing, for football; it was a time for her son who wasn't named Sam.

He stayed there until, dimly, he heard the final gun and had to press against the low wall as the fans spilled over the railing and onto the field. His shoulder was punched, his back was slapped, and he did his best to keep from going down, to smile as if he were delirious at the victory they'd won, until he saw Tracey and she was pointing to the nearest steps.

"God," she said breathlessly when he finally reached her and she fell against him. "You'd think it was the stupid Super Bowl, for crying out loud."

Her uniform was rough to the touch, but his arm slipped naturally around her waist, the rest of him turning to form a shield while she put her instrument away and shoved her music into whatever pockets she could reach.

"You see your folks?"

He nodded stiffly.

"You have to wait or anything?"

"Do you?"

"Nope."

With a "let's go, then" he held her close to his hip and moved toward the gates. It would take a while; there were kids running impromptu races, football players trying to get away so they could change and return to join the celebration, and a handful of band members playing music their teacher never let them try in practice.

"Don," Tracey said then, "what's wrong?"

Joyce applauded and cheered when the final gun sounded, and didn't hear a word Jean Garziana said to her as they headed up the steps toward the exit. Donald was gone, lost in the swirling bodies that spilled over the field, and she hated herself for feeling relieved. Norm was behind her and when she looked back, he gave the lifeless stare he reserved for people he did not know. Jean touched her arm, and she smiled automatically, gestured toward her ears and then at the milling crowd. The woman nodded, and they concentrated on leaving the stadium and heading up for School Street. At the corner it wasn't quiet, but it was considerably less mobbed.

"We're going for a drink," the woman said then. "Would you like to join us?" When Joyce balked, she opened her raincoat to expose a nurse's uniform. "It won't be for long, I promise. I have to go on shift at midnight."

"But I'm not dressed," Joyce protested, looking down at her thin blouse, her wrinkled slacks, the ballet slippers. "I'd feel embarrassed." A nervous laugh—*you know how it is*.

Anthony Garziana came up then with Norman in tow. When Jean explained the ensemble situation, he laughed heartily and slapped Norman's arm. "No problem, ladies, no problem," he said. "Joyce, you go on and change. I want you to have a good time tonight. Norm, you go with her, bring her back, and we'll have a few drinks, we'll talk, what do you say?"

He left no time for an answer. Taking his wife's arm, he turned to the curb just as a limousine pulled up. "The Starlite, okay?" The door opened, and he was gone.

Joyce yanked the kerchief from her head as the limousine pulled away.

"I'm glad you showed," Norman said.

"I'm not that stupid," she told him wearily.

"Funny, I said almost the same thing to Don earlier."

"What?" She grabbed his arm, remembered the people still pressing home, and forced her lips into a meaningless smile. "What the hell do you mean?"

"Don and I had a talk," he said flatly, refusing to look anywhere near her.

"What did you say?"

"That you and I had to have a talk before the night is over." He did look, then, and she would not look away. "We do, Joyce. You know we do, after that stunt you pulled today."

"I—"

"Don saw you."

Something hard and cold settled in her chest. "Oh, shit."

"Yeah."

Blindly she stared at the faces moving rapidly past her, at the cars driving away. "Do we have to go?"

"Yes, we have to."

"Then I'm going home to change."

His fingers curled around her waist, the pads pressing deeply until she tried to pull away. "You'll be there, right?"

"Aren't you walking me home?"

"No," he said. "No. If I do, we'll never catch the mayor."

"I see."

"Do you?"

"Clearly, Norman. More clearly than you give me credit for."

She twisted her wrist free and walked away, feeling the coarse pavement beneath the slippers, gasping once when a group of boys raced by and one stepped on her toes. Tears rose and vanished as she willed the pain away, willed away the limp after only three strides.

Don knows. He knows, and what was she going to do now?

It's stupid, she thought as she waited on the curb and sought a break in the traffic; I'm stupid. Oh, god, what the hell am I going to do now?

She ran across the street and huddled in the shadows, berating herself for reacting to Norman's announcement the way she had. She should have waited until he'd come home and then talked with him calmly; and if not calmly, at least with a certain logic that would show him how foolish he was being. But he kept quoting his goddamn father at her, digging in his heels the moment he sensed her resistance to his running for office—and in her panic at losing what security they had, she'd called Harold. And Harold had responded the way she'd known he would—not with sage advice or calming talk, but by kissing her cheek the minute she'd left the school behind, holding her free hand and kissing the fingers until she'd pulled into his driveway on the other side of town. And once in the apartment, when she tried to explain, he had taken her in his arms and pulled her blouse from her jeans.

The moment his hand spread across her naked back she was lost, it was all lost . . . and Jesus, Don had seen!

When she unlocked the front door, her teeth were chattering as much from the cold as from tension, and from the fear that she wouldn't be able to explain to Norman that her foolishness— no, she corrected harshly as she slammed the door behind her. Not foolishness. Idiocy. Weakness. But not foolishness.

She rushed upstairs and stripped off her clothes, was reaching into the closet for something more appropriate for having drinks with the mayor and his wife, when she heard someone knocking on the front door. Don forgot his key was the first thing that came to mind, and she snatched up her bathrobe and struggled into it on the way back down. And she would have to tell him something. He was so frail that anything near the truth would have to be tempered. Your father and I are having problems—vague, unsatisfying, and something the boy already knew.

She opened the door and immediately clutched the robe's lapels to her throat. "Harry, for god's sake! What the hell do you want?"

Norman watched his wife rush off toward home, then turned, stopped, and found himself alone. He almost laughed—all that posturing, all the snide joy of letting her know about Don, and it was wasted. His dramatic exit spoiled because he had no way to get to the Starlite unless he walked the ten or twelve blocks.

"Nice going, jerk," he muttered, shoved his hands into his pockets, and started to follow her, grinning at the horns that blared out the victory, waving once in a while when someone called his name, staring at the few faces he passed and wondering what in hell there was about a lousy high school football game that made people think all was right with the world.

He paused to light a cigarette, bending away from the damp wind that promised rain later on. The smoke was warm, and he enjoyed it for a minute, then scowled and tossed the butt into the gutter. He licked his lips; he swallowed. He was working himself into a bad, self-pitying mood, and that was hardly the way he had to be when he faced Garziana.

He straightened his back, let his arms swing, and whistled a silent march as he moved on, thinking to call a cab when he got home and have both of them arrive at the lounge in a flourish. A good entrance, first impressions, the mayor would be pleased.

Think about the game, he ordered; think about all that good feeling, all that cheering, the rush when Pratt caught that first pass, the lucky sonofabitch.

His stride lengthened, the whistle became audible, and when

he had to stop at the Snowden driveway to let Chris pull in, he even saluted her and gave her a grin.

And waited.

To watch as she slid out, long legs white in the streetlight, braids slipping and sliding over her chest as she turned toward him and grinned, grabbed her pompons from the backseat and rounded the back of the car.

"Hi!" she said, cheeks flushed, eyes bright.

"Hi yourself."

"Gonna celebrate?"

"Damn right."

"Me too. See ya."

She ran up the walk, up the steps, and he didn't stop watching, knew what he was doing and didn't give a damn. Right now Joyce was fussing with her hair, her makeup, and beating herself to death over what Don had seen. It wouldn't hurt to wait a few minutes, to let her calm down.

"Mr. Boyd?"

He looked. She was standing at the open doorway.

"Mr. Boyd, my father—" And she gestured inside.

What the hell, he decided; a celebratory drink with a rich surgeon wouldn't hurt. Maybe a check for the campaign kitty if he played his cards right.

He made a show of deliberation before nodding and following her into the house.

Where the door closed silently, where the lights were all out.

"Hey, Chris," he said, suddenly nervous.

"I was going to say," she said softly, "that he was out of town, but wouldn't mind if I offered you something to celebrate the great game. Mother wouldn't either. She's in Florida for a vacation."

They were shadows and half-light, and he reached for the doorknob, looked stupidly at her fingers when they caught his wrist and held it. For a second. For two. One by one lifting to release him, the rustle of the pompons as they dropped to the floor.

"Chris," he warned, but didn't reach again.

Dumb, Boyd. Dumb, you stupid asshole.

"I have to change," she said, and walked slowly up the stairs he hadn't noticed on his left. She didn't look back, her hips and legs pulling him as if they were beckoning.

He considered only for a moment what he was doing, what he was getting himself into, then decided with a sharp nod that being a saint hadn't kept him his wife, hadn't kept him his son, and wasn't it about time he took what he wanted, had what he deserved.

So he followed, on his toes, and walked into a dark bedroom where he saw her on the mattress. In dimlight, naked, her hands slipping across her breasts, across her stomach, spreading to either side and kneading the sheet.

He stood at the foot of the bed. He unbuttoned his shirt.

He almost stopped when he saw her smile and thought it was a sneer.

"Celebrate," she said.

He nodded, undressed, and crawled over her legs, held himself above her and looked into her eyes. In the dark they were dark, showing nothing at all; and the smile was still there, the upper lip curled.

"I know what you're doing," he said in a whisper.

She nodded and shifted to bring his gaze to her breasts.

"It won't work."

"Sure," she said, and grabbed for his shoulders.

He resisted just long enough to show her he meant it, to show her who was boss, then lowered himself while she guided him, and heard himself gasp. Felt himself thrust. Looked up at her face and saw her staring at the ceiling.

Falcone pushed in and closed the door, took Joyce by the shoulders and practically dragged her into the dark living room. "He found out, didn't he? The sonofabitch knows what's going on, doesn't he?"

"Of course he does."

"Jesus Christ!" he said, dropping his hands and turning to the bay window. "Joyce, what the hell were you thinking of?"

"Me? All I wanted was someone to talk to. You were the one who couldn't keep his hands to himself."

"I didn't notice you screaming rape," he said quietly.

Streetlight reached weakly into the room, building shadows out of furniture, adding pits and slopes to his profile.

"But you know what you do to me," she answered. "You know, and you shouldn't have."

"Ah, Christ, don't give me that, okay? That's soap opera stuff. You're a grown woman and—"

She saw his eyelids drop into a squint and she leaned around Norman's chair to look out onto the lawn. No one could see in without a lamp on, but he might have seen Donald coming up the walk; or worse, it could be Norman.

"What?" she whispered.

He pointed. "You got me crazy, Joyce. I could have sworn I saw some kind of animal out there."

She laughed. It was going to be all right. Harry was making jokes now; it was going to be all right.

"Look, Harry, this isn't going to work. I've got to get back to Norman, so why don't you—"

"Damn, there it is again."

With a smile she shook her head and moved to his side, looked out the window and saw it in the yard.

Under the trees the slope of its back nearly reaching the lower branches. Around it a drifting fog, snaking through the grass and dropping from the leaves, blurring its outline but not the green glow of its eyes.

"It's a gag," Harry said. "Plaster or something. A costume. Is this one of your kid's things?" His voice hardened. "Is that kid out there playing games with us, Joyce?"

"His name is Donald," she said quietly, and gasped when its head rose and it looked straight at her.

"Jesus," Harry whispered, his head shaking slightly.

A foreleg pawed the grass, and emerald flame curled into the air, strands of green webbing that poked through the fog and reached for the house.

"I haven't been drinking," Falcone said aloud to himself. "I swear to god I haven't been drinking. What the hell is it, Joyce?"

But she was staring up at the ceiling, toward the back where she knew Don's room to be, remembering the poster and the horse that had been there.

"It's a gag," Harry insisted, "and I don't think it's funny."

She looked out the window, and could see the stallion's muscles bunch at the shoulders, shift at its haunches, and she barely had time to scream before it leapt from the grass and came through the bay window.

She dove to one side, her leg cracking against the armrest of Norman's chair, a snowstorm of glass winking over her to the back where it bounced from the wall and fell to the carpet, tinkling like bells in the dead cold of winter. She twisted around as she fell and saw the stallion fill the room, saw Falcone backpedal to the hearth, where he snatched up the poker and brandished it over his head.

The horse looked around and saw her pushing herself into the foyer. It snorted, and the room filled with fog; it lashed out with a rear hoof and Norman's chair was dashed into the corner, collapsing upon itself as it writhed in greenfire; it turned back to Falcone and he swung the poker at its head, missed, and was drawn offbalance a step off the hearth.

A wedge of glass dropped from the ceiling where it had been stuck like a knife blade.

Joyce drew herself to her feet and sagged against the newel

post as the stallion lifted its head, lowered it, and grabbed Harry's jacket with its bright long teeth. He screamed and tried to hit the beast again, but the horse shook him ragdoll side to side; the smoke-fog thickened, greenfire flared, and as Joyce shrieked and took the stairs, she heard the distinct sound of bones snapping, a spine breaking, Harry's body released and slammed against the wall.

"Don," she whispered as she ran to the landing. "Don, save me, please save me."

When she turned to run into the hall, the stallion was in the foyer, green eyes watching, the fog drifting up ahead of it and sweeping around her ankles, filling her with a chill that made her bones ache, that made her eyes widen, that slowed her when she ran to hide in her room.

On the stairs then—hooves against wood, echoing, hollow.

The pool in the oval was calm despite the wind, though every few minutes a gust would escape from the branches and send ripples across it, bobbing the dead leaves and sending some to the bottom. From the boulevard they could hear the continuing victory parade, but they felt no need to join it. Instead, they huddled together on a damp redwood bench and watched the black water.

"Divorce," Tracey said with a sympathetic shake of her head. She had changed into a shirt and jeans and was wearing a light sweater under her school jacket. "God, I don't know what to say."

Don sniffed several times to keep back the tears, determined not to let Tracey see him cry. "They hate me, you know."

"Don't be silly. They do not."

"Well, they don't care, then. All they care about is themselves. Jesus, do you know . . . I can't believe it, but do you know that last week Mom called me Sam?"

Tracey pried one of his hands loose from between his knees and held it, rubbed it to drive away the cold.

"And I'm crazy, Tracey."

"Dumb."

"No," he said earnestly, turning to her, leaning closer. "No, I mean it. I'm crazy." He kept her silent with a look and took a slow breath. Now was the time to do it, but the words he sought were impossible to order, and he shoved himself to his feet and began pacing the oval. Tracey watched him patiently, biting at her lips, lifting her shoulders when the breeze came again.

He stopped on the other side of the pond and faced her, looking up at the trees and the dark above the leaves. "I don't get it," he said with a tremulous smile. "I mean, your folks fight, don't they? I mean, I know what your father is like and all, but they have fights, right? So why don't they get divorced? Why . . . what's the matter with me that Brian can't leave me alone for one lousy minute?" His neck tightened, pulling his mouth down; he lowered his gaze and saw Tracey watching him, her hands deep in her coat pockets and forced together over her stomach. "I did something, Trace," he said softly. "I did something."

She stood and walked toward him, but he held out his hands to keep the water between them. "What, Don? That nonsense about killing Tar?"

He nodded.

"That's stupid. You didn't do it."

He nodded again, and put a hand to his forehead, massaged it, and drove it back through his hair. "You don't understand."

"I understand you're upset about Tar, and Mandy, and now this stuff with your mom and dad. I can see that, Don, but you—"

"No."

The word was quiet, and as effective as a slap. She took a

step back and turned her head away from the wind that engulfed them for a moment in a shower of dead leaves.

And at that moment Don started around the pond toward her, hoping the raw edges of the leaves would cut him to shreds, would bury and smother him, and when they blew away, there would be nothing left but a pile of slow shifting dust.

She met him and embraced him, and he almost decided not to say anything more.

"Don?"

"Tracey, look, let's go—"

She pushed him away and glared at him, black hair fanning over her eyes and fanning away. "Jesus," she said, "do you think you're the only kid with problems? What the hell makes you so special that you're the only one?"

"Tracey!"

"You've never been called a spic, have you? You've never had someone try to feel you up just because you smiled at them."

"Hey, Tracey, please, I didn't—"

"You know why my folks don't get divorced? Because my father is a worse Catholic than the Pope, what's why. Because if it came to it, my mother and father would live together for the rest of their lives hating each other's guts, but god forbid they even think about divorce." She put a fist to her cheek and pressed it in hard. "I have to wear long skirts so you can't see my legs, and I have to wear baggy blouses because my father doesn't want you to know I have any tits."

"Jesus, Tracey, I—"

"It's like living in a convent, Don! I love him, don't get me wrong, but there are times when I want to bust open his head. So . . ." She pointed at him, her hand trembling violently. "So don't you dare tell me you're the only one around here with problems, all right? Don't you dare, Donald Boyd!"

"Tracey," he said, taking a step toward her, "I didn't mean that. I meant—"

"I know," she said, suddenly smiling though there was a tear on her cheek. "I know. But you don't seem to understand there's nothing you can do about it. You can't run away, and you're too good to end up like Brian." She closed the gap and took his hands. "You have to live with it, Don. Like me, I guess. You have to live with it."

She hugged him. She lifted her face and she kissed him, and he tasted the sweet of her, the soft of her, and for a second in that kiss he thought she was right.

But it ended.

And still holding her, he shook his head.

"Tracey, you're wrong."

"About what, Vet?"

"I did something about it."

Joyce dragged the bench from her vanity and shoved it against the door. Then she shoved it away and dragged the vanity over, toppling bottles of perfume and lotion, stands that held her necklaces, a lamp and a pair of china figurines, and she didn't make a sound when an ivory-handled hairbrush slipped and bounced off her bare foot.

She was sobbing noiselessly, cursing the long hair that kept falling into her eyes, cursing Norman for not being here when she needed him.

In the hall—hoofbeats sharp, slow, and steady.

An armchair was next. She couldn't move the dresser, couldn't move the bed and fell to the floor with her hands over her head, not wanting to listen to the thing moving toward the room, not wanting to see the slips and fingers of fog drifting under the door and over the carpet.

Then she heard something else and her head jerked around,

her hands dropped to her robed lap, her eyes widened while her mouth opened in a strangled, gurgling scream.

A whickering, soft and low and deep—the thing in the hall telling her it was coming in.

They were still by the pond, and Tracey was growing angry.

"Now listen," Don insisted. "Just one minute, okay?"

"Don, I'm trying to help. I'm not an expert, Jesus knows, but you—"

"I asked you about wishing, remember?"

Her eyes shifted side to side before returning to watch his face. "Yes."

"Do you know . . ." A hesitation while he waited for something he said to make enough sense to keep that flicker of fear from returning to her eyes. "A wish, I think, isn't just one thing. It's whatever you want it to be. It can be like wishing for a million dollars to fall out of the sky on you, or maybe getting all A's without doing any homework. Or it can be really wanting something with everything you've got— like you and your flute, y'know? You want to make records and do concerts and make the most beautiful music in the world, right?"

She gave him a nod that was touched with confusion.

"And I want to be a vet. I mean, what the hell's wrong with wanting to be a vet? I want it so bad I dream about it, I wear it, for god's sake, and the . . . the only people who understand are my friends on the wall."

He stopped and tried to turn away, but she wouldn't release him, only hugged him once and tightly to force him to go on.

"I talk to them," he continued in an embarrassed whisper. "I tell them things. Everything. My stories, you know? And about Sam, and the folks, and about goddamn Brian and Tar, and even a little bit . . . a lot about you."

A hard look now, to see if she was laughing. She wasn't; she was crying.

"I needed a friend, Trace. Things felt like they were falling apart and I needed a friend, so I picked one out. A poster. A horse. I . . ." He looked over her head to the darkness beyond. "I made him come to me."

He could see it then in her eyes, and the way her lips quivered though she tried to keep them still with the press of a finger. Then her eyes cleared, and he saw something else—she believed him now. She believed he had killed Tar.

When he pushed her away, she didn't argue; when he snapped up a hand to stop her, she did; when he smiled at her to prove he was under control and she didn't have to be afraid, the smile he received in return was rigid and pale.

"All right," he said.

The wind strengthened, and above them, around them, branches clattered, leaves scraped, the surface of the pond distorted their reflections. West of town there was thunder.

He looked across the water and up the path, into the dark lane that led to the ball field. He wasn't sure if he wanted to do this, but it was too late to stop it. Tracey had to know or she would run away like the others, run back to Jeff and leave him alone.

"Come here," he said gently, as if talking to a friend too shy to leave the night for the light that began to sparkle in the cold air.

Tracey glanced toward the exit, her weight shifting to run in case he took a step nearer.

"Come on," he said gently. "It's me, remember?"

White globes danced in the pool to the wind, and there was a moment when the water turned in a circle, stretching his face and chest, merging his body with hers, vanishing in an explosion of pale blue when lightning forked above the trees.

He waited.

Tracey reached out a hand.

"Come on, boy," he whispered, as if talking to a pet.

Tracey blinked back a tear.

It began in the thunder and he wasn't sure he heard it, not until he felt her suddenly at his side, gripping his arm tightly and looking wonderingly at his face.

Slow and steady hoofbeats at the far end of the tunnel lane, part of the thunder and continuing after, unhurried and hollow, iron striking iron.

Tracey pressed her mouth against his arm when she saw it pass through the farthest pool of white. Darker than shadow. Sleek head bobbing, legs lifting as if prancing, fog and greenfire swarming up its flanks.

"Don," she said.

But he was too intent on watching the stallion, seeing it move through its own billowing cloud, seeing the curls and streams of greenfire from its hooves, seeing the greeneyes seeing him and knowing.

The hooves echoed.

The fog thickened.

And when it reached the opposite end of the pool, it stopped and snorted and stamped a foot that lanced flame toward the lightning.

"It's not a trick, is it," Tracey said, shifting until she was partly behind him.

The thunder was louder, nearer, rustling the leaves.

Don shook his head.

It was there, and it was waiting, and it wouldn't take its eyes from him, didn't move a muscle, its mane untouched though the wind blew his hair like needles into his eyes.

"Oh, my god . . . Tar," Tracey whispered, a cry caught in the name. "Oh, god, Don, you weren't lying."

"And I'm not crazy either."

The fog.

Greenfire.

"I wished him dead," Don told her without looking away from the horse. "I wished Tar dead."

Tracey's eyes closed. "Don, tell it to go away."

"It helps me," he said. "It hears me and it helps me."

"Don?"

He smiled, open-mouthed and suddenly. "Damn, Tracey, do you have any idea what this means?"

The horse backed off, into the fog that streamed from its nostrils as it breathed and moved, until its outline was a shadowed blur and its eyes were slanted green.

Then it vanished when an explosion of sirens erupted behind them. They whirled, whirled back and the fog was snaking off into the trees, the pool raising wavelets that slapped against the apron, and they spun about a second time when they heard footsteps racing toward them.

It was Luis Quintero, revolver drawn and followed by three other men. When he saw the two standing next to the water, he slowed and holstered his weapon, but didn't stop until he reached them and grabbed Tracey's arms.

"Are you all right?" he demanded. Then he looked hard at Don. "You. Are you all right?"

"Dad!"

"You told me you would come here. When . . ." He looked at Don and gestured to one of the men. "Take my daughter home at once."

"Dad, what's going on?"

"Don, please come with me." The voice was rough and solicitous, and Don looked over his shoulder at the empty dark path. "Please, Donald, we have to hurry."

"What?" he asked.

More sirens, and the thunder, and the first spatter of rain.

"No more until we get you home."

He balked, suddenly panicked. "Home? Mom? Is it Mom? My father?"

"Until we get you there," Quintero repeated. "Be patient. I will help you."

NINETEEN

A patrol car was parked askew at the boulevard exit, and Don started for it at Quintero's gentle urging. Tracey was already gone, looking through the rear window of a departing cruiser, one palm pressed against the glass, her face obscured in glaring fragments by the streetlights sweeping over it. Then, as a patrolman opened the door and gestured him in, he looked up the avenue and saw two other police cars angled across the mouth of his street, lights spinning while three officers put up a sawhorse barricade.

"Mr. Quintero, what's going on?"

"Don, please," Quintero said.

Don gaped, then looked in the opposite direction and saw the cars, the lights, a handful of people walking hurriedly toward his block. With a cry no one heard he yanked his arm free and started to run, heedless of the traffic as he bolted across to the islands, crashed through the shrubs and out the other side. A bus swerved barely in time to avoid him. Quintero shouted several yards behind.

At the mouth of the street he vaulted the barricade and ran a dozen feet before slowing and taking to the righthand pavement, walking stiff-legged, his arms flapping at his sides.

In the yards his neighbors were standing alone and in small groups, porch lights brightly white behind them and masking their faces; in the street was a fire engine angled in toward his driveway, and at the curb were two cruisers whose radios filled the air with abrupt bursts of static, whose lights bounced off the dead branches, flared off the windows, while an ambulance van backed onto the lawn.

He walked on, half-stumbled, until a policeman grabbed his arm and tried to turn him around. He protested and was released when Quintero barked an order; he breathed through his mouth as he stepped off the curb and stared at his house—at the ragged hole of the bay window, at the lamps on in every room with shadows on the walls, in the garage, at the roof bleached by spotlights on the sides of the cruisers.

"What?" he gasped to Quintero when the man reached his side and laid a hand on his shoulder. "What?"

A siren. Firemen standing around the engine, smoking while they waited for the word to go home. Flashlights. Voices in raised-whisper instructions.

"What, Mr. Quintero?" he said, turning to Tracey's father with anguish in his eyes.

"It is all still very confused," the man said, trying to watch Don and the house at the same time. "Someone—Mr. Delfield, you know him, I think—saw smoke coming out of the house a little while ago. He called us, he called the fire department."

White-jacketed men backed out the front door, stretcher in hand, on the stretcher a green plastic bag tied shut at the top.

"Oh, my god!" Don sobbed, and took a step to run.

"No!" Quintero snapped. "Not your mother, Don."

It was the voice, not the hand, that stopped him again; it was the voice, not the hand that told him who it was.

In his house. That bastard had been with his mother, in his house.

"H-how?"

Quintero scratched his thick mustache nervously. "I don't know. Sergeant Verona is inside. I was for a while, and I saw no fire, nothing charred. Just . . . ." He gestured toward the body being loaded into the van. As it pulled away and another took its place, he said, "Do you know about Tar?"

Don nodded as his hope to believe this wasn't real failed.

"Like that."

The window was smashed inward, and as he watched, a section of frame wobbled and broke free and tumbled to the ground.

A man in a tuxedo started up the front walk, and paused when he saw Don by the curb. He waved and hurried over, and Don felt his stomach begin to lurch. It was Dr. Naugle, and he was talking before he even reached them.

". . . called me and I came right over. Donald, are you all right? Were you—" He looked to Quintero, who shook his head. Then he put a hand to Don's face and felt the cold, the sweat, felt the chest begin to heave. "Bring him over here," he told the policeman, and for the moment Don didn't argue—he let them walk him to the curb, where he was forced to sit down, forced to look over his shoulder at the wreckage of the house, at the station wagon still in the drive. "I'll be right back, Don. Stay right here. Can you hear me, Don? You stay right here."

Don thought he nodded; he wasn't sure.

"Mom?"

"She is not hurt," Quintero assured him. "I promise you, she is not hurt."

"Then where . . ."

"In her bedroom. The door . . . ." He looked around, searching for someone to tell him to stop, to tell him this boy had no right to know how his mother was found behind a barricaded door that had been almost bashed in.

"Dad," Don said suddenly, straightening and looking around.

"He's not here."

He stood and tried to pick out his father's face in the crowd growing on the lawns opposite the house. The voices were clearer now, subdued and excited, a post-game show to keep their spirits high. "Where's my father?" he demanded. "Why isn't he here?"

"Don," Quintero said, seeing the look on his face. "Don, do you know what happened here? Do you know who did this?"

"No!" he said, angry he should be asked, afraid he would be blamed. "No, I was with Tracey since the game ended."

A voice stopped him. He spun to his right and saw Norman skirting the fire engine, nearly tripping over a length of thick hose being wound into place. He ran, and they collided, and his father hugged him tightly, asking over his shoulder what was going on?

"Where were you?" Don asked into the man's neck. "God, Dad, where were you?"

Norman thumped his back a couple of times and turned him away, keeping one hand around his shoulder. "I was at the Starlite with the goddamn mayor. Your mother was supposed to—Sergeant Quintero, what's going on? Will somebody please tell me what the hell is going on?"

The ambulance attendants reappeared at the door, Dr Naugle beside them. Joyce was on the stretcher, only her face visible above the sheet; Norman brushed the police aside as he ran for his wife.

Don started after him, then turned to Quintero. "You said she was all right," he accused through a spray of spittle.

"She is not hurt," the man repeated.

"Then why . . . ?"

The stretcher was wheeled to the ambulance's back doors.

and Norman watched helplessly as they lifted her in. Then he
said a word to Naugle and returned to his son.

"She was sitting on the floor," Quintero said, and said it a
second time when Norman drew near. "Her eyes were open,
but she was in shock. That is all I know, Mr. Boyd," he said
loudly when Norman started to question. "But there is still
the matter of the other man. I—"

"Why didn't you go with her?" Don asked his father.
"Dad, why didn't you go with her?"

Norman's eyes were red-rimmed and puffed, the neck of
his sweater sagging where he'd pulled on it. He looked back
at Naugle standing by the van, then stiffened and Don saw
Sergeant Verona making his way down the walk from the
porch. The detective took his hat off when he saw the Boyds
waiting, and turned it slowly in his hands.

"Who did it?" Norman demanded, one step short of grabbing the cop's lapels. "Who the fuck did this to my house, to
my wife? Was it Falcone? Did he—"

"I don't know, Norm. I came as soon as I got word. Your
wife obviously isn't up to talking just yet, and the coroner
there can only tell me Falcone was—" He stopped and looked
at Don. "The place is a mess. It's like a football team had
practice in there with clubs and bats, for god's sake." He
motioned to Quintero and they moved off, heads together.

"Dad?"

"She's in shock, like he said," Norman answered absently
as he watched the two men conferring. "She'll be all right.
She's just in shock. Jesus Christ, will you look at that house?
They'd better the hell leave someone around to watch it or
we'll get stolen blind."

Don moved off the verge into the lawn and stared in the
window. The mantel was clear, one lamp's shade was cock-
eyed, and he thought he could make out smears and stains on
the back wall. A look to the policemen, the firemen climbing
back onto their engine, their breath steaming, their coats

rippling as the wind dropped under the trees to push down the road. His father came beside him and touched his arm.

"Jesus," Norman said, staring at the house. "Jesus, it looks like somebody dropped a bomb on it."

Don couldn't think because there was too much to think, and he didn't protest when he was pulled across the van, helped into the van. Naugle was perched beside his mother; Norman came in behind and drew the doors shut.

He didn't hear the siren wind up to a wailing; he didn't see the barricades parting to let the ambulance through. He could only watch Joyce strapped under the sheet, all her hair pulled over one shoulder, an IV snaking from its stand to her hidden arm. Her eyes were closed, her complexion sallow, and ever so often Dr. Naugle would pat a handkerchief to her forehead and touch a finger to her neck to check on her pulse.

"Jesus," Norman whispered. "Jesus, what a mess."

The waiting room was small and filled with sculpted plastic chairs, a single plastic couch, a low table stacked with magazines worn and some tattered as if they'd been read. Don stood at the window overlooking the main entrance, one foot tapping arhythmically on the checkered tiled floor. Every few seconds he wiped a hand under his nose or buried it in his hair; every few seconds he would turn to the swinging doors and stare down the hallway toward his mother's room.

The building was quiet. The passage of a nurse or doctor was soundless, and even when one stopped to speak to another, he could see their lips moving and couldn't hear a whisper.

He wanted to leave.

He didn't want to know what Joyce would say when she regained consciousness and saw where she was; he didn't want her talking about a horse or Falcone, didn't want her judged crazy when she insisted on the truth.

And she would be. He knew it, and all of it would be his fault just because he had tried to get things running his way.

And the most terrible part wasn't the dying. That's what frightened him—it wasn't the dying. Something had gone wrong, and he had somehow lost control. If, he thought with the heels of his hands to his eyes, he had even had control in the first place.

His arms lowered slowly.

He stared blindly out the window.

"Who did it?" Norman asked quietly behind him.

Don jumped and spun around, leaning back defensively against the sill. His father was jacketless now, more grey in the hair falling over his brow. "What?"

Norman glanced at the window, at the floor, and leaned a bit closer. "I'll bet it was some of your friends, wasn't it?"

"Friends? Dad, what are you talking about? What friends?"

Norman's fist bunched at his sides. "What the hell did you do to Pratt this time, huh? What did you say to him now?"

"Nothing! I don't understand. I don't know what you mean."

Norman grunted with the effort to open his hands, and dropped onto the couch. "Neither do I, son," he said wearily. "Jesus, neither do I. This is . . ." A forearm wiped hard over his face, a hand plucked at his shirtfront. "Your mother is going to be all right. She's . . . like Naugle said, she's in shock."

Don peered through the door panes. "Did she say anything?"

Norman shook his head. "About who did it? No. Verona's in there now, hoping she'll come around soon. But she isn't going to. Naugle says it's going to take a while."

"Verona? The police?"

Norman leaned forward and picked up a magazine, flipped the pages and dropped it. "Yep. Why not?" He laughed bitterly. "I have drinks with the mayor and we're talking . . well, we're talking, and the next thing I know your mother is in here and Verona is calling me from the school because Hedley—''

Don fumbled to a chair. ''Mr. Hedley?''

''When it rains, it pours, and don't you ever forget it,'' he said in disgust. ''D'Amato found him in the auditorium after the game. His body was on the stage, hidden in the wings.'' Then he slammed his palms to the table, looked up and glared. ''This is crazy! What other town gets rid of one madman and immediately replaces him with another?'' He looked around the room helplessly. ''It's nuts. It doesn't make any sense. Jesus Christ, you try to protect your family, your future, and what help do you get, huh? You don't get any, that's what. You get shit is what you get.''

Don pushed out of the chair.

Norman looked up at him, eyes dark with rage. ''If I find out Pratt had anything to do wth this, I'll kill him, you hear me?''

''Brian doesn't kill people,'' Don said, almost shouting. ''How can you—''

''It could have been an accident.''

''What?''

''Sure. The prick could have . . . well, it could have been something that went wrong, you know.''

''Dad—''

Norman wasn't listening. ''Damned Falcone. Can you believe it, right in my own house? It's crazy.'' He nodded, agreeing with himself. ''It's goddamn crazy!''

Don moved to the door and pushed it open.

''Where are you going!''

''Air,'' he said. ''I need some air.''

''Your mother's in there. Don't you care that your mother's in there? We have to be here when she wakes up.''

''All I need is a little air,'' he said, and let the door swing shut behind him, let his feet take him across the corridor to the elevator. He pressed the button. He watched the door slide open in balky stages. He stepped in just as Sergeant Verona left his mother's room. The detective raised a finger for him to wait a minute, but Don let the doors close and sagged against the rear wall.

He gave the doors a slightly skewed grin.

In a way it was kind of funny. His father was right in blaming him for what happened, but for all the wrong reasons. But that he was blaming him in the first place wasn't funny at all.

The cage thumped to a halt, the doors opened, and he blinked at the lower floor's glare as he followed a short hall into the main lobby. A man ran a polisher over the floors, the machine humming softly; a young woman at the reception desk was reading a book and smoking. Neither of them looked at him as he crossed the gleaming floor, and he could see no police or security guards on duty either at the reception desk or at the revolving doors as he pushed through to the outside.

Cold; it was cold, and he leaned his head back to drink the night air.

"There you are!"

He started and half-turned to retreat inside when, suddenly, Tracey was there and her arms were around him.

"I told Mother to go to hell," she said, half-laughing, half-crying. "She said I had to stay home and I told her to go to hell. God, am I gonna get killed when I get back."

Hesitantly his arms went around her; gratefully he lowered his face to rest against her hair. He didn't care if anyone was watching, but he would have killed the first person who tried to break them up.

Another hug and she said, "C'mon, I want to talk to you." She took his arm and guided him along the arc of the circular drive leading on and off the hospital grounds. To the right was the visitors' parking lot, empty and barely lighted by three-foot pillars at the corners, and they crossed it with-

out speaking, Don only once looking up at the building to see
if he could pick out his mother's room.

At the far, darkest side they found a concrete bench under
a half-dozen skeletal cherry trees and sat down, staring across
the empty blacktop to the brick posts that marked the hospital's entrance. Across the street there were houses as black as
the near-leafless trees that marked the edge of the sidewalk.
No cars passed. No horns sounded. It was a hospital zone,
and no celebrations were wanted.

"How's your mother?" she asked then, covering his hand
with one of hers.

Haltingly, pausing frequently to clear his throat and stretch
his neck to shake loose the obstructions he found there, he
explained what the police had told him and what his father
had said about Mr. Hedley. Then he told her what he knew
had really happened, what they wouldn't believe even if his
mother had seen it and could talk.

"But I didn't do it!" he added heatedly, his insistence
almost begging. "Trace, you know me, I wouldn't wish my
own mother . . ." He remembered. Suddenly, like a sharp
elbow in the stomach, he remembered.

"Don?"

"My father wanted to know if it was one of my friends."

"What? I don't believe it."

"I'm not lying, Trace. He wanted to know if I'd said or
done something to good old Brian to make this happen."

"He couldn't have been serious. I mean, he's worried and
all, Don. He's not thinking straight."

He wasn't sure, and was no longer sure he cared. "He was
with the mayor, can you believe it? He was having drinks
with the mayor while my mother almost died!"

"Mr. Falcone did," she reminded him softly.

"I know." He turned to her urgently. "And you know
why she didn't die?"

Tracey shook her head, changed her mind, and nodded. "The park."

He leaned back and looked up at the sky, wondering what had happened to the rain, what had happened to the thunder. It had been all figured out, and now it was all changed. Even in his own world the Rules didn't stay the same.

"But they do," she said, and he blinked before realizing he had spoken aloud. "That . . . that thing, Don. It's yours."

"But I didn't tell it to kill—"

"I know, I know," she said. "I know, but it's more than you think."

His eyes closed slowly; he was tired. Ashamed because suddenly he was so tired all he wanted to do was curl up in her lap and fall asleep.

"I shouldn't believe any of this anyway," she said quietly, as if talking to herself. "It's not possible. I know what I saw, and I know what you said, but it's still not possible."

"It is," he said, watching stinging colors swirl across his eyelids. "Jesus, it is."

"I thought about it all the way home, and all the way over here. I thought about you making me see things that weren't really there. Like one of your stories. And I thought about how I wanted to help you so much that I'd even see King Kong if you told me to."

Her breath came in harsh pants; he didn't open his eyes.

"I thought about it, but Don, I saw it. So . . . so I thought about it like it was real, and what you said about it—it isn't right, Don. It isn't right."

His head swiveled slowly. "It wants to help me, don't you understand that? It came because I needed help, and it helps me. But I swear to god I didn't say anything about—"

"No, Don," she said, turning her head as well. "No, it's protecting you, and that's not the same."

*   *   *

Norman didn't think he could take another nasty surprise. He slumped back on the couch and stared at the acoustical tiles on the ceiling, only a flutter of a hand or a slight jerk of his head letting the detective know he was still listening. Though why he should, he didn't know. Verona, for all that he was an obvious hard worker, wasn't anywhere near finding the answer to this mess.

"All right," he said finally, rolling to sit upright. "All right, Tom, I've heard enough. It's crazy and you know it." And: crazy, he thought, is getting to be the word around here.

"You're not telling me anything I don't already know." Verona rubbed at a dark pouch under one eye. "But what am I supposed to think? I know it's hard, especially now, but what in god's name am I supposed to think?" He held up one hand and pointed with the other to a finger. "The lab tests show that Don didn't hit that man with the tree branch like he said he did. There was nothing to indicate that Boston had been struck by a car. Adam Hedley looked just like them, and I'll be damned if I'll believe that a car drove into your school, down the aisle, jumped the stage, and ran him over. Then there's Falcone—"

"Oh, Christ, Tom, will you listen to yourself?" Norman picked up a magazine as if he were going to throw it. "One—you can't find the tests. Two—by your own admission there was nothing to show Boston hadn't been hit by a car either. And I refuse to believe that my son, through some mysterious means, managed to subdue two men and a kid and bash them to death, one of them right in the middle of Park Boulevard." He leaned back heavily. "Besides, he was home when Hedley was killed, and he was with Tracey Quintero when Falcone . . ." He choked. He refused to say it one more time.

Verona threw up his hands, more in frustration than in defeat, and Norman almost felt sorry for him. In fact, he knew he did. The man was grabbing for any straws he could find, and only Don's encounter with the Howler and those elusive lab tests gave him any sort of connection.

"Joyce," Verona said, "spoke his name several times."

"Well, Jesus, man, he's her son!"

Joyce had slipped into a deep sleep at last, and Naugle had summoned them both into the room when she began muttering in a dream.

"She also said 'a horse,' if you recall." His smile was brief and mirthless. "Tell you what—I'll go for the car in the school if you'll go for the horse in my house."

"She could have been talking about drugs."

"For god's sake, get serious!"

He was tired. He wanted to go home. The only decent news he had had all evening was that John Delfield had gotten some of the neighbors to help him erect a temporary shield of plywood across the smashed bay window. He reminded himself to drop the man a note, perhaps enclose a check to reimburse him for the materials.

A door squeaked open and Naugle came in, bringing Norman to his feet.

"I gave her an injection," the doctor said. "Otherwise, there's no change."

"A shot? What for?"

"She wasn't asleep deeply enough," Naugle said. "She's having some pretty hairy nightmares, and I don't want her any weaker than she is."

"Great," Norman said, dropping back to his seat. "That's just great."

"You might as well go home."

Norman almost agreed before shaking his head. He wanted to stay. If he left, he might check to see if Chris was still home, still in her bed, still . . . He shook his head and shuddered, and Naugle patted his shoulder.

*　　*　　*

A car pulled into the parking lot, blinding them with its headlamps. Don threw up a hand and cursed softly, but Tracey only patted his shoulder and stood.

"I think it's Jeff," she said, squinting as the beams swung away from them and the car stopped.

"Jeff?"

She started off the grass. "Yeah. I called for a ride home. I sure wasn't going to ask my father."

"Well, I would have taken you, you know," he protested, following her to the door. "God, Tracey—"

She turned and put a hand to his chest. "Not now, Don, okay?"

"But what are we going to do? About—"

She sucked in her cheeks, bit down on the inside. "I don't know. I mean . . . I don't know."

The door opened and Jeff, his glasses catching the light and turning his eyes white, smiled ruefully when Don leaned down to peer in.

"Hey, man, I'm sorry."

"Yeah. It's . . . yeah, thanks."

Tracey slid in and took hold of his hands, pulled him close and kissed him. "There," she whispered with a small satisfied smile. "So there."

"But I need you," he pleaded, ignoring Jeff's puzzled look. "What am I going to do now? I need you, Tracey!"

"I know. And I'll see you tomorrow, okay? If I don't go now, I won't get out of my house until my funeral." She kissed him again, quickly. "Please, Don, just stay here, okay? It'll be all right if you just stay here. I'll be back tomorrow, first thing."

"Promise," he said tightly.

"Promise."

He didn't like it, but he could do nothing about it. She was right, and he knew it, but he didn't have to like it. As he didn't have to like giving a quick report on his mother to

Jeff, who kept leaning over Tracey and asking him questions until, at last, she poked him on the shoulder back behind the wheel.

Then they were gone.

The car swung around and they were gone, and Don tasted the memory of her kiss, the touch of her hand, and felt the frustration begin to rise in his chest.

She should have stayed!

If she loved him . . .

He looked away, looked back to the drive.

Love him?

But how the hell could she love him and still hurt him this way, leaving him when he needed her to keep from going crazy, leaving him when he needed her to help him escape?

His hands slammed into his jacket pockets and he watched his breath turn to fog.

She had to be right, he thought then. She had to be.

The wind tangled in the cherry trees, the thin branches snapping as if torn from their trunks.

But she should be *here*, he argued; she shouldn't leave me alone when I need her the most. She shouldn't! He raised a fist and only with an effort did he bring it to his mouth instead of shaking it at the image of Jeff's car on the drive.

Damn you, Jeff! God damn you, you're supposed to be my goddamned friend!

The wind keened over the hospital. A flare of water rose beneath a light, another on the drive, and he felt a raindrop on his hand.

And heard a hoofbeat behind him, soft on the grass.

He looked down at the tarmac and saw the ghost of a fog slip between his feet.

Turning slowly, he watched the cherry trees dance, narrowing his eyes against the dust the wind raised.

Then he saw the spots of green floating in the air, saw the

sparks rising, saw the shadow of the stallion as it stood there unmoving.

His legs nearly gave way, but the stallion tossed its head, and he staggered toward it, ignoring the pressure growing in his chest, ignoring the needled stinging building in his eyes. He stepped onto the grass, and he reached out a hand.

And the neck was warm, and it was smooth, and the nose when it nuzzled into his palm was the comfort of velvet.

"God," he whispered, neither a prayer nor a name.

It whickered softly, and when he turned his head sideways, he looked into the emerald fire that glowed out of the fog.

"He took her away," he said. "He took her away, and she's supposed to *love* me." He slipped his hands into the mane untouched by the mist and stroked the neck again. A bubble in his chest around a nugget of fire. "You know what?" he said softly. "Dad thinks I did it—the house, Mr. Falcone." He laid his cheek against the warm black mane. "The creep." The bubble grew, and there was heat in his lungs. "The bastard. And you know what else? Do you know what else? That cop is back, and he keeps looking at me like I'm some kind of *freak*." It was hard to breathe, and there in the dark were swirling spots of red. "It was *my* medal, *my* time, and Brian ruined it. Donny the fucking Duck!" He backed away, and the bubble burst. "I can't even get a stupid medal without somebody taking it away! What the hell do I have to do, huh? What the hell do I have to do?"

He turned to walk away, turned back and pointed at the street, his arm so rigid it began to tremble.

"And *she* goes *away* with *him*, just when I need her! What the hell kind of love is that, huh? What the goddamned hell kind of love is that when you . . ."

The fog. And the red. And the black shadow in the trees.

"What am I going to do?" he asked. "What am I going to do?"

A hoof pawed at the ground (greenfire), the eyes narrowed, the head raised.

He stepped away, and blinked, and suddenly knew what he had said when the red vanished and the fire died away.

"No, wait a minute," he said, and stretched out a hand. "God, no, I didn't mean—"

It was gone.

Don's mouth opened, and no sound came out.

It was gone, the fog swirling around black laced with fire, and there no question, now, about what Tracey meant.

It wasn't helping him at all. It was protecting him against hurt, and it didn't make any difference whether he willed it or not. When he hurt, he was rid of whatever had caused it. Imagined or not.

Tracey? Oh Jesus, please not Tracey!

Anguish twisted his features, fear jerked him around, and whatever he cried was lost in the wind, and the sheeting cold rain that bore down on his head.

TWENTY

She saw it in the outside mirror.

The sudden downpour had startled Jeff into slowing, the store- and streetlights broken into kaleidoscopic shards that smeared on the blacktop and ran down the windshield. The wipers worked as fast as they could, but it was nearly impossible to see where they were going, and she was about to ask him if he'd pull over and wait when she rubbed the back of her neck and glanced to her right.

And saw it.

And suddenly it was too late to talk, too late to turn around, and too late to explain why the air in her lungs was suddenly barbed and the rain had suddenly grown intolerably loud.

Twisting around, a hand braced on the dashboard, she saw the empty street behind her, reflections and distortions and blossoms of water short-lived on the tarmac. And the pocket of dense fog that moved steadily toward them, ragged edges ripped away by the wind, its bottom spilling under parked cars to the gutters to mingle with the rain. It reached no higher than the telephone poles, did not spread to the sidewalk—it followed them as though being towed, and when they slipped through a stretch of unlighted shops, she saw in its center the greeneyes, the greenfire, the suggestion of shadow darker than itself.

"Jeff," she said fearfully.

"Boy, he looked terrible," Jeff said, fighting with the wheel to keep the car from sliding on the oil-slick avenue. "God. I don't know how he keeps it together, y'know? If I were him, I'd probably look for the nearest cliff, you know what I mean?"

"Jeff, please."

"Trace, I'm doing the best I can, but I can't pull over here. There isn't any room. You want a bus to come up and bash us into New York? Take it easy, we're almost there."

Thunder was the rain that slammed on the roof; lightning was the flare of swinging traffic signals straining against their wires.

"Jeff, go faster."

He looked at her, amazed. "What? In this? But you just told me to slow down, Tracey!"

"Jesus, Jeff, don't argue!"

He saw her looking out the back and checked the rearview mirror, frowning at the white that filled the back window. "What the hell is that? It can't be spray, I'm not going that fast."

Greenfire that licked and curled toward the car.

Tracey closed her eyes and prayed. Even in talking with Don she didn't believe it, was more inclined to think she had been infected by his own fantasy, his understandable and unnecessary need to get away for a while. She'd known those moments herself, but never so intensely, never so importantly that she'd thought them real.

A white ribbon drifted over her window and she rubbed at it frantically, hoping it was only condensation from her shallow breathing. It didn't leave, she couldn't banish it, and she turned to Jeff and urged him to hurry.

"Tracey, look—"

The fog dropped a strand over the windshield and she muffled a scream, jammed her foot down on his, and pressed the accelerator to the floor.

Jeff yelled in alarm and shoved her away, and the car began to slide from one side of the street to the other, narrowly missing a parked car, a tipped garbage can, the point of a curb. He sawed at the steering wheel, touched and released the brake, his mouth open and swearing while he stared at the road ahead.

Alongside, then. It was coming up on her side and she whimpered Don's name.

"Tracey," he said nervously, "what's going on?"

She had to look away. She had to look at him because of the abrupt fear that pitched his voice high and pulled his lips away from his teeth. His glasses were slipping down his nose, and he kept tossing his head back because he didn't dare release his hands. He was pale, and in the stuffy car his face was running perspiration.

The wind buffeted them, shoved them, and the wiper on her side stuck midway to the top.

"I gotta stop," he said. "We're going too fast, I gotta stop or we'll crack—"

"No!" she screamed, and lunged for the accelerator again.

He swung out a frantic arm and caught her across the throat. She gagged and fell back, gulping for a breath, shaking the tears from her eyes, turned her head slowly and inhaled a scream when she saw the stallion's left shoulder even with her door.

It lowered its head, and she saw the green unwinking eye.

Jeff yelled then and the car swung into a skid, helped by the wind and pummeled by the rain. Tracey slapped one hand to the dashboard to brace herself, put her right hand over the door handle in case she had to leap out.

The car slewed, spun, and they were thrown to the roof when it thumped over a curb, were thrown back, then snapped forward when it crashed into a tree that loomed out of the fog. Tracey's arm took the shock to her shoulder, and she moaned but kept her head from striking the windshield. Jeff, however, had been knocked into the wheel and he was slumped over it when she was able to clear her vision, a sliver of blood at the corner of his mouth, his arms limp at his sides.

"Jeff! Oh, Jeff, please!"

She tugged at him, pushed him, but he only sagged back and slid over, landing partially on her lap. The fog seeped through a crack in his window.

"Jeff, I'm sorry, I'm sorry." She eased him upright, kicked open her door, and fell to her knees into the street. The car was half up one of the boulevard islands, a maple cracked over its top and scraping the roof with its branches. Shading her eyes against the rain, she tried to see how close she was to home, how close the stallion was. But there was only the mist being shredded by the rain and the dark bulk of the car rocking slowly in the wind.

On your feet, she ordered, and did it; find yourself, she demanded, and she did it, gasping when she realized they were far past her street, had jumped the island across from the park's entrance.

The boulevard was empty.

She staggered around the back of the car and held her hair away from her eyes as she reached for the driver's door. The wind kicked her against it, and hot needles of pain spun around her shoulder and spiraled her back. She gasped. Her mouth opened and filled with rain. She spat and reached again, and uttered a short cry.

The boulevard was empty, except for the stallion galloping

down the east-bound lane—neck stretched and greenfire, ears back and greeneyes, billows of smoke-fog filling the air around it, the sound of its hooves replacing the rain's thunder.

Which way? Oh Jesus, which way?

There was no escaping, but there could be stalling, long enough, she hoped, for Don to understand and come after her. And the only place she knew that he would think of right away . . .

With a shriek of hatred at the charging animal, and despair for leaving Jeff, she let the wind push-shove her across the lane and past the wall. Into the park where half the lights had been knocked out. Running toward the pond where the water slapped over the sides.

He ran.

Slapping the rain from his face, ignoring the puddles that grew into lakes, Don ran toward the center of town. It occurred to him Jeff might have taken her home, but he couldn't be sure. By now Tracey knew it was after her, and she wouldn't want any of her family hurt. And there was no place else to go where she was sure he would follow—she had to be at the park, waiting if she were still alive.

He scowled and punched his chest. He couldn't think like that or it was over; he had to know she was alive and somehow avoiding the stallion. Maybe in the trees where it might not be able to maneuver so well; maybe along the wall to keep it between them. But she was alive. She had to be alive. What the hell would be the sense if that damned thing got her?

At home, though, was her father, and her father's gun. He didn't know what could stop it, if anything could, but Tracey would have to be thinking of a weapon to defend her, and the best one would be where her father's guns were kept.

Oh, Christ, he thought; make up your mind!

Stop, he yelled then, without moving his lips; stop, don't do it, it's Tracey and I didn't mean it!

If it heard his hurt, it must hear his pleading; if he was in control, it couldn't not obey. Unless, under the new rules, it protected without question.

Oh, Christ, he thought; make up your damned mind!

He wasn't going fast enough. He would never be able to outrun Jeff's car, or outrun the horse. He had to stretch out, he had to reach, he had to beat the wind to wherever he was going.

He was going too fast and he was going to slip and break a leg if he wasn't more careful; he was going to run out of steam and be too late if he didn't pace himself like always.

A race, he told himself; a race, and there they are, looking out their windows watching, cheering silently, waving flags and tooting horns as he swept under awnings, went with the wind instead of trying to fight it, his sneakers splashing a wake behind him, his arms cutting through the cold rain to give him room to move.

They were cheering because he was Don Boyd, and he was going to make it.

He fell.

The curb was under several inches of water backed up from a storm drain, and he misjudged the edge. His hands raked along the blacktop, the knees of his jeans tore open and spilled blood into the street. He whimpered, and cursed, and kept pushing himself forward until he was on his feet again.

Running.

In silence.

The windows were empty, there were no crowds watching, there were no bands or hurrahs or photographers waiting along the route that had him swerve into the street, using the parked cars now to push him with a slap of his hand, wondering where the traffic was, dodging around an Ashford

Day banner stripped from its mooring and flapping in the street feebly where tomorrow there'd be a parade.

Running.

In silence.

Tempted to swing into the Quinteros' neighborhood, just in case he was wrong, sobbing when he realized he had no time for a choice; the park, or Tracey's house, and if he made a mistake, somebody would die.

She sprinted into the oval, knowing enough not to look behind her in case she lost ground. A globe flickered and went out. The rain was stained silver. She tried to veer around the pond, but the leaf-coated apron shifted under her feet and she went down on her shoulder. Screaming. Writhing. Almost welcoming the dark cloud that crested and settled over her. At least it would dull the pain; at least it would keep her from seeing herself die.

But the cloud lifted and the rain woke her, and she leaned on one hand and looked down the path.

It was there.

Standing in the entrance, oblivious to the storm, head and flanks shining as if coated in thin ice.

Panting against the wind that stole the breath from her mouth, she staggered to her feet and let the wind push her backward. On either side the trees waited, yet she couldn't stop herself from looking as the stallion began to move, legs slowly lifting, head slowly bobbing, the greenfire from its hooves lighting its way.

The park.

It had to be the park, and he didn't know why, and he was close to weeping as he ran past Beacher's, past the theater, and saw Lichter's car canted on the island.

He slowed as he swung up to the wreck and saw Jeff lying on the front seat and Tracey nowhere in sight. He apologized

to his friend by touching the window as if he were touching
his hand, then veered sharply across the lane and ran through
the gates.

The oval was ahead, and he tried to call out, but there was
nothing left in his lungs but the air that moved his legs,
pumped his arms, dried his throat as he opened his mouth to
find one more breath to keep him from stopping.

And once there, it was empty.

He staggered and slowed when the sodden leaves threatened to spill him, his arms out for balance until he reached
the path again.

Then he stopped.

He looked back.

He called Tracey's name, hands cupped around his mouth,
eyes blinking at the rain that tore through the branches and
ran down his back, his chest, filled his sneakers, and made
him still with the cold.

Half sideways, he began to run toward the field, always
checking behind in case he had missed her. Calling. Demanding. Spinning around at a flare of lightning and seeing
her sprawled on the ground . . . seeing the stallion beside
her, teeth bared and hooves pawing.

"No!" he screamed, and Tracey turned and saw him.

"No!" he screamed, and the stallion swung its head around.

He stumbled and flailed across the muddied field, shaking
his head and stretching his hand out toward her without
taking his eyes from the horse that backed away.

greenfire and greeneyes and fog lifting to the storm at his
approach.

Tracey got to her feet and fell against him when he reached
her, but he shoved her behind him when the stallion lifted its
head high.

"No," he said, a palm out to stop it.

Its head, higher; its rear legs slightly bent.

"No!" he shouted, both hands out now as it lifted itself

off the ground, its forelegs outstretched and the greenfire that sparked from them crackled through the rain.

"No!" he screamed. "No! Go away!"

Greeneyes so narrowed they nearly vanished in the fog.

"I don't need you!" Don screamed as the stallion rose higher. "I don't need you, goddamnit! Just . . . just leave me alone!"

Higher still, and blacker.

"Goddamnit! Goddamnit! Leave me alone!"

Higher until Don dropped to his knees, hands out, eyes raging, feeling the blood rush to his face feverish and stinging.

Tracey buried her face in his back.

He screamed again, and again, swinging his arms back and forth to counter the thick mist that poured from the stallion and obscured the greenfire, buried the greeneyes, suddenly scattered like a window shattered by the wind.

Don cowered away from it with a gasp at the touch of its dead cold, shifted, and threw his arms protectively around Tracey. She hugged him tightly, desperately, and they watched as best they could while the storm took over, the rain penetrated the fog and finally pummeled it to the ground.

And when it was gone, they were alone; the stallion was gone.

"Oh, Don," Tracey gasped as he helped her to her feet. "Oh, god, I was so frightened."

"Yes," he said, and headed for the path, pulling her behind him until she had to run to catch up.

"Don! Don, what . . ."

He didn't answer. A single urgent look, and he began to run again, not fast enough to outstrip her, but fast enough to get him past Jeff's car before anyone noticed it was there. He swung left, toward home, and Tracey followed with one hand gripping her torn shoulder. There were no questions, and he was glad because he wasn't sure he really knew what he was doing.

The police were gone. The yards and houses were dark. He puzzled at the plywood nailed over the bay window, but he didn't stop to look. He rushed up the steps and grabbed for the doorknob.

"Oh, shit!" he yelled, thumping the door with a fist. "Damn, it's locked." He turned and started down, hesitated on the walk before pulling Tracey with him into the garage. The door here was open, and he stumbled into the kitchen, staggered down the hall. He didn't look at the living room wreckage, didn't feel the cold saturating the walls, but hauled himself up the stairs and into his room.

Tracey came up behind him, her eyes glazed with pain.

Don switched on the light and looked at the poster over his desk. "Oh, god," he said.

The trees, the lane, and there at the back, the stallion frozen in running.

I'm sorry, he thought; I'm sorry.

And he ripped it from the wall, crumpled it into a ball, and ran downstairs again and into the kitchen. After two hapless attempts he managed to turn on the stove and held the poster over the flame until it caught in several places.

"Don? Don, help me."

When he felt the fire begin to scorch his wrist, he dropped the burning paper into the sink and watched it char, watched it flare, watched it spark and crackle and sink into paper embers.

"Don, please help me."

"Yeah," he said. "Don the Superman to the rescue."

TWENTY-ONE

A cool night in late October, a Sunday, and clear—a bold harvest moon pocked with grey shadows, and a scattering of stars too bright to be masked by the lights scattered below; the chilled breath of a faint wind that gusted now and then, carrying echoes of nightsounds born in the trees, pushing dead leaves in the gutters, rolling acorns in the eaves, snapping hands and faces with a grim promise of winter.

A cool night in late October, a Sunday, and dark.

. . . and so the boy, who really wasn't a bad kid but nobody really knew that because of all the things he had done, he looked up in the tree . . .

"Don, for god's sake, give me a break, okay? I'm not one of those dumb little kids of yours, you know. I don't believe in fairy tales."

He laughed silently at the telephone and snuggled closer to the wall, stretching his legs out until his bare feet were braced against the staircase. The chill of the wood felt good

335

against his soles. "I thought you liked my stories. I thought you needed something to take your mind off things."

Tracey groaned loudly. "I'm in pain, Vet, remember? I am a patient of the only hospital in the world that serves food the Geneva Convention banned from World War Two. And I am not supposed to be tortured."

"Torture?" he said, his voice high-pitched and insulted. "I don't recall you ever thinking I was torture before."

"I didn't say you," she answered softly. "I wasn't talking about you."

"I know," he said just as softly. "That was a joke."

"Oh." A pause. She forced a laugh. "I see. A joke."

Water ran in the kitchen. He looked in and saw his father at the sink, a towel over his shoulder, an unlighted cigarette dangling from his mouth—the same thing he had been watching for the past three days.

"Well, listen," Don said.

. . . and he saw the crow sitting on the highest branch in the biggest tree in the world. A big crow. The biggest crow he had ever seen in his life. And the boy knew, he really and truly knew, that the crow was going to be the only friend he had left in the world. So he talked to the crow and he said . . .

"Enough," Tracey pleaded with a laugh. Then, abruptly solemn, "Please, Don. No more. You promised me no more."

He sighed and nodded. "All right."

"Are you okay?"

"I'm supposed to ask you that, remember?"

"You know how I am. I want to know how you are."

He was fine, he thought, all things considered. After he had taken Tracey to the hospital in the station wagon, fighting the rain that washed in through the broken windshield, he had waited until they had brought Jeff in as well. A concussion and some deep lacerations, he was told, nothing more and his statement to the police had been accepted without question—he had gone for a walk after leaving his father, and saw the results of the accident, ran home to call since it was only a block away, and found Tracey wandering around in a daze. He supposed, when he was asked, they had skidded during the storm.

His mother was still unconscious, and Dr. Naugle had put him in charge of his father. To get some sleep, some food, so he would be ready when she woke up.

"Don, I have to go. The wardens have come with the pills."

"All right," he said. "I'll come around tomorrow."

They rang off, and he wandered into the kitchen, watched his father silently, then went up to his room. He was exhausted, and he dropped onto the bed and fell asleep almost instantly, not waking until after midnight to undress and sleep again.

At school on Monday he spoke to no one, avoiding their puzzled eyes, cutting biology when he saw the substitute at the head of the room. He ran for an hour afterward, feeling oddly distanced from the sound of his feet on the red cinder track, as if he were floating through a tunnel, looking for someone he knew he wouldn't find. Then he went home to fix his father's supper. Norman ate little, smoking as he did, finally pushed his plate away and left the room without a word.

Don didn't follow. He rinsed off the dishes, dried them and put them in the cupboard, then went upstairs to change his clothes for the evening visit to his mother, Jeff, and Tracey. When he came down again, Norman was at the door, impatiently jingling the keys to the car he had rented while the station wagon was being repaired.

"You know," he said as he drove through the wet streets, "you seem awfully calm these days."

Don shrugged.

"And it seems to me you're spending an awful lot of time with that girl."

"She's a friend. So's Jeff."

"And your mother is your mother. I think it would help if you stick around her room a bit more."

"Okay."

He could feel his father look at him, not quite glaring, but he didn't much care one way or the other. He had been trying to sort out everything he felt, and it bothered him that he couldn't make up his mind whether or not he should feel guilty. He was afraid something had happened to him that night in the park, and just as afraid that he might blurt out the truth and be considered a case for the men in the white coats. His father, on the other hand, had spent a lot of time on the phone—with the mayor, with several board members, and with Dr. Naugle. Don was ashamed to think Norman was more worried about the mayor.

On Tuesday Jeff was released and showed up after school to watch him run. There were questions, but he didn't ask them, and Don soon stopped worrying about what the boy had seen. Even if it had been just a glimpse, it could easily be explained as an aftereffect of the accident.

On Wednesday he decided not to use the track but to walk home right after last class. There was homework to do, and his father would have to go to see his mother alone.

"Hey, stranger!"

He stopped and turned around, and shifted his feet when Chris came running up, her hair unbound, her shirt out of her jeans.

"Hi," he said.

"God, you've been a ghost, you know that?" she said. "Where've you been hiding?"

He gestured toward the house, toward the men on ladder fixing the window. "Cleaning up, seeing my mom . . . you know."

"Yeah. Hey, I'm sorry about what happened."

She moved closer, and he could smell the perfume she used.

"Is it true," she said, "that your father is leaving?"

"Yeah. A leave of absence. What with all the trouble and my mom and all, he needs the time, you know?"

"Boy, do I," she said. "Is he really going to run for mayor?"

He shrugged. "I don't know. He's thinking about it, but I have a feeling things have changed." Then he looked at her eyes and saw something missing. Her expression was friendly enough, her tone as gentle, but there was still something missing and he couldn't figure it out.

"Hey, uh, look," he said at last. "It's Halloween this weekend, and . . . well, we kind of got screwed up last week, because of what happened. And I was wondering . . . that is, I—"

He jumped then when a car horn blared behind him, and Chris laughed, tapped his arm and walked over to Brian's car.

"Hey, Duck, what's up with your mom?" Brian asked as Chris opened the door and got in.

"She's okay," he said flatly.

"Good. Tell her I said hi." He cocked a finger-gun at him and gunned his engine, and as he drove away with one arm around Chris's shoulder, Don heard him say "Quack," and heard Chris say, "Quacker quack," and laugh.

"What?" he said. "What are you talking about?"

"Now look," Norman said. "I haven't got time to argue with you. I've done all the figures, and what with the medical expenses and the house, there just isn't enough money. I'm sorry, but I can't pull it out of the air, and I can't spend it when it isn't there. You'll have to start looking closer to home, at the state colleges, where it's cheaper. Besides, the way your grades are going, you'll be lucky to graduate."

Tracey was sitting on the living room couch, her mother in polite attendance. When he told her about his father's dictum, she commiserated and suggested he start looking at scholarships, student loans, and some of the local organizations who sponsor kids in college.

He hadn't thought of it; he thanked her; he wanted to kiss her, but her mother wouldn't leave.

In the cafeteria Jeff groaned and made to dump his tray over Don's head. "What's the big deal with Chris anyway, huh? I thought you and Tracey were . . . you know."

"We are, I guess," he said. "I don't know."

"But you don't want to be tied down, huh?"

He looked up at the bitterness he heard in Jeff's voice. "No, I didn't say that."

"I know you didn't," Jeff said. And pointed a fork at his chest. "Well, listen, pal—Tracey Quintero is one great lady, and you'd better not hurt her. You listening, pal? You'd better not do anything to hurt her or you'll have to answer to me."

He forced a grin. "Hey, is that a threat?"

Jeff didn't smile back. "Whatever."

And he almost gasped aloud when he realized that Jeff was in love with her too.

On Friday he stood at his mother's bedside with his father and watched her easy breathing, watched the IV feed her, watched the screens of the instruments recording her life.

At five minutes to ten she woke up, saw her son, and screamed.

* * *

The room was dark.

Sitting on the desk chair with his back to the wall, he could see them on the shelves and on the posters—the elephants, the hawks, the bobcats, the panther in the jungle licking its paw.

The night was cold.

Downstairs, he could hear his father answering the door, handing out tissue-wrapped packets of candy to the trick-or-treating kids who were roaming the neighborhood in packs herded by parents.

Yesterday his mother woke up.

Today he had stayed home, sitting at his desk trying to make up his mind, and during a wandering through the house when his back grew too sore, he had looked out a side window just after sunset and had seen his father talking to Chris. It looked as if they were arguing, and he wanted to run out and tell her not to get his father mad, not now, for god's sake, or she'll regret it come June.

Then she had pulled a handful of her hair over her left shoulder and started walking toward her backyard. Norman, after a brief hesitation, had followed when she looked back and pouted, and thrust out her chest.

Norman didn't come home for more than an hour.

Harry Falcone and Chris Snowden, and goddamn Sam was dead.

Nothing had changed.

Red.

People were dead, kids were dead, and nothing had changed.

A hazed red, like looking through a distant crimson curtain.

He spoke to Tracey on the phone and had found the nerve to tell her he loved her, and was puzzled enough not to ask why when she told him she liked him, but she wasn't sure yet about loving. Instead, he changed the subject, to school, to Jeff when she asked how he was doing, to the weather and the coming holidays. And when they hung up, he looked at the stairs without seeing a thing.

And a few minutes later he sighed and rubbed his eyes.

She was wrong when she said he was all right now; she was wrong when she said she didn't know about loving. Of course she did. He had heard it in Jeff's voice, and he had just heard it in hers—she was afraid of him now, and she wasn't afraid of Jeff.

So how could he be all right when nothing had changed in spite of what he'd done?

He stood in the kitchen and drank a can of soda, stood in the hallway and stared at the telephone for nearly five minutes before dialing Tracey's number. She was surprised to hear his voice again, and sorry that she couldn't go out with him next weekend because she had already promised Jeff a sample of her father's intensive interrogation. She laughed. He laughed. She suggested that Don call him and give him some hints. He laughed again and told her he just might do that.

And hung up.

And went to his room where he damned them both silently, and wondered what he'd done wrong, wondered where his mistake was?

Change. He would have to change if he wanted to take her back from Jeff; he would have to change if he wanted to get the world straight again.

"No," he said then.

No, he thought, eyes narrowed in a frown.

What was needed, he decided as he heard his father tramp up the stairs, was not a change in him, and not the simple recognition that his problems were no worse than anyone else's. He knew that. He wasn't stupid, and he knew that.

But what he knew that no one else did was that he had the means to do something about it.

Norman knocked on the door and opened it, grunted and slapped the wall switch that turned on the desk lamp.

"Jesus, are you a mole or something?"

"I was thinking."

"Oh, good. It's about time. I'm off to see your mother. You watch the door and hand out the candy. If you think of it, put some poison in the apples."

Don smiled dutifully, and his father gave him a salute, then looked around the room and shook his head.

"Someday maybe I'll understand all this," he said as he took another step in and scanned the shelves and the posters. "Maybe I've been wrong, son. Maybe . . . well, maybe I've been wrong." He lifted his shoulders and scratched his head. "When your mother's feeling better, maybe you and I should have a little talk. I suppose better late than never, huh, son? What do you say?"

Don nodded and accepted the offered hand, didn't protest when Norman put a hand on the back of his head and pulled him close to his chest in a rough approximation of a hug.

And when he was gone, Donald stared at the desk until the moon filled his window, stared at the desk until the swirling red was gone.

Then he smiled and stood up.

No, Dad, he thought; better late is not better. It isn't better at all. And he reached over the bed to pull down the picture of the deserted jungle from his wall.

And when he looked out the window, he whispered *where are you?* to the prowling shapes out there, darker than shadow and waiting for his call.

658 8737

Tony Malziew

— weekend

Info Packet

Family